work in
l time.
f those
an she
spital's
orkers

full of
emedy'

5 4 UL 2014		to put
1 9 JUL 2014	1 2 FEB 2015	
2 0 AUG 2014	2 4 MAR 2015	
	2 3 JAN 2015	today'
0 7 OCT 2014	2 7 APR 2015	
2 5 OCT 2014	0 2 MAY 2015	0 9 JUL 2015
	0 1 AUG 2015	

'Delightful' *Daily Express*

'Utter indulgence' *News of the World*

But don't say we didn't warn you…

'Pick this up at your peril: you won't get a thing done till it's
finishe

P.S. 'Y  *leat*

By Jill Mansell

Jill Mansell

THE UNPREDICTABLE
CONSEQUENCES OF LOVE

headline
review

The right of Jill Mansell to be identified as the Author of
the Work has been asserted by her in accordance with the
Copyright, Designs and Patents Act 1988.

First published in Great Britain in 2014
by HEADLINE REVIEW
An imprint of HEADLINE PUBLISHING GROUP

First published in paperback in Great Britain in 2014
by HEADLINE REVIEW
An imprint of HEADLINE PUBLISHING GROUP

1

Cataloguing in Publication Data is available from the British Library

ISBN 978 1 4722 1612 0 (A-format)
ISBN 978 0 7553 5593 8 (B-format)

Typeset in Bembo by Palimpsest Book Production Limited,
Falkirk, Stirlingshire

Printed and bound by CPI Group (UK) Ltd, Croydon, CR0 4YY

Headline's policy is to use papers that are natural, renewable and recyclable products
and made from wood grown in sustainable forests. The logging and manufacturing
processes are expected to conform to the environmental regulations of
the country of origin.

HEADLINE PUBLISHING GROUP
An Hachette UK Company
338 Euston Road
London NW1 3BH

www.headline.co.uk
www.hachette.co.uk

This book is dedicated to the following fantastic people:

Elaine Worthington
Marie Mason
Debbie Matsell
Amanda Morris
Tina Rashid
Nina Claridge
Kim Jackson
Mel Russell
Juliette Morrison
Deb Kirby
Alison Faiers
Victoria Clarke
Carolyn Abberley
Dianne Trower

Helen Heaney
Trish Davies
Awen Mai Parry-Williams
Bev Symonds
Valerie Jeffery
Caroline Kitcher
Karen Smyth
Marj Flynn
Yvonne Maddocks
Ciara Laverty
Tracy Reck
Denise Lavelle
Jake Christopher Wilmott

Seeing some of these names here may come as a surprise to
their owners, who were secretly nominated by friends and
family. Isn't that just lovely? Thank you so much
to everyone for your generous donations to
Comic Relief – you're all absolute stars!

Chapter 1

In the high-ceilinged drawing room of the Mariscombe House Hotel, Sophie Wells was putting the finishing touches to the setting for the photo shoot.

The original plan, to photograph the Ropers outside and *en famille* in a Marks and Spenceresque summer meadow, had been scuppered by the abysmal weather. The rain had been hammering down all morning and there was no way of postponing the event, as two members of the family were flying back to Australia tomorrow.

But Emma Roper knew exactly what she wanted. On the phone earlier she'd said, 'OK, if we can't be outside, we'll have one of those all-white shoots instead. You know, all modern and cool. And we'll all wear white too. It'll be like one of those Boden ads.' Delighted with herself and her artistic vision, she'd announced, 'So that's sorted. We'll see you at the hotel at three. It'll be great!'

Some clients liked to have the style and setting of their photo shoot suggested to them, while others preferred to make the directional decisions themselves. In Emma Roper's case it was evidently the latter scenario, and Sophie was happy to go along with it. Accordingly, she'd brought with her the lighting system, the white muslin backdrop on stands, and more swathes of muslin for the floor. If Boden-style was what Emma had set her heart on, Boden-style she would have.

1

She stepped back to survey the end result and adjust the lighting as Dot Strachan popped her elegant head around the door.

'Oh I say, I need my sunglasses in here!' Blinking at the brightness of the scene, she went on cheerily, 'Just wondered if you'd like a coffee, darling?'

Sophie wanted to be like Dot Strachan when she grew up. At seventy-two, Dot was effortlessly stylish, with killer cheekbones and light blue eyes that sparkled, offsetting her perma-tanned complexion and swept-back white-blond hair. Of course she had wrinkles, but they were the good kind that came of smiling so much and living well. She worked tirelessly, made running a hotel look easy and had never worn anything frumpy in her life.

'Thanks, but I'd better not.' Sophie pulled a face and indicated the expanse of pristine whiteness. 'Knowing my luck, I'd manage to spill it. Anyway, I'm fine. The Ropers'll be here any minute and we'll be out by four. Thanks again for letting us use the room at short notice.'

'No problem. Any time, I told you before. When they turn up,' said Dot, 'I'll tell Rose to send them through.'

When you'd grown accustomed to the surfing beaches of California, a grey rainswept afternoon on the north coast of Cornwall didn't quite measure up. Weather-wise, it wasn't what you'd call balmy. Josh Strachan had spent childhood summers here in St Carys, but today he was giving the icy waves a miss, leaving them to the diehard enthusiasts.

Like Griff, his grandmother's long-haired terrier cross, currently barking his head off and launching himself into the shallow surf as it rolled up the beach. Josh shook his head, marvelling at Griff's boundless enthusiasm for taking on the waves. OK, enough, the torrential rain was coming down even harder now; time to head back. He stuck his fingers in his mouth and let out a piercing whistle to attract the dog's attention.

Griff determinedly ignored him, like a five-year-old in a playground desperate for one more go on the slide.

Well, he'd only been back in the UK for a week. They were just getting to know each other. Cupping his hands around his mouth, Josh called out with authority, '*Griff*. Here, NOW.' Bloody delinquent animal, he was doing it on purpose. And to think he'd believed Dot when she'd told him the outrageous lie that the dog was well trained.

Josh made his way down to the water's edge, kicked off his deck shoes and at the third attempt managed to grab hold of Griff, snapping the lead on to his collar and hauling him up on to the sand. The tail end of a wave caught them, soaking into the leg of his jeans. He gave the dog a stern-as-possible glare, and Griff returned it with a naughty, unrepentant tail-wag. God, the sea was freezing.

As they made their way back across Mariscombe beach before heading up the steps carved into the cliff that gave the hotel its unparalleled view of the ocean, Josh conjured up mental images of the Californian ones he'd left behind. Santa Monica . . . Laguna . . . Huntington . . . amazing stretches of sand, world-class waves, year-round perfect weather . . .

But it hadn't been the UK, had it? It hadn't been *home*. And most of the time he'd been too busy working with people he didn't even like to take advantage of the surfing opportunities. Which was why he'd taken the executive decision to walk away, leave that artificial, stress-filled world behind him and aim instead for a better quality of life in the company of people he might actually enjoy spending time with.

That was the plan, anyway. After the Go Destry debacle, he never wanted to see another spoilt, whiny American teenager in his life.

'Right, now *you* rest your chin on your left hand, and *you* lean back a bit, and you two tilt your heads up so you can both see your mum . . .' Honestly, arranging five children and an adult could be as complicated as conducting an orchestra. 'And you rest your hands on their shoulders . . . that's it, that's great, now all look at each other and say, "Wow, you're gorgeous!"'

The brothers and sisters yelled it to each other then burst out laughing, and Sophie snapped away, firing off fifteen or twenty shots. 'Brilliant, keep going, say it again to someone else, perfect . . .'

Amid the giggles and laughter and renewed shouts of 'Wow, you're gorgeous,' the scrabbling noise on the other side of the door went unnoticed. Next moment the handle was pushed down, the door burst open and a wildly overexcited Griff launched himself like a hairy torpedo at the immaculate Boden group.

A hairy, wet, mud-strewn torpedo at that.

'AAARRGH.' The teenage girls shrieked and attempted to push the dog away as he scrambled over the boys, tail wagging furiously and paws leaving muddy prints over . . . well, everything.

'No! Griff, *down*,' Sophie shouted with predictable lack of effect. Emma was aghast, the boys had creased up laughing and the white backdrop was now spattered with dark spots where the dog had energetically attempted to shake off some of the mud.

'My dress,' Emma wailed. 'My beautiful white dress!'

'*Naughty* boy.' Putting down her Nikon, Sophie managed to catch Griff and scoop him up into her arms. Although it hadn't been his fault. Shaking her head apologetically at Emma, she said, 'I'll be back in a minute.'

Outside the living room she saw at once what had happened. At the far end of the hallway, by the entrance, a tall figure stood with his back to her. His dark hair was slicked back and wet from the rain, he was wearing a sodden grey and white shirt and jeans and talking rapidly into the phone he was holding in his right hand. From his left dangled a thin leather lead with no dog on the end of it.

As Sophie made her approach, she heard him say, '. . . OK, no problem, I'll get that sorted. Bye.' Then he hung up and slid the phone into the back pocket of his jeans.

She tapped him on the shoulder. 'Excuse me, I think you've lost something.'

He turned, eyebrows raised in enquiry, and saw who she was holding against her chest.

'Oh, right. Thanks.'

Honestly, talk about unbothered.

'You can't just let Griff off the lead, you know, and leave him to cause havoc.'

'I didn't.' Clearly taken aback at her tone, he said, 'I put him in his basket in the back office.'

'He's all wet and muddy!'

'I was about to fetch a towel to dry him off when my phone rang. It was an urgent call.'

'Come with me. Let me show you what he's done.'

'Oh God.' The eyebrows flattened out and he exhaled, following her across the hallway. When they reached the closed door to the drawing room he said defensively, 'Hang on, you can't blame me for whatever's in here. I did check the doors on my way through. They were all shut.'

Sophie knew who he was; of course she did. They might not have met before, but it was no secret that Josh Strachan had just moved back to St Carys and into the hotel he'd bought along with his grandmother three years ago.

Goodness, though, he was attractive. It was actually quite fascinating to discover you could be this mad with someone yet simultaneously so hyper-aware of their looks.

'And are you going to tell me Dot didn't warn you about his party trick?' As she said it, she put Griff down and lightly touched the brass door handle. Like lightning, Griff sprang up and grabbed the end of the handle in his teeth, swinging in mid-air for a moment and furiously twisting his body like a Cirque du Soleil gymnast in order to pull it down. As the door burst open, Sophie grabbed him and said, '*Et voilà.*'

She saw Josh Strachan mouth the words *Oh shit* as he took in the scene of devastation. To his credit, he held up his hands at once and said to the assembled group, 'I'm really sorry, it's my fault, I didn't know he could open doors.'

Most of the assembled group ignored him; they were all far too busy shrieking with laughter and taking photos of each other on their mobile phones. Only Emma, their mother, fixed Josh with a baleful eye and said, 'It's all ruined. Our beautiful photo shoot . . .'

'I know and I'm sorry, but can we rebook it for another day? I'll pay for everything, obviously . . .'

'The twins are leaving for Australia tomorrow morning. So no, we can't. But thanks for wrecking something so important.' Emma's voice had begun to wobble; her eyes filling with tears, she said in a brittle voice, 'I can't *believe* this is happening . . .'

'OK, let me sort this out.' Sophie dumped Griff in Josh's arms. 'Here you are, take him away and get him dried off. Give us five minutes, then bring him back in.'

'*Back?*' Josh looked at her as if she'd gone mad.

'Why would you want that creature back in here after he's done this?' Emma's voice was shrill.

'Just do it.' Sophie signalled to Josh to leave the room with Griff. Then she turned her attention to Emma. 'It's OK, please don't cry.'

'B-but everything's *ruined.*'

'Listen, of course you're upset. But isn't part of all this because your boys are off to Australia tomorrow?'

Emma took a deep shuddery breath and carefully dabbed at her eyes with a tissue. She nodded and said, 'Of course it is. I can't bear it. They're only eighteen . . . they're my babies . . . how am I going to cope without them?'

'I know, but it'll be an adventure.'

The older woman's shoulders sagged. 'An adventure for them, maybe. Non-stop anxiety for me. I kept thinking they'd change their minds and stay at home.' Her voice began to wobble again. 'But it hasn't h-happened. And goodness knows how they're going to cope . . . If I don't leave clean socks out for them every morning, they just put on yesterday's dirty old ones!'

'Ah, it'll be hard for you,' Sophie sympathised. 'But it'll end up being the making of them, just you wait and see.'

'Is she crying again?' One of the boys grinned and shook his head. 'Come on, Mum, just chill out. It's all good.'

Emma managed a watery smile at her son. 'I know, darling. I'm doing my best.'

Sophie collected the Nikon, then drew Emma across the room and sat her down in the window seat. 'Now, take a look at these.' She showed her the initial photos, then the few frames she'd captured when Griff had first burst in on them. The element of surprise had worked brilliantly; formerly stilted and ill at ease, the children's faces had been transformed by laughter and delight. 'Aren't they more themselves? Less self-conscious?'

'And that's why you want the dog back? So we can take more photos like this?' Emma sniffed. 'It's not going to be very Boden.'

'I know, but it'll be more informal and relaxed. They'll be the kind of photos that make people smile. Honestly,' Sophie reassured her. 'They'll be great. Just in a different way. And you won't have to pay for them, either.'

Chapter 2

The family left the hotel forty minutes later. From his upstairs window, Josh watched them run across the car park in the pelting rain and pile into a blue people-carrier. At least they didn't seem too mentally scarred by their ordeal.

Downstairs, he found the photographer energetically tidying the drawing room, restoring it to its normal state. Griff, meanwhile – *how typical* – had exhausted himself and was now dozing peacefully on the rug in front of the fireplace.

Unaware that she was being observed, the girl gathered up the mud-streaked, paw-printed muslin sheets and bundled them into a metal case. Next, she unhooked the backdrop from its stand, efficiently rolled it up and slid it inside a long cardboard cylinder. Her hair was all shades of blond and cut into a choppy style that swung around her shoulders as she worked. The fact that her clothes choice this morning had been a black top and grey jeans meant that Griff's muddy prints didn't show. Her sleeves were pushed up and a collection of silver bracelets jangled on her left wrist. Her top half was natural and her bottom curvy, both attributes Josh approved of, particularly after the years he'd spent in LA, where most of the girls maintained the kind of improbable Barbie-style figures that made it hard for them to stay upright.

'Nearly done . . . oh, it's you.' Turning, she glimpsed him in the doorway and straightened up. Nodding at Griff, she said,

'Have you come to get him? He's shattered now. I've just finished the shoot.'

'I know, I saw the family driving off. And I *am* sorry. Dot did warn me about the door-opening thing,' Josh admitted. 'I just forgot about it. Can I blame it on the jet lag?'

She gave him a look. 'Only if you're a complete wuss. You've had a whole week to get over it.'

Her eyes were bright and sparkling, silver-grey with very white whites. Her well-defined eyebrows were dark but tipped with gold and there was a smudge of mud on her left temple.

It wasn't an expression he'd ever thought of using before, but it occurred to him that she had *joie de vivre*.

'True.' He dipped his head in acknowledgement. 'All my own fault. So how did it go in the end?'

'Come over here and I'll show you.' Leading the way across the room, she picked up her camera and began scrolling through the shots, starting with the half-dozen or so pre-Griff originals, then on through the second stage of the shoot.

'These are great.' Josh nodded at them, genuinely impressed. 'So it ended up not being such a disaster after all.'

'Thanks to me being a complete genius,' she agreed happily.

He liked her attitude. 'What's your name?'

'Sophie.'

'Hi, Sophie. I'm Josh.'

'I know. Haven't you noticed everyone whispering about you since you've been back?'

'Not really. Well, maybe a bit. You don't take much notice after a while.' He paused. 'Do you have a business card?'

She took one from an envelope in the side pocket of her black canvas holdall and handed it over.

Sophie Wells Photography. Portraits, Weddings, Commercial was written in silver on a black background, along with her contact details. Josh noticed that as well as the bracelets on her left wrist there was a key attached to a plain silver bangle. He reached out and touched it briefly. 'What's this for?'

'It's the key to my secret Swiss bank account.'

'Amazing. I didn't know Swiss banks used Yale locks.'

A dimple appeared in her left cheek. 'I started wearing it after I locked myself out of my flat three times in one week.'

'Look,' said Josh, 'I still feel terrible about the photos.'

'No need. I told Emma I'd do them for free.'

'But that means you're losing out. Which is even worse.'

Sophie shook her head. 'They all like what we ended up doing instead. Emma's still happy to pay.'

'But their clothes . . .'

'They live on a dairy farm. She says the mud'll come out in a boil wash.'

'But when I came back here with Griff, she was in tears.'

'I know, but you weren't actually to blame for that. Relax,' Sophie said cheerfully, 'it's your lucky day. You're off the hook.'

Women, he'd never understand them. Still, it was a positive result. Somewhat distracted by her eyelashes – were they also gold-tipped beneath the mascara? – Josh said, 'Fine then. So long as you're sure. Can I ask you a personal question?'

'You can try.'

He was charmed by her easy smile, playful humour and feisty can-do attitude. OK, and her body was pretty amazing too. 'Are you single at the moment? Or seeing someone?'

If she were, he would have to say with good-natured regret, 'Well that's a real shame,' and leave it at that.

'Me? Oh no, I'm not seeing anyone.' Sophie shook her head. 'Completely and utterly single, that's me.'

Excellent. Enjoying her honesty, Josh said, 'So would you like to come out for dinner with me one evening?'

'It would have to be an evening.' Sophie nodded gravely. 'Otherwise it wouldn't be dinner, it'd be breakfast or lunch.'

'Definitely evening,' he agreed. 'We could do it tonight if you like.' *This is going so well.*

'Oh, I can't.'

'Yes, bit short notice. Friday, then? Or Saturday? You choose, whenever suits you best.'

But even as he was saying it, Sophie was shaking her head. 'Sorry, no . . . I mean, thanks for asking, but I can't meet you for dinner.'

'Right.' Taken aback, Josh said, 'Not at all?'

'No.'

'OK. That's fine.' It wasn't remotely fine. What was going on? Did she have a small baby at home, or an elderly relative who couldn't be left unattended? 'Am I allowed to ask why?'

Her eyes sparkled. 'Oh dear, are you offended?'

'Of course not,' lied Josh.

Sophie gave him a who-are-you-kidding look. 'I think you are. Don't be. I'm just pretty busy right now.'

'So maybe in a couple of weeks?' He couldn't quite believe he was still asking.

'Look, thanks again, but no thanks. I just don't really want to go out to dinner with . . . anyone.'

Aaaand another knock-back.

'No problem.' Josh wished he'd never started this now.

'Sorry.'

He managed a rueful smile. 'Hey, all I need is a few months for my ego to recover. I'll be fine.'

'It's not you.' Sophie's mouth was twitching. 'It's me.'

OK, now she was making fun of him.

'Well, *obviously*,' said Josh.

At the exact moment her grandson was being rejected by Sophie, Dot Strachan was fending off a clumsy advance at the other end of the hotel.

Oh dear, it never got any easier. She didn't want to hurt the poor man's feelings, but *really*.

'So how about it, hmm? Sound like an offer you can't refuse? The golf club puts on a jolly good bash, you know!' Edgar Morley's moustache bristled with enthusiasm at the prospect. 'And it's a

1950s theme night. Our era! Everyone dresses up for the occasion. Last year they hired an Elvis lookalike to make the evening go with a swing!'

Was Old Spice aftershave still sold in the shops, or had Edgar bought up crateloads of the stuff years ago and been working his way through it ever since?

Also, the idea of him jiving away in drainpipe trousers was enough to put anyone off their canapés.

But Edgar was lonely. Dot knew this because he'd told her so, many, *many* times. He had been widowed just over a year ago and was desperate to find himself another wife. Yearning for companionship and for someone to look after him because he had no clue how to cook for himself, he'd taken to homing in on any female of a vaguely appropriate age in general, and Dot in particular.

It was sad, and Dot did sympathise, but he was just going to have to badger someone else to accompany him to the 1950s night at the golf club.

'Next Saturday, did you say? Oh Edgar, I'm afraid I have something else booked for that evening.'

'Really? Oh no, that's too bad.' With the air of one suspecting that he was being fobbed off, he said, 'Where are you going?'

'To a party. With Lawrence.' This time it was even true.

The reply sent Edgar's untrimmed eyebrows shooting up. 'Your ex-husband? *Pfft.*' With an air of disapproval he added, 'To be honest, I'm surprised you have anything to do with him. After the way he treated you.'

'Yes, well. It's a party being held by mutual friends. We can either go along separately, ignore each other all night and make things awkward for everyone . . .' Dot paused. 'Or we can behave like adults and turn up together.'

More huffing and puffing from a disappointed Edgar. 'Well he doesn't deserve it, that's all I can say.'

'I know.' Right, time to get back to work. Making a point of checking her watch and looking busy, Dot said cheerily, 'The good thing is, Lawrence knows it too.'

Chapter 3

It was Saturday morning and Tula Kaye was feeling guilty. But not *that* guilty. Otherwise she wouldn't be here now, driving down the M5 from Birmingham to St Carys.

Oh, but how could she resist? For the last three weeks she'd been working crazy hours at the pub; didn't everyone deserve a break? There had to be more to life than slogging from home to work and back again, through the driving rain and grubby streets of Aston. When the miserable weather had abruptly given way yesterday to dazzling sun and temperatures whizzing up into the seventies, everyone's mood had lifted, but somehow it just hadn't been enough. During the afternoon, in the gap between lunchtime and evening shifts, Tula had found herself poring over her computer, checking out the live webcam overlooking Mariscombe beach.

The weather forecast, promising unbroken sunshine for the coming weekend, was what had clinched the deal. The first glorious heatwave of the summer. Picking up her phone, she'd sent a text to Sophie.

Hi, how busy are you this weekend?

She'd forced herself not to get her hopes up. Of course, there was nothing to stop her from paying a visit to St Carys even if Sophie was working, but it wouldn't be the same.

Tinggggg went her phone, signalling the reply:

Couple of hours on Sunday morning, otherwise free. And it's sunny! Coming down???

She shouldn't.

But she was going to.

Yes, she typed back, *if that's OK with you?*

Sophie's reply read: *Definitely. Hooray! We'll have big fun! Xx*

And that had been that; the decision was made. Tula had joyfully dug out some summery clothes, packed a small case and gone back to Bailey's Bar to work the evening shift.

Like a true master criminal, she'd also deftly lobbed in a couple of throwaway comments that would come in handy in due course. OK, what she was doing was bad, but she'd never done it before. Wasn't everyone allowed to pull a sickie just the once? Honestly, some people did it every couple of weeks and didn't even let it trouble their conscience.

So she'd worked really hard all evening, jokily mentioning in passing that her flatmate was cooking a prawn curry and there'd better still be some left when she got home, because she was starving. And at midnight, as they were all leaving the bar, she'd wondered aloud about getting some chips from the takeaway before deciding not to because she was so looking forward to *the delicious prawn curry* that was waiting for her at home.

See? All in the detail.

The trick had been to set off at five in the morning in order to avoid the traffic, which on gorgeous days like this could be a nightmare. After two hundred and fifteen miles and almost four hours of driving, Tula reached St Carys at last. Her spirits soared at the sight before her; no longer viewed through glass on a computer screen but in real life with her own eyes. Oh yes, this was *so* worth pulling a sickie for. Look at the sea, glittering like a turquoise sari, the vivid blueness melting at the horizon into the sky. The shriek of the gulls swooping overhead and the fresh smell of ozone filled her senses . . . she could practically taste the salt on her tongue. And the heat of the sun somehow just magically felt better on her skin down here in Cornwall than it did in Birmingham.

Tula drove down the winding road into the town, left her car in the car park and popped into the bakery on the seafront to pick up a Cornish pasty and four warm apple doughnuts.

Opening the front door and flinging her arms out in welcome, Sophie said, 'Yay, you're here! Fantastic! You're also revolting.' She wrinkled her nose. 'Not even nine o'clock and you've started already.'

'Can't help it.' Tula was unrepentant; buying and eating a proper Cornish pasty on arrival was all part of the experience, her way of celebrating the fact that she was here. Holding the second bag out as a peace offering she said, 'I bought doughnuts too.'

'Ooh. Apple?' They were Sophie's favourite.

'No, cat food and mustard.'

'Perfect.'

By lunchtime the beach was filling up and Tula was developing some colour on her front. Reddish colour rather than brown, sadly, but it was a start, and if she gave herself a good old coating of fake tan, it would all blend together into a rosy-golden glow.

'So what happened with that guy you went out with the other week?' Sophie rolled on to her side and peered at her over the top of her sunglasses.

'Which one?' Tula spoke without enthusiasm.

'Tom, was that his name? You were all excited.'

'Right. Well, turns out I was the only one who was. We went to the cinema.' She grimaced at the memory. 'And he fell asleep.'

'Oh no.'

'Then afterwards we went to get something to eat and I was being all entertaining and vivacious, and he only went and dozed off again. Excuse me, it's not funny.' Tula aimed a swipe because Sophie was battling to contain her laughter. 'I swear to God, I was being brilliant company. He just didn't appreciate me.'

'Maybe he was working nights?'

'That would have been an excellent excuse, wouldn't it? Except he wasn't. He just said sorry, he didn't know why he was so tired, so I said jokingly it was probably because I was so boring.'

'And . . .?'

'And he just shrugged and yawned. Like a complete arse. Seriously, such a let-down.' Tula exhaled in frustration. 'If anyone was boring, it was him.'

'What a pain. Oh well, his loss. How about Danny from work?'

'Danny's great, I love him. We went for a curry the other night.'

'You did? Well that's good.' Sophie nodded encouragingly.

'Good in one way, not so much in the other,' said Tula. 'He told me he was gay.'

'Oh.'

'After I tried to kiss him.'

'Whoops.'

'So then I had to pretend I'd known all along and it had only been a jokey kiss. And he pretended to go along with it, but really we both knew it hadn't been a jokey one. So yet again I ended up making a massive prat of myself.' Tula heaved a dramatic sigh. 'But honestly, how are you supposed to tell? There should be a way. He doesn't act camp or sound camp; there are no *clues* . . . he's just lovely-looking, always so cheerful and friendly, and really easy company; you can chat to him about anything . . . Oh damn . . .' Her voice trailed off as the words sank in. 'Listen to me, how could I have been so stupid? Of course he's gay.'

'So he's a good friend.' Sophie's tone was consoling. 'That's not so bad, is it? Those last longer than boyfriends anyway.'

'Certainly longer than *my* boyfriends.' Tula knew she was her own worst enemy, but she couldn't help herself; when she found someone she liked, she just got overenthusiastic, like a toddler being offered the latest must-have toy. And it inevitably scared off the man in question. Aloud she said, 'How about you? Anyone interesting?'

'No.' Sophie shook her head, as Tula had known she would.

'Are you going to be like this for ever?'

'Who knows?'

'Don't you get lonely?'

'No, I really don't.'

And the thing was, she knew Sophie genuinely meant it. She'd simply banished the idea of boyfriends from her life and didn't appear to miss them at all.

Tula envied her that ability – though not, obviously, the reason behind it.

It had to be good, though, to be so un-needy. If only she could be a fraction as determined and focused on her own career. Not that you could call her job a career.

Still, it might only be bar work, but it paid the bills. Speaking of which . . .

'Ready for an ice cream?' Scrambling upright, Tula dusted sand from her legs and pulled her shorts and T-shirt on over her bikini.

'You don't have to get dressed,' said Sophie. 'They sell them over at the beach café.'

'I know, but I love that shop we went to last year, the one up on the esplanade. Remember the blackberry ice cream?'

Sophie nodded. 'You're right, they're the best. I'll have one of those too. Better get tubs rather than cones, or they'll be melted by the time you get back.'

God, there were a lot of steps. Tula finally reached the top and paused for breath; this was her punishment for telling a lie. But Sophie would be shocked and disappointed if she knew about the sickie – she had such a work ethic, it would never occur to her to skive off.

Plus, Tula knew if she tried to call her boss from the beach, there was the chance of him overhearing seasidey holiday-type background noises and waves crashing on the sand.

To the left was the beginning of the esplanade, crowded with people. To the right was a narrow path leading up to the grounds of a hotel.

OK, the sound of screaming kids would be a giveaway too. Turning right, Tula took the quieter option and admired the hotel's grounds as she wandered through them. Nice place. And here was a secluded bench, set back in a honeysuckle-strewn archway. Perching on the wooden seat, she took out her phone.

A text would be way easier but such a cop-out; only a complete *amateur* would think of texting in sick. Patrick was suspicious enough as it was.

No, it had to be done properly, voice-to-voice.

Well, croak-to-voice.

She pressed call and heard the phone start to ring two hundred miles away in Birmingham.

Now, how would Kate Winslet do this?

'Bailey's Bar.' Patrick's manner was as brusque as his personality.

'Oh . . . Patrick, is that you?' Tula adopted an agonised whisper, as if she were incredibly brave but doubled over in agony and unable to crawl out of bed.

'Tula, what's up?' His voice became even more brusque, if that was possible.

From the back of the hotel, a tall male figure had emerged and was making his way across the lawn in her direction. Not deliberately in her direction, thank God; he was just heading for the path that led down to the beach. Half turning away so as not to make eye contact, Tula whispered, 'I'm so sorry, Patrick, I really don't think I'm going to be able to—'

'What? Speak up, girl, I can't hear you.'

That's because I'm being ill, you wazzock.

'I'm not going to be able to work tonight.' She raised her voice but kept it in death's-door mode. 'I think it's food poisoning from the prawn curry I had last night . . . Oh Patrick, I thought I was going to die; I've never felt so terrible in my life . . .' Out of the corner of her eye she saw the man passing by and swivelled round still further.

'So where are you?' Patrick demanded. 'In hospital?'

Honestly, would he only be happy if she was in the intensive care unit on life support? 'No,' she croaked, clutching her stomach in order to sound more convincingly ill. 'I've just been throwing up all night and all morning. Pretty much non-stop. I mean, if I feel better in the next few hours I'll come in for my shift, you know I hate to let you down, but the way I'm feeling at the moment, I can't see it happ—'

'So you're not going to be in,' he interrupted curtly. 'Well that's just great. What about tomorrow night?'

Miserable bastard. Such compassion. 'I expect so . . . if it's just a twenty-four-hour thing, I should be better by then . . .'

'Well make sure you are,' Patrick snapped. 'And you'd better not be messing me around.'

Honestly, what a cheek. Irritated, Tula croaked, 'I'm *sick*, Patrick. Don't try and make out I'm not. Have I ever let you down before?'

Since there was no answer to that, *because she hadn't*, he snorted and hung up.

Tula watched the man from the hotel as he headed down the steps in the direction of the beach. Broad shoulders, dark hair, rather nice view from the back; she wondered briefly whether the front matched up.

Anyway, blackberry ice creams. Relieved to have the dreaded phone call out of the way, she slid her phone into the pocket of her shorts. Then, spirits lifted, she set off in the direction of the esplanade.

Chapter 4

Lying on her back, Sophie closed her eyes and revelled in the blissful sensation of the sun on her eyelids. She really should do this more often. Somehow, spending a whole day on the beach always felt like a luxury she couldn't afford to indulge in; building up the business invariably took priority. If Tula hadn't come down today, she would have kept herself busy with work.

But she was glad she hadn't now. Taking a few hours off made a nice change. Resting her arms behind her head, she trailed her fingers through the dry, fine sand and listened to the sounds of the waves breaking on to the beach, the seagulls swooping and wheeling overhead. The smell of Ambre Solaire hung in the air and a light breeze was coming in off the ocean.

Sophie stretched, satiated. As well as the blackberry ice creams, they'd had fish and chips and Maltesers. And Diet Coke. It had been a lovely day, spent gossiping, swimming, then later joining in with a game of volleyball on the beach. Now they were enjoying the last couple of hours of sunshine and listening to the chatter and snippets of conversation going on around them. Children were engaged in building sandcastles and digging moats, couples were idly bickering and the group of posh girls directly behind them were eyeing up the talent and providing a running commentary on their various attributes.

'The one in the yellow board-shorts? He's pretty fit.'

'Not bad. I'd rather have the blond one with the tan. Nice abs.'

'But he's got one of those noses. There's big and there's too big.'

'Oh come on, it's only a nose, that can be fixed! See the guy with the long dark hair? He's good-looking but his body's too long for his legs . . . now that's something you're never going to be able to sort out.'

Cue giggles. Sophie opened her eyes and tilted her head to the left to see what Tula was doing. True to form, she was propped up on her elbows, surveying the view. Which included, naturally, the men in question.

Of course it did. Tula would never miss an opportunity to ogle.

Following her line of gaze, Sophie saw Josh Strachan emerging from the sea with his surfboard. He shook water from his hair and glanced over in their direction, prompting a flurry of interest among the posh girls.

'Now that's *much* better, that's what I call a body,' the loudest of them said in admiration. 'How did we manage to miss him before?'

The answer to this was quite simple: for the last hour or so, Josh had been busy surfing, and it was presumably the first time he'd left the water. Sophie, who'd spotted him earlier, watched as he made his way over to the café.

'Unzip your wetsuit, unzip your wetsuit,' one of the other girls chanted quietly. 'Come on now, let's see your chest.'

'Ooh, spoilsport,' said the loud one as Josh disappeared from view with his wetsuit still zipped. 'I may have to go over there and get myself a drink. Show him what he's missing.'

'Hang on, here he is again, and he's got a dog with him now! Oooh, look at that, *sooooo cute* . . .'

Because that was the thing about Griff: he did have the knack, when he wasn't being a mud-spattering, havoc-causing holy devil, of looking ridiculously cute. Sophie, plugging her earphones back into her ears, turned the volume on her iPod up to maximum to block out the chatter of the girls behind them, and closed her eyes once more.

Less than a minute later, someone was licking her toes.

Or, more accurately, *something*. Having done a shuddery, whole-body twitch, Sophie jackknifed into a sitting position and saw that it was Griff at her feet, tongue lolling and tail wagging away happily.

At the other end of his lead was Josh.

'Sorry.' He grinned down at her, evidently not meaning it. 'Thought it was you, earlier. Hello again.'

The last time he'd seen her, she'd been upright, wearing jeans and a top, and her hair had been loose. Today she was prone in a bikini with her hair tied back and dark glasses half covering her face. Lifting the glasses, she said, 'You've been in the sea the whole time. I've been here. How could you know it was me from that far away?'

It had all gone quiet behind her. Josh Strachan looked briefly surprised. At last he replied mildly, 'I recognised your bag.'

Oh. Right. Sophie glanced over at the oversized holdall she carried with her everywhere. Made of bright turquoise leather and studded all over with nuggets of silver that reflected the sun and glittered like camera flashes, it probably was quite . . . standoutish.

Fair enough.

'And how about you?' Josh's tone altered. 'How are you feeling now?'

What? What was *that* supposed to mean? Opening her mouth to ask, Sophie belatedly realised he was addressing Tula.

Which made even less sense.

Tula, clearly thinking the same, said, 'Excuse me?'

'I saw you swimming earlier. And playing volleyball. Seems like a pretty miraculous recovery.' He paused, tilting his head to indicate the carrier bag at her side, containing all the empty drinks cartons and food wrappers. 'After last night's dodgy prawn curry.'

Last night? What was he *on* about? 'You've got the wrong person,' Sophie protested. 'Tula wasn't even here last night.'

Josh smiled and replied pleasantly, 'I didn't say she was.'

22

If it were possible to have an awkward silence on a noisy crowded beach, this was it. Even more bizarrely, Tula had gone bright red. The girls behind them were doubtless agog.

With all the finesse of a five-year-old, Tula shook her head and said, 'I'm sorry, I don't know what you're talking about.'

She never had been able to tell a convincing lie.

'Don't you?' Josh Strachan was evidently finding the situation entertaining. 'So the girl I saw sitting in the grounds of our hotel earlier, the one talking to someone on her phone about how incredibly ill she was, thanks to a prawn curry . . . that wasn't you?'

'Fine,' Tula blurted out. 'Great, brilliant, thanks a lot. The whole point of doing it up there rather than down here, believe it or not, was because I was trying to be discreet.'

'OK. Sorry,' said Josh, although he clearly wasn't. 'Anyway, looks like you're feeling much better now. So that's good, isn't it?'

'Josh! You off?' Another surfer arrived, greeting him with a slap on the back. 'Are we going to see you at the party tonight?' Flashing a dazzling white smile at . . . well, pretty much every girl in the vicinity, he added cheerily, 'Hello, ladies!'

Behind Sophie and Tula, evidently entranced by the sight of two attractive men in wetsuits, the posh girls chorused, 'Hello!'

Sophie hid a smile, because that was Riley Bryant for you: the ultimate charmer in a hello-ladies kind of way. With his long sun-bleached hair, Caramac perma-tan and sea-green eyes, he was Joey from *Friends* personified, only blonder and thinner and with a trace of a Newcastle accent. He loved women, any women, flirted incessantly, and his vanity knew no bounds.

What saved Riley from being insufferable was his talent for self-mockery. Outrageously and unapologetically hedonistic, he lived a life designed to suit only himself. Since holding down a proper job didn't appeal, he survived instead on the proceeds of a trust fund set up by his doting aunt. Any criticism of his choices simply rolled off his back; he had the ability to laugh at himself and didn't take offence. He spent his days surfing, travelling the world, partying like there was no tomorrow and sleeping with girls. If they had the choice, he argued, who in their right mind wouldn't want to do that?

Basically he'd be every parent's nightmare son-in-law. But if you regarded him simply as harmless entertainment, he was always good value and amusing company to have around.

One of the posh girls, evidently coming to the same conclusion, seized her chance and said, 'Actually, you look like the right person to ask. We're just down for the weekend, wondering where's the best place around here to go for the evening. Is there anywhere fun you can recommend?'

Riley raised a playful eyebrow. 'Fun?'

'And lively,' her friend chimed in. 'Some place we can let our hair down.'

Glancing at them over her shoulder, Sophie noted that they did indeed all have plenty of hair, the gleaming, swishy kind. And teeny-tiny bikinis. They were also wearing the full complement of jewellery, fake tan and make-up. Which wasn't something you saw that often down here on the beach.

'Well, we're going to the Mermaid.' Riley turned and pointed in the general direction. 'It's at the far end of the esplanade. A friend's celebrating his birthday there . . . it'll be lively, I can guarantee that.'

'And he wouldn't mind us turning up?'

'Are you kidding? More the merrier, wouldn't you say?' Riley turned to Sophie for confirmation. 'You know what CJ's like. Hardly going to complain, is he, about a bunch of gorgeous girls showing up at his party?'

Sophie shrugged and shook her head, because this was undoubtedly true.

The posh girl in the teeniest pink and white polka-dotted bikini said, 'Awesome!'

Chapter 5

'So what do you reckon?'

Sophie said, 'About what?'

It was nine o'clock in the evening. They'd left the beach at six, showered and changed back at the flat, and had had their first couple of drinks at a wine bar called La Petite Bouteille.

'Where shall we go next?' Tula was twirling the stem of her empty wine glass and doing her best to look innocent, as if it were a completely spur-of-the-moment question.

She was rubbish at it.

Since two could play at that game, Sophie said, 'Ooh, it's quiz night at the Mariner's Arms. Let's go there!'

'Quiz night?' Tula looked horrified.

'It's a really friendly pub. Loads of lovely old fishermen. We'd have a great time.'

'I was thinking, why don't we try somewhere more . . . buzzy?'

'OK. Well, are you hungry? There's a new Mexican restaurant with singing waiters. That's buzzy.' Her smile bright, Sophie added, 'We could have chimichangas!'

'Or maybe . . .' Tula was casting around for inspiration, 'how about giving that other place a go? You know . . . thingy . . . the Mermaid?'

Sooo predictable.

'I think Riley was inviting the other girls.'

'No he wasn't, it was all of us. Definitely.' Tula nodded earnestly.

'And you want to go there because you fancy him? Trust me,' said Sophie, 'you don't want to get involved.'

'I wouldn't! Apart from anything else, I live two hundred miles away. Anyway, I'm not stupid,' Tula protested. 'I can see what he's like.'

Sophie raised a playful eyebrow. 'And when has that ever stopped you before?'

'Look, I just think we'd have more fun at the Mermaid than doing some boring quiz with a bunch of smelly old fishermen. Plus, the other one'll be there too.' As if this was the clincher, she said, 'Thingy with the cute dog.'

'Josh.'

'That's it.'

'You mean the one who overheard you on the phone and caught you out, big time.'

'It's the first sickie I've ever pulled. You have no idea how desperate I was for a break, a weekend away. And it's never going to happen again,' Tula wheedled. 'Oh, don't look at me like that. Anyway, do you find him attractive?'

'Who, Josh? No.' Sophie shook her head; this was the way she'd trained herself to react. She hadn't mentioned to Tula that he'd asked her out.

'Yay, brilliant! So you don't mind if I have a go at him?'

A *go*? Slightly taken aback, Sophie said, 'I thought you lived two hundred miles away.'

'Come on, he's gorgeous. All dark and carved and glinty-eyed.' Tula jumped down from her bar stool and flashed an optimistic grin. 'Not to mention masterful. I can give it my best shot, can't I? Some men are worth the commute.'

'Spoken like a true romantic.'

'But I *am* romantic. If I met the right man, it wouldn't matter to me if he was rich or poor. Although rich would be better, obviously. And if Josh half owns that hotel, he must be doing all right.'

Sophie smiled at this, realising there was something else Tula didn't yet know about Dot Strachan's grandson. 'He's not too strapped for cash,' she admitted. 'He used to manage Go Destry.'

'Are you serious?' Tula's eyes widened in disbelief. '*Go Destry*? You mean . . . he's the one who discovered them? Bloody hell, why didn't you tell me this *before*?'

Sophie shrugged. Hollywood gossip simply didn't loom large on her radar. Or even small, come to that. 'Sorry. I didn't know.'

Every so often, fate and luck conspire together to create synchronicity, and a kind of magic results. It had happened to Josh Strachan three years ago when he'd been making his way through an LA park and had passed a group of teenagers singing and dancing along to a backing track. Their voices were good but not outstanding, their dance moves were by no means perfect and the music was frankly dire, but there was just something about them that made him want to stop, watch and listen.

Somewhere deep down had stirred the realisation that these kids possessed the kind of indefinable charisma that couldn't be manufactured. You either had it or you didn't. And if it was nurtured properly . . . well, then the sky was the limit.

A mixture of restless curiosity, adventure and world-class surfing beaches had brought Josh out to LA years earlier. Through friends and contacts he'd managed to land a decent job working for a small independent record label. After asking the teenagers a few questions and handing them his card, he'd suggested they come into the office the next day.

When they did, however, nerves had got the better of them in a major way and the easy camaraderie that had piqued Josh's interest was lost. The assembled co-directors of the company unanimously declined the opportunity to sign the band, who at the time called themselves – horrendously – Four Ov Uz. Josh did his best to argue their case but was flatly overruled. Setting up another meeting outside working hours, he spoke to the band again and listened to a very average song one of the boys had written for them. He then offered to become their manager, detected what was missing from the song, rejigged it himself and financed the trip to the recording studio.

A month later, he handed in his notice and walked away from the record company in order to manage the band full-time. He worked day and night to crystallise their image; Dizzy, Jem, Bonnie and Cal were two boys and two girls with quirky good looks, complementary personalities and bags of likeability factor. All in their late teens, they were witty, intriguing and exuded *joie de vivre*. The plan was that female fans would fancy the boys and want to be best friends with the girls, and for the males to pretend not to find any of them attractive but grudgingly admit that their music was OK.

The band's name had to go, obviously. After brainstorming for hours without success, Josh went for a drink in a bar and saw a bunch of men watching the horse-racing on TV, yelling at the tops of their voices for the horse they'd put their money on. The horse had ended up winning magnificently by half a length, and Josh named the band after the words the men had been bellowing: Go Destry.

The next six months weren't easy; only Josh's unswerving belief in the band kept them going. Performing in clubs failed to attract audiences. Each new attempt to get them noticed was unsuccessful. Everyone was growing disheartened, running out of enthusiasm for what felt like an insurmountable task. Josh, having taken on the biggest financial gamble of his life, was rapidly running out of cash.

Then somehow, incredibly, it all began to change. A couple of shows went well, clips were posted on YouTube and people finally began to watch them and take notice. A week or so later, the superstar rapper EnjaySeven – known for his own eclectic tastes in music and fashion – became an unlikely supporter, retweeting one of their YouTube links on Twitter and publicly predicting that Go Destry were destined to be massive. This prompted a deluge of attention, with everyone racing to agree with him. The next gig sold out, iTunes sales skyrocketed and the band found themselves being greeted at every turn by fans chanting GO DESTRY, GO DESTRY, GO-GO-GO DESTRY.

It all went bananas after that. Josh's phone never stopped ringing; the band were booked to appear on all the major TV shows. The whole of America fell in love with them, charmed by their winning ways, impish humour and capacity for mischief, as well as by the insanely catchy debut single 'Come Back to Me'.

What had initially been on a par with a cottage industry, became over the course of the next year an unstoppable juggernaut. A huge record deal was struck and top songwriters were hastily drafted in to create an album that would live up to all the hype. A stadium tour was put together. There were advertising deals. A TV series. Movie proposals were thrown at them.

Basically, the world had gone crazy; it was all happening too fast. Realising this, Josh began turning offers down but his protégés found out and objected: how *dare* he decide what they could and couldn't do?

This turned out to be the beginning of the end. As the months went by, being part of an unstoppable juggernaut stopped being thrilling and fun. Like overtired toddlers refusing to give in to their exhaustion and go to bed, the members of Go Destry morphed from cheerful teenagers bursting with gratitude and enthusiasm into irritable twenty-somethings with huge egos, short tempers and a massively inflated sense of their own invulnerability. They became snide, careless and decidedly lacking in the manners department. Despite Josh's best efforts, a couple of them also started dabbling enthusiastically in drugs.

It became harder and harder for him to keep everyone on track. Allegiances were endlessly shifting within the group and rivalries didn't contribute to a calm atmosphere. There were several poor reviews in the press, and the band's popularity showed the first signs of sliding into a decline. Outraged, Dizzy and Cal made their displeasure known and were promptly approached by another management company promising to give them the extra boost they needed to get back on top. Within forty-eight hours, summoned to a meeting with his protégés, Josh found himself peremptorily informed that unless he got his act together, he was out on his ear.

He responded calmly with a comment along the lines of maybe, since they were the act in question, he wasn't the one needing to get them together. He then announced that if this was how they felt about everything he'd done for them, they should sever their business relationship forthwith.

And that was it; after three tempestuous years, the adventure was over. The split caused a storm of speculation, and several other bands approached Josh, desperate to be taken on by him. But he turned them all down; he'd had enough of the entertainment industry in general and spoilt brat pop singers in particular. He'd built up a fortune and frequently worked twenty-hour days in the process. His own social life, due to pressure of work and all the travelling involved, had become pretty much non-existent. He was ready to get out now; there was nothing to keep him in LA any longer and there was definitely more to life and better ways to earn a living than by half killing yourself looking after people who were happy to sell you down the river.

Furthermore, Dot was a marvel for her age, but even she had let slip once or twice that running the hotel single-handedly might soon start to become too much for her.

Josh had made up his mind: it was time to go home to the UK. To Cornwall. To St Carys.

Chapter 6

'Waaah, stop it,' shrieked Tula as Riley scooped her up into the air. 'Put me down! I'm too *heavy* . . .'

'Don't give me that. You're light as a feather. OK, hang on tight . . .'

'*You* hang on tight,' Tula retorted, before letting out another yelp as he expertly threw her over his shoulder in a fireman's lift.

In front of them in the car park of the Mermaid Inn, CJ called out, 'Everybody ready? Down to the beach, around the rocks at the end and back again.' He raised two ominously murky pint glasses like trophies. 'Losers have to drink these.'

There were six couples taking part. Tula was just glad she wasn't wearing a short skirt. But the party was brilliant, everyone was incredibly friendly and the drinking games had been hilarious. So long as they didn't lose this one; God only knew what had gone into making that muddy-looking brew.

'Three . . . two . . . one . . . GO,' bellowed CJ, and they were off.

Urgh, being carried in a fireman's lift was a bumpy experience. Clinging on for dear life, Tula admired Riley's physique; his shoulders were broad and his biceps rocklike as he ran out of the car park and down on to the beach.

'Don't be sick down my back,' he warned as they headed for the outcrop of three rocks exposed by the low tide at the far end of the beach.

'I'm never sick.' Raising her head and seeing the rest of the party cheering them on, her heart clenched with joy at the sight of Josh's instantly recognisable figure among them. He was here; at last he'd turned up, hooray!

It was dark now, but the full moon and the strings of lights looped between each of the street lamps along the esplanade went some way towards illuminating the beach. She could see and hear the white foamy waves breaking along the shoreline. The whoops and shrieks of the other contestants mingled in the warm night air with the yells of encouragement from the pub behind them. Just as they reached the rocks, Riley tripped, lost his footing and stumbled . . .

And then they were lying on the sand, tangled up in each other, and he was saying, 'Sorry, that was the seaweed. Are you OK?'

'I'm fine.' He'd been the one who'd broken her fall; she'd managed to land inelegantly on top of him. 'How about you?'

'Never better.' He was grinning up at her now, his long blond hair spread out on the sand beneath his head. His eyes glinted with mischief as he slid his hand around the back of her neck. 'Well, now we're here, seems like an opportunity too good to waste . . .'

'Losers!' bawled one of the other couples, racing past them.

'That's what they think,' Riley murmured. 'Sometimes losers win.'

'Ooh no, no no no.' Before he could guide her mouth down to meet his, Tula vigorously shook her head and wriggled away.

'No?'

'*No.*' Glancing over in the direction of the Mermaid's car park, she could still see the others outside, watching the racers. And if she could see Josh from here, the chances were that he could see her.

'Oh dear. Someone else you've got your eye on?' Riley's tone was playful.

'No.'

Ignoring her protest, he raised his eyebrows. 'Josh?'

'No!'

'Come on, I saw the way you were looking at him this afternoon. It was pretty obvious.'

'Oh God. Really?' Tula's heart sank; just for once in her life *why* couldn't she be the cool, enigmatic type?

'To be fair, I'm pretty much an expert.' Rising to his feet and brushing the sand off his jeans, Riley added, 'Although I'm usually the one on the receiving end.'

'Sorry.' She smiled at his wounded expression.

'And I really liked you, too. This is crushing.' Holding out his hands, he hauled her upright. 'I've lost all my confidence now.'

'I'm sure you have.'

'I'm not that ugly, am I?'

'You're beautiful,' Tula assured him as her phone beeped.

It was a text from Sophie:

What are you two DOING out there??

Leaning in to read it, Riley said, 'Nothing, sadly.' Then he took the phone from her, switched it to camera mode and held it at arm's length, capturing both their faces on the screen. 'There you go, a little something to remind you of the time we met, that romantic fireman's lift you were given on the beach. In years to come, you'll look at this photo and think, damn, what an idiot I was to turn him down, the one that got away.'

'I had my chance and I blew it.' Tula nodded sympathetically.

'You'll probably regret it for the rest of your life. Your friends will see this picture of us and go, wow, who's *that*? He's gorgeous!'

'They will say that.' If she'd thought for one second he meant any of this, Tula wouldn't have been able to joke about it. 'I'll probably have this photo blown up to poster size and hung on my bedroom wall. I expect I'll cry myself to sleep every night in my lonely single bed.'

Riley slung a companionable arm around her shoulders as they made their way back up the beach to the Mermaid. 'I really hope that happens. It's no more than you deserve.'

OK, downing that drink as a forfeit probably hadn't been the best idea. Having spent the last hour dancing madly along to the band, Tula headed out on to the balcony for some fresh air. It was hot inside the pub. She'd danced with CJ, and with Sophie, and with several other people too, even the posh girls, who were good fun once you got to know them . . .

Hearing low voices on the beach below the balcony, she bent over the wooden railings and saw a couple leaning against the wall beneath her. One streaky blonde, one dark-haired. Their bodies were pressed together and they began to kiss. Smiling to herself, Tula wondered what Riley would do if she were to tip her glass and allow a few drops of icy white wine to land on his head.

Then the door opened behind her and someone else stepped out on to the balcony. Tula's stomach did a giddy flip when she half turned and saw it was Josh. Honestly, the effect he was having on her was just ridiculous. Also, had he noticed her leaving the pub and deliberately followed her out here? Because if so, that *was* exciting.

'Hi.' His smile was brief. Oh, but still bone-meltingly gorgeous.

'Hot.' Bugger, that came out wrong. Fanning herself energetically, Tula said, 'In there. Needed some fresh air. Anyway, hi to you too. Again!' A few drinks and a fanciable man tended to have this effect, rendering her stupid.

'So how long have you and Sophie known each other?'

'Four years now. She moved into the flat above mine in Aston and we've been friends ever since.'

Josh nodded. 'Right. And what's she like?'

'Mean. Nasty. Not a nice person at all.'

He smiled. 'I can see that. So, does she have a lot of boyfriends?'

'No.' Oh, that dismal sinking feeling when you realise he's only talking to you in order to find out about your friend.

'*Any* boyfriends?'

'Why?'

'Just interested. Did she tell you I asked her out the other day?'

Tula shook her head; how like Sophie not to mention it, so as to spare her feelings. 'No, she didn't.'

'She turned me down.'

'Oh dear.'

'I know.' Detecting the note of sarcasm, Josh said wryly, 'I just wondered why.'

'If it helps,' said Tula, 'she did tell me she wasn't interested in you.'

'Right. Well, thanks for that.'

'Just letting you know.' Tula sensed that offering herself up as a willing substitute probably wouldn't be the best idea. Which was disappointing, but oh well. Taking a glug of wine, she changed the subject. 'So, I hear you used to manage Go Destry.'

'That's true, I did.'

'My friend Danny loves them, they're his all-time favourite band.' Was it an unbelievably dorky thing to do? On impulse, Tula took out her phone and said, 'Could I have a photo with you to make him jealous?'

Josh's shrug was good-natured. 'If you like.'

She took the photograph quickly, already embarrassed. Enough humiliation; time to play it cool.

'Right, thanks. I'm going back inside now. Bye!'

If he followed her in, it would be a good sign, wouldn't it?

But all he did was smile, stay where he was and say, 'Bye.'

In her fantasy, this was because he was playing hard to get.

Chapter 7

'Feeling better?' said Patrick when Tula turned up for work on Sunday evening.

'Yes thanks.' She patted her stomach and looked brave. 'Sorry about yesterday. Won't be having any prawns again for a while.'

'You're sure you're OK?' He peered at her face. 'Looking a bit pale.'

This was because she'd covered up the slight sunburn with a hefty coat of ivory foundation. But it was nice of Patrick to be asking, even if it probably just meant he didn't want her keeling over in front of the customers. 'Really,' Tula reassured him, touched by the unexpected concern. 'I'm fine.'

By eleven thirty, she was hot and tired and her legs ached. Between Saturday's dancing and this evening's relentless work, it had been a strenuous weekend for her feet.

Once the cleaning up had been done, Patrick beckoned her into the office. Without preamble he announced, 'Don't bother asking for a reference, as a refusal often offends.'

Tula's heart began to thud. 'Sorry?'

'And spare me the wide-eyed orphan look too. It's game over, OK? You're out of here.'

He knew. Shit. *How* did he know? But even as the question was racing through her brain, Patrick was holding up his phone to show her.

And there it was, the evidence: the two photos she'd posted on Facebook last night. *Like an idiot.*

'Bit of a giveaway,' said Patrick, clearly relishing every second. 'Not very clever of you, was it? Boasting about the great time you were having *down in Cornwall.*'

'But . . .' Tula felt sick. Her privacy settings were friends only. Patrick was about as far removed from a friend as it was physically possible to be. How *could* he have seen the private photos she'd posted on her private account, purely to show off to Danny the fact that . . .

Oh God. Realisation flooded through her. What an idiot. The other day at work, Danny's brother had wanted to see the pictures she'd taken at last weekend's party, and she'd switched the settings to friends-of-friends, meaning to change them back again afterwards.

Except she hadn't, had she? It had slipped her mind. Talk about bad timing. And Patrick, already suspicious, had typed in her name and struck lucky.

Bastard.

On the way home, Tula made the connection. Putting Patrick's name into the search box brought up the name of the friend they had in common, a girl who had briefly worked at Bailey's Bar over Christmas. What she was doing being friends with him on Facebook was anybody's guess. But there it was, the link that had unwittingly connected them and enabled Patrick to catch her out.

And why did he have a Facebook account anyway? The man was in his fifties, for God's sake. He was too *old*.

Arriving home twenty minutes later, she found the sofa occupied, a sci-fi movie playing on the TV and flatmate Coral curled up with her boyfriend Evan. Twisting round to greet Tula, Coral said, 'Hiya, good night?'

'Not so you'd notice.' She may as well come straight out and say it. 'I've been sacked. Patrick found out where I was yesterday.

We were short-staffed, so he made me work the whole shift before telling me.' Tula threw herself down in the uncomfortable chair. 'So that's it, no more job. My life just got even crappier. Go, me.'

Coral said, 'Oh no, what a pain.' Then she looked at Evan and gave him a shall-we-tell-her-now? eyebrow raise.

Evan nodded and Coral smiled before turning back to face Tula. 'Actually, we've got some news too. I checked with the landlord today and asked if it was all right, and he said it's fine by him if Evan wants to live here too. So he's moving in next week!'

Tula froze. Oh God, hadn't she been punished enough for one night? Not this, not now, *not Evan*.

'And it'll help you out too,' Evan chimed in with enthusiasm, 'because your share of the rent will come down. So that's good, isn't it?' His moon face grew moonier. 'Can't say I don't have my uses!'

What could she do? What could she say? The two of them had been so certain she'd be happy about this thrilling newsflash, it hadn't even occurred to them to ask first. And the awful thing was, the fact that the prospect filled her with horror was all her own fault.

Because Coral was wonderful, the best flatmate anyone could ask for. And Evan was lovely too, a genuinely nice person. He was kind and clever, thoughtful and sweet-natured, and not afraid of a bit of washing-up. He was even happy to carry perilously overfilled bin bags down the narrow rickety stairs. In so many ways he was everything you could possibly want in a flatmate.

If only he didn't have some of the most annoying habits known to man. For some reason they didn't bother Coral at all, but these irritating traits drove Tula to distraction. When he ate, he made the kind of sloshing, chomping noises a pig might make. When he wasn't eating, he repeatedly cleared his throat and sniffed. He also breathed really noisily. All the time. And finally, he had a habit of chewing the skin around his fingernails and making tiny wet sucky-bitey noises that meant Tula spent every minute in his company wanting to scream at him to STOP IT, STOP IT, JUST BLOODY STOP IT.

And failing that, to drive a sharpened stake through his heart.

She'd tried discreetly raising the matter in the early days when Coral had first started seeing Evan, but Coral had been genuinely mystified by the idea that anything like that could bother anyone, or indeed be annoying in any way.

And the thing was, Evan was just so *nice*. Concluding that her hypersensitivity and low irritation threshold was her own problem, Tula had gritted her teeth and forced herself to tolerate the various tics and noises, for all their sakes.

But that had been only just about bearable when he was at the flat every now and again. Having him here full time would be more than she could stand.

Snort . . . breathe . . . cough . . . chomp . . . slosh . . .

'Isn't it great news?' Coral was lovingly stroking Evan's arm.

'Yes . . . great,' Tula said faintly, her skin already crawling at the thought.

Help.

Chapter 8

Marguerite Marshall was in her mid fifties, with elaborately coiffed black hair, immaculate make-up and birdlike, miss-nothing dark eyes. Over the course of the last twenty-five years she had written thirty-eight best-selling novels, which had been translated into over forty languages. In the region of twenty-four million copies of her books had been sold worldwide, though it was impossible to announce an exact figure as her devoted fans never stopped buying them; sales just kept spiralling upwards.

Sophie knew this because she heard pretty much the same spiel every time they met. Not for Marguerite the British habit of modesty and self-deprecation; her confidence was breathtaking and she loved nothing better than a captive audience.

Which was why Sophie had allowed an extra couple of hours for today's shoot. She knew from experience that once Marguerite had you on the premises, it wasn't easy to escape.

The house, Moor Court, was an imposing ivy-clad Victorian residence with well-tended grounds and a staff cottage at the bottom of the driveway.

Well, it had originally been a staff cottage. These days it was more of a shag pad.

And it was the shagger himself who opened the door of the main house, greeting her with a kiss on the cheek.

'Morning, angel. She's all ready for you in the drawing room.' Leading the way across the hall, Riley pulled open a second door and said, 'Mags, Sophie's here. I've told her she's going to have to use all her tricks to blur out those bags and wrinkles. You know, you really shouldn't have downed that second bottle of gin last night.'

No one else would get away with speaking to Marguerite like that. No one would dare to even try. But all she did was shake her head and say good-naturedly to Sophie, 'Ignore him, it's all lies. And I certainly don't have bags and wrinkles.'

Riley said, 'That's because you've spent the last two hours covering them with make-up.'

'I've spent the last two hours writing fifteen hundred words,' Marguerite declared. 'And rather brilliant ones they are too.'

He winked at Sophie. 'Whatever you say. Right, anything you want picking up while I'm out?'

'No thanks, darling. What time will you be back?'

'Who knows? See how the day goes. OK if I take the Merc?'

'Fine. Just try not to prang it.'

Riley grinned, raised a hand in farewell and left them to it. They heard the front door crash shut, the throaty sound of the red Mercedes Sport starting up, then the scrunch of the tyres on gravel as he tore off down the drive.

'That boy.' Marguerite shook her head fondly. 'He'll be the death of me.'

And whose fault would that be? Not that Sophie said this aloud, but really, Marguerite had no one to blame but herself. Riley's parents had died in a boating accident nine years ago, when he was twenty. His mother and Marguerite had been sisters. Marguerite, who had married and divorced three husbands, had never had children of her own, nor known a moment of maternal longing in her life. Babies repulsed her and older children were either boring or unendurably tiresome. But when Riley had lost his mum and dad, she'd risen to the occasion with typical magnificence.

Now, almost a decade on, the damage had been done. Having lavished him with love, attention and access to all the money a work-shy, profoundly hedonistic twenty-something could wish for, Marguerite had succeeded in turning him into a feckless Peter Pan figure who was all but unemployable. Officially, Riley was meant to be driving her around to literary events, organising the author tours and public appearances, and handling all the tedious company paperwork. In reality, he appeared to do little other than please himself, and spend his days surfing, socialising and having fun.

Which was undoubtedly nice work if you could get it, but hardly admirable. Riley might be good company, but you couldn't say he possessed the kind of qualities you'd look for in a man. Not that it seemed to bother the girls he brought back to his cottage at the bottom of the drive.

'Right, let's see.' Having finished scrutinising herself in the mirror of the gold powder compact, Marguerite snapped it shut and said, 'Where shall we start? I need new publicity shots for my Dutch publisher. I thought we could have some taken with me standing beside this window, move on to the office, where I'll sit at my desk, then head outside for some garden shots.'

'Sounds good.' There was never any point in trying to tell Marguerite where to sit or stand; she always knew best.

'And look, I've chosen my outfit to match the cover of the new book.' Holding it up and pointing to the glossy green and pink artwork, Marguerite struck the kind of pose last seen on an old episode of *The Price is Right*. 'You see, darling, attention to detail is key. *So* important. It's what marks out the true professionals from the amateurs.'

'It does.' Sophie nodded in peaceable agreement; she would let Marguerite run through her repertoire of poses, then casually take some of her in more relaxed mode. This way, the publishing company could choose which ones to go with.

'I was talking to my US editor on the phone the other day. She was just telling me how she wished more authors could be like me. Because I give my fans what they want, you see – I just instinctively know how to reach out and create a connection between us.' Holding the book close to the side of her face, Marguerite smouldered into an imaginary camera lens in order to demonstrate just how to make that connection. And the thing was, you could laugh all you liked at her towering confidence and self-belief, but the fact remained that her millions of readers weren't laughing; they were too busy buying and devouring her books. They flat-out adored her and believed every boast she made. Some even fainted with excitement when they met her in the flesh.

This was Marguerite's take on it, anyway. To be fair, she'd been in Australia at the time, and her fans had been forced to queue for too long outside the bookstore in a sweltering ninety degrees of heat.

Not for nothing did Riley teasingly call his aunt the Queen of Spin.

For the next twenty minutes Sophie took a hundred or so shots. Then they stopped for a coffee and a break, during which time Marguerite closely scrutinised the photos and insisted on deleting most of them.

After that, it was time for a change of scene. Marguerite arranged herself on the leather swivel chair in front of the computer in her impressive book-lined office. Copies of the Dutch edition of her latest novel were strategically placed on the desk beside a huge crystal vase of stargazer lilies, chosen to continue the pink-and-green theme. Beautifully decorated leather notebooks were piled up next to the computer, alongside a box of fountain pens. Marguerite was famous for taking a notebook with her everywhere she went.

'This is what I've written so far this morning.' She pointed with pride to the text on the computer screen. 'Started at seven o'clock. Because I have the work ethic, you see. And I know my fans are out there, waiting with bated breath for my next book.'

Since Sophie already knew it would be at least a year before the book came out, their breath was going to have to be seriously bated. She took another eighty or so photos of Marguerite tip-tapping away at her computer, then pretending to read her own book in Dutch and finally pretending to admire the vase of lilies on her desk.

Another two hours and a couple more outfit changes later, and the photo shoot was done. Sophie packed away her camera and Marguerite signed a copy of her latest book and presented it to her. 'There you go, something to keep you awake at night! Once you start reading, you won't be able to put it down, guaranteed!'

'Gosh, thanks.' Sophie lived in fear of being interrogated about the plots of the four books she'd already had pressed upon her; she wouldn't put it past Marguerite to test her and make sure she'd devoured every page. And while the books were undoubtedly popular, they weren't her own personal choice of reading matter.

'And how are you fixed for Friday evening?'

'Um, let me think.' Sophie mentally double-checked her calendar and nodded. 'Yes, I'm free.'

'Excellent. The thing is, a local charity is holding a fund-raising dinner at Mariscombe House and they've asked me to be their guest speaker. I did it for them a couple of years ago and they're terribly sweet but a bit clueless . . . the photos they took of me last time were just abysmal. I almost died when I saw they'd printed them in their newsletter and posted them online. So if you could pop along and do the honours, I'd be grateful. Just for an hour or two. Say, turn up at nine?'

'No problem,' said Sophie. 'I can do that.'

'Thank goodness. No more ghastly blink-shots and unflattering angles.' Marguerite breathed a sigh of relief. 'Perfect!'

Tula's little blue Renault, old and pretty decrepit at the best of times, was suffering badly. For the second time in three days it had been forced to make the gruelling journey down to Cornwall and was now crawling into the home straight like an unfit marathon runner in the final stages of exhaustion.

Coaxing it into the pay-and-display car park, Tula dragged her cases out of the boot and skedaddled before the car had a chance to embarrass her publicly by bursting into flames. Loaded down like a pack mule, she made it down the hill to Sophie's flat and rang the bell.

No reply. No car in sight either. And – looking again at her phone – *still* no reply to this morning's texts and emails.

Bum. And her first appointment was in . . . she checked the time . . . thirty minutes.

By the time she'd lugged the cases back to the car park, Tula's hair was sticking to her neck. The heat and the journey hadn't done her clothes any favours either – she looked as if she'd slept in them for a week.

Thinking fast, she unzipped one of the suitcases and took out a clean white shirt and red skirt. Then, having hauled both cases back into the boot, she climbed into the passenger seat of the car and proceeded to change out of one set of clothes and into another.

OK, not ideal, but no big deal either. Besides, what other choice was there? When people stared as they made their way past, Tula determinedly ignored them. It wasn't as if she was naked, for heaven's sake. She still had her bra and knickers on. If she were down on the beach wearing a bikini it'd be perfectly fine and unremarkable.

Which just made it all the more annoying that a group of teenage boys on bikes, having decided to stop to the left of the car, were currently cracking up laughing at her state of undress.

And in her haste to get the shirt on, she'd managed to jam her arm into an inside-out sleeve.

'Waaahh!' She jumped out of her skin as someone rapped on the car window on the driver's side. The unexpectedness of it was what caused her to honk like a startled goose. Which was attractive. Shit, if it was more bloody kids . . .

Grinning at her through the glass, Riley did the winding-down-the-window signal. Tula rolled her eyes and finished shovelling her arms into the sleeves of her shirt. When she was properly decent again, she jumped out of the car.

'Don't stop. I was enjoying that.'

'Of course you were. I needed to change in a hurry.' At least his arrival had seen the teenage boys off. Wryly Tula said, 'Fancy bumping into you here.'

'Your fault for parking next to me.' He jangled his keys and she realised the sporty red Mercedes was his. 'Anyway, I thought you'd gone home to Birmingham.'

'I did, yesterday. And now I'm back again.' She shrugged; there was no time to go into that unfortunate sequence of events now. 'Stuff . . . happened.'

'Ah.' Riley nodded sagely. 'Stuff.'

'I've been trying to get hold of Sophie, but she isn't at home and her phone's switched off.' Checking her watch again, Tula said, 'Oh God, and I've got a job interview in twenty minutes.'

'She's working with my aunt, that's why. And I'm impressed,' said Riley. 'You don't hang around, do you? What kind of job?'

'Just bar work.' She'd trawled the job listings websites last night and called the relevant numbers first thing this morning; luckily in the hospitality industry there tended to be a regular turnover of staff. 'At the Melnor Hotel.'

'The Melnor?' Riley grimaced. 'No way. Seriously, you don't want to work there.'

Which was *exactly* what you wanted to hear when you'd just driven over two hundred miles for an interview.

'Why not?' said Tula. 'What's wrong with it?'

'Run by Melvyn and Noreen. Lots of noise, underage drinking, drug-taking and gang fights. It's the worst hotel in Cornwall, trust me. And the reason they're always needing new staff is because they scare the bejeezus out of the old ones.'

'Oh.' *Oh God*.

'Plus, you don't have nearly enough tattoos.'

'Right.'

'And are you carrying any deadly weapons about your person? No? You see, you just wouldn't fit in there at all.'

'But I need to work. Maybe it won't be so bad once I get there.'

'Sweetheart, it'll be worse. Where else have you applied?'

'To the Coldborough Hotel, but I'm not seeing them until four o'clock. It's got a website,' Tula said defensively. 'It looks OK.'

'I'm sure it's great,' said Riley. 'If you're ninety-six years old. And into biscuits. And *beige*.'

'Oh well. Beggars can't be choosers.' At least she liked biscuits.

'Hang on, someone mentioned something yesterday . . .' Whipping out his phone, he pressed a couple of buttons and said, 'Hi, yes . . . good, thanks. Listen, did I hear Lisa's leaving? She is? So you're going to need someone to replace her? Because I've got a friend here who could be just what you need . . . No, not that kind of friend. You'd like her. And she's keen to get sorted, job-wise. If you wanted to meet her, snap her up before anyone else does, I could bring her along now.'

Chapter 9

When strangers saw Dot and Lawrence Strachan together and learned that they were husband and wife, they invariably assumed that their marriage was wonderful and their lives were filled with love and joy. Why wouldn't they be? They were a striking couple, the connection between them was immediately apparent and their easy camaraderie and laughter indicated how happy they were in each other's company.

Which just went to show, you actually *could* fool all of the people all of the time if you set your mind to it.

Not that it was any secret that they were no longer a couple; it was just what others imagined when they first met them. And they *had* been gloriously happy together for very many years. They had met as teenagers and married at the age of twenty-one, which seemed crazy now but had been more usual all those decades ago. They had been the perfect couple, everyone said so. All their friends envied them. Dot and Lawrence had appreciated their own good fortune and tried not to be sickening about it, but they'd both known how lucky they were to have found each other and stayed so happy together for so long.

Forty years . . .

Until the day Lawrence Strachan had been taking a misty morning stroll along Mariscombe Beach and had seen two huge boisterous dogs racing across the sand, so involved in chasing each other that they failed to notice the woman ahead of them and sent her flying in spectacular fashion.

The woman let out a stifled shriek of dismay and landed awkwardly on one side in the cold, wet sand. The teenage owner of the dogs, in a panic, bellowed at them and legged it, never to be seen on the beach again.

Which left only Lawrence to hurry over and help the damsel in distress. But who wouldn't have done the same? The woman was lying facing away from him, gasping with shock and pain, her fine blond hair spread across the sand, her blue sweatshirt and jeans already soaking up water. Then, of course, the lacy edge of a wave slid up the beach, its icy coldness making her gasp again.

'What hurts?' said Lawrence, bending over her.

'Arm. Elbow. Ow . . .'

Carefully he helped her into a sitting position, then to her feet. The woman managed a brief smile and said, 'Typical, I only started coming for morning walks to get myself a bit healthier. Serves me right for trying. Anyway, thanks.'

She was in more pain than she was letting on. Lawrence guided her over to the nearby rocks and sat her down, then gently rolled back the sleeve of her sweatshirt. Her face fell as they both saw the visible kink in her arm.

'Broken,' said Lawrence.

She shook her head in despair. 'Brilliant.'

'Come on, I'll drive you to A&E.'

'I've been enough of a nuisance already.' Her gaze took in the fact that the front of his shirt was now damp and sandy as well. 'You don't have to.'

'It's no problem. Besides, how else would you get there? Catch a bus?'

Was it fate?

Was it sheer bad luck?

Or amazingly good luck?

Lawrence drove her to the local hospital, discovering en route that her name was Aurora Beauvais. She was forty-eight years old, originally from Edinburgh, recently moved down to St Carys with her husband Antoine, a composer.

By the time they reached A&E, Lawrence realised he was in the grip of something life-changing, inescapable, a *coup de foudre*. Nothing had been said, but he could feel it shimmering between them, a palpable, almost audible buzz in the air. Unbelievably, he knew she was experiencing it too. It was at once horrifying and extraordinary.

He waited with Aurora while she was examined, X-rayed and had her arm put in plaster. By one o'clock she was free to leave the hospital.

'What happens now?' Lawrence asked as he drove her back home.

'I don't know.' Her eyes were huge, her face pale. 'I'm scared.'

'Me too.'

'We must never see each other again,' said Aurora.

'I can't do that.' He stared at her, because the prospect was just so utterly unthinkable.

'I know, but we have to. I'm married. I love my husband.' Her voice wavered. 'Seriously, I'm just not the kind of person who does that.'

'Nor am I. But this is . . . I don't know. I love my wife, too.'

'I wish we hadn't met,' said Aurora. 'I really do. Those stupid dogs have a lot to answer for.'

Dot sat up, dragged back to the present, her attention distracted by the sound of Griff, in his basket under the desk, whimpering as he slept, dreaming of chasing rabbits, paws twitching. Life must be great for a dog, mustn't it? Food, shelter and affection was all they needed to be happy.

When you were human, it became that much more complicated . . .

The reason Dot knew exactly what had happened on the day Lawrence and Aurora had first become aware of each other's existence was because he'd told her himself, in great detail. At first she hadn't wanted to know; the prospect of what was happening was simply too repulsive and terrifying. But eventually, the not knowing had felt worse. Ignorance was no longer bliss. Like touching an electric fence in order to discover just how electrifying it was, she'd asked Lawrence to tell her everything.

Each detail had been more painful than the last, but Dot had absorbed it all in an effort to understand. Because that had been the most extraordinary aspect of it: her husband's bewilderment and sorrow and shame, coupled with a complete and utter inability to countenance giving up this overwhelming new love of his life.

It was eleven years now since it had all happened, but Dot was still able to recall every moment, every word, every emotion of that time. It had been a surreal nightmare, the very worst time of her life; unable to eat or sleep, she had wondered how getting through it could be physically possible. Her husband was distraught and endlessly apologetic but there could be no going back. He'd met someone who meant more to him than she did, and there was nothing either of them could do about it.

The thought of actually meeting her rival was anathema to Dot, but she felt the need to at least see her with her own eyes. One afternoon, she found herself skulking in her car at the end of the street where Aurora lived with her husband, waiting for her to return home from work. Wearing dark glasses and a hat, she sat there for an hour before Aurora appeared.

When she did, Dot marvelled at her ordinariness. Aurora was attractive but not amazingly so. Her fair hair was cut in a no-style style, she was wearing a nondescript green coat over a sensible shirt and skirt. Effortlessly glamorous herself, Dot was astounded by this decided lack of glamour; Aurora didn't fit the bill of husband-stealing femme fatale at all.

Then her heart gave a squeeze of panic as the other woman paused at the front gate of her house and looked directly across the road into Dot's car. The hat and dark glasses might as well have been invisible; there was no question that Aurora knew who she was.

Even more extraordinarily, she stood there for several seconds and waited, with a look of sympathy on her face, letting Dot know that if she wanted to come over and confront her, she could.

If she wanted to scream and yell at her, she could.

Maybe even if she wanted to deliver a resounding slap across the face and rip her no-style hair out, she could.

But having always imagined that she *would* be the kind of woman who would want to confront head-on any form of rival, Dot discovered that she really didn't want to after all. Nothing Aurora Beauvais did or said could make her feel better about the situation. No good could come from any interaction.

Turning the key in the ignition, she had shifted the car into gear and driven away.

The bell went *dinggg* out in reception, and Dot rose to her feet to deal with it, smoothing down her narrow skirt with habitual attention to detail and already breaking into a welcoming smile as she pulled open the office door.

Her smile broadened when she saw Riley waiting at the desk with the girl he'd called about just now. Dot, who relied a lot on instinct and first impressions, liked the look of her straight away; she was pretty and bright-eyed, with small pearly teeth and swingy dark-brown hair.

'Hello, darling.' Riley greeted Dot with a kiss on the cheek. 'Here she is. Her name's Tula.'

'Tula Kaye. Lovely to meet you. Thanks so much for seeing me.' Tula's handshake was enthusiastic.

'Welcome. And I'm Dot,' said Dot, already charmed. Gesturing around the side of the reception desk for the girl to follow her, she said, 'Let's have a chat, shall we? Come along through.'

Well this was all going incredibly well. Tula was ecstatic. The hotel seemed perfect, the couple of members of staff she'd met so far were friendly and she and Dot had really hit it off. Bumping into

Riley in the town car park had turned out to be a massive stroke of luck. Best of all, when she'd mentioned in passing that her friend down here was Sophie, it transpired that Dot knew her too.

'Of course I do! Sophie's a gem, she did all the photos for our brochure. Now, why don't I show you around and you can meet some more people, get a feel for the place . . .?'

'I'd love to.' Tula was scarcely able to believe her luck. Over the last few months, she'd become far more accustomed to everything in her life going pear-shaped.

Less than three minutes later, life reverted to type. Having made their way upstairs to the first landing, they bumped into Josh, who did an unceremonious double-take when he saw her.

'Josh, perfect timing! It looks as if we've got ourselves a replacement for Lisa, isn't that great? Say hello to—'

'Tula. I know. Hang on.' Josh's brow furrowed as he surveyed Tula. 'You haven't seriously applied for a job here, have you?'

'Why not?' Her heart began to gallop. 'It's allowed.'

Puzzled, Dot said, 'Why ever shouldn't she?'

At that moment Tula glanced out of the landing window and experienced the *click* of a final jigsaw piece slotting into place. On Saturday she'd climbed the stone steps from the beach and ended up in the grounds of a hotel whose name she'd paid no attention to. It was where she'd first bumped into Josh Strachan, who co-owned it with his grandmother. But when Riley had driven her here today, they'd parked on the driveway at the *front* of the hotel, and it hadn't occurred to her that he'd brought her to the same place.

'Why shouldn't she?' Josh echoed. 'Because she's not the kind of person you'd want to employ. She lies to her boss, doesn't turn up for work and isn't bothered about letting other members of staff down.' Turning to Tula he said, 'What are you doing back here anyway? Why aren't you in Birmingham?'

Since denying everything clearly wasn't going to work, Tula blurted out, 'Look, it was one tiny mistake and I've paid for it. I hate Birmingham, I can't stay in my flat, and taking that photo of you ended up costing me my job.'

'Ah, so it's my fault?'

'No, I'm just telling you what happened!'

'Fine. And I'm telling you what's *not* going to happen.' Josh was shaking his head. 'You're not going to be offered a job in this hotel.'

'Oh, but—'

'I mean it.' He held up his hand, cutting off Dot's protest. 'Of course you like her, because she seems so nice, but I heard her on the phone on Saturday, calling her boss pretending to be sick so she could spend the weekend down here drinking at the Mermaid and flirting with men.' He paused. 'Chiefly Riley Bryant.'

Although it wasn't the moment to say so, the one she'd most wanted to flirt with had actually been Josh himself.

But the look of disappointment on Dot's face was more than Tula could bear. Her perfect job was evaporating in front of her like dry ice.

'Oh please, it was just one shift. I swear to God I've never, *ever* done it before, and I'll never do it again.'

'You won't be doing it here, that's for sure.' Josh was implacable, unmoved. 'We need people who are honest and reliable. And you don't appear to be either of those things.'

'But I *am*,' Tula pleaded. 'And it was your friend Riley who told me about this job. He was the one who brought me here!'

A brief eye-roll greeted this statement. 'Why doesn't that surprise me?'

She was hyperventilating now. 'Please, I'm a really hard worker. I wouldn't let you down, I *promise*.'

But Josh was already shaking his head; he'd taken charge and was refusing to listen to any more. 'I know you wouldn't,' he said flatly. 'Basically because you aren't going to get the chance.'

That was it; Tula gave up. But honestly, it was at times like this that it would have been handy to know how to do kung fu.

Chapter 10

'Now hold up my book and smile . . . more than that . . . no, lift your chin so you don't look pouchy . . . there, you see, that's *much* better.' Marguerite, who had taken charge as usual, was orchestrating the situation like Steven Spielberg. Nodding at Sophie to begin, she called out, 'Anyone else wanting their photo taken with me, just form an orderly queue over there to the right. Everyone will get their turn!'

Sophie hid a smile and got on with the task in hand, taking care to shoot only from the most flattering angles, as ordered by Marguerite. Resplendent in a bright orange silk dress teamed with zebra-print shoes, Marguerite had actually given a hugely entertaining after-dinner speech. The guests had enjoyed the evening and been thrilled to have the opportunity to meet her. All in all, it had been a good night for the charity.

If less so for Sophie herself; after agreeing to pop in for an hour or two, she'd subsequently been forced to turn down an offer to spend a far more lucrative evening at a silver wedding celebration in Port Isaac. But that couldn't be helped; you took the work as you were offered it.

By ten thirty, when all the photos had been taken, Sophie was packing away her equipment when she became aware of someone standing behind her.

'Oh, hello.' Glancing round, she saw that it was Josh Strachan.

'Hi.' He paused, as if waiting for more. When it didn't arrive, he said, 'Cross with me?'

'Would it make a blind bit of difference?' Sophie clicked shut the fasteners on the camera case and straightened up. 'This is your hotel . . . well, partly. It's up to you who you take on.'

'I know.' Josh gave her a measured look. 'What happened to your friend? Did she go back to Birmingham?'

'No. Nothing to go back to, remember? She's still here.'

'Where's she staying?'

Two could play at being cool. 'On my sofa.'

'Has she found work?'

'Yes.' Sophie wondered where this was headed. 'She managed to reschedule the interview she'd had to cancel in the first place in order to come here.'

'And she got the job.'

'She did. Excuse me a second . . .' Waylaying Marguerite as she swept past in a cloud of orange silk and Guerlain perfume, Sophie said, 'I can send you tonight's photos by Monday, if that's OK.'

'Perfect. Thanks so much for doing this.'

'And I've been here since nine so I'll email you my invoice at the same time.'

'You'll invoice *me*?' Mascaraed lashes batted in surprise. 'Oh no, darling, I'm the guest of honour here tonight! Just send the bill to the charity . . . they'll take care of it!'

And she was gone. Sophie suppressed a sigh, because the tiny strapped-for-cash charity hadn't requested her services and would regard any form of invoice as an expense they couldn't afford. Which meant she was now going to be even *more* out of pocket.

'Where?' said Josh.

'Where what?' Distracted, she dropped her keys.

'Where's Tula working?'

'At the Melnor Hotel.'

You could tell he was unfamiliar with the name by the way he didn't flinch. 'And is she enjoying it?'

'No,' Sophie said evenly, 'of course not. She's hating every minute. It's way over on the other side of St Carys, out on the road to Bodmin, and no one in their right mind goes there.'

'Why not?'

'Because it's an awful drug-infested drinking den for the trouble-makers who've been kicked out of everywhere else.'

Josh said, 'If it's that bad, why's she working there?'

'Why do you think? Because Tula's a grafter who always pays her own way, and anything's better than no job at all. Plus,' Sophie concluded pointedly, 'she wasn't allowed to work here.'

He looked at her. She looked back at him. He really did have incredible cheekbones. OK, and a pretty amazing mouth too.

'She's your friend,' said Josh. 'You're bound to defend her.'

'I'm not defending her. You asked; I'm just telling you the truth. If you'd taken her on, you wouldn't have regretted it.'

'Ooh, there you are.' Dot came rushing up to them. 'Lovely! Have you asked her yet?'

Josh shook his head. 'I was just about to.'

'About Tula?' Sophie feigned innocence. 'I was just telling him, she's working over at the Melnor.'

'Oh my goodness.' Unlike her grandson, Dot was entirely up to speed with the situation. 'Oh *dear*.'

'In fact I'm just on my way over there now to pick her up.'

'I thought she had her own car,' said Josh.

'She does. But by the time she'd finished her shift last night, someone had smashed the passenger window and nicked the stereo out of it.'

'Poor thing, how awful! But maybe that means she might . . . you know . . .' Dot looked meaningfully at Josh.

Reading between the lines, Sophie said, 'What happened?'

'We took on a French guy,' Josh began.

'Ahem, *you* took on a French guy,' Dot retorted. 'And this morning he didn't turn up to begin his shift. When I checked his room, he'd packed his belongings and left.'

'Why?'

'Well, he was quite an intense young man,' Dot confided. 'Took his wine knowledge very seriously. According to the other restaurant staff he got rather upset last night when a couple of customers pretended to be wine-tasting experts and started banging on about top notes of grilled hummingbird and base notes of panda's armpit. It seems he felt they were being disrespectful. Anyway, he's gone.' She didn't look too distraught about it. Raising her eyebrows at Josh, she waited expectantly for him to speak.

Sophie did too. This was fun.

'Fine,' Josh said at last. 'So do you think your friend Tula might be interested in coming to work for us?'

Yay!

'She told me she wouldn't work for you if you begged her on your knees.'

His face fell. 'Really?'

'Not really.' Ha, winding people up was brilliant, especially when they deserved it as much as he did. Watching him relax, Sophie said, 'But it's up to her, not me.'

'Will you ask her?'

'Why don't we drive over to the Melnor now?' She kept a straight face. 'You can apologise first, grovel for a bit, then ask her yourself.'

The Melnor Hotel, modern and unlovely, stood on its own outside St Carys, like the outcast who hadn't been invited to the party. Music was thudding out of the building as they drove into the car park to join the scattering of motorbikes, vans and vehicles with that uninsured look about them. Teenagers in hoodies were hunched along one wall, smoking and swigging out of cans.

'Park over there, under the light,' said Sophie.

'Bloody hell.' As Josh switched off the engine, a fight spilled out of the bar. Scuffling men rolled over in the dirt, yelling and punching and swearing at each other. 'Do you want to wait out here while I go in and get her?'

What, and miss all the fun? thought Sophie. Not a chance. She hopped out of the Audi and said, 'No way, I'm coming in with you.'

The hotel bar was what kept the Melnor in business. Well, that and the drugs Melvyn and Noreen sold to their customers. The younger ones hanging around outside the entrance were enveloped in a cloud of pungent cannabis smoke. Inside, the bar held more customers knocking back pints. The linoleum floor was sticky with spilled drinks, the lighting came from overhead fluorescent tubes and the nicotine-stained walls were bare. Leaning against this side of the bar were people in various stages of inebriation, Melvyn and Noreen among them. Behind it, Tula was working at the speed of light pouring fresh pints and clearing away empty glasses whilst simultaneously avoiding the attentions of the leering bald man attempting to get a good look down her top and defusing an argument between several huge, terrifying-looking drunks.

Alongside Sophie, Josh murmured, 'Jesus.'

'Noreen, who are them two?' A scrawny woman had spotted them, and gave the landlady a nudge. 'Undercover cops?'

Eyes swivelled in their direction. Among this clientele, Sophie realised they looked as ludicrously out of place as a couple of royals – William and Kate, maybe – popping in for a swift half.

Then Tula glanced up from her work and did a cartoon double-take at the sight of Josh.

Chapter 11

'Are you lost?' Noreen demanded abruptly. 'Where are you looking for?'

'It's OK,' Josh announced. 'We've just come to give Tula a lift home.'

Tula's eyes widened in disbelief.

'She ent finished yet. Fill this 'un up, girl.' Melvyn thrust his glass under Tula's nose.

'Listen.' Josh moved towards the bar. 'I'm really sorry about before.'

Tula flushed and said cautiously, 'OK.'

Noreen, swaying on her bar stool, was still eyeing him with suspicion. 'Who is 'e? Is 'e the law?'

Having handed Melvyn his pint, Tula said to Noreen, 'No, he's not the law. It's gone eleven o'clock. OK if I finish now?'

Noreen heaved a sigh of annoyance, because this meant she had to get off her stool and take over behind the bar. Clearly still bothered by Josh, the only man in the place wearing leather shoes rather than down-at-heel trainers, she said, 'Go on then.'

Outside, they intercepted the bunch of hoodies just before they had a chance to set off the Audi's alarm system. Sophie climbed into the back seat, indicating that Tula should sit in the front alongside Josh.

'OK,' said Tula once they'd exited the car park. 'This is all kinds of weird. What's going on?'

'We took on a barman.' Josh got straight to the point. 'He's let us down. We'd like to offer you the job.'

There was a moment of silence. From the back seat, Sophie reached forward and tapped Tula on the shoulder. When Tula glanced round, she shot her a broad you-win grin.

Catching Sophie's eye in the rear-view mirror, Josh said levelly, 'I saw that.'

'Right,' said Tula. 'So let's get this straight. All of a sudden I'm good enough after all? Or are you just *completely* desperate?'

'Your friend here tells me you're a hard worker. Maybe I over-reacted before.'

'So you're desperate,' Tula prompted.

'Not completely. But Dot's keen for you to join us.' He paused. 'And I am too.'

'Do me a favour,' said Tula. 'Could you just say sorry again?'

Another pause. 'Sorry.'

'Really sorry?'

'Don't push your luck.' Josh's mouth twitched. 'I'm offering you a better job than the one you've got now. And accommodation too.'

'Maybe I like staying at Sophie's.'

Sophie gave the back of Tula's seat a swift kick; there was such a thing as pushing your luck.

Evidently thinking the same, Josh shook his head. 'If you're not interested, just say so. I'll find someone else.'

'I'm interested,' Tula said quickly.

'Good. Can you start tomorrow?'

'I don't know about that. I can't let Melvyn and Noreen down.'

He smiled slightly. 'Touché.'

'Then again,' said Tula, 'if you're really desperate . . .'

She took out her mobile, called the Melnor and told Noreen she wouldn't be back. Luckily they were used to members of staff doing a bunk, so the news wasn't as traumatic as it might have been. 'Fine, who gives a toss, plenty more where you came from,' Noreen slurred down the phone. 'Just don't expect to get paid for the last two nights.'

'Sorted,' Tula announced when the call was over.

'Good.'

'Shall I move in tonight? Oh,' her face fell, 'my car's being fixed. I won't be able to move my stuff.'

'No problem,' said Josh. 'We can use mine.' He glanced over his shoulder at Sophie in the back seat. 'Is that OK with you? Taking your friend away from you?'

'Oh, you're welcome to her,' said Sophie. 'She snores.'

'I don't, by the way.' On her knees in Sophie's living room, Tula was busy cramming her worldly goods back into two cases.

'Don't what?'

'Snore.'

Josh looked amused. 'Doesn't matter to me whether you do or not.'

'I know. But I'm just saying.' She couldn't help herself; maybe he wasn't interested in her right now, but she had no intention of giving up yet. It could still happen. And there was definitely more chance of it happening if he didn't think she snored like an old warthog every time she fell asleep.

But anyway, no need to worry about that now; she was going to be moving into Mariscombe House and working for Josh, *hooray*. They could get to know each other gradually, and in time she would win him over with her wit, her sparkling personality and her vivacious charm . . .

Oops, although he might not be quite so entranced by her tangled socks and tights; hastily she shovelled them into the case under a pair of jeans.

Had Josh spotted them?

Dammit, of course he had. Story of her life.

Josh watched idly as Tula buried the armful of underwear in the case before reaching for the rest of her clothes. He turned his attention to the photographs on the geranium-red wall above the sofa Tula had spent the last couple of nights sleeping on. The plainly framed photos were excellent, as you'd expect.

'That one's my favourite,' he told Sophie when she emerged from the kitchen with a plate of toast.

Following the direction of his gaze, she smiled. 'Mine too. Holiday heaven.'

It wasn't a scene that had been carefully designed and set up, which made the resulting composition all the more miraculous. Sophie had taken the photograph on St Carys beach. The sun was high in the sky, small waves were eddying up the beach and people were swimming in the sea. In the foreground, a serious-looking baby sat with his fat legs outstretched while he carefully poked at a sandcastle with a stick. To the left of him was a small girl, presumably his sister, in an oversized white T-shirt. Her hair was a glinting mass of marmalade ringlets and her face an absolute picture of suppressed glee as, having crept up behind him, she prepared to carefully balance a long strand of seaweed on the baby's head.

Finally, to top it all, Sophie had managed to capture the exact moment a Jack Russell terrier with a naughty look in his eye was helping himself to the last sandwich on the picnic plate in the bottom right of the picture.

'I didn't know it was all going to turn out so perfectly,' she said. 'If I had, I'd have taken the parents' details and sent them a copy. They were over there,' Sophie gestured to the right of the photo, 'just out of shot. But I had no idea. It wasn't until I checked the frames on the computer later that night that I realised what I'd got.' Smiling at the memory, she added, 'This is what's so fantastic about photography; you never know when you're going to create a bit of . . . magic.'

Josh watched her hands dance and her eyes light up as she spoke. The way her evident love for her work shone through was oddly touching.

'You have to be good at it too,' he pointed out.

'I know.' Sophie glanced at him. 'I am. But you already know that.'

There was just something about her. She wasn't like other girls. Hiding a smile, Josh said, 'I do.'

Ten minutes later, they were in the car on their way to the hotel. Tula realised she'd sprayed too much scent over herself when she saw Josh inhale, then slowly exhale and lower the driver's window.

'I'll meet you in reception at nine tomorrow,' he said. 'And tell you everything you need to know.'

She beamed. 'Don't worry, I'm a fast learner.'

'Good.'

'And thanks for giving me another chance.'

'We needed someone. It works both ways. But I meant it when I said you mustn't let us down. If I ever catch you doing what you did last week . . .'

'You won't,' Tula assured him hurriedly. 'I told you I wouldn't.'

'Yes, well. If you ever miss a shift you'd better make sure you really are sick.' He gave her a stern look of warning. 'And hang-overs don't count.'

'I know that. You just wait.' With a mischievous grin Tula said, 'I'm going to be the best employee you ever had!' Whoops, the double entendre had been unintentional, but it gave him the opportunity to raise an eyebrow and make a wry, jokey comment. Because if he was changing his mind about taking her on, surely this meant there was a chance he might fancy her just a little bit?

Was it really so unreasonable to think that?

Instead, after a pause Josh said, 'Can I ask you a question about Sophie?'

OK, evidently it was unreasonable.

'What do you want to know?'

'According to Riley, she doesn't have boyfriends. He's never seen her with anyone. All she does is work.'

'And that's a problem?'

He shrugged. 'No, but it's unusual.'

'You mean you can't get over the fact that you asked her out and she turned you down?'

'Not at all,' Josh protested. 'I'm just curious.'

'Maybe she's a lesbian.'

His eyebrows lifted a fraction. 'Is she?'

Entertaining though it would be to pretend this was true, Tula couldn't bring herself to do it. She shook her head and said, 'No.'

'So what's the situation?'

'Why don't you ask her?'

'I'm asking you first.'

And there was certainly no way she was going to tell him. Tula said, 'I think she's just concentrating on building up the business. That's her number one priority right now.'

They'd reached Mariscombe House. Josh pulled into the car park, switched off the ignition and turned to look at her. 'Which means you know, but you're not going to tell me.'

Which in turn would probably only succeed in intensifying his curiosity. But what other choice did she have?

'Maybe it just hasn't occurred to you that you might not be as irresistible as you think,' she said.

His half-smile indicated that he was aware that as far as *she* was concerned, he was. Opening the driver's door, he said, 'Come on then, let's get your stuff up to your room.'

Oh well, the fact remained that he wasn't going to be getting anywhere with Sophie.

Tula discreetly admired Josh Strachan's athletic body as he swung the cases out of the boot of the car. She might still be able to win him over; you never knew.

Chapter 12

Sophie had been twenty years old when she'd met Theo Pargeter in a queue at the local post office.

Ah, the glamour.

It was a very long queue. Everyone else in it was in their sixties and seventies, collecting their pension, renewing their car tax or pedantically counting out small coins in order to buy stamps and post letters off to twenty different countries. The staggering slowness of all involved had Sophie in silent hysterics, and Theo, directly in front of her, soon joined in. By the time she eventually emerged from the post office, he was waiting for her outside. They went for a coffee. Then another. Followed by a walk in the park. And pizza and wine. It turned out to be a long, unpremeditated and entirely unplanned first date.

'From now on,' Theo told her at the end of the evening, 'I'm never going to complain about post offices. Their queues are the *best*.'

Weeks went by and Sophie was happy. Theo was great. They complemented each other so well and everyone remarked upon how perfect they were together. Unlike her last boyfriend, whose hobbies had been football and going out drinking and talking about football with his mates, Theo was charming, kind, thoughtful and empathetic. He was also good company. Things were definitely looking up. Sophie even adored his mum, Betsy, which was just as well, since Theo still lived at home and he and Betsy were a close-knit unit of two. Not weirdly close; just in a good way. It was actually heart-warming to see how well they got on.

The months passed and Sophie's relationship with Theo went from strength to strength. Their friends started to tease them, asking when the wedding was going to happen. Which was crazy, because they were far too young to be thinking of anything like that.

But another year later, completely out of the blue, Betsy suffered a major heart attack, and life as they knew it changed for ever. Theo spent most of his time at her bedside in the coronary care unit, and Sophie visited whenever she could. Betsy, her face whiter than the sheets she lay on, clutched her son's hands and told him how much she loved him. Then she started saying the same to Sophie. One afternoon, her voice croaky and weak, she whispered, 'All I want is to know my boy's going to be happy. He means everything in the world to me.'

'I know.' Sophie stroked her thin arm.

'And you love him too, don't you?'

Sophie nodded and said, 'Yes.' Because she did.

'I just want to be sure everything's going to be OK. You're meant to be together. You are going to get married, aren't you?'

Sophie swallowed; Theo had only left the ward to buy a coffee from the machine in the corridor outside. 'I don't know.'

'But you *must*.' Betsy was shaking her head from side to side in an attempt to convey the urgency in her frail voice. 'You must! Promise me you will!'

At that moment a nurse came bustling over to take Betsy's blood pressure, and Sophie was saved from the awkwardness of having to reply. But Betsy wasn't letting it drop; evidently she'd gone on to discuss the situation with her son. Three days later, taking a break from the hospital visiting routine, Theo took Sophie out for an early dinner at their favourite Italian restaurant and uncharacteristically ordered a bottle of champagne. Well, sparkling wine with a champagne-shaped cork.

Sophie knew at once what it meant; she guessed what was about to happen. Oh God, surely not, please no . . .

'I love you,' Theo said simply, his hands reaching across the table for hers. 'I never want us to be apart. Sophie, will you marry me?'

'Oh, but aren't we too young?' Even as the words were spilling out, she could see the hurt in his eyes. It wasn't the done thing to hesitate, come up with reasons why it shouldn't happen. She was spoiling the moment.

'No.' Theo shook his head vehemently. 'We're not too young. It's *fine*.'

She could hear her own breathing, felt like Darth Vader. 'But . . . are you doing this because your mum told you to?'

His jaw jutted. 'She didn't *tell* me to.'

'Asked, then. Because it's what she wants more than anything. She told *me*,' Sophie whispered. 'The other day.'

'OK, I know, but that's not why I'm doing it. I want us to get married. I thought you would too.'

Oh God, this was awful. Because the thing was, he was right: at any other time she might have been overjoyed. She did love him. And she knew he loved her. But a powerful sense of déjà vu was bringing a memory hurtling back from childhood.

Sophie had been standing in the garden at home, listening to their neighbours arguing. She'd been eight years old. Rob-next-door was very nearly ten. She'd liked him and he'd always been friendly in return. It had been mortifying, therefore, to hear him wailing, 'But Dad, I don't *want* Sophie at my party.' Followed by his father's brusque reply: 'I know, Rob, but she's our neighbour. You *have* to invite her.'

An hour later, the mortification had expanded like styrofoam in her throat when Rob had rung their doorbell and recited without enthusiasm, 'Hello, Sophie, it's my birthday on Saturday, I hope you'll come to my party.'

Before she could answer, her mum had come out of the kitchen and exclaimed, 'How wonderful, that's so kind of you! She'd love to come!'

Afterwards, when she'd tried to explain that she didn't want to go, her mother had laughed and said, 'Oh darling, don't be so silly! They're our neighbours, of course you have to go!'

Sophie shuddered at the memory and looked up to meet Theo's gaze. 'It's just the . . . timing.'

'I know. And if everything was OK, we'd leave it for maybe another year. But everything isn't OK.' His Adam's apple bobbed a bit as he said this. 'Mum's . . . she doesn't *have* another year. I'd do anything to make her happy. Yes, she wants to see us get married, but is that really so terrible? If it makes her happy?'

When he put it like that, it did seem churlish to object. Sophie immediately felt bad. And the middle-aged couple at the next table had definitely heard them; they'd abandoned their conversation in order to eavesdrop.

She did love Theo. It wasn't as if she didn't.

Plus, although there was no way she would say this out loud, maybe they could just vaguely plan on getting married; the chances were that Betsy wasn't going to live as long as it took to arrange a wedding, after all.

Sophie smiled and gave his fingers a squeeze. 'OK then, yes, let's do it.'

His eyes brightened. 'Really?'

'Yes.'

'I love you.' He moved the candle out of the way before leaning across the table for a kiss. The strain of the last couple of weeks melted from his face as she kissed him back.

'Congratulations,' said the wife at the next table.

'Thank you,' said Theo.

The woman raised her glass at them and winked at Sophie. 'You'll be able to choose an engagement ring! That's something to look forward to!'

'Oh, I don't need an—'

'No,' Theo cut in, 'we won't be buying one of those.'

Which had come as a relief at the time. Except she'd wildly underestimated the degree of planning that had gone into this evening's proposal.

Leaving the restaurant at eight o'clock, they headed over to the hospital before visiting time ended. Now she knew why they'd eaten dinner at six. As they entered the ward, Betsy turned her head, the unspoken question radiating from her yellow-tinged eyes.

Sophie saw Theo nod at his mother, and Betsy visibly relaxed, breaking into a smile. The next moment Sophie found herself being manoeuvred round to face him. And there and then, in the middle of the ward, in front of *everyone*, Theo dropped to one knee. Grasping her left hand, he cleared his throat.

'Sophie . . .' His voice was deliberately louder than usual, like an actor on stage, so that all the nurses, patients and other visitors could hear. 'I love you so much. You mean everything to me. Will you make me the happiest man in the world and be my wife?'

She knew why he was doing it like this; it was so his mum could see him proposing, could be a part of it. Which was obviously a lovely, thoughtful thing to do, if pretty embarrassing for her. The back of her neck had gone all prickly and hot.

But what could she do, other than go along with it? The rest of the ward had fallen silent; everyone was waiting. And the smirking teenage boys who were here to visit their gran in the next bed were clearly *longing* for her to say no . . .

'Yes.' Sophie smiled down at Theo and nodded. 'Of course I will.'

And then everyone was clapping and going *aaaahhh* and the smirking teenagers were pulling disappointed faces at each other and Sophie watched in disbelief as Theo took something small from his jacket pocket and began putting it on her finger.

Oh, good grief, he *had* bought her a ring . . .

Then her stomach did a weird little squeeze of dismay as she realised her mistake. No, he hadn't bought her a ring; this one belonged to his mother.

It was small and delicate, in the style of a flower, with a central diamond and garnets for petals. She already knew that Betsy's parents had given it to her on her twenty-first birthday and that Betsy had worn it ever since. OK, maybe this was just for show, for the benefit of their audience. As it slipped into place on her third finger, Sophie said, 'It's your mum's ring . . .'

'Not any more.' Theo rose to his feet and put his arms around her. 'She wants you to wear it. It's yours now.'

He kissed her briefly on the mouth — it wasn't the place for anything more full-on — then led her over to Betsy's bed. There were tears of joy in Betsy's eyes.

'You have no idea how happy you've made me,' she said as they hugged. 'I know it sounds silly when I'm stuck here in this bed, but this is one of the best days of my life.'

And who knew how many days she had left? As Betsy took her hand, Sophie said, 'I can't wear your ring. You must keep it.'

But Betsy was already shaking her head. 'No, no, bless you, I want you to have it. Nothing would make me happier. Look how lovely it is . . . it's just beautiful on you!'

Oh dear. Sophie knew at that moment that there was no wriggling out of it. The ring *was* pretty, but it was the kind of style she would never have chosen for herself in a million years. Her own taste in jewellery was sleek, chunky and modern. This was like asking Lady Gaga to wear a beige knitted cardigan for the rest of her life.

But what else could she do, when it was pretty much Betsy's dying wish?

Chapter 13

The doctors had already warned them that Betsy had only weeks
to live. What no one had bargained for was the effect the word
wedding could have on a potential mother-of-the-groom. Rallying
almost immediately, she began making plans for the forthcoming
nuptials. Theo was overjoyed. Sophie was pleased too, of course,
but at the same time inwardly alarmed that what had only been
meant as a vague promise now appeared to be going ahead. Still
weak, but spurred on by her own enthusiasm, Betsy came home
from the hospital and got busy on her computer, organising the
register office, the reception, her own outfit and dozens of other
must-have items for the big day.

Her recovery was miraculous. Everyone said so.

And three months later, Betsy was there with them when they
got married. Resplendent in caramel silk splashed with pink
peonies, she beamed with pride throughout the ceremony, afterwards telling everyone that she had the best daughter-in-law in
the world.

And yes, of course it had all been down to emotional blackmail,
but Sophie told herself it was OK to have been steamrollered
into the wedding; it was just happening a couple of years earlier
than it might have done otherwise.

Betsy was happy and that was what mattered. Look at the
amazing recovery she'd made. It really *was* a miracle.

Except it turned out, sadly, not to be so. Within ten weeks of the wedding her condition deteriorated once more; she was readmitted to hospital and then transferred to a hospice.

Aware of the prognosis, she told Sophie and Theo to look after each other and be happy. 'I'm going to miss out on seeing my grandchildren,' she croaked, her voice barely audible.

'Oh Mum . . .' Tears sprang into Theo's eyes as he clasped her thin, almost translucent hand.

'And you'll make such wonderful parents,' Betsy whispered, her own eyes filled with love for her son.

'If we have a girl,' Theo promised, 'we'll call her Betsy.'

Feeling like the worst kind of daughter-in-law, Sophie silently amended that if they ever had a girl, Betsy could be her middle name. It wasn't going to be the one that got used every day.

'And if you have a boy,' Betsy went on, 'will you name him after your grandfather?'

Sophie managed a slight smile to cover the horror; Betsy might be dying, but there were limits. No way was any future child of hers going to be called Brian.

Betsy died later that night. The funeral, held a week later, was an emotional affair. Once it was over, Sophie expected Theo to grieve for a while, then gradually become accustomed to no longer having his mother around. After a few months, she thought, he would still miss her, of course, but the worst of the mourning would be over.

What she hadn't imagined was that it would be the other way round; twelve months after Betsy's death, the grief was worse.

And if it had been the hardest year of Theo's life, it had been difficult for Sophie too. They were living in Betsy's house, and she was working shifts in a call centre whilst attempting in her spare time to learn as much as possible about photography. As Theo's wife, it was also her job to help and support him and do everything she could to cheer him up.

But nothing worked; he had neither the inclination nor the wherewithal to cheer up. Six weeks after the funeral he had walked out of his job and had subsequently shown no interest in finding another one. He was clearly depressed, but refused to see a doctor. At times he'd be silent and withdrawn for days on end. At other times he would go out and stay out, drinking too much in an effort to numb the pain. When he was at home he did nothing around the house, nor was he grateful for anything Sophie did. It was like being saddled with the kind of room-mate you'd run a mile from in ordinary life, and it was no fun at all.

Which only made Sophie feel more guilty, because this was her husband and it wasn't his fault. She knew perfectly well this wasn't what he was really like. And they'd exchanged vows: for better, for worse, in sickness and in health. She had to be patient and understanding and help him through this.

Eventually, surely, worse had to become better.

But Theo wasn't making it easy for her. He resented the fact that she was carrying on with life as if nothing catastrophic had happened. He accused her of not caring. Sometimes he told her she was the only thing that kept him going. At other times he announced bitterly that she'd only married him to please his mother.

Which was true, although she never admitted it. But the whole scenario was a nightmare. What was she supposed to do?

And then it took another turn for the worse, with Theo getting it into his head that the reason he wasn't feeling any better was because they hadn't yet fulfilled Betsy's *other* dearest wish.

If they had a child, everything would be resolved.

Funnily enough, the prospect of giving birth to a baby called Brian wasn't a tempting one. Sophie couldn't allow him to think it was going to happen. This was when the arguments escalated; Theo swung between angrily accusing her of not wanting him to get better and begging her to change her mind. Nothing she said could make him believe she wasn't being unreasonable. Eventually Sophie was forced to pretend to go along with what he wanted, while secretly taking the pill in order to ensure it didn't happen.

By now she was feeling trapped in a nightmare with no way

out. Her friends were telling her to leave Theo, but how could she do that to him? If they could just get through the next few months, he might turn the corner and go back to being himself again, the real Theo she'd first fallen in love with.

Then the worst bit of bad luck meant that the truth came out. While Sophie was at work one day, Theo happened to pick up the DVD case of *Bridget Jones's Diary*, which was lying on the carpet beneath her side of the bed. For some reason, maybe wondering idly if the DVD itself was inside it, he'd opened the case and discovered it wasn't. Which just went to show, you might *think* it would be the safest possible place to hide your contraceptive pills, but sometimes even the most watertight plans could go awry.

Sophie never forgot the look on Theo's face when she arrived home from work that evening. He told her she couldn't possibly love him if that was the level of deceit she was capable of sinking to. He then announced that he didn't want to live in the same house as someone who only pitied him. Finally, ignoring her protests, he said it was pretty obvious that the reason she was taking the pill was because she was having an affair with someone else.

Nothing Sophie said could change his mind, which was made up. He loved her but she clearly didn't love him. The marriage was over and she could move out as soon as she liked.

It was horrendous but also, secretly, a relief. Maybe a break, a breathing space, was what they both needed. Who knew, after a few months apart, the situation might improve . . .

Sophie moved out a couple of days later. She rented a tiny flat in Aston; by no means lovely, but at least it was cheap. And she met Tula, who lived in the flat below.

This turned out to be the most fantastic stroke of luck; the two of them hit it off from the word go. Within a week, returning home from work became a joy rather than something to be silently dreaded. What had been an ordeal took on that last-day-of-term sense of lightness and anticipation. It was like turning the corner and discovering a wonderful new world of infinite possibilities.

Guilt mingled with the relief, needless to say. Sophie knew she'd failed as a wife. Everyone told her she'd done her best, but perhaps she should have tried harder to help Theo. He'd announced that since seeing her was just too painful, they shouldn't meet up for a while. Which was probably a sensible idea.

Without the benefit of hindsight, she had no way of knowing the worst was yet to come.

The following Friday was Tula's birthday. She was holding a party in her flat and everyone was invited.

'You have to come,' she told Sophie. 'It's going to be brilliant!'

Delighted, Sophie said, 'Perfect, I'll definitely be there.'

At four o'clock in the afternoon, just as she was arriving home from work, her phone pinged with a text from Theo. Her heart sinking, she opened it:

Hi. Want to come over tonight? Just for a chat?

Sophie exhaled slowly. Any agony aunt would say it was too soon. She'd only moved out ten days ago. Even if she didn't have Tula's party to go to, it would be too soon.

Rather than mention the party – because that would be plain mean – she sent back a text saying:

Sorry, can't make it, have to work late tonight.

She hovered a finger over the x. Every text she'd ever sent to Theo had ended with kisses. As had his messages to her. But he hadn't sent any today. Maybe adding kisses would make *her* look needy, prompting him to think she was desperate for a reunion.

No kisses, then. She would follow his lead. She pressed send and heard the whoosh of the text spiralling out into space.

The next moment Tula banged on her door and called out, 'Will you be an angel and come to the supermarket with me? I need help carrying all the food back for the party.'

Right, stop thinking about Theo. Pulling the door open, Sophie plastered a bright smile on her face and said, 'No problem. Let's go!'

It was a great night. She'd forgotten how it felt to have fun and be carefree. There were new people to meet, slices of pizza to eat, music to dance to and drink to drink. By three in the morning the soles of Sophie's feet burned, her throat was sore from shouting to be heard over the music, and the muscles in her face ached from laughing so much.

It wasn't until you felt young again that you realised you'd spent the last couple of years feeling far too old. She was only twenty-four.

At five in the morning, as the first light of dawn was spreading across the sky, she climbed the stairs to her own tiny flat and fell into bed, happy and exhausted.

Waking up at midday on Saturday, Sophie made herself a cup of tea, then returned to bed and lay there for an hour, idly watching an old rerun of *Friends* on TV and checking her mobile, smiling at some of the photos she'd taken last night.

Just after one o'clock, making her way downstairs to see how Tula was faring, she glanced over the banister and saw a slew of post lying on the mat by the front door.

Thinking there might be some belated cards among them for Tula, Sophie went down and collected up the envelopes. Yes, two were definitely birthday cards . . . She stopped in mid turn, realising that the third envelope was addressed to her. In Theo's writing.

How odd; why on earth would he choose to send her a letter in the post rather than an email? And one with a second-class stamp?

Opening the envelope, she began to read.

And her blood ran cold.

Chapter 14

Dear Sophie,

It's five o'clock on Friday and you've just told me you can't come over. (No kisses at the end of your text – yes, I noticed.) That's OK – I wanted to see you one last time but it doesn't matter. I'm putting this in the post with a second-class stamp so you'll get it next week, by which time I'm sure you'll have heard the news.

Anyway, I'm really sorry to do this to you, but life just doesn't seem worth living any more. I love you so much, Sophie, but I know you don't love me. Nor do you deserve to be stuck with someone you've stopped loving, just because you feel sorry for them. I bet the last couple of weeks have been a lot more fun, haven't they? I'm not saying that in a sarcastic way, either. It's a genuine question.

I love you.

I really love you, Sophie. You have no idea how much. Sorry if me doing this makes you feel sad – you'll get over it in no time. And no need to feel guilty either. Don't let what's about to happen spoil your life – you don't deserve that. I want you to be happy again. Sorry about the whole baby thing too. When the time comes, you'll meet someone else and have beautiful babies.

Right, enough. You're probably bored with reading this

now, if you've even got this far. (I know, why do suicide notes always have to be so *depressing*?)

Anyway, goodbye. I love you too much to want to carry on without you in my life.

Be happy, Sophie. Sorry again.

All my love,

Theo xxxxxx

She hadn't read the whole letter; skimming through the contents had been enough. After that, everything was a blur. She had no memory of doing it, but she had somehow managed to drive – still in her nightdress – across Birmingham to Theo's house.

The front-door key, thank goodness, was still on her key chain.

She vaguely remembered her hands shaking so badly it had taken several goes to unlock the door.

And there he'd been, up in the bedroom, on the bed. Theo, whom she'd loved with all her heart. Waxy-skinned and with his eyes closed, deeply unconscious but still breathing. Just about.

There were empty pill bottles on the bedside table. She called 999. An ambulance arrived . . . and police. The paramedics worked on Theo until he was in a stable enough condition to be moved, then whisked him off to Queen Elizabeth Hospital. No one could say what the prognosis was; it might already be too late to save him. This had been no cry for help; Theo had planned *not* to be rescued in time. He'd undoubtedly wanted to die.

If the second-class letter had arrived when he'd meant it to, he would have been dead long before he was found.

And it could still happen.

The second letter had been almost worse than the first. In the minutes before the ambulance arrived, Sophie had spotted the sheet of paper on the same table as the pill bottles. It was folded in two and had her name handwritten on the front.

Inside, it said:

Hi again, darling,

Had second thoughts after posting that letter. Thought I might walk over and wait for you to finish work. But it turns out you weren't there after all. So I came over to your flat just before midnight. No reply when I rang your bell, but I could hear the noise from the party going on on the first floor.

Then I saw you, through the window. At the party, laughing and dancing without a care in the world. The music was Beyoncé singing 'All the Single Ladies'. Which was appropriate. If you'd looked out of the window, you'd have seen me standing outside on the pavement. But you didn't. Never mind. I'm glad you were having fun.

Txxx

Sophie felt sick. Theo might not have said it in so many words, but the implication was that she might just as well have picked up a knife and stabbed him through the heart.

Oh God, please don't let him die . . .

Time had become meaningless. For the next hundred or so hours, day blended into night as Sophie haunted the ward, the waiting room and the corridors of Queen Elizabeth Hospital.

Theo was comatose in the intensive therapy unit, unresponsive and with his life hanging in the balance. Organ failure was a possibility. So was neurological damage. The doctors warned her that even if he survived, he might wake up and no longer be recognisably himself.

Guilt and terror had her in their grip; she was trapped in a clammy spiral of fear. The medical staff were treating her like Theo's wife, but they knew the truth. It was all there in his medical notes. They were being wonderfully kind and sympathetic towards her, but what were they saying to each other behind her back? Did they despise her? Were they gossiping and speculating over what she might have said or done to make him *that* desperate to end his life?

And yes, she'd explained the circumstances to the doctor who'd asked her, and he'd written them down too, but did anyone actually believe her, or did they secretly assume she must have done something terrible to provoke him?

On the third evening, one of the ITU nurses came over to her table in the cafeteria and said, 'Hi, I've finished with my magazine . . . do you want to read it?'

'Thanks.' Sophie was touched by the kind gesture, even if she wasn't sure she could concentrate on reading anything. But when the nurse had left the cafeteria and she looked at the cover of the magazine on the table, certain bright red words leapt out at her:

ME AND MY NEW MAN JUST WANT TO BE HAPPY BUT MY HUSBAND WON'T LET ME GO!

Was it a coincidence, or was the nurse making some kind of point, silently letting her know that they knew? *Even though they didn't, because there was no other man.*

On Wednesday evening, the first signs of recovery became apparent. By Thursday morning, Theo was beginning to regain some sort of consciousness. Pain caused him to react irritably. Slowly his eyes began to open for short periods. Calling his name elicited a brief response, as did squeezing his hand and asking him to squeeze in return. The hospital staff were cautiously optimistic but continued to warn Sophie that brain damage could be a possibility.

Racked with guilt, she had already silently vowed that if Theo was brain-damaged, she would devote the rest of her life to looking after him. Simply because her conscience wouldn't allow her to do anything else.

But by Friday, the prognosis – thankfully – was becoming brighter. Having been persuaded by the medical staff that he was now out of danger, Sophie spent the night at home. Physically and mentally exhausted, for the first time in almost a week she actually managed a full night's sleep.

Arriving back at the hospital the next morning, she bumped

into one of the doctors, a cheerful Aussie, as he was coming off duty.

'You wait till you see him,' he told Sophie with a broad grin. 'You won't believe the difference. It's like someone flicked a mains switch and he's back.'

Oh thank God, *thank God for that*. As the doctor headed off down the corridor, Sophie held her emotions in check for as long as it took to duck into the nearest ladies' and lock herself inside a cubicle.

Then she burst into tears of relief; more tears than she'd known she possessed. Theo was going to be all right. It was like facing the death sentence, then being reprieved at the very last minute. No longer would she have to bear the unendurable guilt. From now on she would do whatever Theo wanted her to do. If he preferred to take things slowly, fine. But if he wanted her to move back into the house with him . . . well, that was fine too. They could resume the marriage where it had left off. Anything, *anything* that meant she no longer had to feel that terrible weight of guilt.

Entering the ITU, she paused at the sink as always to thoroughly scrub her hands. There was Theo, she could see him from here, sitting up in bed talking to one of the nurses. She was laughing at something he'd just said. Oh wow, they were having a completely normal conversation. Sophie's heart turned over as she dried her hands. She was going to walk over there now and greet him as if everything was fine, as if she'd never moved out, as if *nothing had ever happened* . . .

The next moment the nurse spotted her and said something to Theo. He turned his head to watch as Sophie approached the bed. Her shoes clicked against the polished floor. It felt as if all the staff on the ward had fallen silent.

Her arms were already half outstretched when she realised that Theo wasn't smiling. In fact, he was slowly shaking his head. As she drew to an awkward halt, he said, 'No, no. What are you doing here? I don't want to see you.'

'What?' She felt sick; it was bad enough that all the nurses were watching. Thank goodness the rest of the patients were unconscious. 'But Theo, I'm here because—'

'Don't care.' He shook his head again. 'Not interested. I don't need your sympathy.' Turning to the nurse on the other side of the bed, he said, 'Get her out of here.'

'OK, calm down.' The plump nurse rested a soothing hand on his shoulder. 'But she was worried about you. She's been here every day since you were brought in.'

'I don't care. I wasn't awake then, I couldn't stop her.' The disdain in Theo's eyes and the flat tone of his voice was chilling. 'But I am now, and I want her to go.'

'Sorry, dear.' The nurse's eyebrows signalled to Sophie to do as he said.

'And don't come back,' Theo called after her, his voice rising as she made her way back down the ward that suddenly seemed a mile long. 'I never want to see you again. *Ever*.'

Chapter 15

'Look into each other's eyes and smile,' said Sophie, though it was hardly necessary; the two of them hadn't been able to stop beaming all day.

'Hold your stomach in,' the bride told the groom.

'You hold yours in,' he countered. 'Yours is bigger than mine.'

Even with both of them trying their best, they still looked like a couple of bowling balls. Gloriously happy ones, though. The brand-new married couple were enough to restore the most pessimistic person's faith in happy-ever-after. They'd already told Sophie their story during the pre-ceremony photographs, and it had only made her love them more.

'He moved into the flat below mine,' Hannah cheerily explained. 'With his *trumpet.*'

'And she was upstairs from me,' Owen chimed in, 'dancing along to her blasted exercise videos. And guess when she used to do it? At seven o'clock in the morning before she left for work. I mean, can you imagine the joy I felt, being woken up by that?'

'So he started playing his hideous trumpet at ten o'clock at night. Honestly, I used to fantasise about stuffing it down his throat. I'm a lark,' said Hannah, 'and he's a night owl. You can't imagine how much we hated each other.'

'So how did you end up getting together?' Sophie was busy setting up the gold Lastolite reflectors that would give the photos a warm glow.

'My flat needed rewiring. I asked the landlord how I was meant to cope without electricity while it was being done, and he told me Owen had kindly offered to let me come down and use his flat for the evening.'

Owen said, 'And he told *me* that Hannah had begged him to ask if she could come and spend the evening in my flat.'

'So we were forced to be nice to each other,' said Hannah. 'For six whole hours.'

'And it kind of did the trick.' Owen grinned. 'We both realised the other person wasn't as bad as we'd thought.'

'Well *I* wasn't,' his new wife retorted. 'I still had my doubts about you.'

'But then I won you over.' He surveyed her with affection. 'Even though you didn't want me to.'

'I was thirty-eight,' Hannah told Sophie. 'And completely happy being single. I'd long given up on the idea of meeting Mr Right and having children.'

'That was eighteen months ago.' Gesturing at his wife's hugely swollen stomach, Owen said with pride, 'And look at her now.'

It was a wonder the excitement of the big day hadn't sent Hannah into labour. Giving her husband's own rotund belly a pat, she said gleefully, 'Look at you too.'

By six o'clock everyone was relaxing and enjoying the party, being held in a marquee in the back garden of Hannah's parents' house in Launceston. The speeches had been made, the sit-down reception had finished and now the dancing could begin. Except for those still working, needless to say. But Sophie loved this stage of a wedding, once everyone had stopped being self-conscious about the fact that they were wearing their best outfits. High heels had been kicked off, lipstick had faded and fascinators had slipped as the day progressed. Now the formal photos were out of the way, she could capture everyone having fun. Slipping between tables and watching from the edge of the dance floor, she captured perfect moments in time: one of the tiny bridesmaids with her flowered headband askew, dancing with her grandfather whilst carefully holding on to a half-eaten slice of wedding cake . . . A broad-hipped matronly type in skin-tight lilac satin doing the hokey-cokey to an Abba song . . . A teenage boy stealthily tipping some of his mum's wine into his own empty water glass . . .

'Excuse me, have you seen Riley anywhere?'

Turning, Sophie saw the tall blonde girl who had brought Riley along with her to the wedding. She shook her head and said, 'No, sorry, I haven't.'

'He's disappeared. Just buggered off twenty minutes ago and hasn't come back,' the girl said crossly. 'I can't imagine where he's got to.'

Sophie did her best to look similarly mystified, though when it was Riley you were talking about, where he might have got to was anyone's guess. He could be up to anything at all.

The girl stalked off, clearly annoyed, and Sophie wandered outside to see if Riley was visible anywhere. If he was busy chatting up another girl, she could warn him that the blonde was on the warpath.

But there was no sign of him among the guests in the garden. It wasn't until she crossed to the far side of the lawn to take a few photos of the house and marquee from a distance that she glimpsed a hammock strung between two trees. From the shape of it, the hammock was occupied.

Surely even Riley couldn't have sex in a hammock, could he? Nevertheless, Sophie proceeded with caution. Then she relaxed; all was well, he was on his own. And fast asleep.

Too much champagne, probably.

He did look kind of cute, though, the handsome surfer boy with the sun-bleached hair and killer cheekbones, his habitual casual air at odds with the dazzling white shirt, dark morning suit and highly polished shoes. She was more used to seeing his tanned feet in faded blue flip-flops.

Stepping back and raising her camera, Sophie took a couple of shots of Riley asleep. As the shutter clicked, he opened one eye.

'Hi.' A slow smile spread across his face. 'Sorry, dozed off.'

'Your girlfriend was wondering where you'd got to.' She took one more photo for good measure, just because he was so pretty.

'Ha, don't tell me, and you came out to look for me because you were worried I might be up to no good.'

'Funnily enough, that thought did cross my mind. Can't imagine why,' said Sophie.

He spread his arms in protest. 'And here I am, completely innocent. Not doing anything naughty at all.'

'Apart from having too much to drink, abandoning your girl-friend and crashing out.' She gave the side of the hammock a playful prod.

'It's nothing to do with the drink. I didn't get much sleep last night; it just kind of caught up with me.'

Sophie raised an eyebrow. 'Hmm.'

'And Amelia isn't my girlfriend,' Riley added. 'She didn't want to come along on her own, so she asked me to be her plus-one.'

'She wishes she was your girlfriend.' Sophie had seen the way Amelia had been acting around him all day.

He shrugged, acknowledging the truth of this. 'Well I'm just doing her a favour . . . oh, here she comes now.'

Turning, Sophie saw Amelia stalking across the grass towards them, clearly still not in the sunniest of moods.

'*There* you are. What's going on?'

'I was tired. Popped out for a power nap,' said Riley.

She narrowed her eyes accusingly at Sophie. 'And you said you didn't know where he was.'

Honestly, why did girls never realise how behaving like this made them look? Sophie said, 'That's because I *didn't* know.'

'But now you're out here talking to him.'

'She was letting me know you were looking for me,' Riley said.

'Well you can come back inside. You've been gone for ages.' Her voice softening, Amelia held out her hand. 'Come on, let's go.'

'Hang on a sec. What time are you heading back to St Carys?' Riley turned to Sophie.

'I have to be here until ten.'

'Can I get a lift with you?'

'What?' Amelia looked dismayed. 'But I said you could stay at mine! I'll drive you back tomorrow morning.'

'I know, but I really need to get home. Marguerite called; she needs me to fix her computer.'

This was so obviously not true that Amelia's eyes narrowed. Hauling himself out of the hammock, Riley said to Sophie, 'Is that OK?'

She shrugged. 'If that's what you want to do.'

'Great. Come on then.' Reaching for Amelia's hand to make it up to her, he said, 'Let's go and have ourselves a dance.'

An hour later, another girl approached Sophie and said shyly, 'Could you take some photos of me?'

Sophie smiled. 'Of course I can.'

'Not here in the marquee. Outside.'

In the garden, the girl began to pose for the camera. She was in her late teens, a bit overweight and wearing a Lycra dress that clung like a sausage skin and didn't do her any favours. But she threw herself with gusto into a range of poses.

'Very good,' Sophie said, to be kind. 'You've done this before.'

The girl flushed with pride. 'Yeah, I'm a model.'

Okaaay . . .

'Really?' Doing her best to sound interested rather than downright astonished, Sophie said, 'What kind of modelling do you do?' *Please not the X-rated kind.*

'Well, I'm just starting out really.' The girl assumed a pose with both arms raised high above her head and her pudgy face tilted back. 'I was spotted by a talent scout from a famous modelling agency and he said I was a natural.' She twisted round so she was beaming at Sophie over one shoulder. 'It was, like, the best day of my life. I never thought I could be a model, but he said I definitely could!'

She was a sweet girl, but not the prettiest. Nor was she anywhere near tall enough to work as a model. Her heart sinking, Sophie said, 'And what kind of work has he been getting you?' Although she was fairly sure she didn't want to know.

'Well I haven't done any actual jobs yet, but they've got my portfolio sorted out now, and then they'll start sending photos out to people who need models for, like, photo shoots in New York and Paris and glossy magazines and stuff.'

Oh God. 'Right. And do you have to pay the model agency to be on their books?'

The girl looked horrified. 'No way! That's what the scam agencies do. If they ask you to pay them money, you know they're not a proper business. They were the ones who told me that.'

Oh. OK. Chastened but still baffled, Sophie said, 'Well, good for them.'

'They never do that,' the girl went on. 'Because they're a proper agency you can trust. The only thing you have to put a bit towards is the photos for the portfolio, because they need to be done by a proper professional.'

Ah . . .

Sophie nodded slowly. 'And how much were they?'

'Six hundred pounds. Well, six hundred and ninety-five. But it's, like, an investment,' she added hastily. 'Cheaper ones wouldn't be any good. And my nan and grandad used their savings to help out. They said it was worth every penny if I was going to end up being a supermodel like Kate Moss!'

Sophie told Riley about the scam as they left Launceston behind them and headed back to St Carys. 'It makes me so *mad*. I mean, seven hundred pounds to take a few photos then pretend to be sending them out to magazines. That poor girl. And her grandparents used all their savings . . . poor *them*.'

'What's the name of the agency?'

'She wouldn't tell me. They're based in London, apparently, but they so-called scouted her on a beach in St Ives. And she got defensive when I kept asking questions.' Sophie grimaced. 'Said she couldn't remember the name of the agent. Or the photographer. Honestly, some people are just disgusting, taking young girls' money and getting their hopes up.'

'Leave it,' said Riley. 'Nothing you can do. Anyway,' he changed the subject, 'when are you and me finally going to get together?'

Sophie shook her head in amusement, because Riley was truly in a league of his own. 'Never.'

'Do you realise,' he clapped a hand to his chest, 'that every time you say that, you rip my self-esteem to shreds a little bit more?'

As if.

'The only reason you ask me is because you know I'll say no.'

'Not true. I'm just an incurable optimist. Every time I ask you, I hope and pray that this time you'll say yes.'

'Fine,' Sophie said patiently. 'In that case, yes. Let's do it, let's go out on a date.'

'Seriously?' Riley sat up.

She grinned. 'No, of course not. I just wanted to see the look on your face.'

'Why won't you come out with me?'

'Don't fancy you,' said Sophie. How many times had she said it now?

'How about Josh Strachan?'

'Don't fancy him either.' It was true; she didn't. *I'm in charge of my own emotions.*

Riley raised an eyebrow. 'You know what your trouble is? You don't fancy anyone.'

'And I like it that way.'

'Why, though?'

'Just makes life easier.' Sophie shrugged. 'I don't need the hassle.'

'Who says I'd be hassle?'

She smiled patiently and gave him a look. 'Anyway, I'd rather concentrate on work, building up the business.'

'He's pretty keen, you know.'

'Who?' Though she knew.

'Josh.'

'Not my problem,' said Sophie.

'You're a cruel woman.'

'Not cruel.' She shook her head, amused. 'I call it upfront and honest.'

'Fine then. Talk to me about your friend Tula.'

They'd pulled up at traffic lights. Sophie's smile broadened, because Riley was doing his best to sound casual, which definitely meant he was intrigued. Then again, he appeared to find most girls intriguing. It was pretty much his default setting.

'My friend Tula's had a terrible time with boyfriends. Trust me, the last thing she needs is to have her heart broken again by someone like you.'

'Has she said anything about me?'

'No.'

'You see, there's something weird going on,' Riley protested. 'I actually do like her more than I thought I would. But she's already turned me down. And not in a game-playing way, either. She really wasn't interested.'

'You're not her type,' said Sophie.

He looked outraged. 'Why not? What's wrong with me?'

'Too pretty, too full of yourself, too lazy. Tula grew up with a dad like that . . . well, before he ran off with another woman, and then another and another. She wants a boyfriend she can trust, someone who won't let her down like her dad did. Also,' Sophie concluded, 'someone not afraid of a bit of hard work.'

'Don't tell me,' said Riley. 'You mean someone like Josh.'

Sophie didn't speak. Then again, no answer was really necessary.

With a sigh, Riley tipped his head back and said, 'Yeah, it's OK, I noticed it too.'

Having dropped Riley off at his cottage, Sophie drove home. She uploaded the wedding photos on to the computer and spent an hour checking through them, deleting the immediate disasters and no-hopers and making a note of the ones she was particularly pleased with.

It was one o'clock before she went to bed. Lying back against the pillows and gazing up at the ceiling, she thought about Riley's comments in the car. It was four years now since Theo's suicide attempt, but just thinking about it still caused all the same emotions to come flooding back.

They'd had no face-to-face contact since that day in the intensive care unit when he'd regained consciousness. Having told her in no uncertain terms that he never wanted to see her again, Theo had stuck to that decision. Upon leaving the hospital, he'd put his mother's house on the market and sold it within weeks. He'd then left Birmingham without telling anyone where he was going. The quickie divorce had been conducted entirely through their respective solicitors.

And that had been that.

Lying there in the darkness, Sophie remembered the hatred she'd seen in her husband's eyes that last time, and concentrated on keeping her breathing slow and even. She'd stopped crying years ago. Theo wasn't dead; thanks to the internet, she knew that much. Of course she'd looked him up on Google. He was living in a different part of the country now, nowhere near Cornwall, and running a small independent business. There was a single photo of him on the company's rather basic website looking . . . well, not exactly beaming with joy, but he'd never been relaxed in front of a camera.

What was his life like now? Was he still dreadfully depressed? Rattling with pills and unhappiness? Sophie knew he never wanted her to contact him again, so she would never know the answer to those questions. But every couple of months she found herself checking the website, making sure it was still there, reassuring herself that Theo was still alive.

His actions had succeeded in changing her irredeemably and for ever. The fear and terror and guilt involved in being responsible for someone else's life – or more accurately death – meant she could never bring herself to become emotionally involved with another man.

On the surface, her day-to-day life was happy; she laughed and joked and behaved like a completely normal person. Other people regarded her as cheerful, up for a laugh and extrovert.

But that was on the surface, purely for public consumption. Unaware of her past – simply because it was no one else's business but her own – what they didn't realise was that there was a permanent chunk of ice embedded in the centre of her heart.

Nor was it ever going to melt. Life was easier with the ice in place. Some people might not have been able to stick to the vow she'd made to herself, but Sophie knew she could carry on indefinitely. It was like dieting; most people embarked on weight-loss programmes and gave up within days or weeks, first sneakily wolfing down doughnuts, then abandoning the whole notion of dropping a dress size until the next faddy diet came along. Whereas others made the decision that if they wanted to maintain a low weight, they were just going to have to get used to consuming fewer calories and stick with the plan, because the end result was worth it.

Well, that was what she'd decided. Only instead of giving up chocolate and doughnuts, she'd given up men.

And once you'd made up your mind, it wasn't that hard to do, it really wasn't. In some ways it was quite . . . freeing. Sophie closed her eyes. At least it wasn't as hard as the alternative.

A couple of miles away, on the other side of St Carys, in his cottage in the grounds of Moor Court, Riley finally got to bed at three in the morning. Which was ridiculous when you considered he'd only managed a couple of hours' sleep last night and roughly ten minutes in the hammock earlier. But he was used to it now.

He thought about Tula for a bit, replaying in his mind what Sophie had told him about her.

Basically, Sophie was saying her friend was completely allergic to people like him.

Riley exhaled. It had never bothered him before because it had never mattered, but now he was beginning to sense that it might.

What would Tula think about him if she knew the truth?

Chapter 16

Falling in love didn't always bring happiness and everlasting joy. Lawrence Strachan had discovered this to his cost following the day he'd met Aurora Beauvais on the beach. It had been a *coup de foudre* so powerful and overwhelming his subsequent actions felt as if they were beyond his control. The last thing he'd wanted to do was break up his own happy marriage and decimate the life of Dot, whom he also loved. But it had ended up happening anyway.

He wasn't proud of himself for having done that. But having been the instigator of so much misery, he'd at least imagined that as time passed, Dot would find another man worthy of her, and he and Aurora would carry on being a happy couple. In his more optimistic moments he'd even been able to envisage the four of them socialising together. OK, maybe that was pushing it, but it wasn't beyond the realms of possibility; some couples and their previous partners managed to get along together just fine.

Except it hadn't worked out like that, had it? There'd been no time for any of them to—

The cup slipped from Lawrence's hand, splashing its contents across the café table. Hot coffee soaked into the newspaper he'd just bought and dripped down on to his trousers. Lawrence barely noticed; he was too stunned by the sight of the man who'd just emerged from the shop opposite.

'Oh no, look at you, how did you manage to do that?' The

middle-aged waitress came bustling over with a damp cloth and a roll of kitchen paper. As she cleaned the table and removed the sodden *Telegraph*, Lawrence gazed, transfixed, across the street.

What on earth was Antoine doing back in St Carys?

'Shall I get you another coffee, love?' Lowering her voice, the cheery waitress said, 'Don't worry; on the house.'

'Um . . .' As Lawrence hesitated, barely able to concentrate, he saw Antoine turn and make his way towards the esplanade. Within thirty seconds he would be out of sight. 'No, don't bother, it's OK. Thanks anyway.' Pushing back his chair and getting clumsily to his feet, he threw down a handful of change and left the café.

His previous train of thought had been prompted by the momentary glimpse of someone who'd reminded him of Antoine entering the newsagent across the road. It hadn't occurred to Lawrence for a moment that it could actually *be* him.

But it was. Eleven years after leaving Cornwall and moving back to his native France, Antoine had returned.

With absolutely no idea why he was doing it, Lawrence began to follow him. Keeping close to the shopfronts, he prepared to duck inside one of them if Antoine happened to look round. His heart was thumping inside his chest at the subterfuge; he was like James Bond with dodgy knees and hypertension.

Antoine was undeniably looking well, though. He carried himself easily and had kept himself trim. How old was he now . . . in his early sixties? He'd always been a stylish dresser; not too many British men of that age could carry off a pale pink linen jacket worn with a dove-grey shirt and immaculately tailored dark trousers. He had also managed to hang on to his hair, which was combed back from his tanned face. Basically, he *did* look like Hollywood's idea of a secret agent.

Lawrence, who was currently wearing an old checked shirt and faded navy corduroys, stopped in his tracks as Antoine, ahead of him, paused to take a phone from his jacket pocket and speak into it. Who was he talking to? What *was* he doing here, anyway?

And had he remarried? Presumably, after this length of time, he had met someone else.

Lurking behind a revolving rack of postcards, Lawrence glimpsed his own reflection in the window of the shop currently sheltering him from view. He pulled his stomach in, as he always did when the sight of it caught him off guard. Then the phone call ended and Antoine was on his way again.

This time there were no more interruptions. Antoine walked the length of the esplanade. At the end, Lawrence expected him to turn to the right and take the path leading down to the beach. Either that or turn left and carry on up the road to the main car park.

But Antoine did neither. Instead he took the footpath beyond both those turnings; the one leading up to Mariscombe House.

What?

Why?

Bemused, Lawrence watched as he disappeared from view. When a minute had passed, he took out his own phone and speed-dialled the hotel.

'Hello, Mariscombe House, how can I help you?' It was the new girl, Tula; Dot liked her staff to know how to help out on reception.

'Tula, it's Lawrence. Listen, has a man in a pink jacket just walked into the hotel?'

'Ooh, yes, he has. Would you like to speak to him? I can pass—'

'*No*,' Lawrence blurted out. 'No, don't say anything. I just wondered what he was doing there. Is he meeting someone, do you know?'

'Um, no idea. He's on his own, as far as I can tell. He's just going up to his room,' said Tula.

'Up to his *room*? You mean he's booked in?' Lawrence hadn't been expecting this. 'Who with?'

'Hang on, let me just check. He arrived last night.' He heard the sound of the computer mouse clicking as she searched for the information. 'Ah yes, here were are. Mr Beauvais, room seventeen. No one else with him,' said Tula. 'On his own.'

'And how long's he taken the room for?'

'A week.'

'Right. OK.' Lawrence exhaled. 'Thanks.'

Clearly keen to impress with her dazzling reception skills, Tula said cheerfully, 'You're very welcome! Any time.'

Lawrence ended the call, then turned and headed back along the esplanade.

He wondered whether Dot knew Antoine was there.

Either way, he knew he definitely needed a drink.

They never really went away, but Antoine's return brought the memories flooding back in technicolour detail. When Aurora had broken the news to her husband that she'd fallen helplessly in love with someone else, he had – understandably, perhaps – not taken it well. As Aurora herself had freely admitted, anyone looking at the pair of them would assume that if one of them was going to leave the marriage, it would be Antoine. He was a composer, intelligent, handsome and stylish, with a faint French accent that just made him that bit more irresistible to women. Looks-wise, Aurora had been more ordinary, her way with clothes more haphazard. Their marriage had been happy, but she'd known the outside world considered her to be the lucky half of the partnership.

Antoine had been both devastated and furious. He'd come to Lawrence's home and confronted him, stating quite plainly what he thought of him. He'd said, 'I would like to kill you. The only reason I won't do it is because I don't want to go to prison. But trust me, I wish you would die.' He'd paused, then continued, 'I think that's the only thing that would make me happy. If you were dead.'

It hadn't been a threat; simply the honest truth. And Lawrence couldn't blame him. He'd tried to apologise, but Antoine wasn't interested. He'd left the house, left St Carys, left the UK and returned to France.

Lawrence and Aurora had moved into a seafront flat in nearby Bude and prepared to spend the rest of their lives together; now that the hard part was out of the way, they were looking forward to some happiness.

And they were happy, even though the guilt at what they'd done was overwhelming, and they were aware that after causing so much pain and grief to Antoine and Dot, they didn't deserve to be.

The happiness, however, lasted only seven weeks. Feeling tired and indescribably unwell, Aurora took herself off to the doctor's surgery for an examination and blood tests. Within days she'd been referred to the hospital for scans and X-rays. The diagnosis hit them like a meteor crashing out of the sky. Aurora was suffering from a form of cancer that had been busy metastasising inside her body, silently spreading from its primary site in her left lung and invading her liver. Moreover, it was advancing at speed; this wasn't the leisurely kind of cancer that gave you time to come to terms with it.

Exploratory surgery was carried out, but there was no possibility of a cure. Aurora had lost the battle even before the first symptoms had made themselves known. Weakened and unwell, she longed to live but knew it wasn't going to happen. The happy-ever-after they'd looked forward to had been wrenched away, and not just for a while, either; for good.

The ensuing weeks had been the worst kind of nightmare. Lawrence felt as if he'd forgotten how to breathe. It was like being plunged underwater and never being allowed up for air. He genuinely couldn't begin to imagine how the rest of the world was managing to carry on as if everything was still normal. He spent every possible minute at the hospital, at Aurora's bedside, willing her to astound the medics and get better. Aurora accepted her fate as the punishment she deserved for being the cause of so much misery.

'You didn't make this happen,' Lawrence told her over and over again. 'If we'd never met, you would still have become ill.'

'Would I?' Her face greenish-white against the pillows, Aurora shook her head. 'You think that, but you don't know for sure.'

Lawrence was no longer sure of anything. Aurora had irrevocably changed his life for the better, and now she was changing it for the very-much-worse. When she held his hand and said, 'God, I bet you wish you'd never met me,' he was torn in half. Because this was the woman he loved more than anything, but just seven weeks of being together before the cancer had taken her captive . . . well, it was a pretty rough deal. Seven weeks simply wasn't long enough. He'd been happy with Dot. If he hadn't met Aurora, it wasn't as if he'd be miserable now . . .

Shit, maybe she was right and it was all a matter of karma, nature's way of ensuring the sinners got their just deserts.

It was a salutary lesson for Lawrence. He'd always been a popular man, liked by all. But since abandoning equally popular Dot, he'd experienced the cold chill of disapproval from acquaintances and friends. And he'd completely understood that, accepted it as his due.

Now, though, it was almost unbearable knowing that although no one had said as much to his face, a lot of these same people would be feeling he'd got what he deserved, that maybe now he understood how it felt to have your world ruthlessly torn apart.

As the weeks went by and Aurora's condition worsened, the unthinkable ending drew nearer. In the end, the unthinkable became almost desirable, she was in so much pain. Antoine flew back from France and Lawrence waited outside the hospital while he visited his wife. Whatever passed between them remained private; Lawrence didn't ask what had been said and Aurora didn't tell him.

Was a Frenchman familiar with the expression *Schadenfreude*? Either way, Lawrence recalled the look in Antoine's eyes when his rival had wished him dead. Did Antoine remember that moment too?

And was the curse now set to be all the more painful, with Aurora being the one to die and Lawrence himself left behind, forced to carry on without her?

She succumbed, finally, just two months after the initial

diagnosis. Aurora was now at peace, but for Lawrence the grief had only just begun. He hadn't seen or been in contact with Dot, although she obviously knew what had happened; everyone in Bude and St Carys did. And whilst there was sympathy for his situation, there were also still plenty of people who felt he'd been a foolish man who'd made a foolish decision and ended up – deservedly – managing to lose *both* the women in his life.

But time had passed and gradually he'd got over the worst of the grieving process. Eighteen months after Aurora's death, Lawrence moved back to St Carys. The week before Christmas, he bumped into Dot on the high street.

She looked thinner but was otherwise as elegantly dressed as ever, in a scarlet coat and gleaming navy boots. They were still officially married, but the third finger of her left hand was bare. Which was understandable.

The sight of her made Lawrence's throat tighten. He had missed her so much.

'How are you doing?' said Dot.

He'd shrugged. 'Well, you know, pretty dreadful really. But . . . can't complain.' *Because it's no more than I deserve.*

'No.' Dot hesitated, then said, 'And what are you doing for Christmas?'

Lawrence shook his head and watched as a family made their way past, laughing and struggling to carry a twelve-foot Norwegian spruce. It felt like a hundred years since he'd laughed. 'Same as last year. Nothing.'

It wasn't even as if he and Aurora had happy memories of Christmas; they'd talked about sharing it, but cancer had intervened. It had never happened.

Dot looked at him. Finally she said, 'I don't have any plans either. OK, just an idea, but do you want to come over for the day?'

'What?' He couldn't believe what he was hearing.

'Doesn't matter if you don't want to. If you'd rather be on your own, that's fine, not a—'

'*No*,' Lawrence blurted out before she could withdraw the offer. 'I'd like to. Really, that'd be great. Thank you.'

'Right. Turn up whenever you want after midday. I'll cook the food, you can bring the wine.' Intercepting the question on his mind, Dot said, 'No presents. No funny business. I'm not trying to win you back, if that's what you're wondering. I just think life would probably be easier in the long run if we could get back to being friends.'

Slowly Lawrence nodded; after forty years of happy marriage, of course it would be easier. Grateful for the olive branch – and the generosity of the woman proffering it – he said, 'Me too.'

Chapter 17

Lawrence finished his whisky and left the bar. Needless to say, his feelings for Dot had only intensified after that. Having never actually fallen out of love with her in the first place, he'd spent the last decade hopelessly in love with a woman who steadfastly refused to be anything other than friends with him in return. And to be honest, after the way he'd behaved, who could blame her?

Now, retracing his steps along the esplanade, he turned right at the end and headed down to the beach. There was Josh, paddling out on his board to beyond the surf. Lawrence watched as he turned, waited, caught a wave just before it broke and surfed expertly to the shore. Making it all look so easy, even though it wasn't.

Having spotted him, Josh made his way up the beach. When he saw the troubled look on Lawrence's face, he said, 'Hi, problem?'

He knew what had happened, of course, all those years ago. Josh had been as shocked as anyone when his grandparents – held up as an example to all who knew them as the ultimate perfect couple – had split up. Lawrence was endlessly grateful that their own relationship had survived.

'Antoine Beauvais has booked into the hotel. He's staying for a week.'

'I know.' Josh raked his wet hair away from his forehead. 'He turned up late last night'

'But why? That's the thing. What's going on?'

'No idea,' said Josh.

'Does Dot know? She's not working this afternoon. I tried calling her mobile but it's switched off . . . she's hopeless about answering that thing.'

'Dot knows,' said Josh.

'She does? Right.' Taken aback by this news, Lawrence said, 'So any idea what he's doing here?'

'She hasn't told me.'

Maybe he could track her down and ask her. 'Whereabouts is she?'

'Gone to the hairdressers,' said Josh.

'Oh.' Since Dot generally did her own hair, Lawrence said, 'Special occasion?'

'I don't know about that.' Josh shrugged and hesitated. 'But she's having dinner tonight with Antoine Beauvais.'

It had been another long, hot day, and by five o'clock Sophie was ready to hit the beach. Well, the water. Stripping down to her blue and white striped bikini, she left her clothes and towel on the beach and waded into the sea.

Aaahh, bliss. The water enveloped her, instantly cooling her skin, and she began to make her way out to the diving platform. At this more sheltered end of the beach, the sea was calmer, the waves reduced, and it was possible to swim without getting mown down by an out-of-control surfer.

The diving platform was empty. Hauling herself up on to it, Sophie sat on the gently rocking sun-warmed wood and surveyed the scene before her. It was always great seeing the beach from this angle . . . the swimmers, the paddling children, the sandcastles close to the shoreline and the sunbathers stretched out on their multicoloured towels. Their voices were muted by the waves, and you could see the surfers in their shiny black wetsuits but not identify them from this distance.

The next moment, as a flash of light caught her attention, she realised that the sun was bouncing off the lenses of a pair of binoculars. What was more, they appeared to be trained on *her*. One of the black-clad surfers, standing on the beach close to the café, was watching her through them. And he had dark hair. If it were Josh Strachan, she wasn't sure she liked the idea of being observed from a distance. It felt uncomfortably like being spied on.

Flushing slightly and looking away, Sophie rose to her feet and prepared to dive back into the water. A splash behind her was followed by a sudden rocking movement of the diving pontoon. Turning, she saw someone in red board shorts levering themselves up out of the water. When he raised his head, she saw that the owner of the tanned, tightly muscled body was Josh.

'Hello!' Surprised to see her, he signalled towards the beach and said, 'Sorry, didn't know you were out here.'

He was breathing heavily, had evidently been exerting himself. Sophie said, 'Where did you come from?'

'Just swam around the headland and back.' Josh gestured a crescent shape with his left hand. 'Baz is timing me. He bet I couldn't do it in under thirty minutes.' Checking his watch, he broke into a grin of satisfaction. 'I reckon I did it in twenty-eight.'

He hadn't been sleazily spying on her after all. Neither had Baz, come to that; he'd had those binoculars trained on Josh, not her. Sophie relaxed. 'How much was the bet?'

'Twenty quid. Worth the effort.' Shaking water out of his hair, Josh said, 'Finished early today?'

Flushing slightly, Sophie looked away, tipping her face up to the sun. 'That's the thing with my job. Irregular hours. You work when people ask you to work, do the rest in your own time.'

'So nothing this evening.'

'That's right. But tomorrow I'll be on a job working flat out from midday to late evening.'

'Keeps it interesting. OK, looks like I have to go.'

Shielding her eyes, Sophie saw that Baz was now making strenuous beckoning gestures. 'Why?'

'He's looking after Griff. Maybe he needs to get home.'

And there was Griff, she belatedly noticed, dancing around Baz's legs. Sophie said, 'I'll race you back to the beach.'

'I'm still out of breath,' Josh protested.

'That's why I'm making the bet.' She rose to her feet. 'I'm not stupid.'

'Tenner,' said Josh.

'Twenty.'

'Fine. *Go* . . .'

Griff came doggy-paddling out to greet them as they approached the shore. Sophie beat Josh by a couple of seconds.

'You won,' he told her.

She narrowed her eyes at him. 'Did you do that on purpose?'

'No way, never.' He shook his head, clearly amused by her look of suspicion. 'Wouldn't dream of it. Anyway, where's your towel?'

'Over there.' Sophie pointed to the little pile of belongings twenty yards away on the sand.

Once she was semi-dried and dressed, he came over and tried to give her a twenty-pound note.

'Absolutely not. You let me win.'

'I didn't.' Josh smiled. 'But OK. Maybe you'll let me buy you a drink sometime instead. Just a friendly one,' he added before she could protest. 'Seeing as you don't do dates.'

It was time to leave. Josh was heading back to the hotel. Together they made their way across the dry sand with Griff trotting between them. Plenty of people were still navigating the steps on the path leading down to the beach. A chihuahua on a fluorescent pink lead began to yap furiously at the sight of Griff, who looked bemused.

'Are those dogs going to have a fight?' said a wide-eyed small boy, watching from further up the path.

'Definitely not.' To be on the safe side, Josh bent and scooped Griff up, ready to pass the frantically yapping chihuahua. His bare arm brushed against Sophie's as they both shifted to one side to allow the boy's grandmother to make her way down. Sophie did her best not to notice the physical contact.

As they carried on climbing the uneven steps, she moved further over to the left to make room for a woman approaching with a pushchair. Behind them now, the chihuahua was still yapping. Josh was keeping a firm hold on Griff.

The small boy, clutching the front of his yellow shorts, said in a piercing voice, 'Mum, I need a *wee*,' and the woman with the pushchair said distractedly, 'Ben, wait, you can't have a wee yet . . . no, don't pull your shorts down . . . *oh* . . .'

In her haste to reach out and grab her son's arm, the woman lost her footing and stumbled, letting out a cry of pain as her ankle twisted beneath her and she crashed to her knees. Her grip was wrenched from the handles of the pushchair, which tipped sideways down the next step and promptly bounced, provoking shouts of alarm from those around it.

Sophie realised she was directly in the pushchair's path. She also knew there was only one way to stop it careering down the slope to the pebbly bit of the beach. Since there was a baby in the pushchair, she didn't have much choice. To her right, Josh was holding Griff and otherwise obstructed by an elderly man with a walking stick.

Time appeared to have slowed down, but impact was increasingly imminent. What she wouldn't give for a crash helmet right now. Bracing herself, Sophie held her arms out like a goalie and prayed this wasn't about to hurt as much as—

OOF. Fuck . . . ow, ow, *ow* . . .

Blindly she grappled with the weight of metal and now-screaming baby; so long as they both didn't go crashing head over heels, all would be well. Or as well as could be expected when there was a searing pain in your back and it felt as if you'd just been kicked in the head by a bull.

And now she was sprawled face down in the dusty, stony sand with what felt like warm liquid metal in her mouth and a car wheel pressing down on her head. But both hands – she could feel them, thank God – were still hanging on to the pushchair. Oh please, *please* let the baby be all right.

The next moment the pressure on her head was reduced and somewhere above her Josh was saying, 'It's OK, you can let go now. Let go . . .' She felt her fingers being gently prised free, the pushchair was lifted away and the baby let out an indignant wail.

'Oh thank you, thank you,' gasped the mother, her voice disappearing somewhere over to the right as the pushchair was carried down to the beach.

Sophie felt Josh's hand carefully cupping the back of her head, heard him say in a low voice, 'Are you all right? Can you move?'

She nodded, more out of politeness than conviction, and mumbled, 'Is the baby hurt?'

That was when she realised the warm liquid metal in her mouth was blood and the question had come out as an unintelligible gurgle.

Josh rolled her over on to one side and she spat the blood into a patch of dusty grass. *Ladylike*. From the sharp pain on the side of her tongue, it seemed she'd bitten it, which was at least better than having a couple of teeth knocked out. Repeating the words, Sophie looked up and saw him shake his head.

'The baby's fine. Thanks to you. You've got a lump on the back of your head and a cut on your face. How's the rest of you?'

'My back hurts.'

'Don't try to move. Stay where you are. I'll call an ambulance.'

'No way. I'm fine.' Other people were crowding around, peering down at her. It was like being a circus attraction. Mortified, Sophie held one hand out to Josh. 'And I'm not staying here either. Help me up.'

Seeing that she meant business, he did so. Once she was on her feet, a woman in the crowd handed her a pack of tissues to mop up the blood trickling from her mouth and temple.

The mother of the baby in the pushchair called up to her from the beach. 'You all right, love, are you?'

'Um, yes . . .'

'That's good. Cheers, then!' And Sophie found herself on the receiving end of a breezy thumbs-up before the family turned and headed off across the sand.

'Such overwhelming gratitude,' Josh said drily.

'I wouldn't want overwhelming gratitude.' Sophie pulled out another tissue and marvelled at the amount of blood a bitten tongue could produce. 'Although I wouldn't have said no to an ice cream.'

He relaxed. 'Come on, let's get you out of here. Want me to carry you?'

A brief mental image of how that would look. And feel.

'No. I can walk.'

'Are you always this obstinate?'

'I am when I don't want to look stupid.'

As she slowly limped her way, Quasimodo-style, up the rest of the steps, Josh murmured, 'Because now you aren't looking *at all* stupid.'

And Sophie belatedly discovered that when she shouted with laughter she *sounded* like Quasimodo too.

Back at the hotel, he helped her into reception. Horrified, Tula said, 'Oh my God, what happened to *you?*'

'He threw me down the steps,' said Sophie.

'No he didn't. He wouldn't do that.'

'I fell,' Sophie admitted, 'and got hit by a flying pushchair.'

'She needs to lie down.' Josh handed the other end of Griff's lead to Tula. 'I'm taking her up to my room. Do you know how to call the doctor?'

'I do.' Tula looked proud. 'Dot told me about this morning.'

'I can call my own doctor,' Sophie protested.

'And wait how long before they give you an appointment to

turn up at the surgery?' Josh shook his head. 'We have an arrangement: any problems and the doctor comes here to the hotel. He'll check you over, see if we need to get you to the hospital.'

'Well I'm definitely not going *there*.' Sophie was adamant. 'I've got a big job on tomorrow.'

'You haven't seen yourself in the mirror yet. Maybe you should think about letting the experts decide,' said Josh.

Chapter 18

Coming down the staircase at seven o'clock, Dot saw Tula still working behind the reception desk.

'What are you doing here at this time, darling? You should be off duty by now.'

'It's OK, I offered to stay on. I'm enjoying learning about everything that needs to be done. You look nice,' said Tula.

'Thanks.' Dot put a hand up to her hair, re-blonded and professionally blow-dried. 'Feels a bit weird. Not used to hairspray.'

'Off out somewhere special?'

'Kind of.' Since special didn't really begin to cover it, Dot said, 'I'm going out to dinner with my ex-husband's late mistress's husband.'

Tula's eyes widened. 'Blimey.'

'I know! Mr Beauvais from room seventeen.'

'Wow. He's very good-looking.'

'I know that too. Not that it's relevant.' Dot pulled a face. 'What with him being the husband of my ex-husband's dead mistress.'

'Phew. Well now I get why Lawrence was asking about him,' said Tula.

'He was?' *Ha, good*. So that explained the calls Lawrence had made to her switched-off phone.

Then the lift doors opened and there he was. Antoine Beauvais. Looking, it had to be said, the very picture of a French film star.

Dot wondered if he would even recognise her – they'd only briefly seen each other once or twice all those years ago. This morning he'd left an envelope addressed to her at reception. Inside, he'd explained that he was staying here at the hotel and would be honoured if she would meet him at seven for dinner. No other explanation, just that simple request. No idea why, either.

In all honesty, though, how could she refuse? Dot had been so utterly intrigued, she had said yes.

'Dorothea.' He'd recognised her, thank goodness. Dot found herself being greeted with a Gallic kiss on each cheek. Then Antoine stepped back to survey her. 'It's good to see you again. You look wonderful.'

He was wearing the most divine cologne. 'Nice to see you too.' She didn't tell him he was also looking wonderful; he must already know that.

'I've booked a table at the Rose. Is that OK with you?'

'Of course. I love the Rose.'

'I thought we'd have more privacy than if we stayed here.' He passed his room key across the reception desk to Tula before guiding Dot over to the door. 'Shall we go?'

'Have a nice evening,' Tula said brightly.

And Dot, turning to smile at her, saw Tula giving her a massive thumbs-up.

Once they were seated at their table and had been handed their menus, Antoine said, 'So are you curious?'

'Very.'

'It's eleven years since I left St Carys. My travel agent recommended Mariscombe House and booked the room for me. It wasn't until I looked at the website afterwards that I realised it was your hotel.' He dipped his head in acknowledgement. 'Quite a surprise.'

'We took it over three years ago. Keeps me busy.' Dot smiled at him. 'I love it.'

'We?' said Antoine.

'Me and my grandson, Josh. He put up half the money. He's been living and working over in the States, but now he's back.'

'And . . . how are things with you?'

'Really good, thanks.'

'Not married, I see.' He glanced at her left hand. 'Partner?'

Dot shook her head. 'No. You?'

'Not currently. There have been . . . ladies, of course.'

'Of course,' Dot murmured. How could there not be ladies?

'But for now? Unencumbered. And may I ask what happened to your ex-husband?'

'Lawrence?' Dot said steadily. 'He moved back to St Carys a year or two after Aurora died.'

'I remember meeting him for the first time, confronting him. Wishing him dead.' Antoine paused and adjusted the crisp white cuff of his shirt. 'Ironic that he's still alive and Aurora should have been the one to go. Did he try to get back together with you?'

Dot shook her head. 'I made it very plain that it would never happen. We bump into each other from time to time. But I couldn't trust him again.'

'Does he wish you'd take him back?'

'I don't know.' She did know, but wasn't going to say so. Antoine was a virtual stranger, after all; they were linked only by the fact that their respective spouses had fallen in love.

'And have you forgiven him?'

'Forgiven, not forgotten,' said Dot. 'Because he ended up suffering too, but I'll never forget what he did and the way it made me feel.'

'If your husband had died and Aurora had tried to come back to me, I couldn't have allowed it either.' Antoine nodded in agreement. 'Once the connection has been broken, it can never be repaired, you know?'

The waiter arrived, menus were hastily perused and orders taken. When the wine had been sampled and poured, Dot said, 'So what brings you back to St Carys?'

Antoine smiled slightly. 'The reason Aurora and I moved here in the first place was because we loved it so much. I wanted to see if it had changed. Spending some time back in Cornwall seemed like a nice idea . . .'

'And?' Dot prompted when his voice trailed off.

'Honestly? I made a poor decision.' Silver eyes twinkling, Antoine said, 'There is a rule I should have stuck to, but I did not. The rule that says it isn't wise to become romantically involved with the divorcee who lives directly across the street from you.'

'Ah,' said Dot.

'Ah indeed. Especially when you realise you've made a big mistake, but the lady in question doesn't think so. I ended the relationship a couple of weeks ago and she has taken it rather badly. I made an error of judgement.' His tone was wry. 'And now her feelings are hurt, so she is making my life difficult.'

'Oh dear.' Men, honestly.

'So it seemed like a good time to remove myself from the situation,' Antoine concluded.

'Escape, you mean.'

His mouth twitched. 'Or that.'

'And you're hoping that by the time you head back, she'll be over you.'

'Exactly. Over me, rather than all over me.' His command of English was remarkably good. And there was that shrug again, somehow simultaneously managing to indicate apology and lack of concern.

'You're booked into the hotel for seven days,' said Dot. 'Is that going to be long enough?'

'For what? Ah, I remember.' Another nod and a complicit smile. 'Well, let's see how things turn out. Basically, I can stay as long as I want.'

There'd been no need to head over to the hospital, thankfully. Called out to check Sophie over, the doctor had given her the all-clear. After applying butterfly stitches to the gash on her temple, he'd told her to take things easy for a while. Reassured and dosed up on painkillers, she'd promptly fallen asleep in Josh's bed.

Now, opening her eyes and checking her watch, she saw that it was nine in the evening. Outside, the sun was setting behind the trees, washing the sky with a fiery shade of pink tinged with apricot. *Beautiful.* Inside, various parts of her were throbbing painfully and there were smears of dried blood across the formerly pristine white pillowcase.

Sophie eased herself with care out of the bed, hobbled over to the mirror on the opposite wall and gazed at her reflection.

Oh dear, not beautiful at all.

She'd wrenched her back and shoulder muscles. There was a sizeable lump on the back of her head. Her tongue had been bitten and there was the stitched cut on her left temple, accompanied by an emerging blue-grey bruise. Blood from the cut had dried on her cheek and in her hair. Basically, she looked as if she'd picked a cat fight with . . . well, a bunch of big angry cats.

The door opened as Sophie was experimentally poking out her tongue and assessing the puncture marks her teeth had made.

'You're awake,' said Josh.

'Nothing gets past you, does it?'

'How are you feeling?'

'Better. Thanks for letting me sleep in your bed. Sorry about the pillowcase.'

'No problem.' Watching her flinch as she bent to pick up her bag, he said, 'You're welcome to stay here if you don't want to go home. Just climb back into bed, I'll have some food sent up, you can get some rest, watch TV . . .'

'Thanks, but it's OK.' Tempting though it was to just crawl back under the covers and be waited on, Sophie slowly straightened up. 'I have emails to go through, photos to print off. Could you pass me those painkillers?'

'Are you sure you'll be all right?' Josh was still surveying her with concern.

She nodded. 'Honestly, I'll be fine after a shower.'

But there was an element of bravado to this statement. On their way out to Josh's car, Sophie could feel that the muscles in her back and shoulder were stiffening up. Getting into the car had them squealing. When they reached her flat, Josh had to help her up the stairs. OK, this was getting ridiculous.

'You can't work tomorrow,' he said flatly. 'No way. You'll never do it.'

'What was that you mentioned earlier about me being obstinate?'

'But—'

'If you really want to help,' Sophie indicated the bathroom, 'you could run me a bath. Stick some Radox in too. Honestly, that'll make me feel loads better.'

She checked her emails while Josh ran the bath for her. When it was ready, he said, 'Look, I'm going to wait out here until you're out. Just to make sure you're OK.'

'Do you think I'm going to drown?' Sophie raised her eyebrows at him. 'Because I'm not.'

'I know. Just humour me.'

'Fine, then. But I'm locking the door.'

Chapter 19

Twenty minutes later, steamed and rested in the foamy green water, Sophie realised she was in trouble.

Three times now she'd attempted to grip the sides of the bath and haul herself upright. And three times she'd failed miserably. Her back had seized up; instead of the sprained muscles relaxing, they appeared to have gone into spasm. She was stuck here in the water, unable to get out.

On the plus side, Josh was in the living room.

On the minus side, he was in the living room.

Plus, she was naked.

OK, this was officially awkward.

She tried one last time to lift herself out, without success. The pain just made it impossible. Light-headed with the effort of holding her breath and not shrieking aloud, she sank into the water once more.

Then she tilted her head back and called out, 'Josh?'

Footsteps. Then he was there on the other side of the door. 'Yes?'

'You know what I really hate?'

'What?'

'When you're right and I'm wrong.'

'I see.' There was a pause. 'So basically, you can't get out of the bath.'

He sounded as if he *might* be finding the situation amusing.

Well, she supposed she couldn't blame him. Sophie said, 'Basically, that would be correct.'

'Riiiiiight.'

'It's not funny.'

'No, of course not. Have you completely seized up?'

'Completely.'

'And you locked the door, did you?'

'Of course I locked the door, I'm not stupid!'

Now he was definitely laughing.

'OK, do you have a screwdriver?'

'Not *on* me at this moment, no.'

'Well that's probably a good thing. How about out here in the flat?'

'There's a toolbox in the cupboard under the stairs.'

He was back less than a minute later with the necessary Pozi screwdriver. Sophie watched from the other end of the bathroom as one by one the four screws and the exterior door handle were removed. Then he was able to reach the locking mechanism and release it. There was a satisfying click and the door was unlocked but still closed.

'Right,' said Josh. 'Before I open the door, how do you want to do this?'

'You could call the hotel, see if Tula can come down here.'

'Or I could close my eyes,' Josh countered. 'Which would be quicker.'

Oh help. Sophie closed her own eyes, mentally weighing up the options. After several seconds she said, 'OK, listen. In my bedroom, in the second drawer of the chest of drawers, there's a big grey T-shirt. And on the top shelf in the wardrobe are some winter scarves.

'Are you cold?'

'Get the black knitted scarf down. Go and do that now.'

'Please,' prompted Josh.

Bastard. Despite her predicament, Sophie smiled. 'Please.'

A minute later he was back. 'OK, now what?'

'Tie the scarf around your head so it completely covers your eyes.'

'Couldn't I just keep them shut?'

'No. When you've done it, bring the T-shirt into the bathroom.'

She watched the door open. Josh entered the room, blindfolded with her scarf and carrying her T-shirt. Hesitating, he said, 'You'll have to talk me towards you.'

'Straight ahead . . . right a bit . . . forward again . . . left a bit.' OK, this felt really weird. She was naked, but he couldn't see her; it was all very *Fifty Shades*. Getting a bit flustered at the thought, Sophie said, 'Hold the T-shirt out in front of you . . . down a bit . . . and left again . . .' *Got it.* 'Now move back and wait there.'

It felt all kinds of wrong, putting a T-shirt on in the bath. Finally she'd managed to get her arms through the arm holes and pull it down over the rest of her until she was covered to the knees. All the while Josh stood there with the scarf over his eyes and a hint of a smirk on his face.

'Right, you can look now,' said Sophie.

'Are you sure? I'm scared. What if I take the scarf off and you're still naked?'

'Ha-de-ha. Are you terrified I might launch myself at you?'

'You never know.' Smiling, he removed the scarf. 'What if you're only pretending you've hurt your back?'

'I wish. OK, how are we going to do this?'

'Hold your arms out,' Josh instructed. He leaned over, placed his own arms around her and braced himself against the side of the bath. 'Now hang on tight, I'm going to lift you up . . .'

Sophie was acutely aware of her lack of underwear. Water sloshed over the sides, and for a moment it seemed they might both end up in the bath. Then with a superhuman effort he had her upright, if disconcertingly pressed against him.

Oo-er, chest to chest and no bra . . .

'Thanks.' She managed to lift her legs out, then steadied herself and surveyed his now-sodden shirt front. 'Sorry.'

Josh fetched the bath towel and wrapped it around her. 'Don't mention it. Need a hand with anything else?'

'No thanks.'

'Want me to stick around?'

'I'm fine now. There's no need.'

'What are you going to do about tomorrow?'

'Cope.' This was a combination of bravado, desperation and mind over matter. It was a major job and she couldn't let down the people who'd hired her.

'OK, but would it be useful if you had an assistant?' Josh raised his hand. 'Think about it before you just say no out of habit.'

Sophie closed her mouth and considered the offer. Her gaze wandered past him, through the open bathroom door to the boxes of photographic equipment piled up against the wall in the hallway.

'Yes.' She smiled slightly. 'An assistant would be . . . great.'

'Right.'

'Thank you.'

'Don't mention it.'

'It's going to be a whole day.'

'I know. You already said.'

'And you're sure you can take that much time away from the hotel?'

'You're assuming the assistant will be me,' said Josh.

'Oh! Sorry . . .'

'I need to get back and check the diary, see what's happening. If I can't make it tomorrow, I'll find someone else who can. What time will you need to set off?'

'No later than eleven.'

'Fine. You get some rest. Call me if you need to. I'll see myself out,' said Josh. 'And good luck for tomorrow.'

'Thanks.' Sophie was still feeling stupid for thinking he'd been volunteering himself to help her. 'Sorry about getting your shirt wet.'

'No problem. Always happy to help.' As he left the flat, Josh added over his shoulder, 'Especially when it proved that you were wrong and I was right.'

Lawrence had carefully positioned his car in the car park to give him a view of both the driveway and the entrance to Mariscombe House. If Dot and Antoine had gone out to dinner at seven, it stood to reason they'd be returning to the hotel before too long.

He felt like a private eye. It was ten fifteen and he'd already been sitting out here in the dark for an hour. God knows why he was even doing it, but there had just been an inner compulsion to know what was going on. His stomach had been in knots too; it was that teenagery pre-exam sensation of knowing that what happened next had the power to change your life.

And then he saw the headlights of a car coming up the drive. Sinking down in the driver's seat, he watched as it was driven into a parking space over to the left of the hotel.

Yes, it was them. Antoine Beauvais emerged from the car, moving around and opening the passenger door for Dot. *Smooth bastard.*

When you'd been married to someone for decades, opening car doors for them became a nicety that fell by the wayside. Watching with a tortured mix of envy and guilt as Dot smiled and said something to Antoine, Lawrence realised he was holding his breath.

OK, exhale.

The two of them made their way to the entrance of the hotel. Once inside, he viewed them through the lit-up windows as they faced each other, exchanged a few more words, then parted company. Antoine Beauvais headed up the staircase whilst Dot, turning away, disappeared in the direction of the bar.

Thank God, thank God for that. She'd done her duty and now it was over; she'd got rid of him. Overcome with relief, Lawrence jumped out of the car; after all this private-investigating, he definitely deserved a drink.

'Hello, hello, fancy bumping into you two here!' He beamed at

Dot, who was chatting to Spike, the barman. 'Thought I'd pop in for a quick one. Dot, let me buy you a drink. I say, your hair looks fantastic. Now, what are you having, how about a glass of Cloudy Bay?'

'Lawrence, you don't need to—'

'Oh, come on, just the one. I like what you're wearing, too. Is that a new dress? The colour suits you. I'll have the same, Spike.'

'I've been out to dinner, Lawrence. And don't pretend you don't know who with.'

The trouble with Dot being such a popular boss was the way people always told her everything. Oh well.

'I do know. I just saw the two of you come back. Pretty awkward evening, was it? What was it all about, anyway?'

'What makes you think it was awkward?' said Dot.

'You got rid of him pretty sharpish.' Lawrence shrugged. 'He went up to his room, you came in here. What did he have to say?'

'He went up to his room to put his phone on charge. And if you're really that interested in finding out what he had to say,' Dot went on, 'why don't you ask him yourself?'

Shit. She was looking behind him. Lawrence took a swift glug from his just-poured glass of wine. He heard the sound of footsteps, breathed in a waft of expensive-smelling cologne.

'Antoine, look who's here. And what a coincidence, after we were just talking about him earlier.'

Lawrence turned, by now really wishing he hadn't come along.

'Hello, Lawrence.' Antoine's tone was even but polite. He didn't sound as if he were about to pull out a duelling pistol and aim it at his head.

Then again, how could you tell?

Chapter 20

Lawrence said, 'Hello, Antoine.'

'You're looking well,' the other man said.

Still no sign of those duelling pistols. 'Thanks. You too. May I offer you a drink?'

Antoine inclined his head. 'A small cognac. Thank you.' He hesitated, then added, 'I'll be staying here at the hotel for a while, so we may as well be civilised. It's been wonderful seeing Dot again. We've had an excellent evening, haven't we?'

'Fantastic,' Dot said happily. 'And the food at the Rose was great too. I had the most amazing scallops in Pernod.'

'You and your scallops.' Lawrence smiled, because she'd always had a thing for them. What he really wanted to say was, what does *that* mean? You had a fantastic time with the smooth Frenchman and the food was great too?

But if he did, it was unlikely to go down well. Instead he forced another pleasant smile and said, 'Well, glad the food was good. D'you remember that lunch we had at Gidleigh Park?' Turning to Antoine, he explained, 'I took Dot there on her birthday last year. Now that was a meal to remember.'

'You didn't take me there on my birthday,' said Dot. 'It was the following weekend.'

'But that's what we were celebrating,' Lawrence reminded her. 'And it was worth it, wasn't it? Spectacular place,' he told Antoine. 'The chef has two Michelin stars.'

'Ah.' Antoine nodded. 'Michael Caines. I've heard great things about him and his restaurant. If you recommend it so highly,' he said to Lawrence, 'maybe I should take Dot there too.'

Bastard, *bastard*. 'Absolutely. I warn you, though, it's pretty pricey.'

'That won't be a problem, I assure you,' Antoine said with a brief smile.

'And what Lawrence isn't mentioning is the reason it ended up being so pricey,' Dot chimed in. 'Basically, because he was too vain to wear his reading glasses.'

Oh shit. 'Don't—'

'He looked at the wine list and decided he liked the sound of the Perrier Jouet Belle Epoque 2004.' Dot wasn't to be stopped. 'Didn't realise thirty-five pounds was for a glass of the stuff, not a bottle.'

Thanks, darling.

'For Perrier Jouet Belle Epoque 2004.' Antoine was now visibly struggling to keep a straight face.

Lawrence said defensively, 'I'm not that wild about champagne. I don't read up on it.'

'Clearly not. Anyway, thank you for the drink.' Antoine paused, then raised his cognac glass. 'Your health.'

Which was either a simple salutation or a Mafia-style warning to make the most of his health while he still had it.

'*Santé*,' Lawrence murmured, before taking a drink. 'So, are you here for long?' *Please say no.*

'Haven't decided yet. Just seeing how things go. I'm working on a movie score at the moment, but that's the joy of computers. These days you can create music anywhere you like. And when I'm not doing that,' Antoine said pleasantly, 'I can enjoy my free time in Cornwall, take a look around, see how the place has changed.' Briefly resting his fingertips on Dot's waist, he added, 'And I have an expert offering to accompany me, which makes it even better.'

This evening wasn't turning out *at all* as Lawrence had planned.

'It's still warm out on the terrace.' Dot was smiling up at

Antoine. 'Shall we go and sit outside?' She glanced across at Lawrence. 'You're welcome to join us if you like.'

Said in such a way that it was blindingly obvious she was only being polite.

'Thank you,' said Lawrence. 'So kind, but I'll leave you to it.' A part of him wanted to acknowledge the past, to apologise to Antoine for what he'd done, but he'd tried before, without success. It had, in fact, only made an intolerable situation worse. Which meant that this evening, here in this hotel, it was immeasurably easier to avoid the subject.

Sometimes the right words simply refused to present themselves.

Sometimes an apology wasn't – could never be – enough.

Antoine Beauvais hopefully understood that.

'I owe you a drink,' he said now. 'Let me get—'

'No, no, not necessary.' Lawrence was firm as he put down his half-finished glass of wine. 'I have to go. You enjoy the rest of your evening.'

Dot, sashaying out on to the terrace with Antoine in tow, said gaily, 'Don't worry, we will!'

The car pulled up outside the flat just before eleven the next morning. Sophie looked out of the window and felt her heart do a Pavlovian skip of pleasure.

OK, this was something she was going to have to keep an eye on. Enjoying someone's company was one thing, but it mustn't be allowed to get out of hand.

Then again, anyone with half a brain would agree that spending the day with Josh was preferable to being stuck with some stranger who chewed gum with their mouth open and was bored to tears with doing a job they hadn't volunteered for.

Just stay in control and everything'll be fine . . .

'Morning. How are you feeling?' Josh followed her into the flat.

'Better than last night.' Possibly because she'd taken more painkillers. 'Thanks for doing this.'

'No problem. Tell me everything you need to take with you and I'll start loading up the car.'

For the next few minutes Sophie pointed out the bags and cases of equipment and waited in the hallway while he carried them outside. It had taken ten minutes to ease herself out of bed this morning; a long day at work was the last thing she needed, but she'd do it if it killed her.

Although hopefully it wouldn't.

The sun was out; it was a warm and breezy day with cotton-wool clouds scudding across the sky. 'It's the opening of a new restaurant in St Austell,' she told Josh as they sped across country towards the south coast. 'I'm taking photos of the place itself, then the food being prepared in the kitchen, plus pictures of the staff; that's for the brochures and the website. Then there's the party in the evening, with local dignitaries and as many glamorous guests as they can rustle up, and those photos are going to be published alongside a piece about the restaurant in one of those lifestyle magazines.'

'Which is why you couldn't let them down,' said Josh.

'It's a big deal for me,' Sophie said candidly. 'I didn't want to miss out on a chance like this. Those kinds of magazines usually use their own photographers. If I do a good job, they might hire me again.'

'Let's hope you do a good job, then.'

'I will. I always do.'

'Modest.'

'Focused and professional,' said Sophie.

'All work and no play . . .'

'Call me dull if you want. I don't care. This is the career I've always dreamed of and making it work is my number-one priority. I'm not going to do anything to risk messing it up.'

'I can see that.' Josh nodded 'And what did you do before setting up the business?'

'Worked in a call centre.'

'Right.'

'Exactly. It wasn't my dream job. But I saved every penny, started buying photographic equipment and learned as much as I could. And I've got this far,' said Sophie. 'I'm doing OK. Plenty of satisfied customers who recommend me to their friends. You can't understand how much that means to me.'

They were driving across Bodmin Moor; miles of uninterrupted countryside empty of people and golden with gorse. Josh slowed the car as they encountered a flock of sheep wandering like indolent teenagers across the narrow winding road ahead of them.

'What?' said Sophie, aware that he'd turned his head and was watching her.

Josh's eyes were glinting with amusement. Finally he said, 'You're definitely not dull.'

The restaurant, Pierrot, was done out in shades of bottle green and deep purple, with white-painted floors and sleek modern tables. The lighting was an eclectic mix of futuristic spotlights and antique French candelabras. The owners, Maddy and Max, had thrown all their money into the venture and were in a frenzy of excitement that the launch date had finally arrived.

'This is Josh, my assistant,' Sophie told them. 'He's untrained but willing to learn. I had a bit of an accident yesterday, put my back out. That's why he's here.'

'Poor *you*,' Maddy exclaimed. 'And look at your poor *face*!'

'I know,' Sophie said with a grin. 'But try not to stare at him. He can't help it.'

After the initial setting-up, the next couple of hours were spent on photographing various aspects of the restaurant, the staff and the food being prepared in the kitchens. At three o'clock they stopped for a break outside.

'I could get used to this,' said Sophie. 'Sitting back and bossing you around, making you do all the hard work.'

'That's what I used to do with the kids from Go Destry.' Josh shielded his eyes from the sun. 'Drink coffee, watch them perform, tell them what they needed to do to be better. Money for old rope.'

Sophie smiled, because on their way over here, they'd talked about his time managing the band and it had been anything but easy.

'Good news!' Maddy emerged through the French windows clutching her phone and doing a little victory dance. 'I didn't want to jinx it so I didn't say anything before, but we've just had the call to confirm it's happening. Perry Elson's coming along to the party!'

'Ooh.' Sophie was impressed. 'The actor?'

'He's a friend of a friend, over from the States for a few days and staying in the area. It'll up the coverage no end.' Maddy's eyes were shining. 'People will be that much more interested in a place if they think celebs like him have been here. And we've got him for a whole hour.' She beamed excitedly. 'You'll have to take *loads* of photos of him.'

Sophie conjured up a mental image of the young actor, who had starred in a couple of unexpectedly successful films last year and fell into the category of fast-rising star still new enough to appreciate it. He was intelligent, quirkily attractive, as yet unspoiled by fame and universally considered one of the good guys.

Since it would be fun to photograph someone properly famous, she said, 'Don't worry, I will.'

Chapter 21

For the next couple of hours they carried on working, capturing the food being crafted in the kitchen, the cheery atmosphere among the staff and the spectacular views from the windows of the restaurant. Josh uncomplainingly shifted tripods, fetched and carried boxes of equipment and held up reflector boards as instructed. By the time Sophie finally had everything she needed, it was six o'clock and the first of the evening's invited guests were starting to arrive.

'How are you doing?' Josh watched as she surreptitiously arched her back and pressed her knuckles into the area around the base of her spine.

'OK. Holding out.' She'd been moving slowly, taking care not to put any more strain on the torn muscles, but they were really starting to burn again now.

'Want me to give you a massage?'

Sophie thought about it. A massage would help; it would be perfect, just what she needed right now. She imagined how it would feel, those warm, firm fingers kneading away the pain, the unhurried physical contact of skin on skin . . .

Oh wow.

She looked at Josh.

Who was looking at her.

Probably best not to.

'No thanks, I'm fine.'

He raised an eyebrow. 'Except you aren't.'

Sophie eyed him steadily. 'I still don't want a massage. You might make it worse.'

And now he was giving her the kind of look that signalled how ridiculously easy it was to read her mind. Finally he said, 'OK.'

Phew.

The guests had begun to arrive. Flutes of chilled Prosecco were served, trays of canapés were brought out from the kitchen and the buzz of anticipation gave way to the sounds of a jolly party in progress. Thankfully the sun was still out and the wind had dropped, so people were milling around outside in the garden too. Sophie moved between them, taking her favourite informal shots. Everyone was having fun, the hosts were happy and the noise level of chatter and laughter was steadily rising.

Then Maddy and Max's friends turned up with the evening's star guest in tow, and the excitement in the air accelerated to the next level. Everyone was casting barely noticeable glances in their direction whilst pretending not to be remotely star-struck. Which was the good thing about being a professional photographer: when you were the one with the camera, it kind of meant you had to look; you didn't have a choice.

Perry Elson had short tufty dark hair, a cute nose, warm hazel eyes and a winning smile that by some miracle hadn't yet been subjected to a Hollywood dental surgeon's makeover. He was wearing a sea-green shirt and black jeans, and was currently busy being introduced to people. Keeping in the background, Sophie carried on unobtrusively snapping away as instructed. Then Maddy brought him over to her and said, 'Perry, this is Sophie, who's taking the photographs this evening.'

'I'd noticed.' His eyes glinted with amusement. 'Always worth being extra nice to the photographer. Hi, good to meet you.'

He had a just-right handshake and a way of looking at you that made you instantly feel special. It was this quality that had undoubtedly contributed to his success.

'You too.' Sophie marvelled at his ability to exude charisma;

it was indefinable but just . . . *there*. 'Maddy wants me to take lots of pictures of you, I'm afraid.'

'Be kind, please. No drunk shots.' He pulled a comedy eyes-half-closed, mouth-hanging-open face. 'Or double chins.'

'I promise.' He didn't have a double chin.

Evidently keen to move on with the introductions, Maddy said, 'And this is Sophie's assistant.' She shook her head at Josh by way of apology. 'I'm *so* sorry, I've forgotten your name . . .'

'Josh Strachan,' Perry supplied helpfully.

Maddy looked as stunned as if one of the canapés had sat up and spoken.

'It's OK, we know each other.' Breaking into a grin, Perry said, 'Josh, how you doing? Great to see you again. This is crazy, I knew you'd left LA, but had no idea you were here. And you're a photographer's assistant now?' He tilted his head in Sophie's direction. 'I mean, I can understand why, when the photographer looks like this, but . . .'

'I had a bit of an accident yesterday.' Sophie indicated the stitches on her forehead. 'Hurt my back. He's just here helping me out.'

'OK, I get it.' Perry nodded. 'That makes sense. And are you two a couple?'

'Definitely not,' said Sophie, at the same time as Josh said, 'No.'

'Well, what a coincidence, you two knowing each other!' Maddy was enthralled and wildly curious.

'Josh used to manage the band Go Destry,' Perry explained. 'I was cast in the movie they made, back when I was a nobody. We used to play pool in our spare time, that's how we got to be friends. Man, it's good to see you again!'

'Goodness, that's amazing.' Eyeing Josh with new respect, Maddy said, 'I'm *so* sorry I didn't recognise you before. Maybe we can get some photos of you too?'

Josh, watching as Sophie leaned against the wall in order to take the next series of shots, saw the effort she was putting into

131

concealing the amount of pain she was in. No one else knew, but he could see it in the way she held herself, the measured way she moved and the occasional fleeting wince when a muscle spasm caught her by surprise.

Yet she'd spent all day playing down the symptoms, insisting she was fine. For Sophie, pride and professionalism were paramount. Which was what had made last night's experience in the bathroom all the more endearing and enjoyable. Lifting her out of the bath and briefly experiencing her half-naked body pressed against his had been a defining moment, a highlight of their . . . well, whatever it was they'd shared so far. A friendship, yes, hopefully that. A relationship . . . not the kind of relationship *he* would have chosen, that was for sure. But for the first time yesterday he'd sensed that the one-sidedness of the situation might not be entirely one-sided after all. Maybe he'd imagined it . . . or *wanted* to imagine it . . . but something had told him Sophie might not be as utterly unaffected by him as she'd been making out.

Which was both a good sign and utterly frustrating, because why would she persist in refusing to relax and enjoy a relationship that had the potential to be fantastic?

From across the room he watched as Perry chatted with a group of people clustered adoringly around him. Glancing up and catching Josh's eye, Perry charmingly excused himself from the group and came over to join him.

'You're doing great,' said Josh. 'Good job.'

'Oh man, they're nice people.' Sitting alongside him on the window seat, Perry discreetly massaged his jaw. 'What no one ever realises is how tiring it is, being nice the whole time. My face aches from smiling. My brain hurts from saying all the right things, making polite conversation instead of coming out with whatever I want to say.'

'I know.' Josh nodded; the members of Go Destry had told him the same thing on so many occasions. Being endlessly on show was both an occupational hazard and an exhausting process.

'Anyhow, not for much longer. I can leave soon.' Checking his watch, Perry said, 'A couple of days off, then it's back up to London. So what's the situation with the girl? I saw you just now, watching her.'

'If you ask her out, she says no,' said Josh.

Perry laughed. 'You mean *you* asked her out and she said no.'

'Not just me; others have tried and failed. She's just not interested. Allegedly.'

'But you think she might be?'

'I have no idea.' Josh shrugged. 'And I just hate not knowing.'

'Why don't I ask her?'

'I don't think she'd tell you.'

'OK then, why don't I ask her out? See what happens?'

Josh hesitated. Now this was a scenario he wasn't sure he was comfortable with. He'd asked Sophie out and been turned down, but the rest had been hearsay. Riley and Tula had both told him she wasn't the dating kind, but what if she were to say yes to Perry Elson?

Because if she did, he'd look completely stupid. And wouldn't feel too good about it either.

Then again, at least he'd have his definitive answer. Like it or not, he would *know*.

'Fine,' he said. 'Try it. But be subtle.'

'Hey, I can do subtle.' Perry gave him a nudge. 'I'm a movie star, remember? An *actor*. And guess what else I am?'

'No idea.' Already beginning to regret this, Josh said, 'What else *are* you?'

There was the playful movie-star grin. 'Absolutely fantastic in bed.'

Sophie moved the vase of freesias on the table so the sunshine was streaming between their swan-necked stems, while in the background a young girl in a pink dress dreamily enjoyed a spoonful of apricot ice cream. Her white-blond hair was haloed with sunlight and her elbow on the table exactly mirrored the angle of the spoon in her hand. Sophie took a few more shots, aware that someone was standing behind her. Finishing, she turned and saw it was Perry Elson.

'Hey, I'm leaving soon. Maddy and Max wondered if you could take some more pictures of me outside the restaurant before I head off.'

'OK.' Straightening up, she smiled at the little girl and said, 'Thanks, sweetie, you were great.'

Outside, Perry leaned against the whitewashed rough stone wall with the restaurant's name on the plaque next to his left shoulder.

'Take some close-ups,' he told Sophie as she moved around him in search of angles.

'I will.'

'Closer than that.'

'I don't need to get closer,' Sophie reminded him. 'I have a camera lens to do that for me.'

He smiled his million-dollar smile and she captured it for posterity. 'You're smart. And pretty. Are you free tomorrow night?'

'For work?'

'Actually, I was thinking more of pleasure. I'm single,' said Perry. 'I hear you are too. I was wondering if you'd like to meet up in a camera-free situation.' He shrugged lightly. 'Could be fun, couldn't it?'

'You're inviting me out? On a date?'

'Why not?'

Sophie put the Nikon down and gave him a long, steady look. 'OK, three things. One, the answer is no.'

'But—'

'Second, I'm guessing your friend Josh put you up to this.'

Wide-eyed, Perry said, 'I don't know what you mean.'

'Oh I think you do.' His too-innocent expression was *such* a giveaway. 'You're a Hollywood star, over here for a couple of days. There's no way you'd ask out a girl like me, with a bad back, covered in bruises and,' she pointed to her temple, 'with a load of stitches holding together a big ugly cut on her face. Whereas

134

Josh can't get over the fact that he asked me out and I turned him down flat. So it stands to reason that he'd get you to do this to test me.'

'You're good,' Perry acknowledged. 'Very good.' He nodded in appreciation. 'What's the third thing?'

'I'm glad you asked me that.' Sophie paused, then added, 'I know I said no, but I'm thinking it might be fun if you told him I said yes.'

Breaking into a grin, Perry said, 'Want to know what I'm thinking? That you're a bad, bad girl. But also a bit of a genius.'

Chapter 22

Josh watched the two of them make their way back inside. He wasn't able to tell what had happened. Perry headed over to rejoin his hosts and Sophie resumed taking photos of the other guests.

Had Perry done it? Please God let her have turned him down. Josh experienced an unfamiliar jolt of alarm at the unwelcome prospect of being proven wrong. OK, on the up side, at least he'd know. But on the down side, it would be a real kick in the teeth.

Ten minutes later, having charmed everyone, Perry made his excuses and said his goodbyes to those around him. Before leaving, he came over to Josh and said breezily, 'Sorry, mate. Some you win, some you lose.'

Was this it? Josh felt himself tense. 'Meaning?'

Perry winked and said, 'Turns out it isn't men in general she's not interested in. Just you.'

Bloody hell. 'What did she say?'

'Hey, she said yes, what else? We're going out tomorrow night. No need to congratulate me.' Perry looked modest. 'You've either got it or you haven't. See you around, man!'

And with that he was off, pausing only to exchange a discreet smile with Sophie on his way out. Josh saw him mouth *tomorrow* at her and Sophie shyly nodded before turning away.

For crying out loud, this wasn't supposed to happen; he

hadn't meant for Perry to go ahead and actually *make* a bloody date.

By ten thirty, Sophie had done everything she could do, taken hundreds of photographs both formal and reportage-style, and captured the feel of the restaurant, its food and clientele. Now it was time to go home, and she'd never been more glad of it. Resting on a padded blue and white chair outside while Josh packed all the equipment back into the car, she watched as the remaining guests danced in the garden beneath the twinkling multicoloured glow of the lights strung in the trees overhead.

It had been a good party. Everyone looked so happy. A couple in their thirties who'd been dancing together earlier were now sitting at the next table. Married, by the look of their matching wedding rings. He was holding her left hand while with her right she scrolled through a message on her phone.

'Oh brilliant!' Her face lit up. 'Pearl's having a party at her place next Saturday and we're invited!'

'Saturday? Well we can't go to that.' Her husband shook his head. 'We'll be at Mum's.'

It was the intransigence of his tone that did it. Sophie felt a trickle of ice slide down her spine.

'But we go to your mum's every week,' his wife protested. 'Surely she wouldn't mind if we went to see her on the Sunday instead, just this once.'

He exhaled. 'I don't want to go to the party anyway. It'll be noisy.'

With a slight air of desperation, the wife said, 'But she's my friend! How about if you visit your mum and I go to the party? I mean, that would suit both of us, wouldn't it?'

Her husband's jaw was set and he was shaking his head again. 'Except the last time you went out with Pearl you said you'd be home by midnight, didn't you? And what time did you get back?'

Sophie watched as the man's wife visibly deflated. 'I know it was a bit later than that, but we weren't doing anything wrong. Just having fun.'

'One o'clock in the morning.' His eyes were steely now. 'And I didn't know where you were. You might call that a bit late, I call it selfish. Tell Pearl we can't make it. We're going to my mother's instead.'

His wife belatedly sensed Sophie's gaze upon them and turned her head away. The husband, having brought the matter to a satisfactory conclusion, resumed idly stroking the back of her hand with his fingers. Except what had seemed like a loving, romantic gesture of affection now looked sinister and not romantic at all.

Sophie shuddered at the overpowering sensation of déjà vu. Oh yes, this was how it happened: after weeks or months of the old memories fading, she would see or hear something – something like this – that brought all the old feelings crashing back. Together with the urge to stop it happening to other people.

Should she? Could she? Sophie took several breaths; recognising the passive-aggressive signs always made her feel sick, but was there actually anything she could say that would make a difference? Or would it just make a bad situation worse? Like drug addiction, maybe it was something the person had to recognise and deal with by themselves. The beginning was insidious and it might take a while to realise what was happening, but understanding you had to take a stand needed to be a personal decision.

Not something to be blurted out at you by a complete stranger while your over-controlling husband was sitting right next to you, holding your hand.

'All packed away.' Josh reappeared in the doorway. 'Ready to go?'

'Yes.' With difficulty she hauled herself up out of the chair.

'Need a hand?'

'I'm OK.' Like a geriatric duck, Sophie waddled after him. She glanced across one last time at the married couple and saw the wife hastily look away again. The husband smiled pleasantly and said, 'Hope you feel better soon.'

'Thanks.' It took all her self-control not to turn to his wife and say, 'Go to your friend's party, *please*.'

They'd been driving for some twenty minutes before Josh said, 'What did you think of Perry, then?'

Twenty-one minutes actually. Sophie checked her watch and smiled into the darkness; she'd had a mental bet with herself that it would happen inside half an hour.

'He seems nice. Down to earth.' She shrugged. 'Fun.'

There was a pause. Ha, *this* was fun.

'So . . .' Josh said finally, 'what are you doing tomorrow night?'

'Me?' She turned to look at him. 'Why?'

He glanced across at her. 'Did Perry ask you out on a date?'

'What?' Sophie blinked. 'Maybe.' She fiddled distractedly with the silver bangle on her wrist. 'OK, yes, he did.'

'And?'

'And what?'

'Did you turn him down?'

Straight to the point.

'No, I didn't. I said yes. We're going out tomorrow evening.' She said it with a mix of bashfulness and pride, and watched the expression on Josh's face.

'I thought you always said no.'

See? The fact that he'd asked her out and been rejected definitely still rankled. What she couldn't work out was whether he really liked her or just couldn't handle the idea that *anyone* was capable of turning him down.

She suspected the latter. Men with high opinions of themselves tended to get competitive.

'I always have said no.' She shrugged. 'But this time I said yes.'

'And what made you change your mind?'

Ooh, definitely competitive.

'Well, like I said, he's really nice. Good-looking. And fun! I thought, why not just go for it?'

Josh's tone was even. 'And he's made a few movies.'

'I know, but that isn't why I said yes. He's just really easy to talk to. Good company.'

'OK, but don't get too overexcited. He's heading back to LA in three days.'

She smiled. 'Thanks for that. Then again, a lot can happen in three days.'

'Hmm.'

Ha, *such* a sore loser.

They travelled on in silence after that. After another twenty minutes, Sophie unzipped her silver-studded turquoise shoulder bag and took out one of the restaurant's business cards. When they next pulled up at a junction, she passed it to Josh.

'What's this?'

'Read what's written on the back. It's a message from your friend Perry.'

He took it from her and switched on the overhead reading light. She watched him read the words scrawled across the back of the card.

In sloping black handwriting Perry had scrawled: *Just kidding. She said no. Dammit!*

Josh's expression was unreadable as he handed the card back to her. Then he switched the light off and she could no longer see more than a faint outline of his face.

'So you turned him down.'

'Yes.'

'But you said you hadn't. Why?'

'Come on. You set the whole thing up to see what I'd do. It seemed only fair to get you back.'

'And you did. You got me. Well done.' He was smiling now; she caught the white gleam of his teeth. 'I have to say, I'm glad you aren't fantasising about some falling-in-love-in-three-days scenario in which the movie star ends up whisking you off to LA.'

'Thanks.'

'Oh, you know what I mean. That sort of fairy-tale stuff doesn't happen in real life.'

'But you thought I might fall for it anyway. Cheers.'

'I didn't think that,' Josh pointed out. 'You were the one who said a lot could happen in three days.'

'And you assumed it involved the handsome prince carrying Cinderella off to his Hollywood castle. Whereas I could have meant both of us staying here in Cornwall.'

'Which would make an even better ending for a film. OK, this is crazy,' Josh said abruptly. 'Now we're arguing about something that's never even going to happen.'

'True.'

'Because you refused to go out with a Hollywood film star.'

'Technically,' Sophie reminded him, 'he didn't want to go out with me. He only asked because you told him to.'

'Because you turn down everyone who asks you,' said Josh.

'Also true.'

He braked to let a fox slope across the road ahead of them. 'Why do you do that?'

'You asked me that question before. Did I give you an answer then?'

'No.'

'Exactly. So why would things be any different now? It's my choice, my decision, my life. I choose to concentrate on my career.'

'You could have both,' said Josh.

'I'd rather not.'

He glanced across at her. 'Can I ask a personal question?'

'What, another one?'

'Were you attacked? Assaulted?'

Sophie shook her head. 'No, never.'

'Are you sure?'

'Truly. Nothing like that.' It gave her a jolt to realise that this was the conclusion he'd drawn. Did other people think it too? It hadn't occurred to her that there might be speculation about her decision. Her voice softening, she looked at him and said, 'I promise. It was just a decision I chose to make. Relationships aren't the be-all and end-all. They go wrong. Most of the time they're more trouble than they're worth. There's more to life.'

'Right.' He paused. 'If you say so.'

'I do. And please don't think I'm covering up something sinister,' Sophie reiterated. 'Nobody tried to hurt me.'

Which was true, more or less, wasn't it?

Theo had only tried to hurt himself.

Chapter 23

Tula was loving working at the Mariscombe House Hotel. Moving down to St Carys had definitely been the right thing to do, to the extent that she shuddered at the thought of how it so easily might not have happened. If she hadn't been caught out by Facebook, she could still be in Birmingham now.

But she *had* been caught out and she was no longer there; she was here instead. Doing a job she adored, in a gorgeous place, with friendly people.

And, *cough cough*, a very good-looking boss.

OK, officially Dot was her boss, but she didn't mean Dot. Having a crush on Josh Strachan just made working at the Mariscombe that much better. It was a definite bonus knowing he was around, unexpectedly hearing his voice, looking up and catching sight of him as he passed by.

Every single time she saw him, Tula's heart did a little double-beat. Sometimes he stopped for a few words and sometimes he didn't, but simply finding herself on the receiving end of a momentary glance, a nod of acknowledgement or a brief smile brightened her day. She'd even found herself acting as if he were watching her when he wasn't, just in case he secretly *was*. It was extra thrilling, like being in a film, aware of the cameras but pretending they didn't exist.

And here he was again now, heading out on to the terrace in jeans and a green and white striped shirt, talking rapidly into his phone and swinging his Ray-Bans from his free hand. Skippety-skip went Tula's heart as he nodded his head in greeting, ended his call and came over to the tables she was laying before dinner.

'Hi, where's Dot?'

'The Nelligans' taxi didn't turn up in time, so she's given them a lift to the station.' Shaking out a freshly laundered cloth in an attempt to billow it into the air before letting it settle gracefully over the table, she misjudged the angle of the shake and ended up covering her own head instead. *Ach.*

'Here, let me.' Josh solemnly lifted the white cloth off her and helped her smooth it over the tabletop. 'How's the job going? Settling in?'

'Yes thanks. Everyone's lovely.' *Especially you.*

She didn't say that last bit, just thought it whilst polishing a wine glass with a vivacious flourish. *Just like a girl in a film.*

'What time do you finish your shift?'

The sun was shining on to his face; she could see the glints of gold in his dark brown eyes and the tiny lines at the outer corners of the eyelids. His mouth was beautiful, so cleanly edged it looked as if it had been carved, and there was dark stubble peppering his jaw . . . OK, probably best to stop staring.

'Six. But I can stay later if you want me to.'

'That wasn't why I was asking. Seeing Sophie tonight?'

'No, she's got a job on. I was just going to have a quiet evening. Well,' Tula amended, 'apart from Sophie, I don't really know anyone else to socialise with yet.'

'Ah, don't worry. I'm sure you'll make friends soon enough.'

'Unless you'd like to come out for a drink with me?' The words popped out of her mouth almost of their own accord. Tula was as startled to hear them as Josh evidently was. Then again, why not? *Carpe diem* and all that.

'Well . . .'

'Just a drink to keep me company, a friendly gesture, that's all . . . It's a beautiful sunny evening; better than staying in and watching a load of rubbish on TV. Not too much to ask, is it?'

Oh help, and now she was burbling; almost as impressive as flinging a tablecloth over her own head.

Josh hesitated. The next moment, amazingly, he said, 'OK then. We can do that if you want. How about seven o'clock? I'll meet you out here on the terrace.'

Oh my God oh my God oh my GOD . . .

'Seven. Perfect.' It wasn't *that* perfect, what with only giving her a single measly hour in which to do herself up, but never mind, she'd just have to go at warp speed. Throwing him a dazzling smile, Tula said, 'See you then!'

Adrenalin. Excitement. Time for the sixty-minute makeover. Fizzing with excitement, Tula ignored the hunger pangs in her stomach and jumped into the staff quarters' shower. If it was a choice between eating and getting herself Josh-ready, there was no contest.

Shower, hair, teeth, legs, scent, nail polish, make-up, redo hair, more make-up, pale yellow sundress, high heels, low heels, flip-flops, medium heels, pink espadrilles. And one last coat of mascara for luck.

Ta-daaaa, all done with one minute to spare. And giant squirmy butterflies in the pit of her stomach. Tula took one last look in the mirror, then left her tiny room and raced down the back stairs.

'Wow, you look nice.' Carol, one of the older waitresses, gave her an approving nod. 'Doing something special?'

Ha, just a bit. Unable to keep such enthralling news to herself, Tula feigned a casual air and said, 'Just off out with Josh.'

Carol did a gratifying double-take. 'Who? *Our* Josh?'

Tula nodded proudly. 'Drinks first, then we'll probably go on somewhere for dinner.' OK, that bit hadn't actually been agreed on, but it had to be a possibility, didn't it? She was hoping so anyway.

'Lucky you.' Carol, who was in her fifties and married to someone whose nickname was Shrek, said enviously, 'He is lush.'

'I know.' Feeling a fresh burst of butterflies, Tula said, 'Wish me luck! I'll tell you tomorrow how it went.'

By eight thirty, the jug of Pimm's was empty and Tula had a suspicion she'd drunk most of it. Then she belatedly remembered Josh was drinking San Pellegrino, which meant she'd sunk the whole lot.

It was the fruit, basically. She was hungry, so she'd eaten the slices of apple and cucumber and orange by way of a meal replacement. And drunk the accompanying punch, obviously. Well, it was a hot evening. By the time they'd reached the Mermaid Inn she'd been thirsty. And being in the company of Josh Strachan – finding herself on the receiving end of his undivided attention – had been so nerve-racking she hadn't even realised she was knocking the stuff back until . . . hmm, well, until it was all gone.

But they'd been having such a good time. It had been thrilling as well as nerve-racking; Josh was smiling and asking her loads of questions about herself – which was good because it meant he was interested in knowing all about *her*. And in turn she'd told him stories of her childhood, those tricky teenage years, the disastrous boyfriends . . . then had hastily backtracked for fear of sounding like a complete loser and regaled him with tales of wild parties, fantastic holidays and completely lovely boyfriends who'd *adored* her.

In return she'd learned details of Josh's own upbringing, despite having already heard the gist of it from the other girls working in the hotel. Essentially it hadn't been the happiest of childhoods, which only served to massively ramp up his level of attractiveness. Then he'd moved on to the stays in Cornwall with Lawrence and Dot, interspersed with his time at university. By the time he'd finished telling her about the crazy years in Hollywood and even crazier experience managing Go Destry, the jug was miraculously empty.

Spotting her glance in its direction, Josh said, 'Ready for another drink?'

'I probably shouldn't.' Tula was feeling light-headed and *probably* hadn't been the easiest word to get her tongue around; it had come out sounding like *prolly*. Oh, but she didn't want to hurt his feelings. Nor did she want him to think she wasn't enjoying herself in his company. If he got the idea into his head that the evening wasn't a success, he might end it and take her home.

In the unromantic sense.

Which definitely mustn't be allowed to happen. This was their very first date, after all. Whether or not he was aware of it.

'OK, just one more. I'll have a glass of wine this time.' Tula beamed enthusiastically. What the heck, there were worse things in the world than being a teeny bit tipsy on a first date.

'Red or white?' said Josh.

'Wed.' Oops, bit of a Freudian slip. '*Red*.' She emphasised the choice with a sensible nod; but really, they were getting on *so well* together. She'd been doing that thing the dating experts always told you to do, mirroring the other person's gestures and casually making physical contact at opportune moments. And it was actually working brilliantly, for once in its life; it was as if there were some kind of magical connection between them. She sat in a haze of happiness, elbows on the table and chin resting on her hands, as she watched Josh make his way back inside the pub . . . whoops, elbow off table . . . oh well, never mind, look at how gorgeous he was . . .

At the bar, Josh was wrestling with his conscience. Yes, he'd had a plan, but it certainly hadn't been this. Initially, when Tula had invited him to have a drink with her, he'd been caught by surprise. But they'd got off to a rocky start last week and she was turning out to be an incredibly hard worker. A mixture of guilt and sympathy had made him unexpectedly say yes, coupled with the fleeting idea that if he were a bit kinder to Tula, he might perhaps go up a notch or two in Sophie's estimation.

In his mind he'd pictured Tula and himself sharing a couple of drinks out on the terrace back at the hotel. In his mental image, she'd worn a casual shirt and shorts, and maybe a dab of make-up.

Instead, she'd bounced out to meet him this evening done up to the nines, and said brightly, 'Let's go somewhere nice!'

Which hadn't been his intention at all.

They'd ended up at the Mermaid. Whereupon, instead of asking for half a lager or a glass of wine, Tula had spotted the sign for Pimm's, said *Ooh, Pimm's, how lovely, let's get a jug of that* and promptly proceeded to glug her way through it.

She was now, predictably, three sheets to the wind and for some reason copying everything he did. It was bizarre, like when small children found it funny to repeat every word someone else said, except Tula, as far as he could tell, didn't appear to be doing it to be funny. When he rubbed his jaw, she rubbed her jaw. When he picked up and idly turned over a beer mat, she did too. He'd started leaning forward and raising his eyebrows in a quizzical fashion, just to see if she'd mimic him. And she *had*. He had no idea what was going on, but it had kept him entertained for the last hour.

Anyway, moral dilemma. Of course he didn't want to take advantage of a girl who'd had too much to drink. Then again, when he'd earlier attempted to bring Sophie's past into the conversation, Tula had changed the subject. But with her tongue now loosened by alcohol, this could be a golden opportunity to find out just what it was that Sophie was hell-bent on not telling him.

Which could possibly be regarded as underhand tactics, but he was doing it for the right reasons, wasn't he? Basically, he needed to know.

Chapter 24

God, this red wine was completely delicious. Really mustn't have any more after this one, though. The good thing was, the hunger pangs had disappeared – those slices of orange and cucumber had definitely done the trick.

'We should probably head back soon,' said Josh. 'You said you're working the early shift tomorrow.'

'I'll be fine.' Tula beamed at him. 'Don't worry, I won't let you down. Shall we have another drink?'

'Better not. It's getting late.'

'But it's only ten thirty. That's not late at all.' She didn't want the date to be over. 'I know, let's go for a walk along the beach!'

Josh nodded and smiled in that heart-melting way of his. 'OK, good idea. Let's do that.'

Whoops, sitting down had been easy; walking across soft sand was way trickier. And her head was spinning a bit more too, but never mind. The good thing was that after a couple of stumbles, she now had Josh's arm around her waist to steady her. Oh yes, this definitely counted as a blissful experience . . .

'So you wouldn't say any of them had broken your heart.'

She'd been telling him some more about the boyfriends she'd had in Birmingham. Josh, bless him, was sounding concerned.

'No, not broken.' Picking her way over some complicated pebbles, Tula shook her head. 'A few dents and bruises maybe, but nothing permanent. Nothing I couldn't get over. These things happen, don't they? You just keep on looking till you find the one who's perfect for you.' Glancing up at him with a bewitching smile, she said, 'And then one day it just happens. There he is. And you know it's meant to be.'

'And everyone lives happily ever after.' Josh carefully steered her past a clump of gleaming brown seaweed, its frilly fronds sprawled like octopus tentacles across the sand.

'Well we *hope* they do. Except it doesn't always work out that way. Look at Dot and Lawrence,' said Tula. 'Look at Sophie.'

After a moment, Josh said, 'Sophie needs to let go of the past. She shouldn't let what happened affect her life the way it does.'

'I know,' Tula nodded vigorously, 'but she just *can't*. I've tried telling her that so many times, but it's like she's made up her mind and there's no going back. Once you've been married to someone and they do that to you . . . well, it's not something you get over in a hurry.'

'I know, but she has to, for her own good.'

'I didn't know she'd told you.' *Oops.* Tula nearly stumbled again. 'She never tells anyone about Theo. Honestly, though, what a nightmare. First his mother, then the whole suicide thing . . . I mean, God, no wonder she's so messed up.'

Silence from Josh. Finally, in a voice that was overly casual, he said, 'No, no wonder. So . . . how long ago did he die?'

Tula stopped walking and peered up at him, her brain swirling with alcohol. But she wasn't so far gone that she didn't realise he'd been bluffing. Honestly, why couldn't he just relax and enjoy the evening without veering off on other subjects that weren't anything to do with him?

'Let's not talk about Sophie.' Entranced by the way he was looking at her and the sensation of his arm firmly encircling her waist, Tula breathed in the intoxicating smell of him. 'Why don't we talk about us? You're so beautiful, do you know that? The first time I saw you, I could just *feel* it, you know? You seemed so right. And now we're here on this beach and it's all so . . . romantic. Do you know what I'm thinking?'

'Hang on, could you just stand upright a minute? Before we both fall over.' Not that she would have minded falling over with him, but Tula found herself being firmly rebalanced on her own two feet. Taking a step back from her, Josh said, 'No, I don't know what you're thinking, but—'

'The last time I did this, it all went horribly wrong,' Tula babbled. 'There was this guy I really liked at work, and when I tried to kiss him, he told me he was gay. But I'm pretty sure that's not going to happen again, because you're definitely not . . . Oof . . .'

This time she lunged towards him and Josh was forced to catch her. Taking advantage of the gathered momentum, Tula puckered up, aimed her mouth at his and managed to get his jaw. Not perfect, but better than nothing. Plus she was now plastered against his front, which had to be good.

Sadly Josh didn't seem to think so. Once more she found herself being peeled off.

'Oh come on,' Tula protested; it was so frustrating, being thwarted at every turn. 'You know you aren't gay.'

'I'm not gay,' Josh agreed, 'but it still isn't going to happen.'

'God.' She huffed out her cheeks in disappointment as he began to march her back in the direction of the hotel. 'You're such a spoilsport.'

Sounding suspiciously as if he might be laughing at her, Josh said, 'I know.'

The alarm went off at ten past six and Tula wondered if it was possible to die from the sound of a too-loud alarm. Her head felt like an egg about to give birth to a full-grown dinosaur. Her heart was hammering with nausea. Which was now rising in a tidal wave up her body . . . Oh help . . .

Falling out of bed, she only just made it to the bathroom in time.

Jesus, was there anything worse in the world than feeling like this?

'Blimey.' Spike was making himself a coffee when she stumbled into the staff kitchen and filled a glass with cold water at the sink. 'You look rough.'

'I'm a girl barely alive.' Tula swallowed; her legs were like jelly, her hands trembling. Even drinking water was fraught with risk.

'Good night, was it?'

'Not really.' *Stay down, water, please.*

He peered at her with interest. 'You know when milk gets left out and it separates and goes that weird yellowy-green colour? That's the colour of your face.'

'Don't,' Tula murmured. Just the thought of gone-off milk could do it.

'Are you going to faint?'

'No.' It was a distinct possibility.

'You need to go back to bed,' said Spike.

'Can't.'

'There's no way you can work a shift.'

Tula wanted to cry; did he think she didn't know that? Except there was no way she could not turn up for work. Her current state of near-death was self-inflicted, and she'd be out of a job faster than you could say *super-strength Nurofen*.

Plus . . . Oh God, her brain had been quailing and veering away from even thinking about the goings-on of last night, but it was a situation she was going to have to address. Memory was patchy so far, but amidst the grey blur was an all-too-vivid technicolour recollection of her launching herself at Josh like a heat-seeking missile, doing her damnedest to kiss him — and missing — before being smartly fended off.

The shame, the terrible terrible shame of it. Somehow she'd managed to misread the situation and make a complete fool of herself. Wild optimism had overcome common sense. In the cold, hung-over light of day, it was mortifyingly obvious that he wasn't the least bit interested in her. His number-one priority was evidently still Sophie.

Who in turn wasn't remotely interested in him. For goodness' sake, couldn't he see how futile his stupid crush on her was?

Anyway, at least she hadn't been caught out by those sneaky questions he'd asked at the beginning of the evening. Sophie's secrets were still safe.

Then the blanketing grey clouds of her memory parted just fractionally and a single word slipped out, causing the breath to catch in Tula's throat. The word felt as if it might be *suicide*, but her brain had already skittered off in terror. Oh God, oh God, *please* don't let her have said it out loud last night . . .

'Whoops.' Spike hastily pulled out a chair, grabbed her by the arms and steered her towards it. 'You'd better sit down. You look like you've seen a ghost.'

Somehow, by some miracle, Tula made it through her shift. Pale and shaky and feeling unbelievably ill, she nevertheless managed to stay upright, smile at the guests, serve breakfast and generally behave as if she wasn't teetering on the verge of death.

After lunch she went in search of Josh. 'Could we have a private chat?'

Josh led the way into the empty office behind reception, eyeing her with interest. His tone dry, he said, 'Well done. I didn't think you'd manage it. Feeling any better yet?'

'No.'

'Sit down. Why not?'

As if he didn't know.

'OK, I'm sorry about last night. I didn't mean for any of that to happen.' She may as well get all the humiliating bits out of the way first; let's face it, having to apologise for trying to kiss him was less shaming than the actual attempt itself. Tula rubbed her forehead and said, 'Sorry about everything, the grabbing you and stuff. I can't believe I did that. It'll never happen again.'

'You've said that before,' Josh pointed out.

'I know, but about something different. That was bunking off work. This was trying to kiss my boss. And I couldn't be more embarrassed, but it's not even the worst thing I did.' She stopped and took a deep, shuddery breath; during the course of the morning, the memories of last night had made their patchy, terrifying return. 'I told you some stuff I shouldn't have told you, about Sophie. I'm pretty sure I didn't say too much, but . . . please don't tell Sophie, OK? Please. I promised I'd never say anything, and she'll be so upset if she finds out I've let her down.'

His expression was inscrutable. 'Oh. That's a shame. I was going to ask more questions.'

Tula's neck prickled with panic. 'Well don't! And there's no point anyway, because I'm not saying another word. Promise me you won't tell her,' she begged. 'She's my best friend. *Please.*'

'Fine. You didn't say much.' Josh shrugged. 'But OK, I promise. She won't hear it from me.'

'Thank you.' The relief was overwhelming; her eyes unexpectedly smarted and she covered her mouth. 'Really, thanks.'

'Are you going to be sick?' He reached for the waste-paper bin under the desk.

'No.' Tula took her hand away and wondered how it would feel to hear him say it with genuine concern for her, rather than for the office carpet. She was just going to have to accept that as far as Josh Strachan was concerned, she wasn't The One.

Oh well. Maybe in time Josh would come to terms with the realisation that as far as Sophie was concerned, he wasn't hers either.

When Tula had left, Josh remained in the office, lost in thought. Sophie had been married. And her husband had committed suicide. This information had been ricocheting around inside his head since last night.

Well, he'd known there had to be some reason for her being the way she was, but he hadn't been expecting *that*.

Talk about a bolt from the blue. He had no idea what had happened or the circumstances leading up to it, but he certainly understood now why she was so determined to protect herself from further pain.

Feeling responsible for another person's death — even if you *hadn't* been responsible for it — had to be one of the worst experiences in the world.

No wonder Sophie preferred to keep it to herself.

And now, thanks to Tula's impassioned plea not to ask her any further questions, he wasn't likely to find out more.

Before going off duty Josh checked his watch. Sophie would be here any minute. It had been Dot's idea; upon being told by a party of guests yesterday evening that before booking into any new hotel they liked to check out the photos of the people who ran the place, she had exclaimed, 'Oh no, I can't believe we haven't done it; there aren't any pictures of Josh on the website — we need to sort that out at once!'

And while he'd been out at the Mermaid with an increasingly inebriated Tula, Dot had been calling Sophie to get her up here this evening for a short-notice photo shoot.

The next moment, prompt as always, there was a knock at the office door.

'Hi.' Sophie was smiling, and the sight of her — coupled with the knowledge of what he'd discovered last night — caused something in his chest to tighten. She was wearing a purple shirt and faded jeans, and looked happy and utterly relaxed. Except he knew now that she wasn't. There was a carefully constructed guard there that never came down.

OK, just act normally. If she can do it, so can you.

'Hi. Just so you know,' he warned her, 'this is worse than the dentist for me. I hate having my photo taken.'

Sophie laughed. 'So do lots of people. Don't worry, I'll make it quick and painless.'

'Shall we go outside to get it done?'

'No.' She shook her head. 'I want you . . . sitting at your desk.'

It had been one of those accidental, meaningless pauses while she considered the options, but just for a millisecond it had sounded as if she were saying: *I want you.*

Ha, if only.

Mildly curious, he said, 'Why?'

'I have my reasons. Sit,' Sophie instructed, pointing to the chair and already reorganising the items on the desk. 'I need you looking all businesslike and efficient and grown-up.'

Something was going on; her eyes were sparkling as she moved the computer a fraction to the left. Josh sat down and said again, 'Why?'

'For contrast.' Grinning, she pulled a folder from her bag and opened it, taking out a photograph. 'It's Dot's idea. She wants to show everyone how you are now, compared with how you used to be.'

He saw the photo and groaned. 'Oh God.'

'Don't be like that. It's a fabulous idea.'

'Easy to say that,' Josh said drily, 'when you're not the one being publicly humiliated.'

It was a photo he hadn't seen in years, taken by Lawrence during a trip to the beach. In it, Dot was sitting on a rock in a stripy dress, looking glamorous as always and laughing at his antics. And there *he* was, about nine or ten years old, skinny and tanned and wearing bright blue shorts and a yellow snorkelling mask pushed to the top of his head. There were lime-green flippers on his feet and his dark hair was dripping wet. In his left hand he held a shrimping net and in his right he was brandishing a live crab as, beaming with pride, he showed it off to the camera.

'It's a gorgeous photo,' said Sophie. 'I love that expression on your face. Look at you, so pleased with yourself.' Mischievously she added, 'All smug and scrawny.'

'Hey. Less of the scrawny. I was . . . athletic.'

'And you weren't afraid to have your photo taken. OK, let's do this, shall we? Roll up your shirtsleeves and sit forward a bit. Rest your elbows on the table. Give your head a shake. More than that.'

'Why do I have to shake my head?'

'Because your neck and shoulders are tense. You need to loosen up, channel your inner ten-year-old.' Sophie pointed to the photograph on the desk. 'You were relaxed back then. Look at that brilliant smile.'

Was it any wonder he wasn't relaxed now? Josh watched as she adjusted the settings on the camera, took a few test shots and moved around the office searching for the best angles.

'How's your back?' She was still carrying herself carefully, limping a bit.

'Mending, thanks. Pretty spectacular bruise, but it's getting better. OK, look at me and smile.'

Easier said than done. Sophie was behind the camera now, taking photos, issuing gentle suggestions and being persuasive, doing her best to get the shot she wanted.

Oh, but just the fact that he knew she was studying him intently through the camera lens made it almost impossible. Maybe if it wasn't Sophie taking the photos he'd be able to relax more.

She stopped to change the lens, and said good-naturedly, 'You really aren't enjoying this, are you?'

'I know. Sorry. I once broke up with a girlfriend because of it.'

'You're kidding. How?'

'It was a girl in LA.' Maybe if he talked about his past relationships, it might encourage her to do the same. 'Her name was Janine and she was an actress. We got on pretty well, but she was just *obsessed* with taking photos of herself and anyone she happened to be with. I mean, *all* the time. Wherever we went, whatever we were doing.' Josh shook his head at the memory. 'She'd just whip out her phone, hold it at arm's length, strike a pose with her other arm round me and, God, do this pouty sultry smile into the camera. Exactly the same smile every time.'

'And that was it, you were mentally scarred for life.'

'Well no, I hated it before that. But it didn't help. And after a few weeks I couldn't stand it any more. Had to break up with her. She even took a picture of herself then,' Josh marvelled, remembering the occasion. 'Seriously. *While* she was crying.' He shook his head. 'You can't tell me that's not a weird thing to do.'

'It's pretty weird.' Sophie sounded entertained. 'Maybe it's an LA kind of thing.'

'Well I went out with a few girls while I was living there. None of the rest of them were like that.'

'But they didn't last either. So what was wrong with them?'

'I don't know. They were nice enough, just not . . . completely right.' He grimaced. 'Some of them took themselves too seriously. Some were self-obsessed. Some were a bit over-keen on lettuce and yoga . . .'

'Can you pick up that pen? That's it, and write something on this.' Sophie pushed a blank sheet of paper towards him.

'Write what?'

'Anything you like.'

What should he write? Maybe: *Talk to me about your husband, tell me how he died* . . .

'OK, hang on a sec.' Evidently thinking better of it, Sophie took the pen back, quickly scrawled something on the sheet of paper and put it into his hands, with the writing facing away from him. 'Now hold it up, show it to the camera.'

Josh did as he was told, then peered over to see what she'd written.

It said: *I hate having my photo taken.*

He sat back, burst out laughing and Sophie fired off another series of shots.

'There it is.' Having paused to scroll though and examine them on the screen, she pointed to show him. 'That's the one.'

Josh looked. She'd done it, captured the perfect moment. Against all the odds she'd relaxed him and caught him off guard. 'You're good at this.'

'I'm better than good. I'm brilliant.' Sophie checked her watch. 'There you go, the seven-minute photo shoot. Told you I'd be fast.'

He nodded and smiled. What was more, Dot had been right; the before and after photos would look great on the website. A family-run hotel needed a couple of family photos to entertain the clients. 'Thanks.'

'No problem.' Sophie was putting her camera away in its case; in another minute she'd be gone.

'What about your ex-boyfriends?' Josh kept his tone light. 'Any unusual reasons for having to finish with them?'

She snapped the case shut, not fooled for a second. 'Only if they asked too many questions.'

Ouch. Touché.

'Fine.' Josh raised his hands in defeat.

'No problem.' Sophie broke into a dazzling smile, swung the camera case over her shoulder and pulled open the office door. 'I'll email the photos through later,' she said cheerfully. 'Bye!'

Chapter 25

In an effort to take his mind off the Dot and Antoine situation, Lawrence had come along this evening to a party at the golf club to celebrate the ruby wedding of people he wouldn't have particularly counted as friends. Trevor and Val Corbett loved to flaunt their wealth and boast about their marvellous lives. Their sailing boat was the best in the harbour, their grown-up children had never done *anything* wrong and their home had once been rented by a film company and featured in a movie starring Kate Winslet – it was *that* perfect.

But they were also well-meaning and did a great deal for the local community. Besides, anything was better than sitting at home on your own, wondering what kind of evening your ex-wife was having with Antoine bloody Beauvais. And at least there were plenty of people at the golf club to keep his mind off that subject.

Spotting him, Val came bustling across the function room, plump arms outstretched.

'Darling man, how *are* you?'

Lawrence found himself being thoroughly embraced. Big and round, with soft white skin, Val resembled a strawberry Pavlova at the best of times. This evening she was actually wearing a necklace composed of strawberry-shaped crystals, and a matching hair ornament was perched jauntily atop her bleached white-blond curls.

For a moment, Lawrence was speared with sadness. If Dot had

been here, she would have got the joke at once; without saying a word, they could have exchanged a glance and a complicit smile.

Except she wasn't here, was she? Dot was at Gidleigh Park right now, eating world-class food whilst being schmoozed by a Frenchman who knew *everything* there was to know about champagne.

'I'm good,' he told Val, who held him at arm's length and gave him a look of cow-eyed sympathy.

'Yes, but how are you *really*?'

'Fine.' Oh God, she wasn't going to give up.

'We've heard all about it, Antoine being back. Josie Mason-Law bumped into him yesterday – she says he's looking wonderful!'

How was he supposed to react to that?

'And she told us Dot seems *very* smitten. They were having dinner together at the Rose, you know.'

Josie Mason-Law was a meddling old witch. Lawrence forced a smile and said, 'Of course I knew. The three of us met up for a drink afterwards.'

'You did? Goodness, how very . . . modern.' Still sympathetically stroking his shoulder with her pudgy fingers, Val said, 'It must be all so complicated, though. Broken marriages and new relationships. Incredibly painful. If only everyone could be as happy as Trevor and I. Soulmates, that's what we are! Love at first sight, and in all these years we've never had a cross word!'

'Marvellous.'

'Trevor always says he took one look at me and knew he'd found the girl he wanted to spend the rest of his life with. So he snapped me up before anyone else could beat him to it!' Val beamed, powdered chins aquiver. 'I just feel so sorry for all you people who haven't been as lucky as we have. Especially you, darling . . . I mean, after the mess you made of your own marriage!'

At that moment Trevor called her over to greet some new arrivals and Lawrence was reprieved. He took a deep breath, wondering if coming here had been a massive mistake. Maybe he should just slip away and—

'Here you go, get this down you.' A glass was thrust into his hand and Marguerite Marshall said, 'When people say something that really annoys me, I like to get my revenge by putting them in a book.' Her dark eyes gleamed. 'I find it helps.'

'Good plan.' Lawrence smiled briefly. 'The thing is, she doesn't mean it.'

'I know, she's just monumentally tactless. Last year Val said I must have had some terrible Christmases in my time, what with having had so many failed marriages. When I mentioned once that I'd put on a few extra pounds, she told me it was because I was comfort-eating. And the other week, when Trevor overheard me making some jokey comment about feeling old and decrepit, he handed me his little brother's business card, winked and said he could sort me out, no problem. I thought he was doing a spot of matchmaking, setting me up with a younger man to lift my spirits.' Marguerite grimaced. 'Turns out his brother's a cosmetic surgeon who specialises in facelifts.'

Lawrence laughed; when she wasn't busy being intimidatingly bossy and grand, Marguerite had a nice line in self-deprecating humour. 'What the hell are we doing here, eh?'

'Well personally I'm on the lookout for husband number four,' said Marguerite drily. 'At least, that's why Val invited me. She said I should come along because I might meet someone nice for a change.'

'Decent of her.'

'Whereas in reality I'm here because there's nothing on TV tonight and I can't figure out how to set up the new DVD player.'

'Can't Riley do that for you?'

'He probably could, but he's gone out. Skirt-chasing, I imagine.' Marguerite rolled her eyes good-naturedly. 'As ever.'

Lawrence said, 'You're too soft with that boy.'

'I know. But he makes me laugh. Anyway, how about you? What brings you here tonight?'

'Boredom. Loneliness. All the usual reasons for the single man.'

'Still, could be worse. At least we haven't spent the last forty years married to Val and Trevor.'

They sipped their drinks and watched as Trevor, in the centre of the room, demonstrated a practice swing with an imaginary golf club while Val, shrieking with laughter, called out, 'Well done, Pumpy, lovely shot! Hole in one, ha ha ha!'

Lawrence felt sad again. It was easy to make fun of them, but they *were* a happy couple; just because he wouldn't want to be married to Val didn't mean he didn't envy them.

As if reading his mind, Marguerite said, 'You never really know, though, do you? People can put on a good show. Maybe Trevor's spent the last forty years having torrid secret affairs with really thin women.'

'Or men.'

Marguerite transferred her glass from one hand to the other. 'Lawrence, can I ask you something?'

Taken aback by the abruptness of her tone, Lawrence said, 'Fire away.'

'What are you doing next weekend?'

He prevaricated. 'I'm not sure. Why?'

'I'm appearing at a literary festival in Scotland. I just wondered, if you're free, if you'd like to come along with me.'

Bloody hell, talk about a bolt from the blue. He'd known Marguerite for years and there'd never been any hint of interest from her before. Personally he'd always found her rather too full of herself and demanding; her habit of plain speaking and thinking of herself as a bit of a star could be both terrifying and comical. Startled by the unexpectedness of this turn of events, he said, 'Well . . . um . . .' and saw her expression change.

'Doesn't matter. Forget I said anything. Just a thought, if you were at a loose end, that's all.'

It belatedly occurred to Lawrence that he *did* have something on. 'It's not that, I've just realised there's another event I'm meant to be going to. A friend's daughter's holding an art exhibition in Newquay and they invited me . . . I've already said I'm going, so I can't let them down.' This was true, all true, but it didn't *sound* true, even to his own ears. It came across as the most

163

desperate excuse. And he could tell Marguerite didn't believe him for one minute.

'Art? I like art.' There was a note of challenge in her voice. 'What's her name?'

Shit. 'I can't remember,' said Lawrence. 'She uses her married name. But her father's called Ted Bishop.'

'It's fine.' Marguerite finished her drink. 'It was just an idea. If it doesn't appeal, all you have to do is say no.'

'But—'

'Oh look, there's Celia, I must go and say hello.' And that was it, he was summarily dismissed and she was off, in a swirl of perfume and Parma-violet silk.

Lawrence headed outside to the long terrace overlooking the emerald velvet putting green, and sat down at an empty table. He wondered how Dot and Antoine were getting along at Gidleigh Park. He took out his phone and made a quick call before heading back to the party. There were plenty of people he knew here; it wasn't as if he didn't have other friends to talk to.

Forty minutes later, he found himself close to wanting to commit actual bodily harm.

Maybe it was like not being bothered about helping yourself to another cake . . . until you realised there was only one left. Or a small boy who hadn't touched his remote-controlled car for months, until his younger brother suddenly decided he wanted a go.

Lawrence exhaled. OK, that sounded bad, but he honestly *had* been considering his options in a quiet, biding-his-time kind of way. What he hadn't counted on was Edgar Morley turning up and metaphorically crashing the party.

For the last thirty minutes Edgar had been preening, peacocking and engaging Marguerite in flirtatious conversation. Worst of all, she appeared to be enjoying it. Over and over again their laughter rang out, and the sound of them having fun together was like nails being dragged down a blackboard. Edgar Morley was over-keen and periodically made advances towards Dot, who effortlessly rejected him. Desperate to replace his late wife, he was about as subtle as a rhino. He was also a stalwart of the golf club and a complete bore; how he was managing to entertain Marguerite was anyone's guess.

The next moment she glanced across the room and Lawrence found himself caught watching her. For half a second he held her gaze, then broke into a rueful half-smile. Turning, he headed back outside. There were steps down from the terrace and a path leading around the clubhouse to the car park; maybe he'd slip away unnoticed and avoid having to say all those tedious goodbyes.

But once outside, he heard the tap-tap of high heels behind him and inhaled the familiar waft of heady, patchouli-based perfume.

'What was that look for?' demanded Marguerite.

He stopped and turned. 'Sorry?'

'Were you laughing at me?'

Beneath the super-confident exterior there definitely lurked a modicum of insecurity. He'd never even known it existed before.

'Not at all.'

Her eyes glittered. 'I don't like being laughed at.'

'I can tell. But that's not what I was doing.' Before he could censor himself, Lawrence said simply, 'If you must know, I was jealous.'

'What?'

'You heard. Where is he now?'

'Waiting for me to go back in there.'

'Has he asked you out?'

'Edgar? Oh yes.'

'Are you going?'

'No. He's the world's biggest bore.'

'He was making you laugh,' Lawrence pointed out.

'Wrong. He was making himself laugh. I just chose to go along with it to be polite.'

'You were going along with it for a long time.'

'I'm a writer, Lawrence. It's in my nature to study characters.'

'Anyway, there's something I want you to see.' Taking out his phone, he showed her the screen. 'I called my friend. This is his daughter's website. And there's the date of her exhibition.'

'Why did you do that?'

'Because you thought I was making up some excuse. And I wasn't.' He puffed out his cheeks. 'It just sounded like I was.'

'It really did.' Marguerite nodded.

'And I promised I'd go. Can't let them down.' Lawrence paused, feeling like a teenager. 'But I'm free any other evening this week, if you'd like to . . . meet up.'

There, he'd said it. The ball was now well and truly in her court. God, this was scary stuff.

'Sounds good.' Another nod. 'Meet up for what, exactly?'

'Anything you like. Company. Conversation. Food.'

'At a restaurant?'

'Certainly at a restaurant. Trust me, you wouldn't want to risk eating anything I'd put together.'

Marguerite smiled. 'In that case, how about if I make something for us? I'm a great cook.'

Home-cooked food. Lawrence, who was hopeless in the kitchen and lived off whisky and supermarket ready meals, said with feeling, 'That would be the most tremendous treat.' He added, with some surprise, 'I had no idea you enjoyed cooking.'

'One of us has to be able to do it. And it certainly isn't Riley. We'd live off cereal and sandwiches if it were left up to that boy. Oh Lord, here comes Edgar.' Marguerite grimaced. 'How about Thursday, then? Come over at seven.'

'Thursday.' Suddenly feeling a whole lot better but at the same time wondering what he was getting himself into, Lawrence said, 'Thanks. I will.'

Chapter 26

It was breezy on the beach. Tula tied her hair back from her face, shook out the rug she'd brought with her and settled down on the sand to eat her ice cream and read her book. Riley was out there in the water, leaping around in the waves like a dolphin, his own streaky blond hair and smooth butterscotch tan making him look more Californian than ever. He was playing up to the attentions of a couple of girls in tiny bikinis. Tula wondered idly which of the two he'd go for. He spotted her and waved, and she waved back, privately deciding he'd choose the one with the bigger boobs and the khaki bikini.

She was halfway through her ice cream and engrossed in her book when a fine spray of seawater landed on her bare legs. Tula looked up and said patiently, 'Shaking your head like a dog to annoy people is what kids do. You should probably have grown out of it by now.'

'Well I haven't.' Unrepentant, Riley grinned. 'Never gets old, that game. It's my favourite.'

'If you make the pages of my book wet, they'll go all wrinkly. And I hate that.'

'Show me who wrote it?' Bending down and tilting the cover towards him, Riley said, 'Ah, you don't want to be reading that anyway.'

'I do. It's brilliant.'

He tut-tutted. 'Written by one of Marguerite's deadliest rivals.

They did an event together a few years back and she kept interrupting Marguerite, cutting her off every time she opened her
mouth to speak. I mean, can you imagine being brave enough
to do that? So Marguerite gave the woman's next book a poor
review, and that was it: fountain pens at dawn. Every time she's
in a bookshop now, Marguerite hides the old witch's books at
the back where no one can see them.' He tapped the paperback
in Tula's hand. 'And I bet she does exactly the same to
Marguerite's.'

'So mature. Anyway, what are you doing over here?' said Tula
as he threw himself down on to the sand beside her. 'Your girls
are waiting for you.'

'I know. Pretty, aren't they?'

'Very.'

'Envious?'

'No. Actually, you can settle a bet. Which do you prefer?'

His smile playful, Riley said, 'You.'

Tula gave him a look. 'Out of those two.'

'Hmm. Not sure. OK, the dark-haired one.'

'In the khaki bikini? Ha, I was right.' She nodded in
satisfaction.

Riley cast a mystified look up and down the beach. 'And who
were you having the bet with?'

'Just myself. I knew you'd prefer her. Bigger boobs.'

'Really? I hadn't noticed.'

'Yeah, right. Soooo predictable.' Keen to get back to her book,
Tula reopened it. Riley nudged her ankle.

'Come on, couldn't you at least be a little bit jealous? Were
you watching? She was practically throwing herself at me.'

'Why would I be jealous?'

'Maybe because you're secretly starting to fancy me a bit?' He
sounded hopeful.

'Oh. But I'm not.'

'I know, you're making it pretty obvious.'

'Sorry.'

'It's just so frustrating,' Riley complained. 'I told you before. I *really* like you.'

'God knows why,' said Tula.

'Exactly! I don't know why either.' He shook his wet hair out of his eyes. 'It's driving me nuts. You're not my usual type at all.'

'I don't have big boobs.' She pointed to her flat chest. 'Or swingy model hair. I don't wear false eyelashes on the beach.'

'And you're argumentative,' said Riley. 'Very, *very* argumentative. But somehow none of that seems to matter. You know when you walk into a clothes shop and there are tons of different things on the rails but you see this one shirt and know that's the one you really want? You just have to have it, even though it's a style and colour you've never been interested in until now? Well,' he went on with a helpless shrug, 'that's what it's like with you.'

'Oh great,' said Tula. 'So now I'm a mustard-yellow shirt with a weird sticky-up collar and funny sleeves.'

He nodded in baffled agreement. 'You kind of are.'

'Cheers. Your chat-up lines could do with a bit of work, by the way.'

'If I got myself some better ones, would they help me with you?'

'Nope,' said Tula.

'Why not? I don't get what the problem is,' Riley protested. 'Everyone else fancies the pants off me.'

'I know they do.'

'You're definitely the odd one out.'

'I know that too.' She smiled. 'And don't get me wrong – I'm flattered you like me. But I told you before, you're not my type.' This was just a bit of light flirtation on the beach; now wasn't the time to delve into her past and explain her reasons for not wanting to get involved with someone like him. Having grown up with a mother who had lurched hopelessly from one ill-advised relationship to the next, Tula was determined not to make the same mistake. Charming, lazy partners who didn't work and could never be relied on had been her mum's speciality. They were certainly never going to be hers.

'You mean because I'm not Josh,' said Riley.

Tula flushed; how much had he heard? 'I like successful, hard-working men. Not ones who spend all their time surfing.'

'Josh surfs.'

'I know, but he's only just come back from the States. He's taking things easy for a few weeks. Not like you,' Tula pointed out. 'You've been taking things easy for the last ten years.'

'So what you're saying is, if I were a mega-successful busi-nessman, you'd change your mind about me and decide I wasn't so bad after all.'

'OK, now you're just making me sound like a gold-digger, and that's not true at all. Successful's nice, but hard-working's way more important. It's putting in the effort that counts. I want someone with a job.'

'I have a job.' Riley looked wounded.

'I'm talking about a proper job. Occasionally helping your aunt out by driving to the post office to buy stamps doesn't count.'

'I do more than that,' he protested.

'You pick her up from the train station. Every now and again you unjam the printer. It must be exhausting.'

'It would be, if I knew how to unjam a printer. We usually call an expert in to do that. Kidding,' said Riley. 'I'm brilliant. It's my speciality.'

'Well, I'm just saying. My number-one priority is a man with a strong work ethic. That's the only way I can explain it.' Tula shrugged. 'It's a deal-breaker for me. If someone doesn't have that need to work, I don't fancy them, simple as that. I just can't find them attractive.'

Riley surveyed her with a soulful expression for several seconds. Finally he said, 'Not even if they do a huge amount for *charidee*?'

She smiled. 'Except you don't.'

'Dammit, I knew I should have run that marathon. Shall I leave you in peace now to read your book?'

'Probably best. Your girls are getting impatient.'

They both glanced across at the two girls, now ostentatiously doing aerobics in their minuscule bikinis whilst keeping a diligent eye on their errant prey.

'You know something? You're breaking my heart.' Riley said it with a rueful smile.

It was undeniably nice to be in this position for once in her life. Inwardly revelling in it, Tula said good-naturedly, 'I don't think I am. You're just a spoilt boy feeling a little bit peeved.'

Riley rose to his feet and broke into a beautiful grin. 'You could be right. Maybe I should do something about it.'

'I wouldn't worry. Everyone else seems to love you just the way you are.'

'True. But you never know, one day I might surprise you.'

And with that, to the visible disappointment of the two stunning girls exercising on the sand thirty metres away, he cast a mock-salute in their direction and left the beach.

Chapter 27

It was a warm, grey, misty morning. Woken by the alarm at five thirty, Sophie showered and dressed and left the house just before six, feeling like a spy on a secret mission. As the weather forecast had predicted, it began to rain as she drove the short distance out of St Carys along the southbound coast road until she reached the turn-off for Mizzen Cove.

A dark grey Toyota Corolla was already parked in the lay-by on the other side of the road. Sophie pulled up behind it and saw the driver's door open. A short, plump woman in a bright yellow oilskin coat and sou'wester jumped out and came bustling over.

'Hello, you came! Jolly good! Shall we head on down there? Sorry, how rude of me, I'm Elizabeth Sharp. Thank you so much for agreeing to this at such short notice. You know how it is, sometimes you have one of those light-bulb moments and just want to get on and do it straight away.'

'No problem.' Sophie was instantly charmed by the woman's manner. Elizabeth Sharp had called her yesterday and explained what she was after. In person, she was overweight and pink-cheeked, with squirrel-bright eyes and a button nose. Touched by the little she'd learned during their phone conversation, Sophie had been more than happy to do the honours today.

Leaving the cars behind them, they wended their way along the narrow, overgrown path. The rain was light, currently nothing more than drizzle, and a hazy sunshine was just beginning to brighten the grey sky towards the horizon. The sea was pale pearl and as smooth as glass. Apart from the wavelets breaking on the sand, there was absolute silence. Mizzen Cove was the least accessible beach in the area, tiny and only reachable via a steep, difficult-to-negotiate zigzagging pathway. Sophie took care not to slip and do more damage to her back, now thankfully beginning to mend.

'Sorry to drag you all the way down here,' Elizabeth panted as they reached the shale. 'But I'm no supermodel. Don't want to frighten the horses!'

There were no horses, no animals of any description and no other humans in sight. The cove couldn't be seen from the road. Unless a submarine periscope suddenly popped up out of the water, they were completely hidden from view.

'Did you really just decide to do this yesterday?'

'Thought about it for a while, made my mind up yesterday.' As she spoke, Elizabeth removed her rain hat, tossed it on to the pebbles and ruffled her short fair hair. 'I'm fifty-three years old, Sophie. I've spent the last thirty years teaching history in comprehensive schools to bored teenagers who thought I was ancient even before I was forty. All this time I've been a model citizen and – I hope – a nice person. My husband didn't want children, so we didn't have them. Six years ago he left me for a much younger woman and they now have two-year-old twins.' She paused for a moment, then shrugged away the pain. 'Anyway, I carried on with my life and everyone told me how brave I was being. Then I was diagnosed with breast cancer and had to go through all sorts of treatment. And my friends and colleagues just keep on telling me how marvellously I'm dealing with everything, what a *stalwart* I am, with my stiff upper lip and my sensible attitude . . . so basically, this is my way of shaking them all up a bit. I'm doing it for me, but secretly I'm looking forward to shocking a few people too.'

With a flourish, Elizabeth finished unfastening the front of her bright yellow oilskin coat and removed it to reveal the unclothed body beneath. Folding the coat, she placed it on a rock, then straightened and lifted her face to the sky. Sophie opened her bag and took out the camera, giving the older woman time to become accustomed to her naked state.

Within a couple of minutes she was ready to get started. Elizabeth nodded, her pale skin spangled with drizzle. There was no need to tell her to relax; she was already beaming from ear to ear.

'Oh my goodness.' Her eyes were closed, her arms outstretched. 'This feels *amazing*.'

Angling the camera to make the most of the natural light, Sophie began snapping away. Over the sea, shards of sunlight sliced through the grey clouds as Elizabeth surrendered to nature, dancing joyfully across the wet sand. She wasn't a beautiful woman, just average-looking, with the body of so many women in their fifties. Her legs were short, her stomach protruded a bit and one breast was missing, replaced with flatness and shiny scar tissue extending under the arm, but her air of freedom and delight made the images memorable. She'd survived everything life had thrown at her and now she was celebrating it, dancing naked in the rain.

'You look so happy,' Sophie told her when they stopped for a break.

'I am. I wish I'd done this years ago.' Unselfconsciously touching the scars on the left side of her chest, Elizabeth said, 'But then I wouldn't have had these, and they're all part of it. And my hair's growing back curly, after the chemo.' She rubbed her hand over her scalp. 'It always used to be straight. I'm different now.' Her face lit up once more. 'But I'm so glad I'm doing it. Can I have a look at what you've taken so far, is that OK?'

'Of course. Come and see.' Sophie showed her some of the images she'd captured, scrolling through in search of the best ones. Then she paused and said, 'This one's fantastic.'

In the shot, Elizabeth was almost turned away from the camera, standing on tiptoe like a ballerina with her arms stretched above her head. She was looking back over her left shoulder, laughing with sheer joy, and the scars on her chest were just visible, illuminated by the thin rays of sunlight shining down.

'You're right, I love it.' The older woman smiled at the sight of herself. 'I'm the shape of a Teletubby and I don't even care. Childbearing hips that never got to bear any children . . . oh well. And look at those arms, bingo wings ahoy! But none of that matters, because I'm still here and that's actually more important than having a model figure. I'm alive,' she said, 'and I'm so glad we've done this today. It feels . . . *great*.'

'Good,' said Sophie. 'I'm glad we did it too.'

'Although technically, *we* didn't.' Elizabeth raised her eyebrows. 'I did. You just took the photos.'

'Well yes, that's what I meant. It's kind of my job.'

'So have you ever tried it yourself?'

Did this mean what she thought it meant? Amused, Sophie said, 'What, stripped off for the camera? Can't say I have.'

'You should give it a go. You don't know what you're missing.'

Sophie laughed.

'I mean it.' Elizabeth gestured expansively around the cove. 'And what better time than now?'

OK, was she actually serious? 'I couldn't.'

'Why not?'

Ha, ask a silly question.

'Well, because I'd feel . . . *naked*,' said Sophie.

'Naked in the rain. It feels incredible.' Elizabeth's eyes were shining. 'Honestly, it's the best thing I've done in years.'

'But . . . but . . .'

'There's nobody to see you. I won't tell anyone, if that's what you're worried about. No one's ever going to know, except us.' Holding up her hands, she said, 'It's not even as if there'll be any photos!'

Sophie looked to the sky, where a lone early-morning seagull was wheeling lazily overhead. The rain was still falling, as light and barely detectable on her face as warm silk. Elizabeth was certainly right about one thing: if she was ever going to do it, you really couldn't ask for a better time than now, here in this hidden cove, visible to no one.

As if sensing that she was weakening, the older woman said lightly, 'I dare you.'

Except it wasn't weakening, was it? It was emancipating, surely. Strengthening . . . celebrating . . .

'OK.' Sophie shrugged off her unbuttoned blue shirt and unlooped the camera strap from around her neck. Handing the Nikon over to Elizabeth she said, 'Do you know how to use one of these?' Because really, if she was going to do it, there might as well be photos.

'Just show me which button to press.' Surveying the camera, Elizabeth said cheerily, 'And don't worry, you won't regret this. I promise!'

Chapter 28

It was earlier than he'd usually be up, but Josh had offered to drive the Carter-Laings to Newquay airport to catch their flight back to Edinburgh. As they'd been leaving the hotel, Griff had jumped out of his basket and followed them out to the car, whining and pleading to be allowed along for the ride. Which had seemed like a decent enough idea; after dropping off the Carter-Laings, he could take the dog for a proper run along the beach before breakfast.

But as he'd been heading back along the coast road, Josh had come across something unexpected: there was Sophie's car, parked up in a lay-by in the middle of nowhere behind a dark grey Toyota Corolla.

Did this mean it had been stolen? Was that likely? Had she broken down? Where was she and what could she be doing at this time of the morning? Puzzled, Josh parked in front of the Toyota and switched off the ignition. It was the sheer oddness of the situation that propelled him to push open the driver's door. He had to know for sure that Sophie was all right.

As he made his way across the wet grass with Griff bounding joyfully along at his heels, Josh took out his phone and called Sophie's mobile. When it rang and rang and wasn't picked up, his level of concern ramped up a couple more notches. Had a deranged killer flagged her down, dragged her out of the car and thrown her off the edge of the cliff on to the rocks below?

He speeded up, blinking rain out of his eyes. It had to be over a decade since he'd last visited Mizzen Cove; it was too much like hard work for all but the most hardy and determined beach-finder. The thought that something sinister could have happened to Sophie was making his mouth dry . . .

Josh held his breath as they approached the cliff edge, needing to know but not wanting to look. The next moment he heard a shriek of laughter and saw her.

Sophie, wearing no clothes, none at all. She had her back to him but it was unmistakably her, dancing across the golden sand with her arms stretched wide and her blond hair streaming behind her. Jesus, thank goodness she was alive . . . and look at her, *just look* . . .

Relief at not finding an inert body lying broken on the rocks instantly gave way to admiration; basically, the last thing he'd expected to see was Sophie dancing naked on the beach, being photographed by a plump older woman who was similarly unclothed.

Josh smiled at the incongruous sight of the two of them. He had no idea what the photos might be in aid of, but the fact that Sophie was up for such an adventure was enough to make his day complete. And who knew, this could be a regular thing; maybe these days Mizzen Cove was a designated naturist beach and people came here every week to shed their clothes and their inhibitions.

'Woof woof woofwoof WOOF!' Pricking his ears up, Griff wriggled with delight as he recognised Sophie. The next moment he'd launched himself down the steep zigzagging path, eager to join the fun being had by the naked people on the beach below.

Shit . . .

Looking up and spotting him, Sophie appeared to share the sentiment. She let out a muffled shriek and attempted to cover herself with her hands. As she turned away, he saw the blue-grey bruise on her back from last week's fall. Griff, scrabbling down the last bit of the overgrown path, reached the bottom and raced across the sand, leaping around her in wriggly circles and yapping like a lunatic.

'Oh my God, Griff, *go away*,' Sophie wailed. Which had the exact opposite effect; tail wagging furiously, he attempted to launch himself into her arms.

Josh yelled, 'GRIFF! COME HERE THIS MINUTE.' Which, predictably, had no effect whatsoever.

The other woman on the beach stood with her hands on her hips and called up, 'If you can't control your dog, young man, you really should keep it on a lead.'

Mental images of Griff rampaging around the all-white room at the hotel the other week flickered through Josh's brain. Talk about déjà vu.

'I would have done if I'd known I needed to.' The woman had the in-control manner of a teacher and had just called him *young man*. 'I saw Sophie's car back there and wanted to make sure she was OK. I was worried about her,' he insisted, because the woman was giving him a raised-eyebrow look.

'I'm here because I'm *working*,' Sophie protested. Having moved like lightning, she was now back in her denim shorts and buttoning up her blue shirt.

'Of course you are. Sorry.' Josh managed to keep a straight face. 'For some reason it didn't occur to me that you wouldn't have any clothes on.' Unable to resist it, he added, 'Again.'

Sophie shot him a look. 'OK, OK. You can come and get Griff now. Actually, no.' She turned to her companion. 'Do you want to get dressed first?'

The plump woman beamed, utterly unfazed. 'Don't worry, I'm fine as I am.'

Griff continued cavorting around with a carefree gleam in his eye and a long strand of seaweed trailing from his mouth. As Josh climbed down to beach level, he noticed Sophie wince with pain as she knelt and discreetly stuffed her bra and knickers into her camera case. Eventually he persuaded Griff to return to him and give up the prized tangle of seaweed.

'So,' said the woman, who'd been eyeing him with interest, 'you and Sophie know each other.'

'We do.' He tucked Griff securely into the crook of his arm.

'I'm Elizabeth, by the way.' Stepping forward, she held out a hand for him to shake. 'Good to meet you.'

'Josh. Nice to meet you too.' Her remaining breast jiggled as they shook hands.

Her tone conversational, Elizabeth said, 'Ever seen a mastectomy scar up close before, Josh?'

'Er, well . . . no, can't say I have.'

'And does it look horrendous?'

OK, if she could be this upfront about it, so could he. Josh studied her chest and shook his head. 'No, not horrendous. It's just scar tissue. It's fine.'

Elizabeth beamed. 'Thank you. They offered me a falsie . . . you know, reconstruction, but I don't think I'm going to bother.'

'Good for you.' Josh smiled; she might be as mad as a box of rabbits, but there was something refreshingly honest about her.

'We came here to do the photographs because we thought we'd be uninterrupted. I wasn't sure how I'd feel about a stranger seeing me in the buff like this – a civilian, I mean, not one of the medical staff at the hospital.' She shrugged, smiled and spread her hands. 'But now it's happened, you're here. And it's no problem at all!'

'Excellent,' said Josh. 'Happy to help.'

'Ever done it yourself?' Her head was tilted enquiringly to one side.

'Run around naked on a beach? Not since I was two years old.'

'You should give it a try. Really. It's wonderful!'

'I'm sure it is.' She was definitely mad.

'You could do it now,' said Elizabeth.

'No, I definitely couldn't.'

'Oh go on,' Sophie chimed in, braver now she had her own clothes back on. Innocently she said, 'I could take photos of you. I'd be discreet.'

'Is this how she got you to do it?'

Sophie smiled. 'Yes. And it actually *was* great, until you came along. The rain on your skin, the feeling of freedom. Being at one with nature.' Up close, her grey eyes were flecked with silver and danced with mischief. 'I dare you.'

Griff was gazing up at him too, his tail wagging in encouraging collusion. It was definitely time to get out of here. Josh said, 'Thanks for the kind offer, but not in a million years.'

Sophie and Elizabeth watched as Josh and Griff made their way back up the steep path, reached the top and disappeared from view. A minute or so later, they heard the sound of his car driving away.

'Well,' said Elizabeth. '*He's* rather gorgeous.'

Sophie grinned at the look on her face. 'You think?'

'Hey, just because I'm a single-breasted middle-aged history teacher doesn't mean I don't notice these things.' Elizabeth did a playful hip-shimmy followed by jazz hands. 'I'm not dead yet.'

Chapter 29

Tula was working in the restaurant serving breakfast. She did a double-take when she glanced out of the window and saw one of the gardeners mowing the lawn at the rear of the hotel.

Except it wasn't one of the gardeners; it was Riley. Which was a bit like being wheeled into the operating theatre to have a kidney removed and discovering your surgeon was the guy who worked behind the counter at the post office.

Spotting her in the window watching him, Riley nodded briefly and carried on mowing, the effect only slightly spoiled by a near miss with the old stone sundial in the centre of the lawn.

What the hell?

By the time breakfast was finished, Riley had moved on to the strimmer, and was enthusiastically trimming the edges of the lawn. As well as quite a few of the flowers in the borders that had strayed too close to the edge.

Tula headed outside and said, 'What are you doing?'

Riley switched off the strimmer. 'What does it look like I'm doing?'

'Murdering poor defenceless flowers, mainly.'

'Sshh, only one or two.' Leaning over, he scooped up a handful of decapitated heads and dropped them out of sight behind a clump of foxgloves.

'Where's Edward?' Edward was the real gardener.

'Over on the other side. Doing some mulching. Whatever that may be.'

Tula said suspiciously, 'Do Josh and Dot know you're here?'

'Of course.'

'But why? I don't understand what's going on.'

'Oh my God, I can't *believe* I have a crush on a girl who's so dumb. Think about it,' said Riley. 'You said you couldn't respect someone who didn't have a proper job. So this is me, doing a proper job.'

Tula eyed him with suspicion. 'Seriously?'

'Seriously.' In an ostentatious gesture he wiped the perspiration from his forehead and heaved a long-suffering sigh. 'If you want, you could look more impressed.'

'You're working here?'

'Since eight o'clock this morning. I set my alarm for *seven*.' This was said in the manner of someone only distantly acquainted with the purpose of alarm clocks.

'You absolute hero. But why would Dot pay you to do the job when she could get someone who actually knows what they're doing?'

'I'm going to stop surfing and messing around and wasting my days flirting with girls in bikinis,' said Riley. 'I'm just going to work here instead. Prove to you that I can do it.'

'You didn't answer my question,' Tula prompted.

He exhaled. 'OK. She's not paying me.'

'You're doing it for free. That's not a proper job.'

'Hey, I happen to think that makes it better than a proper job. I'm not doing it for money,' said Riley. 'I'm doing it for you.'

Which would be *so* romantic if it were anyone else saying it.

'OK, great. Anyway,' said Tula, 'I have to get back now.'

Riley looked hopeful. 'Want to meet up for a drink this evening?'

Honestly, he had the attention span of a toddler. Tula said, 'To be honest, if you're going to be gardening all day, you'll be too shattered to want to go anywhere tonight.' She turned and waved. 'But good luck with the job!'

By five o'clock Riley was indeed shattered. Considering he regarded himself as pretty fit and a day of surfing was no effort at all, this came as a shock. Bloody hell, though, gardening was a lot less fun. He was hot and dusty and his hands were stained green. There were blisters on his fingers from using the various clippery things, huge lethal shears and vicious secateurs. The worms in the soil had repulsed him. He'd come *this* close to lawnmowering a frog. The sheer number of insects flying and crawling around made him squirm. Even chopping down an old tree had only been fun for the first fifteen minutes, then all the sawdust had got really irritating, flying into his eyes and throat.

All in all, gardening definitely wasn't his thing. It was disgusting in every way and so *dull*.

He found Tula upstairs in the staff kitchen, off duty now. Barefoot and changed into denim cut-offs, she was eating custard creams and flicking through a magazine while she waited for the kettle to boil.

'Hi.' God, just the sight of her had the most bizarre adrenalin-y effect on him. 'I did it.'

'Good for you.'

'Nine hours, pretty much non-stop. *Look!*' He held out his grass-stained hands.

Tula glanced at them. 'It's like you're a superhero.'

But she was saying it with a smile. Encouraged, Riley said, 'And I'm still awake. So, want to come out with me tonight?'

'Because you worked for one whole day?' Tula shook her head in disbelief. 'You see? This is what you're like. Do the job for a year and I might be impressed.'

A whole *year*? She'd be lucky.

'So it's a no?'

'It's a definite solid gold no.'

Damn. Nine hours of work for nothing. What a waste of time *that* had been.

'Fine, then.' Riley examined his scratched, dusty forearms. He needed to go home, get in the shower and scrub himself clean. 'In that case, may as well go out and get laid.'

'Nice jacket,' said Dot.

'Thank you.' Lawrence brushed the lapel of the midnight-blue Jaeger jacket, possibly the smartest item of clothing he owned.

'Chosen by someone with impeccable taste.'

Lawrence smiled, but experienced an inner pang; she'd bought it for him twenty years ago while they'd been spending a long weekend up in London. At the time, he'd baulked at the price and received a lecture from Dot on the subject of cut, quality and false economies. Good things were more than worth the extra cost, she'd explained, and he'd thought it was a load of tosh, an argument evolved over time by women who weren't happy unless they were paying eye-watering amounts for the clothes in their wardrobe. But two decades later, the Jaeger jacket continued to garner compliments.

Yet again, she'd been right and he'd been wrong.

'It still looks as good as new,' said Dot.

'Unlike its owner.' Lawrence pulled a face.

'Can I just say something? A white shirt would have been better than a brown one.'

'Would it? Damn.' Matching colours had never been his strong point; all those years spent married to a style guru, and none of it had managed to rub off.

'Where are you going?'

'Over to Moor Court. Marguerite's invited me for dinner.' This was the reason he'd popped into the hotel for a quick drink beforehand, so he could casually tell someone who'd then tell Dot. Bumping into her himself had been even better.

'Oh.' Dot looked suitably impressed. 'Big dinner party? How many going?'

'Small dinner party. Just the two of us.'

'*Oh.*' Her eyebrows went up.

Lawrence shrugged. 'Apparently she's a very good cook.'

'Really? Well I never.' Amused, Dot said, 'So what's this about? You and Marguerite.'

Yes. She was curious.

'Just dinner.' Another shrug. 'Who knows?'

'Didn't think she was your type.'

'Maybe I've changed my mind.'

'You used to call her Bloody Scary Spice.'

Dammit, he had.

'Look, she's a very successful, very attractive woman. She invited me to fly up to Edinburgh with her,' Lawrence added recklessly. 'To go to a literary thing.'

'Well if you're going to start going along to things with people who are good with words,' said Dot, 'you'd probably be better off learning not to call them *things.*'

She might be hiding it well, but she was rattled, he could tell. Having achieved what he'd come here to do – and feeling simultaneously mean and relieved – Lawrence finished his drink. 'Well, me and my wrong-coloured clothes had better be making a move. How was Gidleigh Park, by the way?'

'Wonderful. We had some pretty good champagne.' Dot smiled slightly.

'I should hope so too. Nothing but the best for you, sweetheart.'

An infinitesimal shake of the head and a sigh. 'Don't call me sweetheart.'

'Sorry, just slipped out. Anyway, how's Antoine?' He said it in last-minute, throwaway fashion.

'Very well.'

'I bet he'd never be seen in public in a blue jacket and a brown shirt.'

'No,' Dot said evenly. 'He would not.'

He'd never seen Marguerite in dressed-down mode before. She'd always been wearing her look-at-me clothes.

'Come in, come in.' She opened the door wide and greeted him with a kiss on each cheek. Instead of vibrant flowing silk she had on a pale grey plain jersey top and matching casual trousers. Her feet were bare, the jewellery was minimal; even the perfume hadn't been sprayed on with its usual force. She was still wearing make-up, just far less of it. It made her seem softer and less intimidating. More attractive.

'I know,' said Marguerite, evidently reading his mind. 'Shocking, isn't it?'

'You look great.'

'Without my armour. Not many people get to see me like this. Thank you.' She took the bottle of wine he was holding towards her. 'Come on through to the kitchen. Do you want to take off your jacket?'

'Probably best. I've just been told it doesn't go with my shirt.'

Marguerite's dark eyes glittered with amusement. 'Who said that?'

'Dot.'

'Of course. And is she a good cook?'

'Not bad.'

'Hmm, sounds as if I might be better. I'm excellent.'

She wasn't kidding. For the next two hours, they sat at the kitchen table drinking red wine and talking and laughing their way through garlic mushrooms followed by cottage pie and vegetables.

And if it sounded ludicrously simple, it wasn't; every last mouthful was sublime. Marvelling at her skills, Lawrence said, 'How did you learn to cook food like this?'

'I was poor before I was rich. I had plenty of practice in my early days. And I'm good at most things I turn my hand to.'

'Well this has been a treat.' He genuinely meant it. 'I can't cook to save my life.'

As a door opened and closed elsewhere in the house, Marguerite smiled and said, 'You're like Riley. He's hopeless too. The last time I went away, he lived on takeaways, toast and Cheerios.'

'I smell food.' The kitchen door opened and Riley came in, wearing an old T-shirt and jeans. 'Hope there's some left for me.'

'Of course.' Marguerite watched fondly as he helped himself to a massive portion of cottage pie. Lawrence, who'd secretly harboured hopes of being allowed to take the leftovers home with him, inwardly cursed her lazy nephew's gargantuan appetite.

'I didn't realise you were here.' He kept his tone jovial. 'What are you doing this evening, then?'

'Having a night in for a change.' Riley showered ground pepper over the mountain of food on his plate. 'Watching *Star Wars*.'

'Oh? Which one?'

'All of them.'

'He's seen them so many times,' Marguerite marvelled, as if it were a wonderful achievement.

'Has to be done.' Grabbing a can of beer from the giant American fridge, Riley winked at them. 'See ya later. Be good!'

'Do you need me to tell you how spoiled that boy is?' said Lawrence when Riley had left the kitchen.

'No. But he's the light of my life. And he's not hurting anyone.'

'Apart from all those girls whose hearts he's broken.'

'That's their problem. If Riley weren't around, they'd find someone else to break their hearts.'

'He should be working.'

'He's my personal assistant. Anyway,' said Marguerite, 'don't criticise. I don't want him to move away. I'd rather let him have an easy life here than a proper job in some other part of the world. I'd never get to see him.'

'I know, but he needs to learn to stand on his own two feet.' Much as he liked Riley, who possessed charm by the bucketload, Lawrence felt compelled to say it.

'You don't understand. He's my only sister's only son. I need an assistant to help me run my life, and I'd rather employ Riley than some complete stranger. It works out well for both of us. So that's what I do.'

She wasn't angry, simply stating her opinion. Any criticism rolled off her like Teflon. Lawrence said, 'OK, fair enough,' and thought how nice it was to see Marguerite without her meet-the-public face on. Impulsively he said, 'I'm having a good time. I like you better like this.'

'Like what?'

'When you aren't being a best-selling author.' He accompanied the phrase with jazz hands.

Her mouth twitched. 'Have you ever read any of my books, Lawrence?'

'No.' Except . . . did that sound rude? Hastily he added, 'I did try one once, but I only managed a couple of pages. *Ach*, that's probably the wrong thing to say too.'

But Marguerite was choking with laughter, in danger of spluttering red wine across the table. When it was safely swallowed, she said, 'I like it that you haven't read my books. I wouldn't expect you to. Not that they aren't fantastic, you understand . . .'

'And you're writing one at the moment?' Eager to redeem himself for what had surely been a faux pas, he changed the subject to her side of the business.

'Always,' said Marguerite. 'The machine never stops turning. As soon as I finish one book I make a start on the next. My fans demand it. They're inexhaustible. I get letters every day from people begging me to write faster.'

'How did you start?'

'Well, I wrote the first novel as my way of escaping a miserable marriage. My first husband was so jealous of other men, he wouldn't let me go to the library. I was so bored with no books to read, I started writing one of my own.'

'I can't imagine you being married to a man who told you what you could or couldn't do.'

'I know. I was young and incredibly stupid.' Marguerite refilled both their glasses. 'And I thought it meant he really loved me. Don't worry, it didn't take me long to come to my senses. As soon as I got my first publishing contract, I upped and left the bastard.'

'And then?' He knew she'd been married three times but had never paid close attention before.

'Oh well, a couple of years later, I found husband number two. And because I was determined not to make the same mistake again, this time I made sure I married a man who was the complete opposite of number one.'

'Ah.' Lawrence nodded, acknowledging the error.

'Exactly,' said Marguerite. 'Jeremy was a complete wimp. He wasn't kind and thoughtful, just weak and spineless. It was a whole new kind of nightmare, and entirely my own fault. Of course I lost all respect for him. And he knew it. Three years we lasted. God only knows how. Cost me a fortune, that one.'

Lawrence cut himself a wedge of the oozing Camembert she'd brought to the table. 'And how long was it before you met number three?'

'Oh, a while.' Marguerite shook her head at the memory of him. 'Third and worst of the lot,' she said drily. 'But again, I should have known better. Basically, when you meet a man sliding piles of chips across the roulette table in a casino, you pretty much know what to expect.'

Lawrence vaguely recalled Nathan. Several years younger than Marguerite, he'd been the quintessential playboy, good-looking and charming on the surface but essentially selfish and incapable of loving his new wife more than he loved gambling and bedding other, younger women.

'I can't remember how long you and Nathan were married.'

'Eighteen months. It was good fun for at least the first fortnight. The shine tends to go off a relationship,' Marguerite drawled, 'when you come back from an author tour to find another woman's empty pill packet in your en-suite bathroom bin.'

'Where is he now?'

'Austria. Currently living with someone far older and richer than me. They have his 'n' hers matching facelifts. And he's lost almost all his hair,' she added with a flicker of satisfaction.

'Poor chap.'

'I know. So there you go, that's when I gave up collecting marriage certificates. Jolly expensive, and frankly they're more trouble than they're worth. I might be great at writing books, but when it comes to husband-picking, I'm a lost cause.'

'Are you happy being single?'

'I'm used to it. And at least I have Riley here. Not quite the same kind of companion, but it's better than rattling around this place on my own.'

'Do you ever get lonely?' said Lawrence.

'What do you think?' Marguerite raised an eyebrow. 'Why else did I go along to Val and Trevor's smug-fest anniversary party the other night?'

He shrugged. They were in the same boat.

'I wonder if it's worse for you.' Marguerite was watching him.

'In what way?'

'I chose three bad husbands. You chose one perfect wife.'

Lawrence took another drink; did she think she was telling him something he didn't already know? He nodded and said, 'So true.'

'And? Do you regret what you did?'

'At the time I didn't feel I had any choice. I just couldn't help myself. We had to be together. Of course, we didn't know how little time we'd have.'

'And you've paid the price ever since,' said Marguerite.

Lawrence nodded. 'Oh yes. The ultimate karma.'

'Do you still love Dot?'

'I never stopped loving her. Hard as that may be for some people to believe.'

'And now Antoine's back on the scene. What's going on there, then?'

'I have no idea.' Lawrence spoke with feeling, then saw the way she was looking at him. 'Oh God, are you going to put my story into your next book?'

'Maybe I already have.' Marguerite smiled slightly, her eyes bright. 'You wouldn't know. You've never read any of them.'

'Touché.'

'How does it make you feel, Antoine paying all this attention to your ex-wife?'

'How do you think it makes me feel?'

'Poor Lawrence. You made your bed and you've been lying in it on your own ever since. It's a hard life,' she observed. 'Especially knowing that everyone's thinking it serves you bloody well right.'

'Thanks.' He lifted his glass to her. 'Kind of you to point it out.'

'Sorry, I'm a bit blunt sometimes.'

'Really?' Lawrence raised his eyebrows at her. 'I hadn't noticed.'

Lawrence left Moor Court at midnight. Marguerite had dismissed the idea that Riley might drop him home, saying, 'Don't bother asking; once he's engrossed in those films of his, it's best to just leave him to it. I'll call a taxi.'

And now it was waiting outside the front door. He gave Marguerite a hug and kissed her goodbye on each cheek. 'Thanks for a fantastic meal. You were right about being a great cook.'

'I'm always right. About everything.' Her tone was playful. 'Pretty much.'

'Apart from deciding who might be good to marry.'

'Well, there definitely aren't going to be any more weddings. I've learned *that* lesson.' Marguerite paused. 'But I've had a nice time tonight. Better than I expected.'

'So you thought this evening was going to be a complete disaster?'

'Stop it. I thought it would be good.' Her eyes glinted with amusement. 'I'm just saying, it exceeded expectations.'

'Right.' Wondering how to proceed, Lawrence found himself briefly at a loss for words.

Marguerite, who wasn't, said, 'Want to do it again?'

'Could do.'

'Such enthusiasm.'

'Sorry. I mean yes, I'd like that.' Lawrence smiled as he said it. 'I've enjoyed myself too, I really have.'

The taxi departed with Lawrence in it. Marguerite surveyed the mess in the kitchen and took the decision to leave it for now; she'd clean up tomorrow.

Before heading upstairs, she popped her head around the door to say good night to Riley.

He glanced round at her. 'How was that, then? Have a good time?'

'Surprisingly good. Are you going to be staying up all night?'

'Most likely.' He pushed his fingers through his dishevelled hair and nodded. 'You off to bed now?'

'Yes.' She crossed the room, rested a hand on his shoulder and dropped a kiss on top of his blond head. 'Night, sweetheart. Keep on doing what you're doing.'

But she'd lost his attention; Riley's gaze had already slid back to the screen. She was evidently interrupting a good bit. Distractedly he nodded and said, 'Yeah, don't worry, I will.'

Chapter 30

It was no good; like a dentist's appointment you'd been trying hard not to think about, the date of the wedding was almost upon them now and the time had come for Tula to do something about it.

She found Dot working behind the reception desk. 'Hi, I've asked Carol and she's fine with it, so is it OK if we swap shifts this weekend?'

'No problem, my darling.' Dot reached for a pen and pulled the shift planner across the desk towards her. 'So she'll be working on Saturday, yes? And you'll do Sunday.'

'That's it.' Tula watched as the schedule was altered accordingly.

'Off somewhere nice?'

'Yes. Well, kind of. It's an old friend's wedding.'

'Ooh, nothing lovelier than a wedding.' Dot looked sideways at her. 'Except I can't help noticing you're not looking that enthralled.'

'I know. And it *will* be lovely.' Hesitating, Tula pulled a face. 'It's this girl I used to work with. She was always better than everyone else, you know what I mean? The kind who makes you feel a bit inferior?'

'Oh no!' Dot looked appalled. 'Really? How *mean*.'

'She's actually really nice. It's the thing about her being so pretty and lovely that probably makes me feel second best. I was thrilled she included me as one of her friends,' Tula explained.

'She didn't have to. Some of the others were a bit iffy like that, but Imi never was.'

'And who's she marrying?'

'Someone equally perfect in every way. Of course. Good-looking, heaps of money, adores her. They're getting married in the middle of Wales at this amazing hotel.'

'Well I think it sounds wonderful,' said Dot. 'But there's still something not quite right. Are you going to tell me what it is?'

Honestly, was she a witch?

'It's all my own fault.' Tula heaved a gusty sigh and began unwinding a paper clip. 'I've always been a bit rubbish when it comes to boyfriends. Imi and her crowd used to joke about it. Her best friend said it was like a sum that didn't add up, I was pretty enough to get someone decent but somehow it never happened.'

'Well *she* definitely sounds mean,' Dot announced.

Tula bit her lip; the comments had always been made in such a way that if she'd got upset, everyone would have said *but we didn't mean it like* that, *it was just a bit of fun!*

Even though the implication had been that there must be some deep-down attribute she was lacking in, something she was getting badly wrong.

'Anyway, so I kind of hinted that I was seeing someone gorgeous now and Imi said I must bring him along with me to the wedding. Which made things kind of tricky, but it was a while back. I kind of hoped that by the time the day came around I might have found myself a gorgeous boyfriend,' said Tula. 'Except now it has. And I haven't.'

'Ah.' Dot nodded sagely. 'The perennial single-girl problem. Well, you'll just have to say he can't make it, he's had to fly off to Amsterdam on some hugely important business trip.'

'I know, that was my plan too. Except I texted Imi last night to say I'd be coming to the wedding on my own because my boyfriend couldn't make it. She was out with her friends at the time.' Tula flinched at the memory. 'Imi called me back and was saying oh no, what a shame, but I could hear the other girls laughing in the background, making jokes about my imaginary boyfriend. One said, "I'll feel bad if he really does have to work," and someone else said, "Oh come on, don't be so gullible, he doesn't *exist*."'

'That's so cruel!' Dot was indignant on her behalf.

'I know.' Tula had fashioned the paper clip into an agitated spiral. She said gloomily, 'So cruel. But also true.'

The next moment Dot clapped her hands and said, 'Luckily, I'm a genius!'

'Oh?' Tula didn't get her hopes up; her own last idea had been to wonder if she could stick a moustache on Sophie and pass her off as a man.

'Josh,' Dot exclaimed. 'He'd do, wouldn't he?'

OK, this was possibly *the* most rhetorical question in the world.

'Apart from anything else,' Tula reminded her, 'he's up in London this weekend.'

'Ah, but that's the thing, he isn't going any more. His friend's father died last night so the party's been cancelled. Which is sad, obviously,' said Dot, 'but could be brilliantly handy for you.'

It was a thrilling prospect, but realistically not likely to happen. Tula wondered how much Dot knew about her unreciprocated crush on Josh. She unwound the paper clip and shaped it into an angsty zigzag. 'He wouldn't do it.'

'Why ever not?'

Tula shrugged. 'Just wouldn't want to.'

'He might,' said Dot, 'if I ask him.'

Oh God, imagine their faces if she were to turn up at the wedding with Josh. It would be the best moment of her whole life. Her mind working overtime, Tula realised it was like the storyline in that film *The Wedding Date* where the girl from *Will & Grace* ended up falling for Dermot Mulroney and they had their own happy-ever-after.

Because that was the magical thing about weddings, wasn't it? *Anything* could happen . . .

'Let me go and talk to him now,' said Dot.

She could be awfully persuasive when she set her mind to something.

'Go on then.' A Disney squiggle of excitement bubbled up inside Tula's chest. 'Doesn't hurt to ask.'

'No,' said Josh when she'd finished outlining her plan. He knew from experience that the thing with Dot and her powers of persuasion was to stand firm and not show a moment's weakness.

'Don't just say it like that. You'd be doing a tremendous favour for a friend.'

He carried on replying to emails on his laptop. 'Still no.'

'But darling, you'd be doing *me* a favour. And I'm your grandmother.'

'Come on. Emotional blackmail?' He looked up and raised his eyebrows, marvelling at her wily skills. 'Really?'

'I like Tula,' said Dot. 'She's one of those girls who means so well and always manages to land up in awkward situations. And you're not doing anything else on Saturday.' She tilted her head. 'Why can't you help her out?'

'Because then I'd be the one in the awkward situation.' He gave up on the emails and shook his head. 'It wouldn't be fair on Tula either. Do you know she has a crush on me?'

'Does she?'

'Quite a big crush.'

'Oh. Well you're not *ugly*,' Dot conceded. 'I imagine lots of girls do.'

'But it would make things . . . awkward. Embarrassing. Especially if everyone thinks we're a couple. They'd expect us to be . . . you know . . .'

'Honestly, I can't believe you're being so selfish. Poor Tula. Trust me, there's nothing worse than having to turn up at an event without a partner.'

'OK, that's more emotional blackmail,' said Josh. This was what she was like; no tactics were off limits.

'But she doesn't want to go on her own.' Dot's light blue eyes were pleading with him now. 'Can't you understand that?'

'I can. It's just that it shouldn't be me. Bad idea all round. Plus, Riley wouldn't like it. He's pretty keen on Tula . . .' The beginnings of the idea unfolded as the words were coming out of his mouth.

Dot perked up too. 'He is? And how does she feel about him?'

'Thinks he's a lazy bum. Can't imagine why.' Reaching for his phone, Josh said, 'Although this could be the chance he needs to come to her rescue.'

'And he's good-looking enough to impress the other guests. Oh, this is an excellent idea,' Dot said brightly. 'They wouldn't need to know he's a lazy bum.'

'Exactly,' said Josh. *Hallelujah!* Now he was off the hook.

Having punched out Riley's number, Josh waited. And waited. Finally he said, 'Hey, lazy bum, it's midday. Don't tell me I woke you up.'

Tula, covering reception, felt her mouth go dry as she watched Dot making her way back down the staircase. Oh wow, she'd spoken to Josh and now she was smiling. That could only mean one thing . . .

'Don't look so nervous,' Dot said gaily. 'You have a date for the wedding!'

Yaaaay! 'Really?'

'Really. Except . . . it's not Josh.'

Oh. *Flump*, went Tula's heart, like a deflated soufflé.

'He couldn't make it after all,' Dot went on, 'but he's found someone else to do it instead.'

OK, Lawrence was a lovely man, but please don't let it be him. Almost scared to hear the answer, Tula said, 'Who?'

'Riley! Which is actually better, when you come to think of it. If you want to make those other girls jealous, Riley's far more the kind of boyfriend to do it. He's so much fun, and he'll charm the socks off them!' She was saying it like a mum persuading a small child that the sandwiches were actually *much* nicer than the cakes.

'OK.' Tula exhaled, awash with disappointment. Dot might be right in one way, but she'd so badly wanted it to be Josh.

'Oh dear. Don't you want to go with Riley?'

She gathered herself. 'Sorry, I know he's fun. It's just when they ask him what he does for a living, he'll say, "As little as possible," and look pleased with himself. He's not bothered that other people might look down on him for not caring that he doesn't have a job. And then they'd be secretly laughing at me for going out with such a loser.'

'Darling, it's only for one day. Tell everyone he's a merchant banker or a physicist or something! Anyway,' Dot reached for the mouse and refreshed the computer screen, 'Josh can't make it on Saturday. He called Riley and Riley said he's happy to go along with you, but if you'd rather not . . .'

Tula was no longer listening; she was staring at the screen, now showing the most recent bookings. One name was leaping out at her, the name of someone booked into the hotel next week. Surely, *surely* it couldn't be him. Oh God, but what if it was?

'Hello?' Sensing she'd lost her attention, Dot waved a hand in front of Tula's face. 'All OK?'

'I'm not sure. This one.' Tula pointed to the screen. 'T. Pargeter, booked in to room seven. Any idea what the T stands for?'

'Oh, do you think it might be someone you know? I booked him myself last night. Hang on a moment, let me have a think . . .' Dot tapped her index finger on the desk and closed her eyes. 'It's almost there . . .'

'Theo?' Tula blurted the name out, her voice a bit high. 'Is it Theo?' Because if Sophie's ex-husband was booked into the hotel . . . well, Sophie definitely needed to know.

'Terence! That's it.'

'Terence? You're sure?'

'Oh yes. I can picture him now. He stayed with us a few months back.' Dot mimed a huge stomach with her arms. 'Quite overweight. Twinkly eyes, big red nose . . . I was terrified I might accidentally call him Toby, like the jug. But his name isn't Theo,' she concluded. 'Definitely. My word, you do look relieved!'

'I am.' Tula fanned herself.

'One of your exes?'

'Not mine, someone else's. Let's just say I'm glad it isn't him.' She grinned. 'Could have been awkward.'

Changing the subject, Dot said, 'So what are you going to do about this wedding, then? Take Riley along or just go on your own?'

The phone on the desk began to ring and Dot waited for her to reply before picking up the receiver.

Tula mentally ran through the options. Riley had offered himself, and if she turned him down, it wasn't as if Josh would suddenly change his mind and decide to accompany her. Plus, she did hate turning up at social events as a singleton.

'I'll go with Riley,' she said, and saw the look of satisfaction on Dot's face.

'Excellent.'

'And thanks,' Tula added.

In a situation like this, let's face it, any fake boyfriend was better than no fake boyfriend at all.

Chapter 31

'Oh my God,' Tula wailed when the red open-top Mercedes finally crunched to a halt on the gravel outside the hotel. 'You're late! Where have you *been*?'

'Getting petrol. There was a queue.' Riley flashed his trademark carefree smile. 'Hey, don't panic. We're leaving too early anyway.'

If you were a punctual type of person, was there *anything* more frustrating than having to travel in the company of a non-punctual one? Tula had triple-checked with Google: from St Carys to Brecon was one hundred and eighty-seven miles, and the journey took four hours. The wedding was due to start at three, and she'd factored in an extra hour for safety. Which was why she'd told Riley to make sure he was here no later than ten o'clock.

It was already ten fifteen.

Riley saw her check her watch and said, 'Calm down.'

'I told you. It takes at least four hours to get there.'

'According to Google. Who drives like a little old lady in a bonnet. I bet I can do it in three.'

Tula exhaled; there was a limit to the amount of complaining she was allowed to do. Riley was helping her out, after all. He was also driving, which was good of him, even if this was only because she knew he couldn't bear the prospect of spending hours cooped up in her rickety old car.

She forced herself to relax. 'OK, sorry. I just hate being late for things.'

'You won't be, I promise. And you're looking fantastic, by the way.'

'Am I?' Mollified, Tula looked down at the geranium-red dress she'd discovered just yesterday in the vintage shop in one of the narrow cobbled lanes behind the esplanade. It fitted like a dream, made her look a bit Audrey Hepburn-ish and exactly matched her favourite red shoes. Modesty aside, she was looking pretty amazing.

It was also really nice to be told you were.

'Is it linen?' said Riley.

'Yes!' Even more impressed, she lovingly stroked the skirt of the dress. 'I can't believe you know that! I've never had anything linen before.'

'You need to change.' He was shaking his head.

'What? Why?' Horrified, Tula stared at him.

'For the journey.' He grinned. 'Linen creases like nobody's business. It'll look awful if you wear it now. Change into something else and put the dress on just before we get there. That's what Marguerite always does before an event.'

'Oh God, really? But we're already late . . .'

'We're not. And you want to look good in front of your friends. Go and change,' Riley ordered. 'It'll take less than two minutes.'

Two minutes later, Tula raced back downstairs wearing flip-flops, denim cut-offs and a grey and white striped T-shirt. She waved the carrier bag containing the dress and shoes and said, 'Won't it get creased up in here?'

'Yes, it will. That's why you're going to lay the dress across the back seat, along with my suit.'

'Oh. Right.' Tula shook the dress out of the bag and did as he said. There, much better.

'Look at our clothes, all cuddled up together. Don't they make a great couple?'

'Don't even think about it.' She briskly tucked the bag containing the shoes into the corner.

'There, sorted.' Riley ostentatiously tapped his watch. 'Can we finally set off now, please? Otherwise we're going to be *late*.'

They made their way inland, passed Okehampton, then reached Exeter and joined the M5. The sun continued to shine; speeding along in the Mercedes with the top down, they were drawing envious glances from fellow travellers, and Tula felt herself begin to relax. She had her best sunglasses on and her hair was streaming out behind her, movie-star style. Riley was a skilful driver. He was also good company. It was going to be a fantastic day.

'OK, we need to get our stories straight.' She had to raise her voice to be heard above the noise of the car engine and the air rushing past them. 'We got together just a couple of days after I moved down here, and it was pretty much love at first sight.'

'So far, so true. What's my name going to be?' Riley looked hopeful. 'Can it be Cedric Moose Hufflepuffington the Third?'

'Let's stick to the truth wherever we can. We just need to know a bit more about each other, in case people ask questions. Now, favourite music,' Tula demanded.

'Barry Manilow.'

'No, really.'

'Really. He's amazing. Can't beat a bit of "Copacabana".'

She rolled her eyes. 'The whole point of this exercise is that I *don't* end up a laughing stock. Favourite film?'

'*Amélie.*'

'Are you serious?'

'Ha, what am I, some sort of girl? Anyway,' he said cheerfully, 'you already know my favourite film. *Star Wars.*'

Oh God.

'Fine. Now, I want you to have a proper job.'

Riley looked appalled. 'What kind of proper job?'

'Something that sounds impressive. How about corporate banking?'

'I don't know anything about corporate banking. And they

might. Can't I be an international spy? Like James Bond?' An eyebrow went up. 'Oh come on, Mish Moneypenny, please let me be a shpy.'

'Because that wouldn't sound made up at all. No,' said Tula, 'that's stupid.'

'I could be a brilliant world-class surfer.'

'What don't you understand about the words *proper job*?'

'Fine, then,' said Riley. 'I'll be a research scientist specialising in clinical neurophysiology and electroencephalography.'

'Say that again?' Tula blinked; it was like hearing a small child suddenly launch into fluent Russian.

Riley rattled the words off again and winked. 'I know. Pretty good, eh?'

'Just a bit. Where did you get it from?'

'It's my party trick. Last year of uni, I shared a flat with a guy who did that for a job. It was a great pick-up line, because no one ever had a clue what it meant. He just told them he had the ability to know everything that was going on in their brains. It never failed to impress. So I learned a bit more about it, and the two of us used to go out on the pull together, pretending we were *both* research scientists specialising in clinical neurophysiology and electroencephalography. And let me tell you, it worked like a charm every time.'

'But what does it mean, exactly?'

Riley shrugged. 'Doesn't matter. You just make it up, say anything you like. Nobody knows any different.'

'Fine.' Tula gave up; if anyone could blag their way through a bizarre job description it was Riley. 'But make sure – *oh shit . . .*'

Ahead of them, brake lights were coming on. Riley slowed the car. Within thirty seconds, three lanes of traffic had ground to a halt and Tula's intestines had wound themselves into a tight, anxious knot. There must have been an accident up ahead.

'Why does this always have to happen to *me*? I *knew* we should have set off earlier.'

'OK, deep breaths. See all these cars?' Riley gestured around them at the gigantic traffic jam. 'It's happening to everyone else too. And look on the bright side: at least we aren't the ones who had the accident.'

Which succeeded in making her feel ashamed, even if he was probably only laying on the guilt trip to divert attention from the fact that it was his fault they were late.

'If we'd left at ten, we wouldn't be stuck here now.'

'You're right.' Riley nodded. 'We might have been involved in the crash. We could be lying injured or dead now.'

See? Bastard.

'Of course. We're still alive. Hooray for us, we're *sooo* lucky.' She exhaled. 'How long do you suppose we're going to be stuck here?'

'The first rule,' said Riley, 'is there's no point in worrying about something you can't do anything about.'

'That's the stupidest rule I ever heard. You're telling me that if you were in a plane that was about to crash, you wouldn't be worried about it?'

'OK, plane crashes are different. Although there still wouldn't be any point in worrying. It's not going to help. Anyway, open the glove compartment.'

'Why? Do you have a mini motorbike folded up in there?'

'Better than that,' said Riley. 'Liquorice Allsorts. We can have a picnic.'

'I don't like liquorice.' Tula pulled a face.

He reached across her and opened the glove compartment himself. 'Brilliant. More for me.'

Police cars and an ambulance whizzed past them up the hard shoulder. The minutes ticked by. Riley ate his way through most of the bag of Liquorice Allsorts and Tula impatiently played patience on her phone. After thirty minutes that felt more like thirty hours, the traffic began to move again at approximately one mile per hour. Another half an hour later, they finally crawled in single file past the site of the accident, in which a trailer had tipped on to its side, shedding a full load of hay bales.

Not a multi-car pile-up, then. Hopefully the driver was all right.

'We'll be fine. I can make up the time, no problem,' said Riley as the Mercedes gathered speed and they resumed their journey. Before long they'd be passing Bridgwater, then Weston-super-Mare, then Bristol . . .

Twenty minutes later, Riley murmured, 'OK, we could have a slight problem.'

Tula's head shot up like a meerkat's. 'What? What kind of a problem?'

'Think we've got a flat.'

'A flat what?'

He gave her a look. 'Well it isn't a flat can of lager.'

'We've got a flat tyre? Oh my God, stop the car!'

'Not completely flat. It's just feeling a bit heavy. There's a services ahead; we'll pull in there and get it sorted.'

'I can't *believe* it,' Tula fretted. 'This is crazy. How long's it going to take to change the wheel?'

'Don't get wound up. Not long at all.'

Having slowed right down, they took the next exit and crept into the service station. Riley parked in a distant corner, where there was enough room to perform the changeover.

Out of the car, they both stood and surveyed the visibly flat tyre.

After twenty seconds of surveying, Tula said, 'Are you mentally *willing* it to inflate? Because that probably isn't going to work.'

This earned her another look. Finally Riley opened the boot and took out the necessary bits of equipment. Then paused again.

Tula said, 'We haven't got all day.'

'OK, there's the jack. Why don't you do it?'

'Because it's not my car. And I don't know how.'

'Look, shall we call the RAC?' said Riley.

She turned to stare at him. 'You mean *you* don't know how to do it either?'

He exhaled. 'It's my phobia, OK?'

206

'You have a phobia of changing wheels on cars? Tell me you're joking.'

'I was seventeen, I'd just passed my test and I was driving on my own up to Scotland. At one o'clock in the morning I got a flat tyre. The car was old, it was dark, I couldn't see where to put the jack and it ended up going through a rusty bit. The car crashed down on my arm and broke it. So there I was, stuck on a deserted road for the rest of the night. And that's why I have a phobia about changing wheels on cars.'

'So what do we do now?'

Riley said, 'I told you. Call the RAC.'

Tula wanted to cry. 'But how long will they take to get here? It could be *hours*.'

He spread his hands. 'It might not.'

'Oh my God, this is—'

'Hello there! Problem?'

Tula swung round to the dusty red builder's van that had just pulled up behind them. A thirty-something male with curly fair hair was surveying her with bright-eyed interest from the passenger seat.

'We have a flat tyre and he doesn't know how to change the wheel.' If she was selling Riley down the river, she didn't care.

'No? Nice car.' The man jumped out of the van and admired it. 'Want a hand?'

'That would be fantastic!' Oh, the *relief*. 'That's so kind of you . . . We're on our way to a wedding in Wales and we can't be late . . .'

'No problem at all. We can do that for you, can't we?' Curly hair checked with his companion, who was tall and bald. Neither of them were what you'd call lookers, but they had nice cheery faces.

And they weren't scared to change a wheel . . .

'We've got time.' The bald one checked his watch. 'We can manage it. Don't fret, Cinderella, you shall go to the wedding.'

Tula clasped her hands in gratitude and decided she loved them both.

Next to her, Riley said, 'That's great. Thanks so much.'

The two men set to work as a team. They knew exactly what to do and they got on with doing it. Realising that the next bathroom break could be a while away, Tula said, 'Back in a minute.' She headed over to the service station building, leaving them chatting about cars to Riley.

By the time she returned, five minutes later, the job was done and the two men were driving off. The curly-haired one leaned out of his window and called, 'Bye, love. Have fun at the wedding!'

'We will! Thank you so much!' She waved back at them before jumping into the Mercedes.

Riley, already revving the engine, said, 'Happier now?'

'Yes, I am. Thanks to them. Red-van men to the rescue.' Tula fastened her seat belt. 'Aren't some people just lovely? So *kind*.'

'They did ask for payment.'

Oh. 'How much?'

'Thirty.' He paused. 'I gave them fifty.'

It was a cheap shot but she said it anyway. 'You could have done it yourself if you didn't have your phobia.'

Ahead of them, the red van took the third exit off the roundabout and began making its way south towards Exeter. Riley took the first exit heading up to Bristol. Without looking at her, he said, 'I know.'

'Sorry.' Tula felt the need to explain. 'It's just . . . I get stressed sometimes.'

'Do you really?' He kept his tone deadpan.

'The thing is, you see, my dad wasn't a great dad. If anything was broken and needed mending, he could never be bothered to fix it. Then when I was ten he left us, and you'd think my mum would have gone for someone a bit more capable instead. But she didn't, she just carried right on choosing hopeless men. They never held down jobs, never did anything useful and always ended up buggering off. At the moment, she's running a bar in Corfu with a complete loser who gambles away all the profits . . .' Tula paused and shrugged; that was enough. 'So anyway, that's why

I'm the way I am. In case you were wondering. I love my mum to bits, but I never want to end up like her.'

Riley had listened without interrupting. Finally he said, 'Right,' and nodded slowly. 'I do see now. Thanks for letting me know.'

The sun slid behind grey clouds as they crossed the Severn Bridge into Wales. While they were queuing to pay at the tolls, Riley pressed the button to automatically bring up the roof of the Mercedes. It was a good call; within minutes, the first fat raindrops began to spatter on to the windscreen.

'Saved your hair getting wet,' he said.

'Are we definitely going to get there in time?'

'Stop worrying. Of course we will.'

Chapter 32

By the time they reached Newport, the rain was hammering down and the traffic was heavy. It came as a relief to leave the motorway and head up quieter roads through Cwmbran, then Pontypool and Ebbw Vale.

'Right,' said Riley, when they'd been driving for several miles through the Brecon Beacons National Park. 'You're going to need to direct me now.'

'I've never been here before. How am I supposed to direct you?' Tula pointed to the black screen on the dashboard. 'Use the satnav!'

'Satnav doesn't work. Marguerite broke it last week.'

'And you didn't think to mention it until *now*?'

Riley said evenly, 'I thought you'd have printed out a map.'

'*What?* I thought you'd have functioning satnav!'

The wedding ceremony was due to start at three. It was already two thirty. They reached a junction and Tula saw two unpronounceable Welsh place names on the road sign. The windscreen wipers swished back and forth, sluicing away the heavy rain, and Riley stopped the car. Simultaneously they took out their phones . . .

No signal.

So typical.

They were in the middle of nowhere, in the midst of an almost biblical downpour, and about as lost as it was physically possible to get.

'You choose,' said Riley. 'Left or right?'

'I don't want to choose.'

'You mean you'd rather I did, so that if I'm wrong it'll be my fault and you can put all the blame on me.'

'Pretty much.' Even Tula had to smile at this admission. She gave her phone a shake. 'Are you sure you don't have any signal?'

'Not a smidgeon. OK, here goes.' He turned right and they resumed the journey that felt as if it would never end.

Twenty minutes later, another sign loomed ahead of them.

'This is it! This is the village!' Tula almost bounced out of her seat. 'Oh my God, we've found it!'

'We?' said Riley.

'OK, you found it. I'm sorry I got in such a panic. You're a genius. And look, there's the church!' She pointed to a spire, just visible between the trees.

'Even better, here's a pub.'

'Are you mad? We don't have time for a drink. The service starts in five minutes.'

But Riley was ignoring her, pulling into the pub car park. 'We need to change our clothes,' he reminded her. 'We can do it in here.'

'Good point. Ha, nearly forgot.' Giddy with relief, Tula pinged her seat belt undone and twisted round to grab her stuff off the back seat. 'Oh. Where did you put them?'

'Put what?'

'Our clothes. And my shoes.' They'd been there before and now they weren't. For a moment, Tula wondered if these super-duper hi-tech vehicles had the ability, when the roof came over, to somehow magically transfer the items from the back seat to the boot of the car.

Then she saw the look on Riley's face and knew they didn't. He turned, gazed at the empty seat and said, 'Oh fuck.'

'You mean while we were driving down the motorway, my dress and your suit went flying out of the back of the car?' Tula's voice rose. '*Or what?*'

Riley was shaking his head. 'Those thieving bastards.'

'The builders? But how could they have done it? You were there the whole time, watching them!'

'The curly-haired one called me over, made me look under the car so he could show me where the jack needed to go.' Riley's jaw tightened. 'That's when the bald one went to get something out of the back of the van. Except he wasn't, was he? He was putting stuff into it. The absolute fucker.'

Tula couldn't speak. She wanted to cry, to scream, to smash up the car. Her *beautiful* red linen dress . . . her best shoes . . . Five hours of unbelievably stressful travelling just to get here . . .

And now this.

'I'm sorry,' said Riley.

Tula closed her eyes for a second, nails digging into her palms as she clenched her hands.

'You gave them fifty pounds and they did that.' More than anything, she wanted to murder the two builders and drive over their mutilated bodies.

'I know.'

'Well we may as well just go home.'

'Hey, you're upset now. But you'd be more upset if we did that.'

She gave him a look. 'And the alternative is?'

'We've come all this way. How about we stay and style it out? One of the reasons I like you so much is because you're funny, you have a sense of humour.' Riley was doing his level best to persuade her that she did, anyway. 'It isn't our fault we don't have our clothes. But we're not *naked*. All we have to do is explain what happened and people will understand. And we'll have a great time. We'll end up laughing about this, I promise.'

Tula listened to the sound of her own breathing. The events of the day had built up and up inside her chest, and her sense of humour had long since vanished. Her clothes would have given her much-needed confidence; this was what Riley couldn't begin to understand. He'd never met Imi's intimidating friends, with their knowing looks and those sly, smirky smiles they liked to exchange whenever someone else said or did something that amused them.

Plus, Riley was wearing a pale pink polo shirt and battered but sexy-as-hell jeans, OK, it might be a casual outfit, but he still looked fantastic.

Whereas her own denim shorts had been chosen for comfort rather than style and her baggy striped T-shirt, post-Snickers bar, now sported a chocolate stain down the front.

He gave her a nudge. 'Come on. Shall we do it?'

Tula pulled down the sun visor and surveyed herself in the tiny mirror. It could be worse; at least her hair was OK and her make-up was still on.

She nodded at Riley, managed a smile and said, 'Let's knock 'em dead.'

By four o'clock, unbelievably, Riley's prediction had come true.

Sitting through the service in the church had been the worst bit. Arriving too late to be able to explain the situation to anyone, Tula had been mortified by the surprised glances cast in their direction. It was like showing up at a funeral in a clown costume complete with honking nose and manic painted-on smile. People couldn't quite believe they were so inappropriately dressed. There had been nudges and whispers and a fair amount of head-swivelling.

Sloping out in shame would have been the desirable option, were it not for Riley at her side, effectively blocking her exit from the pew.

But then the ceremony had concluded, everyone had spilled out of the church to find it had stopped raining, and Imi's friends Lucy and Kat had made a beeline for the most embarrassing couple at the wedding.

'Oh my God, what's going *on?*' shrieked Kat. 'We couldn't believe our eyes when we saw you!'

Needless to say, they were glamorously attired and immaculate in every way.

'Let me explain, seeing as it's all my fault. Anyway, hi, I'm Riley . . .'

And that was it; within seconds, he had launched into the whole story, making it funny, doing all the voices, flashing his inimitable smile and charming the pants off Lucy and Kat.

If they were even wearing any.

Other curious guests gathered round to listen, and by the time Riley had finished, everyone was on their side. Even Imi dashed over between photographs and exclaimed, 'I just heard what happened, you poor things! But at least you're here, that's what matters – I'm so glad you didn't give up and go home!'

'So this is your new boyfriend,' Lucy purred in Tula's ear. 'I can see why you're with him. He's *delicious.*'

This was true; Riley was doing a brilliant job. He'd effortlessly won everyone over. Feeling like a proud mum, Tula said, 'I know.'

'How did you manage to bag this one?' Kat was visibly impressed. 'I mean, no offence, but . . . *look* at him.'

The concept of keeping your voice down wasn't something Kat had ever grasped.

Riley turned and said, 'Actually I can answer that one. By treating me mean and making me think I didn't have a prayer. Isn't that right?' He slid his arm around Tula's waist and gave her an affectionate squeeze. 'She gave me the proper brush-off at first, said I wasn't her type. But it just made me all the more deter-mined to win her over. Hard work, but I managed it in the end.' Stroking a stray strand of hair off her cheek, he added, 'And she's worth it.'

Oh wow, this felt weird, playing boyfriends and girlfriends. Riley's fingertips brushed the side of her face again, but she wasn't allowed to pull away. Even more weirdly, she was discovering she didn't want to. Being the focus of Riley's attention, being the girl on his arm, actually felt amazing. And it was kind of exciting, too; witnessing the effect he was having on all the women here appeared to be making his attractiveness contagious.

Once the outside-the-church photos were out of the way, the

wedding party proceeded across to the hotel where the reception was being held, Riley still trailing admirers in his wake. It was like following the Messiah, thought Tula.

And then they were drinking champagne, sitting down to eat at circular tables decorated in silver and white, getting into the celebratory spirit of the occasion.

'So how long have you two been an item?' Lucy was seated to Riley's right.

'It's been a few weeks now. I fell for her the first weekend she came down to St Carys. Not that it was reciprocated.' Riley grinned.

'But why not? Why didn't you fancy him right away?' This from Kat on the other side of the table.

Tula shrugged. 'Just thought he wasn't my type.'

'Then she moved down, saw me again and decided I wasn't so bad after all. OK, so maybe I had to beg for a bit.' His eyes crinkled with laughter. 'Or even a lot. But it worked, and we've been inseparable ever since.'

Inseparable. Oh, even the way he said the word sent a quiver of longing through her. Tula's hand tingled as Riley's fingers brushed against hers, deliberately so the others could see him doing it. It was hard not to look smug. The envy in Kat and Lucy's eyes was as thrilling as winning a Nobel prize. Well, probably.

The food was delicious, as was the wine. When it came to the speeches, Imi's father and the best man both singled out Tula and Riley for their determination to be here at the wedding of the year. They were made to stand, take a bow and receive the applause that was their due. Phones were held up and photos taken – it was like being Angelina Jolie arriving at the Oscars. Riley, taking shameless advantage of the situation, gave her a hug and a brief kiss on the mouth before they sat down again.

'You're loving this, aren't you?' Tula murmured.

'Every last second.' He raised a playful eyebrow and kissed her again. 'You have no idea.'

'Honestly, you two, get a room,' said Kat.

'No, don't get a room,' Lucy protested. 'Stay here and talk to us. So, Riley, we want to know all about you. What do you *do*?'

Tula found herself tensing up; this was the moment when Riley trotted out his utterly obscure made-up career and someone else at the table said, 'Wow, what a coincidence, that's my job too!'

'I'm an international spy,' said Riley.

Everyone else laughed.

'You know, you really could be,' said Kat. 'Like the ones on that TV show. All super-cool and glamorous.'

'I wish.' Riley smiled at her. 'Actually, I work in clinical neurophysiological research. Electroencephalography. The mysteries of the human brain.' His shrug was self-deprecating. 'Fascinating, but hardly glamorous.'

Tula braced herself; *this* was the moment when he'd be found out . . .

But no, everyone was instantly enthralled. They asked questions and Riley answered them in a completely convincing fashion. He threw in long medical words, told amazing anecdotes, and basically managed to make clinical neurophysiology sound a *far* more thrilling occupation than being some boring old international spy.

Tula found herself watching and listening with equal fascination and growing respect; after such an awful start to the day, Riley had come spectacularly good. He'd exceeded all expectations. As his supposed girlfriend, she was the envy of Imi's friends, which was a heady experience and something that had certainly never happened before.

She was also, somewhat surreally, starting to view him through their eyes and believe that this was the real Riley. That tantalisingly brief kiss he'd planted on her mouth was still playing on her mind too, and not in a bad way . . .

When the meal was over and the band started tuning up on the stage, Kat said, 'I hope you're going to let me have a dance with your boyfriend.'

'Of course you can.' Tula was generous; she could afford to be magnanimous in victory.

Kat eyed Riley and said, 'I bet you're a good dancer.'

'Not bad.' His shrug was modest. 'Not as good as Tula. She's fantastic.'

Oh God, listen to him; he was saying it as if he loved her.

'Could you excuse us for just a second?' Pushing her chair back, Tula gave Riley a nudge and indicated the double doors. She turned to Kat and added apologetically, 'We won't be long . . .'

Chapter 33

Tula found a secluded high-walled rose garden in the grounds to the side of the hotel. The early evening sun was streaming through the trees, the flagstoned path was drying out and butterflies danced among the roses. It was like something out of a film.

'I didn't want us to be overheard,' she explained.

Riley said, 'Now I'm really starting to feel like an international spy.'

'I just want to say sorry for being such a cow before. I was stressed out and grumpy and I can't believe you didn't boot me out of the car.'

'That's OK. Although don't think it didn't cross my mind.'

'And thank you for doing this and for being so completely brilliant.'

He half smiled. 'Have I exceeded expectations?'

'Yes,' Tula nodded, 'you really have. You've been amazing.'

'Good.' He paused. 'Why are you looking at me like that?'

Oops, was she? She'd just been remembering that brief kiss on the mouth and wondering what a proper one would feel like. Aloud she said, 'I'm not.'

'Yes you are.'

He had the kind of colouring that meant his tanned skin was darker than his lips. Tula's breath caught in her throat at the thought of kissing him again. And the way his mouth curved up at the corners in a nearly-smile every time he turned his attention on anyone . . . well, that was what bowled the girls over, wasn't it? It was all part of his overwhelming charisma . . .

'You're still doing it,' Riley murmured. 'And can I just say? It's killing me.'

He wanted her to kiss him. And here she was, badly wanting to do it. Maybe it wasn't wise, but sometimes you just had to give in and act on impulse.

So she did. And it was every bit as fantastic as she'd thought it would be.

Eventually Tula pulled back and said, 'Probably shouldn't have done that.'

'Glad you did.' Riley's eyes were bright. 'So does this mean I may not be as a bad as you thought?'

Stay in control. 'I was just curious.' Lightly she said, 'Remind me again how long you stuck out that gardening job at the hotel?'

He grimaced. 'You wouldn't have liked it either. There were *worms.*'

'Oh dear, that's terrible.'

Riley smiled and said, 'Don't make fun of me. I'm an expert in clinical neurophysiology.' Then he kissed her again and this time she didn't pull away for some time . . .

Until they heard a giggle behind them and Tula spun round to see that they'd collected an audience. Lucy, Kat and a couple of their friends were clustered at the entrance to the walled garden.

'So this is why you two slipped away.' Kat grinned at them. 'So you could get up to all sorts!'

'I don't blame you,' Lucy chimed in. 'I'd be doing the same if I had someone gorgeous to get up to all sorts with.'

'We weren't spying, by the way,' said Kat. 'Just came out for a sneaky cigarette. Don't mind us, feel free to carry on canoodling!'

Riley took Tula's hand in his, which also felt wonderfully romantic and sent zingy sparks up her arm. 'Thanks,' he said easily, 'but we'd rather canoodle in private. Some things are too nice to share.'

As they made their way back to the hotel, leaving the others lighting up their cigarettes, Tula heard Lucy say, 'God, he's so gorgeous. Looks *and* brains. Why can't I find someone like that?'

She also heard, very faintly, Kat retort drily, 'I bet Tula can't believe her luck.'

Up on the stage, the wedding band were playing. Noise levels ramped up, more drink was taken and hair was let down. Everyone was having a great time; proud grandmas danced with grandsons, dads danced with daughters, starry-eyed girls danced with boys and Riley danced with Tula.

When the music slowed down, so did they. Tula could feel the heat of his body against hers. And she liked it.

Hopefully her eyes weren't too starry.

'It's eight o'clock. We need to leave soon.' As she said it, she could see Kat over by the bar, watching them. Which also felt fantastic.

'Unless you'd rather stay. We could, you know.' Riley shrugged. 'If you wanted. This place still has a few rooms available.'

She looked at him. 'You asked them?'

'I overheard someone else asking at reception.'

Oh God, it would be so nice . . .

But no. She wasn't going to. She shook her head. 'You've spent all this time not drinking so you can drive home.'

'I don't mind. You can't use that as an excuse.'

'And I'm on the early shift tomorrow. Seven o'clock start. We really have to get back.'

'That's a shame.' And now he was smiling down at her, giving her that look again.

'I know.' This was *so* tempting. Maybe she could call the Mariscombe Hotel and see if someone wouldn't mind switching shifts . . .

A tap on her shoulder signalled that Kat had joined them on the dance floor. Raising her voice to be heard above the music, she beckoned and yelled, 'Hey, come on over to the bar, I've got something to show you!'

The moment they joined the gaggle of Imi's girlfriends, Tula felt the little hairs on her arms begin to prickle with unease. The atmosphere had altered and there was a collective glint in their eyes that smacked of barely concealed triumph.

'OK, this could be a bit awkward, but I'm going to go ahead and say it, because I think you deserve to know.'

Awkward didn't come into it; Kat was clearly revelling in the moment, delighted to be saying whatever it was she was about to say. Tula felt Riley's fingers tighten around hers. The about-to-sit-an-exam-you-haven't-revised-for sensation was rising inside her chest.

'I took some photos earlier and posted them on Twitter,' Kat began. 'You know, just to show my friends and—'

'Can I just say,' Riley interrupted, 'we're all here having a nice time at your friend's wedding. Wouldn't it be kinder to just leave whatever it is for another time?'

'Oh, I'm sure you'd prefer that.' Kat's face was aglow with *Schadenfreude*. 'But I don't think it'd be terribly fair on Tula. Some things just need to be got out in the open.' She held up her phone. 'I have to say, we did *wonder* if you were too good to be true.'

'Meaning?' Tula squeezed Riley's hand and saw Lucy glance down at their entwined fingers.

'I've just had a text from one of my friends who saw the photos.' With a tantalising flash of her phone's screen, Kat said smugly, 'I suppose when you have as many Twitter followers as I do, this is the kind of thing that can happen. She recognised your wonderful boyfriend, I'm afraid.' Heavily mascaraed eyes fixed on Tula. 'Sorry about this, but she met him when she was down in St Carys two weeks ago. They slept together.'

Everyone turned to stare at Tula. She swallowed, and carried on staring at Kat.

'Her name's Jess. Tall, blonde, *very* pretty. She's a French teacher.' Kat raised an enquiring eyebrow at Riley. 'Ring any bells? And you can't try and dump the blame on her either. You told her you were single.'

'Because that's what men like you do,' Lucy swung in. 'Poor Tula, she thought she'd finally landed herself a decent boyfriend. But all she got was another lying, cheating bastard who thinks he can do whatever he wants just because he has a pretty face.'

'Oh yes, and all this stuff you've been spouting to us about your amazing job.' Kat could barely contain her glee. 'Jess says that according to your surfing friends, you don't even *have* a proper job; you're nothing but a beach bum who does bugger all and just sponges off his rich aunt.'

Imi, the beautiful bride, chose this moment, of course, to come up and greet them, slinging her arms around Kat on her left and Tula on her right side. 'Yay-yay, it's my wedding day! Is everyone having the best time *ever*?'

'We just caught Tula's boyfriend out.' Realising that she now had quite an audience gathered around, Kat raised her voice and pointed dramatically at Riley. 'He has sex with other women behind her back.'

'Oh no!' The happy smile melted from Imi's face; she looked as if she was about to burst into tears. 'Oh darling, how could he *do* that to you?'

Tula blinked. Honestly, was it possible for one day to swing quite so dramatically from disastrous to brilliant and then go crashing back to abject disaster again? And now *everyone* was staring at her in stunned silence. Even the band had stopped playing and appeared to be listening with interest.

'It's fine.' Somehow she managed to find the words. 'We talked about that. He only did it because he found out I'd slept with my boss. It was just one of those silly tit-for-tat things, with him trying to get his own back.'

'She was nothing compared to you.' Riley shook his head. 'I love you so much.'

'I know. I love you too.' Turning to Imi, Tula said, 'Thanks so much, it's been a brilliant wedding. But we have to go now.'

And hand in hand they left, to the sound of Imi's grandmother remarking loudly, 'Honestly, what is it with young people these days? *Obsessed* with sex.'

'Sorry,' said Riley as they left the village behind them.

'That's OK. Not your fault.'

'You were brilliant, by the way.'

'I did all right. They'll be gossiping about us for the rest of the night now.'

'What are the odds, eh? Of all the girls in all the bars in St Carys, I had to sleep with that one. God, I wish I hadn't.'

'Me too.' She paused. 'Slut.'

'Me or her?'

'You!' She smiled. 'Anyway, doesn't matter. I'm planning never to have to see Imi's awful smug friends again. And it won't be any hardship.'

Riley looked at her. 'Did you really sleep with Josh?'

'No.' Tula shook her head. 'Of course I didn't.'

'D'you wish you could?'

She didn't need to reply. They both knew the answer to that one.

Riley carried on driving; retracing their earlier journey was easier than making it in the first place. After a while he said, 'I liked being your boyfriend this afternoon.'

'Good fun, wasn't it?'

'I really liked everyone thinking you were my girlfriend.'

'They were jealous,' said Tula. She'd liked it too. And the kissing bit.

As if reading her mind, Riley pointed to a whitewashed cottage up ahead with a B&B sign hanging outside. 'We could still stay if you want to.'

And the fact that she *did* kind of want to made it seem all the more vital that she shouldn't. Before, his beach-bum idleness had acted like a fire blanket, efficiently extinguishing any flicker of attraction. Now that she found herself liking him more as a person, there was a danger of that overcoming common sense.

And then where would she be?

Oh yes, back to square one, having her heart broken all over again.

They'd almost reached the whitewashed stone cottage now and Riley was glancing at her, waiting for her reply.

'No.' Tula shook her head. 'I still have to work tomorrow morning.' She willed the newly awakened sensations in her body to go back to sleep. 'We need to get home to St Carys.'

Chapter 34

While Riley and Tula were still on their way from Wales back to Cornwall, Josh was making a mug of builder's tea for his grandmother.

'Ah, bliss. Thanks so much, darling. Just what I need.' For the first time in weeks, Dot was neither on duty downstairs nor off out for the evening with Antoine Beauvais. She'd swapped her elegant outfits for a caramel cashmere dressing gown and cream slippers. Relaxing on the sofa in front of the TV, she was make-up-free and greedily devouring a plate of cheese on toast.

'Supermarket white bread,' Josh observed. 'Not very gourmet. Antoine would be shocked if he could see you now.'

'But he can't. Anyway, I don't care. I love ready-sliced bread.' Dot's eyes were bright with mischief. 'I snuck out this afternoon to buy it and smuggled it back up here in a John Lewis carrier bag.'

Josh smiled. Ready-sliced had no place in the hotel; their head chef would be as mortally offended as Antoine. 'I won't tell anyone.'

'I've had it up to here with gourmet.' Dot picked up another slice and dipped it in the puddle of tomato ketchup on the side of her plate. 'Every time Antoine takes me out, we have fancy-pants food, served with jus and foam and micro herbs and aromatic reductions . . . I know it's wonderful and tastes delicious, but after a while it all becomes too much. You just want one thing that tastes normal.' She beamed, unrepentant. 'I bought Jaffa Cakes too.'

Josh definitely approved of Jaffa Cakes. 'And where is Antoine tonight?'

'Having dinner in Padstow with a couple of music bods down from London.'

'And fancy-pants food.'

'Absolutely. More fool them. I'd rather be here having this.' Having swallowed a mouthful of toast, Dot took a slurp of hot strong tea.

'How are things going with you two?'

'Oh, very well! He's lovely, so charming. Listen to me, moaning about the incredible restaurants I've been taken to . . . how ungrateful does that sound? Next thing you know, I'll be complaining that my diamond shoes are too tight.' Dot smiled and waggled her furry slippers. 'No, Antoine's excellent company. I'm having a fabulous time. He's perfect in every way.'

'Good. You deserve someone to spoil you.' Josh stirred his own mug of tea. Was there an element of revenge in the way Antoine Beauvais had returned to St Carys and made a beeline for Dot? Possibly. It had certainly put Lawrence's nose out of joint. Then again, could anyone entirely blame him for that? And it wasn't as if Antoine didn't have feelings for Dot; he was clearly besotted with her. Annoying Lawrence was simply an added bonus.

On the TV screen, an actress in an ivory lace wedding dress was dancing with her new husband. 'That reminds me,' said Dot. 'I wonder how Tula and Riley are getting on in Wales. Let's hope he's behaved himself and hasn't tried to get off with one of the bridesmaids.'

'He wouldn't. He's mad about Tula.'

Dot sighed. 'If only he could sort himself out. I do love Riley, but you can understand why Tula wouldn't want to get involved.' Her clear blue gaze fixed on him. 'She'd rather have you.'

That again. Josh said, 'Not going to happen.'

'Why not? Who would you rather have?'

He didn't reply.

'Oh come on, don't try that with me,' said Dot, amused. 'As if I couldn't guess.'

After all these years, she still hadn't lost her witchy ability to know things other people wouldn't have the first clue about.

Relentlessly she pressed on. 'It's so obvious.' Maybe she *was* a witch.

'Not to most people.'

'But it is to me. Sophie, right?'

She knew him so well. Josh nodded and heard his phone ping, signalling the arrival of an email. He left it where it was, face down on the coffee table.

'Well, you usually get what you want,' said Dot. 'Why isn't it working this time?'

'Because she wouldn't rather have me.' What the hell, if he was going to discuss it with anyone, it may as well be his all-knowing, all-seeing grandmother. 'She'd rather have . . . no one at all.'

'And we don't know why. Something happened to that girl.' Dot shook her head sympathetically. 'I can't imagine what it could have been.'

After a moment's hesitation, Josh said, 'Tula did accidentally let a couple of things slip one night. Don't ever tell anyone, but she said something about Sophie's husband . . . his name was Theo. She mentioned suicide. Must have been pretty traumatic, losing him like that. I imagine it's enough to put you off wanting to get involved with anyone else.'

'And that's all you know? No more details? Oh, the poor darling . . .' The diamonds in her bracelet flashed rainbow dots of light as Dot put down her second slice of cheese on toast. Then she frowned and said, 'Hang on, Sophie's husband was called Theo? Definitely Theo?'

'Yes. Why?'

'Well I'm pretty certain he's not dead.'

Josh sat forward. 'What makes you think that?'

'Because the other day Tula saw a name on the computer

227

screen and did a huge double-take. I'd written T. Pargeter and it knocked her for six . . . she was desperate to know the full name. Well, I couldn't think of it for a few seconds and she said in a panic, "Is it Theo?" Then I remembered that it was Terence, and she was *so* relieved.'

Josh had spent the last two weeks thinking that Theo had died and Sophie was a widow. This new information was going to take some getting used to. He said, 'Maybe she just thought it was a horrible coincidence. Like, spooky.'

'No, no, it was absolutely on the cards that it could have been him. I asked if he was one of her exes and she said no, he was someone else's. Hang on, let me think . . .' Dot closed her eyes in order to concentrate. 'OK . . . she said she was glad it wasn't him because it could have been awkward. And that was it; we went back to talking about the wedding in Wales.' She looked over at Josh. 'But from what was said, this Theo chap definitely isn't dead.'

Josh's head was buzzing with possibilities. So Sophie's ex-husband was still alive. And now they knew his surname, too.

Theo Pargeter.

'What are you going to do?' Dot looked doubtful. 'Because whatever it is, you need to be subtle. Sophie's really not going to appreciate it if you start interrogating her.'

Did she seriously think he didn't already know that? Josh shook his head; whatever he did with this new-found information, he was aware that he'd need to tread with the utmost care. Sophie had closed down that part of her life for a reason.

Her life with Theo Pargeter.

Aloud he said to Dot, 'Don't worry, I won't.'

Chapter 35

Sophie was working on a shoot with a family so annoying you couldn't have made them up. Mind-blowingly wealthy, with homes scattered around the world, they were currently occupying the stunning penthouse apartment of a new hotel up on the clifftop overlooking St Ives. Here in Cornwall for a week – squished in between visits to their villa in Cannes and friends who owned a palazzo on the banks of Lake Como – they'd decided to mark the occasion with a family photo shoot. As you do, apparently, when you occupy that kind of world.

'If the pictures are good enough, we might use one of them for this year's Christmas card,' Julia generously explained. A rake-thin Californian in her fifties, she'd been surgically altered to resemble a waxwork model of a thirty-year-old. Her husband, a plump British entrepreneur, wasn't remotely interested in being photographed but had been coerced into going along with it in order to keep the peace.

The two teenage daughters had expensive drawly transatlantic voices with upturned intonations. They also had shiny curtains of waist-length blond hair and teeny-tiny bodies that they kept loudly insisting were fat. A hair and make-up artist had been hired for the occasion, as well as their stylist, who'd arrived with armfuls of clothes and accessories from their London home. So far the preparations had taken three hours, and Sophie was still waiting to take her first shots of the day.

'Mom, my lashes still aren't right,' whined the younger daughter, Jemini.

'OK, honey, calm down.' Julia gave the make-up girl a blank look that would most likely have involved eyebrow-raising if Botox hadn't rendered such a feat impossible. 'Can you please do them again?'

'Yes. Sorry.' The girl flushed and nodded, visibly mortified.

'Remember the time that one in Monte Carlo did my eyebrows all wrong?' The eldest daughter, Jezebel, spoke without glancing up from her crystal-encrusted mobile phone. 'It was, like, *so* annoying.'

Sophie exchanged a glance with the make-up girl, who was now battling through a fog of cigarette smoke in order to redo Jemini's lashes. What a life this family led, yet they seemed so utterly bored with it. Having finished texting, Jezebel was now chatting on her phone to a friend. 'No, I'm the size of a whale . . . I weigh, like, *ninety-seven pounds.*'

'Sshh, baby,' her mother protested. 'Don't tell everyone. We'll get you some lipo, it'll be fine.'

'Not the turquoise ones.' Jemini waved away the skyscraper-heeled shoes the stylist was showing her. 'I wore those for last week's shoot. Isn't it your job to keep track of these things?'

The stylist looked as if she'd love nothing more than to stab her with a turquoise stiletto heel. Oh yes, this family was evidently a joy to work for. Sophie's phone vibrated in the back pocket of her jeans and she stepped through the French windows on to the wooden wraparound balcony.

'Sophie? I need you to come over here and settle an argument!'

After enduring the whiny, nasal tones of Julia and her spoilt daughters, it made a nice change to hear Marguerite's forthright voice.

'What kind of an argument?'

'You know the ash tree in my garden? The one with the wicker cocoon seat attached to it?'

'OK, yes.' Sophie nodded, remembering the shoot they'd done last year for Marguerite's Romanian publisher. Had they not been happy with the shots? 'You need some more photos of you on the seat?'

'Not of me. There's a bird nesting in the upper branches and I need to know what it is. Lawrence is insisting it's a blackbird, but I'm sure it's a Cornish chough, even though I know they usually nest on cliffs. *Pyrrhocorax*, that's the Latin name. They practically disappeared from Cornwall in the fifties, but there's been a bit of recolonisation in the last fifteen years.'

'Right. Wow,' said Sophie. 'I'm impressed. I had no idea you were such an expert.'

'One of my awful exes was a birdwatcher. He made me go on a bird-spotting holiday with him once. And only once.' The shudder in Marguerite's voice was audible. 'It was horrendous. Everyone had beards and wore chunky knits. Anyway, I've tried taking photos with my phone, but it's useless. That tree's thirty metres high.'

'You need a long lens,' said Sophie.

'*I* don't. You do. Can you come over and see if you can get some decent shots of it?'

'Well I can, but not today. Tomorrow's pretty busy too.' Sophie mentally scanned her diary for the next few days. 'But I could maybe squeeze in a visit between appointments . . .'

'I tell you what, just come over whenever you can. I'm going to be out and about a fair bit myself,' said Marguerite, 'but it's only the garden, so you don't need me to actually be there. A couple of photos good enough to identify the bird, that's all I'm after. And please God let me be right and Lawrence wrong, otherwise I'll never hear the last of it.'

'I'll do my best.' Sophie smiled. 'If all else fails, there's always Photoshop.'

'Ha, that's my girl. Excellent plan. Why be a failure when you can cheat your way to victory?' Marguerite gave a bark of laughter. 'Joking, of course.'

'I'll be over sometime this week.' As Sophie said it, a wail rang out from inside the penthouse apartment: 'Aw, I don't *believe* it, a freakin' crystal just fell off my phone!'

With characteristic bluntness Marguerite said, 'What a ghastly screeching noise. Are you watching *Housewives of Orange County*?'

'Actually, it's one of my clients.'

'Good grief, poor you, she sounds a complete nightmare. I bet you wish everyone was as nice as me.'

Sophie heroically managed to keep a straight face. 'Oh, I do.'

The preparations continued. Julia's husband made endless business calls while the rest of his family readied themselves for the shoot. Julia was on the phone to her nail technician in Los Angeles, debating at length the shade of polish she should try next. Jezebel was noisily chewing gum – chomp *chomp* – and surfing the internet on her iPad.

'OK, so we're starting to narrow it down now.' Julia yawned, mid-conversation with the nail technician. 'The pale green Dior, the Chanel Peridot or that dark shimmering one by—'

'Aaaaarrrgh!' Jezebel jackknifed upright and began making dramatic retching noises. 'Oh my God, that is so *gross!*'

'What? What is it?' Jemini gestured at the hairdresser to move back so she could lean across and see the hideous grossness for herself. 'Oh Jeeeeeez, that just makes me want to barf . . . It's like something out of a horror movie.'

'Oh. Maybe it is from a movie.' Jezebel, her face still contorted with distaste, looked at Sophie and demanded, 'Well? Is it?'

'Sorry?' What were they on about now?

'This!' Jezebel held up the iPad so she could see. 'Is it, like, all done with make-up?'

Sophie studied the screen and realised that Jezebel had been exploring her website. Having scrolled through pages of sample photos, she'd stopped at one of the most recently added.

Elizabeth Sharp had been so proud and delighted with the end result of their visit the other week to Mizzen Cove that she'd posted her favourite photo on her personal blog. Word had soon spread, a local journalist had contacted her and Elizabeth had ended up being featured in several newspapers, with the picture attracting yet more attention and widespread praise. When Sophie had asked if she could include it in the photo gallery on her own website, Elizabeth had said, 'Darling, of course you can! My pleasure!'

There was no hint of pleasure on Jezebel and Jemini's faces. Jemini was shaking her head in disbelief.

'*Is* it special effects?' Jezebel evidently couldn't contemplate the possibility that the photograph might be real.

'Her name's Elizabeth. She's a history teacher,' said Sophie. 'She had breast cancer and she's celebrating still being alive.'

'But . . . but look at the scars! And her breast is, like, totally *gone*. She's all flat on that side.' Jemini's glossy upper lip curled in disgust. 'Why would she let them *do* that to her?'

Sophie said evenly, 'To get the cancer out.'

'But why didn't she make them do a reconstruction?'

'As far as Elizabeth's concerned, it's not a priority.'

'Well I'm sorry, but it's totally gross. *And* she's naked. Some people have no pride,' exclaimed Jezebel. 'I mean, look at how *old* she is. And as for her body, what kind of a state is that to get yourself into? She's all fat and round and . . . eurgh, saggy!'

Jemini pointed to the screen. 'And she's got cellulite.' She exhaled a stream of smoke and narrowed her eyes at Sophie. 'Like, not being funny or anything, but you're the photographer. Shouldn't you have Photoshopped all that stuff out?'

'It's like she's just flaunting all the icky stuff,' Jezebel chimed in. 'Why would anyone want to do that?'

Sophie's jaw was aching from keeping her teeth gritted. 'Actually, she's a friend of mine.'

'Are you serious?' Jezebel twisted round to gaze at her. 'And you put her on your website looking like *that*? If she's your friend, what kind of photos would you take of someone you didn't like?'

'What kind of photos is she gonna take of *us*?' murmured Jemini.

'Don't worry.' Sophie shook her head. 'You're not going to get the chance to find out.'

Everyone stared at her. Jemini said, 'Huh? What's that supposed to mean?'

It was no good; there was no going back now. After the things they'd said about Elizabeth, Sophie knew she couldn't go through with the shoot.

'I told you she was my friend and you just kept on saying that awful stuff. Trust me, you wouldn't be happy with any photos I took of you.' She was dimly aware of the stylist and the make-up artist surveying her with a mixture of envy, horror and glee. 'Besides, I don't want to take them.'

'You're cancelling? You can't do that!' Jemini shrieked. 'We've spent all this time getting ourselves ready!'

'You have phones. You can take photos of each other. It'll be fine.'

'OK, this is crazy. Mom, tell her she has to do it!'

'I don't have to and I'm not going to.' Sophie moved around the sitting room collecting up her equipment. She wouldn't get paid, but sometimes you just had to make a point. Luckily, she was busy enough with other projects to be able to stand the loss.

'Daddy, you have to stop her!'

Sophie said, 'He can't.'

'Oh, just you wait,' bellowed Jezebel. 'He's *so* gonna sue your ass!'

'Your *fat* ass,' Jemini added; it was evidently the worst epithet she could think of.

'Guess what?' Sophie smiled equably at the sisters as she flicked shut the locks on the metal equipment trunk. 'Me and my fat ass can't wait.'

The girls' father caught up with her as she was packing the equipment into her car. Sophie forced herself to stay calm. 'If they say anything publicly about me backing out, I'll tell everyone why I did it.'

The poor harassed man shook his head. 'I'll make sure they don't. And I won't sue you. Look, I'm sorry. I've worked so hard all these years to make money.' He gestured helplessly up at the hugely expensive penthouse apartment. 'To give my family the best life I could. And you know what? I sometimes wonder why I bothered. They've lost touch with reality. They see a flaw and it has to be fixed. The people they mix with, they're all the same.'

He might not have had facelifts, but his teeth were astonishingly even and white, like mini marble tombstones. Sophie felt for him. 'Well, I'm sorry too. I've never walked out on a job before, but you know . . .'

With the weary sigh of a man only too aware that he was somehow going to have to sort things out and make alternative arrangements, Jemini and Jezebel's father took out his phone and said, 'I do know. It's OK, I understand.'

Chapter 36

Traffic was heavy on the way back and the journey took two hours. Approaching St Carys, on a whim Sophie turned left up the lane that led towards Moor Court. If it wasn't to be a completely wasted day, she may as well see if she could spot the mystery bird.

She pulled in halfway up the driveway. Marguerite's sporty red Mercedes was missing, which meant she was probably out. Anyway, as Marguerite had said, there was no need to ring the doorbell. Jumping out of the car with the necessary long lens fixed to the camera around her neck, Sophie took a short cut through the trees leading round to the back garden.

She came out around forty feet from the back of the house. And here it was, the enormously tall ash tree with the cocoon-shaped wicker seat hanging from one of the lower branches.

Peering up, craning her neck and squinting as the bright sunlight flickered through the swaying leaves, she managed to spot the nest, way up high and half hidden amongst the blur of greenery. She hoisted the Nikon into position, adjusted the elongated lens and brought the nest into knife-sharp focus. That was it, perfect, but there was no sign of any birds, either parents or chicks.

Sophie leaned back against the silver-grey trunk of the tree and lowered the camera, but kept her attention on the nest. Through either luck or patience, she would catch a few shots of the bird when it decided to put in an appearance.

Fifteen minutes later, she gave her aching neck a rest and massaged her knotted-up left shoulder. Looked like it was going to be down to patience rather than luck. She was hot, and the back of her shirt was sticking to her spine, but . . .

A tiny movement at the very periphery of her vision made Sophie glance across at the house. For a moment she couldn't work out where it had come from; then it happened again, and she realised there was someone in Marguerite's office.

Not Marguerite, though. The hair was messy and blond, not sleek and dark. It was Riley, wearing a white T-shirt and sitting at the desk scrutinising the computer screen in front of him.

He didn't know she was out here. Only mildly curious as to what he might be doing, Sophie instinctively raised the camera once more to eye level and refocused the lens until she had him in her sights.

There he was, every last tiny detail of his face as clear as if he were an insect under a microscope. Even after all these years, it never failed to amaze her that a lens had the ability to make something far away appear so close you felt you could reach out and touch it.

Sophie made one final minuscule adjustment and turned her attention to the computer screen.

When she realised what was on it, and slowly worked out what appeared to be going on in the room, she felt all the hairs on the back of her neck prickle in disbelief.

Surely not.

It couldn't be.

Could it?

Josh was driving back to the hotel after a meeting in Padstow. He'd reached St Carys, and slowed to let a girl push a twin buggy across the road, when he happened to glance across at the mini supermarket on his right.

Clearly visible through the glass frontage was Sophie, surveying the shelves of wine.

237

Sometimes fate intervenes and offers a helping hand, and it would seem rude to refuse it. Josh waited until the twin buggy had reached the pavement, then promptly parked up on the double yellows. Within twenty seconds he was entering the shop, executing a surprised double-take as he recognised a familiar face.

'Hello!' Did that sound OK? Suitably casual? God, sounding casual was hard.

Sophie swung round and said, 'Oh, hi!'

'Can't decide?' She'd been holding a bottle in each hand, studying the labels. *Look at her, so beautiful* . . .

'They're both the same price.' She pulled a face, holding up each bottle in turn. 'This one sounds nicer. But *this* one's on special offer and has a prettier label.'

'Go for the first one. It's what they're like on the inside that counts.' He liked Sophie inside *and* out. 'Off somewhere nice?'

She shook her head. 'No.'

'Celebrating, then?'

'Kind of the opposite. Commiserating with myself. I walked out of a job today and there's still a chance I could get into trouble over it. Long story,' she added drily. 'Anyway, what are you doing here?'

'Just dropped in to pick up some . . . biscuits.' It was the first thing that came into his head; he could hardly say *I only came in here because I saw you.*

'You live in a hotel. Surely you must have biscuits?'

'Not the kind I wanted. I had a sudden craving for Garibaldis.' He saw the look on her face. 'It's OK, I'm not pregnant.'

Sophie laughed. 'I haven't had a Garibaldi for years.'

Was this fate? Seizing the moment, Josh said, 'I'll share mine if you share yours. Fancy a walk along the beach?'

He saw her hesitate, then make up her mind. 'Yes, I do. Although . . .'

'Although what?'

'Will we take turns swigging out of the bottle? Because it might not be the classiest look I've ever gone for.'

Josh made his way down the left-hand aisle and picked up a packet of Garibaldis, then moved on to the tiny kitchenware section, there to provide emergency supplies for holidaymakers staying in tents and caravans in the area.

'They don't have glasses.' He rejoined Sophie in the queue for the till. 'Will these do?'

She surveyed the two cheap china mugs, one blue and stripy, the other pink and decorated with teddies and hearts. 'Perfect. Yours is the pink one.'

'Funnily enough, I thought it might be,' said Josh.

Sophie sat and wiggled her bare toes in the sand, hyper-aware of Josh's forearm millimetres away from her own. They'd walked to the furthest edge of the beach. Now Josh was opening the bottle – hooray for screw caps – and pouring red wine into their mugs. They both knew they could have gone to the Mermaid, where there were comfortable seats and proper wine glasses to drink from, but they'd taken the beach route instead.

'Cheers.' Josh clinked their mugs together, the side of his hand brushing against hers. *Zinnggg*.

'Cheers.' She took a sip and said, 'It's nice. You were right.' Had he felt the zing too?

'I'm always right.' His eyes crinkled with amusement. 'So, what happened to make you walk out on your job today?'

Sophie told him. The outrage bubbled up; recalling Jemini and Jezebel's reactions made her furious all over again on Elizabeth's behalf. When she'd finished ranting, she said heatedly, 'It just makes me so mad. Elizabeth's worth fifty of them!'

'I agree.' Josh was nodding.

'Life's so unfair. Why does bad stuff have to happen to people who don't deserve it?' It would be poor form to suggest that people who *did* deserve it should be the ones to get cancer, but the thought was there in her brain. She took a bigger glug of wine and said, 'Some people swan through life without realising how lucky they are.'

'Also true.'

'Why are you looking at me like that?' He definitely had a particular expression on his face.

'I like how you get indignant on other people's behalf.' He smiled. 'You're so . . . principled.'

'So principled that I lost out on the best-paid job I've had in months.' She grimaced. 'Ah well, never mind. It's only money.'

He paused, gazing steadily into her eyes. 'There's something I'd really like to know. What happened to put you off men?'

Her stomach clenched; they weren't here to discuss *her*.

'You've asked me that question before.'

'I know I have. Still waiting for the answer.'

'You'll have a long wait, then. I told you, it's private.'

'I'm a good listener. And pretty unshockable.'

'That's irrelevant.'

'Is it?' Josh shook his head fractionally. 'You're a beautiful girl. I like everything about you, apart from the fact that I asked you out and you turned me down. I didn't like that bit at all.'

'Poor you. Heartbreaking.' In order to keep her own emotions in check, Sophie resorted to flippancy. 'You could always ask Tula out. I'm sure she'd say yes. She likes you.'

'And you don't?'

It was her turn to give him a long look. 'You shouldn't ask questions like that. The answer may offend.'

'Did he hit you?'

'Who?'

'The one who caused all of this.'

He was watching her intently. Sophie said, 'No, never. And that's as much as you get. I'm not saying any more.'

'But—'

'Wait.' She held up her hand to stop him in his tracks. 'It's private, OK? I'm not going to talk about it. Ever. Apart from anything else, it isn't my story to tell.'

Josh was still watching her, looking as if there was something else he wanted to say. In return, Sophie silently signalled that it would be a pointless exercise. OK, time to change the subject, to the reason she'd agreed to come down to the beach with him in the first place . . .

What a situation to find yourself in. Josh glanced at the bottle stuck at an angle in the sand and saw that it was almost empty. They'd been sitting out here for an hour now. And all he'd wanted to do the whole time was pull Sophie into his arms and kiss her senseless.

Meanwhile, what had she been doing? The answer to that was: her level best to find out as much information as possible about Riley.

Which was pretty frustrating, to say the least. Every time he'd attempted to steer the conversation on to other subjects, Sophie had deftly steered it right back again. She wanted to know whether they had been good friends all those years ago when Riley had first come to live in St Carys and Josh himself had been returning here during breaks between university terms. Had Riley always been as lazy and hedonistic as he was now? What had he taken his degree in? Did he genuinely have no ambition at all, or did Josh think there could possibly be more to him than met the eye?

It was a virtual interrogation.

'Why are you so interested?' He didn't want to sound like a bad loser, but if she was asking all these questions because she was attracted to Riley Bryant . . . well, he wasn't at all sure he could keep his feelings about it to himself.

Sophie shrugged easily. 'Just curious.'

'He wouldn't be your type.'

She glanced sideways at him, amused by his tone. 'You don't know that. He might be.'

'I do know. Riley's just . . . Riley. He's good fun, great to spend time with, but what you see is what you get. It doesn't go further than that.'

Sophie still wasn't looking convinced. 'You don't think he might have hidden depths?'

Josh poured the last of the wine into their mugs. 'No,' he said flatly, 'I don't. And relationships aren't his thing. Nothing ever lasts longer than a week. More often it's a matter of hours.'

Her choppy blond hair was being blown across her face. Sophie tipped her head back, shaking the strands out of her eyes. 'Maybe that suits some girls.'

OK, did she mean *her*? Was she hinting that she wouldn't be averse to a night with Riley? Experiencing a tightening inside his chest, Josh said, 'When I asked you a while back, you told me you weren't interested in him.'

'Did I?' Sophie smiled, checked her watch and finished her wine. 'Wow, it's later than I thought. I need to get home.'

Josh rose to his feet, brushed the sand off his jeans and reached out a hand to haul her upright. For a moment they were facing each other, their bodies almost but not quite touching; he could see his own face reflected in her clear grey eyes. The urge to draw her closer was stronger than ever. He longed to trace the dimple in her left cheek, to breathe in the scent of her, to push his fingers through that tousled blond hair and feel the warmth of her skin at the base of her throat.

And more than anything else, he wanted to kiss her, *hold her and kiss her* . . .

OK, more than *almost* anything else, but let's not get carried away. One step at a time.

'Well, I'd better get back. Lots of work to do.' Breaking contact and shaking dry sand from her own clothes, Sophie handed him her empty mug and said cheerfully, 'Here, you take it, it's yours. Thanks for the chat, it's been nice.'

She stepped back, moving away, the empty wine bottle swinging between her fingers as she carried it over to the rubbish bin. Once it had been disposed of, she turned, waved and called out, 'Bye!'

And now, with the setting sun behind her, she was heading for the steps, making her way home, presumably to assimilate all the newly gathered information she'd inveigled from him about Riley Bryant.

Josh exhaled, marvelling at his own misguided plans. So much for not getting carried away and taking things one step at a time.

If Riley took advantage of Sophie and then ditched her, he would want to kill him.

Then again, if Riley took advantage of Sophie and *didn't* ditch her . . . well, that would just make him want to kill him *more*.

Chapter 37

It was eight thirty the following morning when Sophie returned to Moor Court. She parked the car where she'd left it yesterday, retraced her footsteps around the side of the house and emerged through the trees in the same place as before.

Was this how it felt to be a spy? She had the camera, her reason for being here, clutched in her hands. The odds were slim, surely, but some sixth sense had brought her back here this morning . . .

And ha, she'd been right. There he was. Sitting in the same chair, wearing the same T-shirt, as engrossed in his task as before. Unbelievable.

Sophie's heart raced as she raised the camera and focused the lens again. Riley certainly looked as if he'd been up all night; his sun-streaked surfer's hair was sticking out all over his head. There were four opened Coca-Cola cans and three empty coffee cups on the desk to the left of the computer. As she watched, he sat back and yawned, flexing his back and briefly stretching his arms above his head before getting back to work.

And yes, it was work. Zooming in on the computer screen, Sophie watched the words appear as Riley typed them. Yesterday afternoon he'd been on page 273. This morning he'd reached page 282 She was able to read what he was writing. She could see him pause to consider the next line of dialogue. He clearly wasn't just copying out someone else's words; he was choosing them himself.

She didn't take any shots of what she was seeing. Apart from anything else, standing in the garden photographing someone inside their own home without their knowledge breached all kinds of privacy laws. Instead, she retreated through the trees, then made her way back to the driveway and up the front steps to the main entrance of the house. She rang the doorbell and waited.

It took a while, but eventually there was the sound of the door being unlocked. It opened to reveal Riley blinking in surprise at the sight of her.

'Sophie! Fancy seeing you here.' He yawned, looked at his watch and said sleepily, 'What time is it?'

'Almost nine o'clock.'

'What?' He looked horrified. 'That's practically the middle of the night.'

'Sorry, did I wake you? I thought you'd be in your cottage. Where's Marguerite?'

'She had dinner with her publisher last night. Stayed up in London. When she's away, I sleep here,' Riley explained. 'Rather than leave the place empty.'

'You're dressed.' Sophie indicated his T-shirt and jeans.

'Never got undressed.' His smile was crooked. 'Fell asleep on the sofa watching the new Bond DVD.' Another yawn. 'Bloody good film, actually.'

God, he was good. So completely natural, such an *easy* liar. Marvelling at his skills, Sophie said, 'Can I come in for a minute? Would that be OK?'

'Sweetheart, of course. Where are my manners? Come through, I'll put the machine on, we'll have some coffee.' He ushered her inside, through the hall and into the kitchen. 'But I'm not expecting Marguerite back before noon. Did she book you for another photo shoot?'

'No, don't panic, she just asked me to pop over and see if I could get some pictures of a mystery bird she's seen in the garden.'

'Oh, the bird . . . right, she mentioned it a couple of days ago.'

Riley was nodding. 'She and Lawrence had an argument about what it could be.'

'That's the one. I'm guessing she spotted it from her office window,' said Sophie. 'So I thought I might get a good view of the nest from there. OK if I take a quick look?'

There was a millisecond's hesitation before Riley shrugged and said, 'Of course you can, no problem. Let me just go and clean it up before you—'

'Hey, no need. It's only me.' Sophie smiled at him. 'I've been in there loads of times before.' As she said it, she headed for the office.

Riley came with her, murmuring, 'But she's not always very tidy when she's in full flow.'

He opened the door to the office. The screensaver had kicked in on the computer. Riley tut-tutted and collected the empty Coke cans, lobbing them into the bin beneath the desk. He piled up the coffee cups and said, 'See what I mean? You only ever see this room when it's been tidied up. Sorry, I should have cleared this lot away after she finished work yesterday.'

'Relax, I'm not a hotel inspector. I haven't come in here checking for dust.' Amused, Sophie held up her camera and made her way over to the window. 'Now, let's see if I can find it . . . Ah, there's the ash tree . . . and that must be the nest!' Delighted by her own brilliance, she fired off a few shots and said, 'OK, no sign of any birds at the moment, but at least I know where it is now. I can lie in wait outside.' Turning back, she knocked her hip against the edge of Marguerite's desk and saw – *bingo!* – the computer screen shimmer into life.

And there it was again, the work in progress: Chapter 19 of Marguerite's next novel.

'You know, she really should save and log out when she finishes work for the day,' said Sophie.

'Tell me about it.' Riley rolled his eyes in good-natured despair. 'I'm always reminding her. She just gets carried away and forgets.'

'Well you need to remind her again, before she manages to

lose a whole lot of work. Oh look, I'm sorry I woke you up. Don't worry about that coffee . . . I'll head on outside and wait for the bird to turn up. You still look shattered.' Sophie patted him on the arm. 'Why don't you go back to sleep?'

Well, she'd been right about one thing. As soon as Sophie was out of the house, Riley saved the work and emailed it to himself for extra security.

Then he checked his inbox and saw that an email had just come in from Marguerite:

> Hi darling, just a quick note to let you know that Sophie will be dropping by in the next couple of days to try and photograph that bird in the garden. So be aware. See you later – home around 3.
>   M x

Oh well, better late than never. Riley glanced out of the window at Sophie, who was now leaning against the trunk of the tree, aiming her camera up at the nest. Then he closed down the computer and left the office, rubbing his hand over his gritty, over-tired eyes as he made his way through to the kitchen. A cup of tea and a slice of toast was what he needed right now, followed by some long-overdue sleep.

It had all started quite suddenly, six years ago. Up until then Marguerite had never faltered. The words had flowed from her; she'd been a magnificent one-woman book-producing machine. In the three years he'd been living down here with her, he'd seen for himself how hard she worked. In almost two decades she'd produced thirty novels, putting in the hours, creating unput-downable reads that would satisfy her millions of fans around the world. Intellectual literary fiction it wasn't; Marguerite's aim was to entertain and enthral, and that was what had always been her forte.

Until the day the tap had been abruptly switched off. Riley

247

remembered it with crystal clarity. He'd come back from surfing and had cheerily asked Marguerite what her word count had been for the day. It was a routine exchange; she always liked to try and outdo herself.

But Marguerite, mystified rather than alarmed, had said, 'Zero. Well, a few words, but I deleted them. Just couldn't seem to get into it today.'

And he'd made a joke about it, distracting her with stories of his own afternoon at the beach. They'd each assumed that tomorrow all would be well again, back to normal, back in the old routine . . .

Except it hadn't happened. Marguerite had sat and gazed at her computer screen for ten hours straight without writing anything.

The next day she tried pacing around the house with a pen and notebook. That hadn't worked either.

By the end of the seventh day she was in a state of full-blown panic, unable to understand what was going on and petrified of what it meant . . . of what it could mean. Riley had taken charge, ordering her to stop worrying and packing her off on a luxury cruise around the Med. For two weeks, he told her, she mustn't even think about writing, and when she came back she'd be raring to go again, guaranteed.

It hadn't happened. Marguerite returned as blocked as ever. Fear of not being able to write then morphed into fear of writing, of trying to do it and getting it wrong, of making the sickening discovery that the talent she'd taken for granted for so long had fizzled up and died . . .

And coupled with the overwhelming fear had come shame, because losing the ability to write meant losing her sense of pride in herself. Years of supreme self-confidence threatened to be swept away by her own abject failure.

And the more she panicked, the more entrenched the mental paralysis became.

Riley was at as much of a loss as Marguerite. He wanted to

be able to help her, but how? She flatly refused to speak to anyone else about it, convinced that admitting the problem would have disastrous consequences; her agents and publishers around the world would lose confidence in her, other writers might pretend to be sympathetic but would be secretly celebrating the downfall of a rival, her friends would gossip endlessly and word would spread . . .

The weeks went by, the writer's block settled like cement around Marguerite and her agitation escalated. Finally, out of desperation, Riley sat down and read his way through the half-written manuscript she'd abandoned mid-sentence. Her heartbreaking refrain was 'I just don't know where it's *going*.' All these years she'd written without plotting ahead, simply immersing herself in the story and experiencing the twists and turns along with her characters.

Riley wrote her a detailed chapter-by-chapter synopsis of the story so far and made up his own mind as to what might happen next. He worked through the night, describing everything that needed to take place in order to keep the characters on track. The next morning he showed Marguerite what he'd written and said, 'See if this does the trick.'

Marguerite was grateful, but it didn't drag her out of her numbed state. Despite liking the ideas he'd come up with, she was still stuck.

'All the characters are there, I can see them *waiting* for me . . .' She shook her head in despair. 'But I just can't make them speak. I don't know them any more . . . it's like they *hate* me and they're refusing to do or say what I want them to do.'

It hadn't been the answer he'd hoped for. Riley looked down at the pages and pages of notes he'd so painstakingly compiled. Marguerite might not feel as if she knew her characters any more, but in his own mind they were completely fresh and full of life, bursting to carry on where she had left off, abandoning them like puppets frustratingly frozen in time.

'Sorry,' he said. 'I was just trying to help.'

'I know, darling, and it's sweet of you. But you can't.' Marguerite, who never cried, blinked away a tear. 'That's the thing; no one can. God, look at me.'

Riley grabbed a tissue from the box on the shelf behind him. 'Here, you're OK, mascara hasn't run.'

'No, I mean *look* at me.' Marguerite indicated the paused YouTube clip on the computer screen, filmed at a hugely popular book festival last year. She pressed play and they both watched the confident, glamorous version of Marguerite Marshall, author extraordinaire, being interviewed up on the stage in front of a jam-packed audience.

'. . . and you're known as a plain-speaking woman,' the interviewer continued. 'Tell me, what are *your* views on the subject of writer's block?'

He was asking the question because a particularly pretentious and generally disliked literary novelist had been banging on in the broadsheets about the tortuous process of having to produce words to order when the muse refused to comply.

'Ha!' With a dismissive snort of laughter, Marguerite said, 'Well, I'm sure we all know who you're talking about. And my reply is that the man in question needs to get a grip, pull himself together and stop being such a ridiculous whingeing drama queen.' This statement was greeted with laughter and the beginnings of applause, but she didn't stop there. 'Seriously, whining and making a fuss like that . . . it's just attention-seeking nonsense. Real writers don't suffer from these namby-pamby problems, let me tell you. We just work our socks off, put our heads down and jolly well get on with it. Writer's block is nothing more than an excuse for failure.' With glittering eyes and utter disdain in her voice, she concluded, 'Trust me, writer's block *simply doesn't exist*.'

On the screen, the audience applauded wildly. Another tear rolled down Marguerite's cheek as she closed the link. Without looking at Riley, she shook her head. 'I sounded like Margaret Thatcher. I can't believe I sat there and said all that. Talk about karma.'

There was simply no answer to that. She was right. Unaccustomed to so much reading and intense concentration, Riley rubbed his eyes and said, 'OK, sorry. I tried.' Another huge yawn almost dislocated his jaw. 'I'm going to bed.'

But despite his exhaustion, sleep had proven elusive. Eventually he'd dozed, waking every so often to the sound of Marguerite's characters in his head.

Bloody ridiculous. What were they doing pestering *him*?

At lunchtime he got up, jumped into his car and drove along the coast road to Mariscombe Bay. The sun was out, the wind was up and the waves were crashing on to the beach. Conditions were perfect, and there were plenty of surfers already out there, taking advantage of an unexpectedly good day.

Riley surfed for a grand total of twenty minutes before giving up, peeling off his wetsuit, climbing back into the car and making his way home again. His friends couldn't understand what on earth had got into him. *He* couldn't work out what had got into him; all he knew was that the voices were still there in his head, the characters were . . . God, it felt as if they were *harassing* him, demanding impatiently to be allowed to get on with whatever was about to happen next in their lives.

It was almost scary; when people with mental illnesses got arrested for doing something bizarre, didn't they always say it was the voices in their heads that had made them do it?

And that was kind of how it felt; like being taken over, possessed. Back at Moor Court, Marguerite had gone out, leaving a note as she always did on the kitchen table: *Giving retail therapy a try. Home by seven. If anyone calls, tell them I'm working and can't be disturbed. M x*

Riley made himself a strong coffee and took it through to the office. He sat down in front of the computer, switched it on and took several deep breaths. Then, refusing to allow himself to panic that this was crazy, of course he couldn't do it, he began to type.

Two hours later he noticed the untouched mug of coffee next to him on the desk.

At six thirty, he sat back and stared at the screen with a mixture of befuddled achievement and disbelief. According to the computer, he'd produced two thousand two hundred and seventeen words. The last time he'd written anything longer than a text or a quick email had been . . . God, it must've been when he was back at university. As for fiction, he had a vague memory of writing a short story for the school magazine about a stunning female chemistry teacher seducing a young male pupil called . . . ahem, Riley. When the headmaster had refused to allow it to appear in the magazine, that had been the end of his literary efforts. He'd *read* plenty of books in his time, but it had never once occurred to him that he might have the ability to write one.

He scanned the screen, reading the words that had poured out of him this afternoon. At times his fingers hadn't been able to keep up with the ideas in his head; there were typing errors all over the place. A couple of repetitions jumped out at him too . . . he'd used the word *shouted* twice in one paragraph there. But the characters felt right . . . they seemed real, and as far as he could tell, they sounded like the same people Marguerite had created.

Whether or not he was right about that, only time – and Marguerite – would tell.

For the next twenty minutes he corrected the errors, tidied up the manuscript and printed off the pages. At ten past seven, Marguerite returned loaded down with expensive shopping bags. When she'd kicked off her shoes and thrown herself down on the sofa in the living room, he handed her a stronger than usual gin and tonic and a folder containing the pages.

Then he left the room and waited. What he'd written was probably rubbish. And if that were the case, at least he knew Marguerite wouldn't be afraid to point it out. Suffering fools gladly had never been her forte. As she'd so often announced to her adoring public, she simply didn't *do* shilly-shally.

Oh well, if it was that bad, maybe this would give her the jolt she needed, spur her on to show him how it should be done.

Which would be the very *best* outcome, of course.

Although even as he was thinking this, Riley inwardly experienced a twinge of unease at the prospect of Marguerite taking over what now felt like *his* cast of characters. Because what if she made them do and say the wrong things, took them off in directions he didn't want them to go?

The kitchen door burst open and Marguerite appeared, white-faced and trembling with fury. 'You *told* someone. I asked you not to and you did it anyway.'

'What?' Startled by the venom in her voice, Riley said, 'I haven't told anyone.'

She shook the sheaf of pages at him. 'So who wrote this?'

'I did!'

'*You?* But you can't have!'

'Well I did.'

The outrage had given way to utter disbelief. Marguerite was staring at him as if he'd just turned into a hobbit. 'But . . . but you don't know *how.*'

'I know.' He shrugged. 'I just gave it a try. So, does it make you want to rip it up and rewrite it yourself?'

'No.' She shot him a suspicious look. 'Did you get someone to help you?'

He shook his head. 'I didn't, I promise. I wrote every word myself.'

'How? Just . . . *how?*'

'I got to know the characters. Then I listened to them. They started doing stuff . . .' God, it was hard to explain how it happened. 'And I kind of wrote everything down. Is it awful?' He had to ask, needed to know.

'No. It's not perfect, but it's a damn good first draft. I still can't believe you did it.' Her expression softening, Marguerite said, 'You've got the voice right, that's the extraordinary thing. It sounds exactly like me.'

'I've spent long enough listening to you. I know what you sound like.' Emulating her direct, punchy style had been surprisingly easy.

253

If she'd been a writer of very light romantic fiction, he'd have found it harder.

'Well. I'm in shock,' Marguerite declared. 'How long did it take you to write this?'

'Five hours.'

'Good going.'

'It just came out of nowhere. I didn't want to stop.'

'I remember that feeling.' Her tone was wry. 'And what happens next? Do you know?'

Would she be offended if he said yes? Would it sound like he was barrelling in and taking over, wrestling the characters out of her control? After a moment's hesitation, he said, 'Kind of.'

'Yes or no?'

What the hell. 'Yes.'

'Fantastic.' Marguerite broke into a huge smile. 'My God, this is incredible. Can you carry on doing it, do you think?'

Could he? He was already itching to get back into the story. The characters were giving him grief, hassling him to pay them some attention. He smiled back and said, 'I'll give it a go.'

Chapter 38

That had been six years ago. Riley glanced up at the bookshelves above the computer, packed with hardbacks and various foreign editions of Marguerite's novels. Unbelievably, he'd now written nine books under her name. And if that sounded easy . . . well, it hadn't been. Sometimes it had turned out to be the hardest thing in the world. On rare occasions the words poured out unstoppably as they had on that first day, and other times they refused to cooperate. Structuring an entire book could also be a nightmare – keeping the various plot threads under control was like fighting to squash an octopus into a bottle. When it was going badly, you despaired of ever getting through to the end. Luckily, when it was going well, there was nothing better.

Marguerite had never got her writing mojo back, but she critiqued his work rigorously as he went along. Which was annoying, of course, but undoubtedly necessary. Her editorial suggestions always made good sense. And when each book was finished, she went over it again with a fine-tooth comb, altering words and phrasing to ensure the end result sounded *exactly* as if she'd written it herself.

No one else must know; that had been the remit from day one. Marguerite had insisted upon it and he'd understood why; she simply couldn't *bear* the thought of people learning the truth. Her whole persona revolved around confidence and can-do achievement. Admitting to failure wasn't something she could bring herself to do.

And so the deception had begun and been rigorously maintained. Marguerite continued to play the part of the beloved best-selling author. Her various editors, agents and many publishers had no idea she was no longer writing her own books. They continued to shower her with praise and promote her all over the world, while Marguerite in turn carried on delighting her fans and promoting herself. Confiding in even one person was out of the question; such an enthralling item of gossip might too easily become public knowledge.

Their secret was still a secret because only the two of them knew about it.

And up until now Riley hadn't minded at all. Marguerite was his only living relative and he loved her. When his parents had been killed, she had stepped up to the plate, and not because there was ever likely to be anything in it for her. Aware that he owed her everything, he'd vowed never to let her down.

And it had genuinely never been a problem, not receiving any public praise or acknowledgement for having written nine best-selling novels. Nor had it bothered him that everyone who knew him thought Riley Bryant was a lazy, work-shy, pleasure-seeking hedonist. He'd enjoyed playing the part, immersing himself in the role . . . which was, after all, pretty much an extension of how he'd been spending his time since university.

The brutally sudden loss of his mum and dad had hit Riley hard, prompting a couple of wild and reckless 'gap years', followed by another one for luck. In all honesty, he'd been privately starting to wonder what the future held. If Marguerite's catastrophic attack of writer's block hadn't come along, who knows how much more of his life he might have frittered away? In one way, becoming her ghostwriter had been the making of him.

Except now there was this situation with Tula, and although there was absolutely nothing he could do about it, being rejected by her was really starting to get him down. There was no way he could impress her with a proper job as well as writing the books; everyone else might think he slept all the time and wasted his days, but he was actually putting in a good sixty hours a week. It was no picnic.

Even more ironically, when Tula had moved down here, he'd been the one who'd encouraged her to go for the position at the Mariscombe. Now, seeing her almost daily and having to cope with her utter lack of interest in him, he was beginning to wish he hadn't.

This was killing him . . .

After two unsuccessful attempts to photograph the mystery bird, Sophie had begun to wonder if it was ever going to happen. Then the next morning there it was, high up in the branches of the towering ash tree. Within minutes of arriving at Moor Court, she had what she'd come for. Third time lucky.

But the curtains in the office were tightly closed; if Riley was hard at work, she wouldn't interrupt him again. And there was still no sign of the sporty red Mercedes on the driveway, which indicated that Marguerite was out.

Oh well, no hurry. She had the photos of the bird, that was the important thing. Flushed with success, Sophie jumped into her own car and headed back to St Carys.

She hadn't been expecting to bump into Marguerite at the Mariscombe House Hotel when she dropped in shortly afterwards to return a book she'd borrowed from Tula, but there she was. Looking quite astonishingly glamorous and grand as she sat alone at a table out on the terrace. Her hair was immaculate, she was wearing full make-up and her outfit was *very* mother-of-the-bride, a fitted gold silk dress with translucent turquoise and gold jacket. Even from this distance you could see her jewellery glittering in the morning sunlight. As far as Marguerite was concerned, more was definitely more and simple understated outfits were for wimps.

Sophie collected her camera from the car, then made her way out to where Marguerite was sitting.

'Hello!' Marguerite greeted her with a heavily perfumed kiss on each cheek. 'Sit down, sit down, keep me company for a bit – I'm being interviewed for one of the glossies and the journalist just called to say that her train's been delayed for thirty minutes. Whereas *I've* been up since six, writing away, then getting myself ready and here on time. All I can say is it's a good job I'm not a diva.'

Sophie somehow managed to keep a straight face. She said, 'Not being interviewed at home this time?'

'My last few photo shoots have all been at home. I thought we could do with a change of scenery. The magazine's sending its own photographer,' Marguerite explained. 'Sorry, darling, I do my best to support local businesses but I can't use you all the time.'

'That's fine. Anyway,' Sophie held up the camera, 'I've just come from Moor Court. I was going to email you the photos, but I can show you them now. Finally got some shots of that bird.'

'Really? Excellent! Let me see.' Marguerite's eyes lit up as she leaned over for a look. 'And?'

'You were right. Lawrence was wrong.'

'Ha, marvellous. I knew it!' She clapped her hands in delight; it was clearly all about the winning for Marguerite. She peered at the camera's screen and said triumphantly, 'There it is, clear as day. Red beak, different-shaped head . . . and look at the curve of the wing. Honestly, Lawrence is an idiot if he thinks that even looks like a blackbird. I told him he was talking rubbish!'

And she'd gone to considerable lengths to prove it. Sophie said, 'I'll email these to you. You can show him.'

Pausing on her way past with a tray, Tula said, 'Morning, ladies. Everything OK? Anything else I can get you?'

'Another pot of tea, please, I think. Sophie? Can you stay for a cup? And we'll have some lemon cake.'

'Good choice. Coming right up.'

'I like your friend.' Marguerite watched as Tula made her jaunty way back inside. 'Lovely smile, always cheerful.'

'Riley's pretty keen too.' Sophie settled back on the cushioned chair. 'He has a total crush on her.'

'A crush? Why doesn't he ask her out, then?'

'He has. She said no.'

Marguerite looked shocked. 'What? No one says no to Riley. Why would she do that?'

'Well . . . you know.'

'Tell me.' Marguerite was indignant. 'Why would any girl not like him?'

Sophie hesitated. She hadn't told Tula what she'd seen the other morning at Moor Court; she hadn't shared her discovery with anyone. Oh well, may as well be honest. 'Tula likes him,' she explained. 'Everyone *likes* Riley. I think she just doesn't respect him. You know, too much playing around, not enough work ethic.'

'He has a job.' Marguerite's spine stiffened, the lioness protecting her wayward cub. 'He works for me. I need someone to organise my life, and that's what he does.'

There was clearly no way in the world Marguerite would admit what had been going on. Sophie said mildly, 'I know. I'm just saying that's the way she feels.'

'If she likes someone, she should accept them for who they are.' Twisting round in her seat as Tula reappeared, Marguerite said, 'I've been hearing all about your views on my nephew.'

'Really?' Tula grinned as she rearranged the china on the table. 'Are there asterisks involved?'

'He's a lovely boy. You couldn't ask for better.' Marguerite was clearly taking the rejection badly on Riley's behalf. 'He even took you to that wedding in Wales!'

'I know,' said Tula.

'All the girls adore him. Yet I hear he asked you out and you turned him down.'

'He's great fun. Just, you know, not my type.'

'Well I have to say, I'm surprised. Wouldn't have thought you'd be that fussy. You're not exactly his type either.' Marguerite's gaze flickered over the tied-back dark hair and cocoa-brown eyes, the lack of supermodel slenderness. 'He usually goes for stunning blondes.'

Ouch.

Not remotely offended, Tula said cheerfully, 'I know he does! And they go for him too. Look, I think Riley's brilliant, but I've been out with my share of hopeless types . . . there's no way I'm ever going to do that again. He's not *hopeless*,' she hastily amended, glimpsing the light of battle in Marguerite's eye. 'I'm just saying he's not the type you'd ever really want to rely on. He's just . . . more for fun, kind of thing. Anyway, I need to get back to work before Josh sees me slacking and gives me my P45. Honestly, he's such a slave-driver!'

When she'd disappeared, Marguerite exhaled and said curtly, 'Maybe she deserves to be sacked.'

'You don't mean that,' said Sophie.

'Hmph. Don't I?' Marguerite wasn't the backing-down kind, particularly where defending her nephew was concerned.

'No.'

'He's a good boy. Couldn't ask for better. She shouldn't be writing him off.'

Writing him off. As the irony of the choice of phrase struck them both simultaneously, bright spots of colour flared in Marguerite's cheeks and she turned away abruptly.

'I'll email you these photos.' Sophie felt a rush of sympathy for her.

'Yes. Thank you. And put a good word in for Riley if you get the chance. But just . . . you know, be subtle about it.'

Which was a bit like Simon Cowell asking her to let someone down gently and be really careful not to hurt their feelings.

'OK,' said Sophie. 'I'll try.'

Chapter 39

It was three in the afternoon by the time Marguerite arrived back at Moor Court. The journalist had been apologetic and easily charmed, and the male photographer had taken some good shots of her in and around the hotel. The interview had gone well – talking about herself was never a hardship – and hopefully the piece, when it appeared in the magazine, would result in increased sales for the upcoming hardback.

Letting herself into the house, she found Riley hard at work in the office.

'How's it going?'

He sat back and rotated his shoulders to ease the knots from them. 'Well Chapter Twenty-Eight's been a bitch; I've re-written the last scene four times. But it's done now. Take a look at it and tell me what you think.'

'I will. Later.' Marguerite indicated the curtains pulled across the window. 'You don't have to keep those closed any more, by the way. Sophie's got the shots she was after. And I was right about it being a Cornish chough.'

'You're always right.' Riley half smiled. 'I don't know how Lawrence ever dared to disagree with you in the first place.'

Marguerite was used to being revered and looked up to. She'd already spoken to Lawrence on the phone and informed him of his mistake; somewhat to her frustration, he had simply roared with laughter and said, 'You mean you actually hired a professional photographer to *stalk* the poor bird and prove me wrong? Priceless! How much did that cost you?'

Which had actually made her feel a tiny bit foolish. She also suspected he wasn't bothered by his mistake . . . and that he'd only been teasing her all along when he'd insisted it was a blackbird.

And what would Sophie charge for her visits? Fifty or sixty pounds, at a guess. Oh well, she'd just have to call it research for business purposes and offset the bill against tax.

'Anyway,' said Riley, 'how did the interview go?'

'Fine. No problems. One of the questions she asked was how would I cope if I ran out of ideas and could no longer write.' Marguerite pulled a face.

'What did you say?'

'That it was my worst nightmare, but luckily nothing like that would ever happen because I have a million ideas bursting to get out of my head.'

'Right.'

'And she said that was a relief, because otherwise my legions of fans would be thrown into a panic.'

'I'm sure they would be.' Reaching for the can on the desk, Riley took a gulp of Coke.

'I had a nice chat with Sophie.'

'Yeah?'

'And with Tula.'

If this had been a TV sitcom, Riley would at this point have spluttered and choked on his drink, maybe dropped it on the computer keyboard or somehow managed to fall off his chair and into the waste-paper basket.

Since this wasn't a sitcom, he didn't do anything like that, but what did happen was almost more interesting. The changes were subtle, but Marguerite was an expert at detecting micro-expressions. There was the brief pressing-together of his lips, the increased tension around the eyes, the quickening of his breathing.

More significant than anything else, however, was the height-ened colour in her nephew's face. And this was Riley, for goodness' sake: outrageous, flirtatious and utterly unembarrassable in every way.

She'd never seen him blush before, but it was happening now. This was the effect Tula had on him.

Extraordinary.

Marguerite said, 'Keen on her, are you?'

Discomfort was radiating from him like heat. Feigning a casual shrug, as if he could barely recall who they were talking about, Riley said, 'Who, Tula? Not particularly.'

'Seems to me that you are. And she says she likes you, just not in *that* way. Any idea why that is?'

He shook his head. 'No.'

How had she known he wouldn't admit the real reason? 'Must be annoying, though.'

Another shrug.

'Don't you find it a bit . . . upsetting?'

'Why would I? Hey, there's a million more girls out there, plenty to choose from. You know me.' Flashing his irreverent lady-killer grin, Riley said, 'What am I going to do, mope?'

'You? Never.' Marguerite smiled; that was it, the old Riley was back in control. But how illuminating had that brief glimpse beneath the surface been?

Very interesting indeed.

She said, 'Print off what you've written and I'll read through it later. So, where are you off to tonight?'

'Don't know.' Riley's streaky blond hair fell over his forehead as he bent the Coke can's ring pull this way and that until it snapped in half. 'Just . . . out.'

Picking up girls was easy.

Riley checked his watch; he'd come out at nine o'clock. It was now eleven thirty and he'd achieved what he'd set out to do.

Piece of cake.

Her name was Lauren and she was almost as tall as he was, an elegant blonde with a discreet tattoo at the nape of her neck. She was wearing a peach silk dress that slithered over her hips and showed off her long legs. She smelled of Chanel No. 19 – over the years he'd had plenty of practice learning to recognise the more popular perfumes – and worked as a dental hygienist in Coventry.

To be fair, she did have excellent teeth.

Together they left the Mermaid and headed for the holiday cottage Lauren and her sister had rented for their week's holiday down here in St Carys.

'It's OK, Jen's gone out to dinner with some friends from the yacht club,' Lauren explained as they made their way along the narrow cobbled streets. 'She's not going to be back before one, so we won't be disturbed.'

They would be alone in the cottage. Something didn't feel quite right. Riley hesitated and said warily, 'Look, maybe I shouldn't come in.'

She stopped dead in her tracks in the middle of the road. Beneath the golden glow of the street lamp her face registered disbelief. 'What? Why not?'

'You don't know me. You shouldn't be inviting strangers home with you.'

'Oh don't be such a wuss – I met your friends, didn't I? Everyone in that pub's known you for years. Besides,' she smiled flirtily and leaned up against him, 'I asked the girl behind the bar about you.'

'And?'

'She said you're absolutely fantastic in bed.'

OK, this was mad. The barmaid's name was Ellen and all she'd ever done was smile shyly at him over the counter. Riley said, 'I haven't slept with her.'

'I know, but she says she knows plenty of girls who have. Don't look like that,' Lauren chided playfully. 'It's a huge compliment!'

'Is it?'

'Well it has to be better than everyone saying you're rubbish.' She laughed and tucked her arm through his. 'Come on, nearly there. We're just on the left.'

It was one of the typically tiny Cornish cottages rented out for a few days at a time. Lauren put some music on, poured out drinks and kicked off her high heels. Riley attempted to ignore his own unease, but the sense of claustrophobia was getting to him. What was more, it had nothing to do with the lack of space.

'We were going to have a week in Padstow.' Lauren flashed her excellent teeth at him. 'I'm glad we came here instead.'

He smiled, attempted to relax. 'When d'you have to go home?'

She pulled a mock-sad face. 'Tomorrow. This is our last night.'

Sex, that was all she wanted. Where was the harm? A mutually enjoyable couple of hours in bed, followed by a cheery goodbye. After that, they wouldn't see each other again.

I mean, look at her, she was stunning. What was *wrong* with him tonight?

'Tell you what, why don't I give you a guided tour of our little palace? Come on . . .' And now she was taking his hand in hers, pulling him towards the narrow staircase.

Up they went in single file, with Lauren leading the way, slinking up the stairs like a starlet. When they reached the landing, she drew him into her room and kissed him enthusiastically on the mouth. Like a *hungry* starlet.

For a couple of seconds Riley was on the verge of pulling away. Then he forced himself to go along with the kiss. It was easier, he discovered, if he closed his eyes and pretended it was Tula.

Except it wasn't Tula.

It was no good; everything about this felt miserably, horribly wrong. He'd lost count of the number of times he had relived that kiss with Tula at the wedding. He could recall every last technicolour detail of the way she'd felt, the warmth of her mouth, the electrifying sensation that had spread through his body . . . He knew how crazy it sounded, even to his own ears, but it had been a kiss like no other he'd ever experienced.

It had just felt so right, so completely . . . perfect.

Closing his eyes and pretending the girl he was kissing was Tula, Riley belatedly discovered, didn't work at all. It actually made him feel stupid for imagining it might have done.

He broke away and said, 'Sorry.'

'For what?' Lauren wasn't showing any signs of wanting to let him go; her fingers were digging into his shoulder blades.

'I can't do this.' He shook his head.

'Why not?'

'There's someone else.'

'No there isn't. You told me you didn't have a girlfriend. And I double-checked with that barmaid. She said you're definitely single.'

OK, this wasn't a scenario with which he was in any way familiar.

'I know,' Riley said helplessly. 'But there's this girl. I think I'm in love with her.'

Lauren's jaw jutted. 'OK, could I just give you a word of advice here? This probably isn't the best time to be admitting something like that.'

'I know, I'm sorry. It's never happened to me before. I don't know what to do about it.'

'You mean she's not interested in you?'

'No.' What else could he say? Lauren didn't want to hear the whole story.

'In that case, may I suggest that the best way to get her out of your system would be to have some fun with someone else? Like, for example . . . ooh, I don't know, *me*?'

She was reaching for him again; Riley took a step back. 'Thanks, but it doesn't feel right. It wouldn't *be* right.'

'Seriously?'

'Seriously.'

'OK, now look, this is the last night of my holiday.' Lauren tossed back her long hair. 'My ex-boyfriend has a new girlfriend. They're probably at it right now. I just want to feel as if someone wants *me*.' Slightly desperately she added, 'I wouldn't say anything,

I promise. It's not as if it'd ruin your chances with whoever this girl is. No one would ever know.'

Not that he was remotely tempted to change his mind anyway, but Riley couldn't help recalling the last time he'd thought that. Until his photograph had been posted on Twitter and the truth, coming back to haunt him, had succeeded in ruining Tula's day too.

He shook his head at Lauren and said, 'I'm sorry. I just . . . can't.'

Hell hath no fury like a woman discovering you didn't want to sleep with her after all. It turned out that the words *I won't say anything, I promise* only applied if the evening ended as she'd hoped it would.

Instead, Riley found himself being ejected from the cottage to the ringing sounds of Lauren scornfully announcing: 'Bye then, so-called stud, what a shame you couldn't manage to do anything! Never mind, if you go online you can order tablets to help with that little problem of yours. Ciao!'

She'd timed it well, too, making sure it was heard by a group of passers-by. Better still, they were local, so they all knew Riley and cracked up. Which was nice of them. Especially Marnie, who, as luck would have it, worked as a receptionist at the local surgery and yelled, 'Ooh no, don't go ordering those things off the internet. Want me to book you in for an appointment tomorrow, pet? Sounds like it's something you need to get sorted out!'

Everyone might be killing themselves laughing, but that didn't mean the rumour wouldn't spread throughout St Carys in no time at all. Riley grimaced as Lauren triumphantly slammed the front door of the cottage shut behind him.

Great. No sex, no Tula and a laughing stock to boot.

What better end to the night?

Chapter 40

It had been ridiculously easy to track down Theo Pargeter on the internet. There were only three people with that name in the UK, and one of them was eighty-six years old, a retired priest living in Aberdeen.

Not likely to be him.

The second Theo Pargeter was fifteen, lived with his parents in London and was keen on skateboarding, thrash metal and hanging out with his mates at the local skate park.

Even less likely to be him.

The third and final Theo was thirty years old and ran a garden craft business on the outskirts of Bristol. The website showed what was sold there: gates, wooden and iron, outdoor furniture, stone urns, paving slabs, wall plaques, statues and water features.

On the home page were a couple of photographs taken outside the shop. One of them featured Theo. He was wearing a khaki shirt, jeans and desert boots and was half smiling for the camera with the air of someone not entirely relaxed about being photographed. Medium height, slim build, short brown hair, pretty good-looking . . . yes, it was easy to picture younger versions of this man and Sophie choosing to be with each other. Until something had happened to end the relationship, something calamitous enough to cause Sophie to steer clear of *all* men as a result.

Suicide had been mentioned, but no one had died. Had Sophie been the one who'd attempted to end her own life? And why?

Josh shuddered; the mere thought of it was enough to cause his stomach to contract with fear. What if she'd succeeded?

The only other thing he knew was that Theo hadn't physically hurt her.

Could he phone him? Just pick up the phone, ascertain that he was speaking to the Theo Pargeter who'd once been married to Sophie Wells, then ask him straight out what had happened between them?

Except how likely was it that this would get him the result he was after? Why on earth would a complete stranger tell another complete stranger such an intensely personal story over the phone?

No, this definitely wasn't the way to go. Josh took out his mobile, brought up Google maps and found the location of the shop in Bristol. It wasn't too far from the M5. He had a couple of unavoidable meetings tomorrow morning, but once they were out of the way, there was nothing to stop him from jumping in the car and driving up there himself.

He had no idea what he would say, or if he stood the remotest chance of getting an answer. But it was the kind of conversation that definitely needed to be carried out face to face.

At two o'clock the next day, Josh was getting ready to leave.

'What's this?' Dot saw the car keys in his hand. 'Where are you going?'

She sounded alarmed. He'd already decided that telling her what he was planning to do ran the risk of increasing the alarm. Not wanting to hear that confronting Sophie's ex-husband might be a terrible idea, he said casually, 'Just heading into Exeter to pick up a few things.'

'What kind of things?'

OK, now he couldn't think of *any* kind of things. 'A birthday present.'

'Whose birthday is it?'

'Seriously, what is this? Twenty questions?'

'Well anyway, you can't go,' said Dot. 'I need you here.'

'Why?'

Now it was her turn to look shifty and hesitate in search of a plausible answer. Honestly, if they'd been a couple of criminals, they'd have given themselves away in no time flat. At last Dot shrugged and said, 'I can't tell you. It's a surprise.'

'What sort of surprise?'

She shook her head. 'Now we're going round in circles. I'm just trying to do what I was asked to do and make sure you're around when . . . the thing happens. It's going to be any time now.'

Josh looked at her and wondered what *the thing* could be. His thoughts went instantly to Sophie. What if she loved him and couldn't hide her real feelings a minute longer? Never mind what had happened in the past; none of that mattered. All he needed to know was that he meant the world to her and *please* could they just be together forev—

'Oh my giddy aunt,' squealed Tula, hurtling up the steps into reception. 'There's a limo coming up the drive that's almost as *long* as the drive! Is Beyoncé coming to stay and nobody thought to tell me?'

Josh looked at Dot. 'Who is it?'

'I told you. A surprise.' Her light blue eyes sparkled with relief at not having to keep the secret any more. 'Go and see for yourself.'

OK, if there was one thing he was absolutely sure Sophie *wouldn't* do, it was turn up in a stretch limousine in order to declare her undying love for him. But just on the off chance, he followed Tula outside anyway.

Because wasn't that what made surprises surprising?

It wasn't just any old stretch limo either. Finished in silver chrome with the sun bouncing off its polished surfaces, it was blindingly bright, the kind of effect favoured by the more flamboyant look-at-meeeee Premiership footballers.

'This is so *exciting*,' breathed Tula, to the left of him. 'If it was my car, I wouldn't have blacked-out windows, though. I'd want everyone to see me in it!'

The limo slowed to a halt, its doors flew open and out leapt three people. Predictably, none of them was Sophie.

To the right of him, Dot smiled and said, 'There you go. That's why I couldn't tell you – they wanted it to be a complete surprise!'

Josh looked at Jem, Bonnie and Cal, three of the four members of Go Destry. Only Dizzy was missing. Jem's hair was even blonder, Bonnie's was much longer and Cal's, shaved at the sides, was spiky and silver-tipped. As always, they were dressed to be noticed in the kind of outfits most people wouldn't leave the house in.

Josh waited. There had been no contact between them since the day they'd sacked him as their manager. Basically, he'd neither planned on ever seeing them again nor expected it to happen.

The awkward little moment was broken by Jem breaking into the kind of skyscraper-heeled run that could so easily have resulted in a broken ankle. She stopped less than a metre away from him, her huge sapphire-blue eyes swimming with tears, and said in a voice trembling with emotion, 'Oh God, Josh, you have no idea. We've missed you *so much*.'

It was all very Disney. Josh was perfectly well acquainted with Jem's ability to cry on cue. But he did the decent thing and greeted them as if they were old friends. Then, because all eyes were upon them and Griff was now barking and leaping up and down like a mad thing on springs, he ushered them inside the hotel and into the empty drawing room.

Ironically, the room that had been the cause of his first-ever encounter with Sophie.

So much for his trip to Bristol this afternoon; he had a feeling that was no longer going to happen.

'OK, cards on the table,' Jem announced; out of the three of them, she'd always been the one who'd done most of the talking. 'We're sorry. We messed up big-time. We thought we were doing the right thing and we were so, so wrong. Our new management guys suck.'

'I could have told you all that.' Josh shrugged. 'In fact I did. But you didn't listen.'

Bonnie said, 'You're, like, a zillion times nicer than them. They treat us like total idiots.'

Sometimes no reply was necessary. A look sufficed.

Well, it would suffice if the people on the receiving end didn't think so highly of themselves that the possibility of irony wouldn't even occur to them.

'*They're* the ones who are idiots,' Jem exclaimed. 'They're making all these terrible decisions, forcing us to do stupid things . . . we're going to end up a laughing stock!'

'Right.'

'You should hear the tracks they want us to record for our next album,' Cal joined in. 'It's all so lame, like music for little kids. And the prototypes for our new dolls are just crappy. Mine makes me look like a complete *dick*.'

'That's very sad.' Josh eyed them gravely. 'But I don't know why you're telling me this. You need to speak to your management about it.'

'Except they don't listen.' Bonnie fixed him with a pleading gaze. 'Not like you used to.'

'OK, so here's the thing,' said Jem. 'We don't want them looking after us any more. We want you.'

'We're *so* sorry.' Bonnie clasped her hands together as if she were praying. 'For everything. All we're asking is for you to take us back.'

'And we'll work so hard for you,' Cal said earnestly. 'Swear to God, no more messing about and backchat and giving you a hard time. None of that stuff.'

'We didn't appreciate you before.' Jem looked as if she might be about to burst into tears; her bottom lip was doing its quavery thing. 'But that's because we were stupid and took you for granted. We wouldn't make that mistake again.'

'Where's Dizzy?' said Josh, though he had an inkling.

Bonnie shook her head. 'He's just taking things easy, having a bit of a rest . . .'

'He's in rehab.' Cal was blunt. 'Drying out, getting himself clean. But he's going to do it. And he wants you back, same as the rest of us.'

'We've stopped all that too,' Jem added. 'No more messing ourselves up. It'll be a fresh start. We want to come back bigger and better and stronger than before. And with you managing us, we can do that, we know we can.' Her eyes lit up at the thought of it. 'Go Destry rides again!'

'Look, it's nice of you to make the offer. I'm flattered.' Josh surveyed their hopeful faces. 'But I'm not interested. I've moved on. I'm living back here now and—'

'Not so fast,' said Cal. 'What d'ya think of the limo?'

'It's very . . . silver.' Well, it was better than saying it looked like a giant toaster on wheels.

'It's yours.' Cal nodded his spiky head in triumph. 'You can have it. And it's called chrome-wrapped, not silver. Anyhow, if you come back to us, it's all yours.'

Josh envisaged the chaos he would cause attempting to manoeuvre the ultra-stretched limo through the narrow cobbled streets of St Carys. It would be like attempting to fit a brontosaurus into a rabbit hutch.

Then again, if he went back to managing Go Destry, he wouldn't be here in St Carys, would he?

He looked at Cal. 'You don't own the limo. It's hired.' Apart from anything else, it had been driven down here by a uniformed chauffeur.

'I know that. But on the way down, we found out how much it'd cost us to buy it.'

'I live here now. I'm helping to run this hotel.'

'But we need you,' said Jem. 'We really do. Even if it's just for the next couple of years . . .'

'We flew all this way to ask you,' Bonnie added. 'We made the effort so you'd know how serious we are.'

'And we've changed.' Jem's heart-shaped face was both saintly and penitent. 'We're better people now. I guess we were kind of idiots before, but we've learned our lesson.'

Josh nodded. 'I'm sure you have, but the answer's still no.'

Cal said, 'But—'

'OK, listen to me.' Jem's voice rose above the others' clamour of protests. 'Don't say no yet. You need time to think about it. We're gonna give you forty-eight hours, how about that? And after you've considered all the angles, *then* you can tell us what you decide.'

'What will you do in the meantime?'

'Just hang out here, I guess. Chill for a couple of days.'

'And where will you stay?' said Josh.

'This is your hotel, right? We'll stay here.'

Josh silently marvelled at their assumption that there would be rooms available; it wouldn't occur to them that they might need to book ahead. Luckily, there'd been a cancellation.

'I'll need to check with reception. You girls will have to share,' he told them.

'Cool, I guess we can do that. Just like in the old days.' Bonnie's smile was bright and brave. 'When we were poor.'

'Is there much to do here?' Cal was gazing out of the window, sounding dubious. 'Not exactly Caesar's Palace, is it?'

Jem gave him a sharp nudge. 'Shut up. This is Josh's place.' She turned back and said cheerily, 'So we'll do that, shall we? Ask that old woman on reception to fix us up with a couple of rooms? It'll be great!'

They were evidently at a bit of a loose end; with their lead singer tucked away in rehab, there wasn't a great deal else the rest of them could do. Go Destry without Dizzy was like the Rolling Stones without Mick.

'Fine, then,' said Josh. 'But the old woman on reception is my grandmother. And if you really want to live until the weekend, it might help to know that her name is Dot.'

Chapter 41

Summer days didn't get hotter than this. Well, maybe they did, but not here in Cornwall. On the crowded beach, Sophie was listening to an overexcited Tula and doing her best to conceal her own emotions behind her sunglasses.

Basically her own emotions were in turmoil. Hearing about Go Destry's arrival in St Carys and the offer they'd made Josh had given her quite a jolt. She now knew how she felt about him . . . the feelings were too strong to ignore. But acting upon them was something else entirely; breaking her own rules and getting properly involved . . . well, she still couldn't allow it to happen.

Which meant that Josh leaving St Carys would in theory be an excellent scenario. With him safely out of harm's way, she would no longer have to face the temptation of seeing and interacting with him on a regular basis. Which would make life a whole lot easier.

Then again, the idea of *not* seeing him filled her with panic. Just knowing that he was around made her feel better. He was like a drug she wasn't sure she could live without. Which in turn obviously meant it would be for the best if he *were* to move back to California.

Oh God.

'Honestly, they're hilarious; it's so weird having them staying here in the hotel.' Tula was far more entertained by the arrival of Go Destry. 'You'd think they'd have breakfast in their rooms, but they didn't, they came down and sat out on the terrace. Everyone was staring and taking photos of them!'

'Fancy that.' Sophie's mind was still on Josh.

'And they've hired a couple of bodyguards. You know, to keep the fans under control.'

'So what do you think's going to happen?' Sophie meant did Josh seem likely to accept their offer and head back to the US.

'Well I lent them the hotel's badminton set. Cal said they're going to be coming down here as soon as the girls have finished their reiki healing.'

'What do they need reiki healing for?'

'Jet lag.'

Jet lag. Of course. There was a smudge of Ambre Solaire on Sophie's sunglasses. She took them off and began cleaning them with a corner of her beach towel. The next moment, glancing up, she saw someone looking at her.

It only took a moment to place the girl. Her name was Alice, and she was the slightly overweight teenager who had been so eager to pose for those modelling-type photos at Hannah and Owen's wedding in Launceston the other week.

'Oh hello!' Sophie waved up at her.

'Hi.' Alice had just paid a visit to the café and was holding three drinks cans.

'Did you see the photos I took of you? I sent them to Hannah and asked her to pass them on.'

'Yeah, thanks, I did. They were nice.' She hesitated, looking a bit awkward, as if wondering whether to say something else. 'Can I ask you a question?'

Bless her, such a sweet girl. 'Of course you can.'

'Do you really think I could be a professional model?' Alice's cheeks had turned pink. 'I mean, you can be honest.'

Oh. That question. Sophie said carefully, 'Well the trouble with models is they're supposed to be tall.'

'And pretty,' said Alice. 'And thin.'

OK, may as well cut to the chase. Sophie said gently, 'What happened?'

'Well, you were right. It wasn't a proper model agency. Their phone number stopped working and the website's not there any more.' She puffed out her cheeks. 'I didn't know people did things like that, but it turns out they do.'

'Oh dear, poor you. And what a rotten way to find out.'

'I know. My nan and grandad said it didn't matter about the money. But I just felt so bad for them. And so *stupid*.' Having decided to confide in her, Alice was evidently now finding it hard to stop. 'I can't believe I really thought I'd been spotted by a talent scout from a real agency. My friends said the same thing,' she went on. 'Turns out they'd been laughing their heads off behind my back because they're really beautiful and like they said, why would someone like me ever get chosen to be a model when I'm not nearly as pretty as them?'

Tula, who'd been listening, snorted and said, 'Charming!'

'Well they don't sound like very good friends to me,' said Sophie. 'I'd think they were the kind you could probably do without.'

Alice was flushing again. 'They don't mean it. It's just the way they are.'

'Honestly?' Tula's dark eyes glittered with disdain. 'They sound like complete bitches.'

Alice shrugged helplessly. 'We're all in the same class at school, though. There isn't really anyone else to be friends with.' As she said it, she glanced down towards the water and Sophie realised that these were the friends she'd come here with today. Two girls in multicoloured micro bikinis were emerging from the sea, peering around in search of someone.

And yes, they were skinnier and prettier than Alice.

'I'd better get back to them. They'll be wanting their drinks.' Alice indicated the cans she'd just bought from the café. 'Thanks anyway.'

'Listen.' Sophie longed to reassure her. 'If you ask me, you're a much nicer person than they are.'

Alice looked anxious. 'You won't say anything to them, will you? Promise?'

'Don't worry, of course we won't.' Sophie shook her head. 'It was good to see you again.' She smiled up at the teenager in her crumpled pink T-shirt and too-tight denim shorts. 'Bye, Alice. Have a nice day.'

'Here they come,' announced Tula forty minutes later. Sitting up like a meerkat, she waved excitedly at the little group making their way down the steps to the beach.

Sophie twisted round to watch them: three famous young Americans and their minders, all hyper-aware of the attention they were garnering with their arrival.

Would they end up taking Josh away from here? From *her*? Who knew? They'd already attempted to sweeten the deal with a stretch limo; what was to stop them making an even more extravagant offer he couldn't refuse?

'Hey, there she is!' Spotting Tula, Cal changed course and headed over towards them. He was lithe, tanned and swaggery, wearing a white cowboy hat, mirrored shades and electric-yellow board shorts.

As you do.

'Hi.' Tula was beaming, thrilled to have been singled out for attention. 'Did you bring the badminton stuff down with you?'

'Sure did.' He swung an imaginary racquet. 'I've never played this game before. What are the feathery things called again? Shuttledicks?'

'I told you what they were called.' Tula gave him a look.

'You did.' He broke into a grin. 'And you said it's played like tennis, either two players or four players.'

'That's right.'

'But there's three of us. Me and the girls. So we're gonna need someone else to make up the numbers.'

Practically everyone on the beach was watching them now. Including, thirty metres away, Alice and her so-called friends from school. Sophie heard Tula say, 'Well, if you're desperate . . .' And then she heard Cal say, 'You wanna play? Cool, let's do it.'

'Hang on.' Sophie reached for Tula's wrist before she could scramble to her feet. 'Cal, can I ask you something?'

He looked dubious. 'What?'

Sophie decided to take the plunge; it was a long shot, but wouldn't it be amazing if it came off? 'You could do something that would be so brilliant. Don't look now, but there's a girl over to your right, and if you asked her to play badminton, you'd make her year. More than a year. You'd make her whole life.' She gave Tula's wrist a squeeze. 'Wouldn't he?'

Tula was looking like a toddler having her Christmas presents snatched away.

'Please.' Sophie looked at her.

'Which girl?' said Cal.

'Teenager. Pink T-shirt, denim shorts, sitting on a green beach towel. Be discreet,' said Sophie.

Cal turned and slowly scanned the entire beach, as if admiring the view. Turning back, he murmured, 'OK, I see her. Couldn't I ask one of her hot friends instead?'

'No, you couldn't.' How had she guessed he'd say this? Sophie shook her head.

'But the others are way prettier.'

'That's the whole point; it's what they'd expect you to do. Anything good that happens, they just take it for granted.' She was doing her best to make him understand. 'But if you ask the one in the pink T-shirt, she'll feel better about herself for the next fifty years.'

Cal removed his mirrored shades and surveyed her speculatively through narrowed eyes.

'Did Josh ask you to do this? Is it some kind of secret test, to see if I pass?'

Sophie looked at Tula. Tula looked back at her. Sophie returned her attention to Cal and said, 'No.'

She was saying no, but making it sound as if the answer was actually yes.

Cal assimilated this information for a couple of seconds. Finally he said, 'OK. Leave it with me.'

'Be subtle,' said Tula.

Together they watched him turn and make his way back to join Bonnie and Jem.

'Thanks,' Sophie murmured.

''S okay. Poor kid. I bet she feels like I always did around Imi's friends. But worse.'

'That's what I thought.'

They watched as the minders set up the badminton net. To give Cal his due, he did a good job of casually looking around before wandering over to Alice and her companions. After chatting to them for a couple of minutes, he said something to Alice that caused the other two girls to stiffen in disbelief.

'Oh yes,' Tula whispered triumphantly. 'Bingo.'

And while Alice finished double-checking that it wasn't a joke and he really did mean her, the expressions on her friends' faces said it all. Reaching out a tanned arm, Cal helped her to her feet. Then he led her over to join his fellow band members, who greeted her with cheery enthusiasm and handed her the fourth badminton racquet.

'I feel like a proud mum,' Sophie said twenty minutes later. Alice was acquitting herself surprisingly well on the makeshift badminton court. She was also visibly having the time of her life, whilst a short distance away her friends sat with their cans of drink, hunched over, bristling with jealousy and pretending not to watch.

When the game was over, Alice said something to Cal and he beckoned her friends over to join them. They posed for photos together, using their mobile phones, and chatted for a minute or two before the members of Go Destry each gave Alice a hug and a kiss, then left the beach.

Half an hour later, Alice paused beside Sophie and Tula on her way to the café again. Without preamble she said, 'Did you make him do it?'

'We didn't *make* him do it.' Sophie shrugged. 'Just wondered if he'd like to.'

Alice beamed. 'That's so nice of you. Thanks. This has been the best day of my life.'

Chapter 42

Heavy traffic on the M5 meant it had taken three hours to reach Bristol. Josh had spent the entire journey thinking about Sophie and wondering what he was going to say when he came face to face with her ex-husband.

Assuming that Theo Pargeter *was* her ex-husband. For all he knew, they could still be married.

Anyway, almost there. Yesterday's planned visit had been scuppered by the arrival of Bonnie, Jem and Cal. Which had been frustrating at the time, but never mind. That was then, this was now.

Less than a kilometre to go. In the glove compartment, Josh's phone beeped with a message. He carried on down the road, then turned left at the mini roundabout.

And there it was, the entrance to the business, looking just as it had on the website. Rather than drive in through the gates, he parked outside and climbed out of the car. Took a few deep breaths. What if Theo refused to talk to him when he learned why he was here?

Once through the gates, he saw that there was a small house to the left, the shop to the right. There were no cars in the parking area and the high fence surrounding the outdoor garden was padlocked shut.

The shop wasn't open either. A handwritten note taped to the door announced: *Sorry, due to unforeseen circumstances we are closed today. Open again as usual tomorrow. Apologies for any inconvenience caused. T.P.*

Inconvenience? Any inconvenience caused? Why ever would he think he might be causing any inconvenience?

Shit.

Just to be sure, Josh crossed the deserted parking area to the house and rang the doorbell. No reply.

If he'd come yesterday, Theo Pargeter would have been here. But he hadn't, he'd come today instead.

Oh well, nothing to be done about it. Hopefully the M5 would be clearer on the way home.

Back in the car, his phone beeped plaintively again like an abandoned baby bird. Josh leaned across, took it out of the glove compartment and saw that Cal had sent him an email. There was a photo attached. He opened it and stared at the screen. For some utterly bizarre reason, Cal had chosen to send him a photo of himself on the beach with an arm draped casually around the shoulders of a short, plump teenager whose pink beaming face exactly matched her too-tight T-shirt.

Cal had written: *See? And she wasn't even pretty!*

Josh shook his head. God only knew what he meant by that. He'd better not have slept with her and be boasting about it.

Not that Cal's behaviour was his concern any more. Go Destry might have given him forty-eight hours to come to a decision, but he had no intention of taking them back. Putting the band out of his mind, he switched from emails to the calendar app on his phone. So many meetings, so much on; who knew when he'd be able to get up here to Bristol again.

Well this was turning into a pretty weird evening. When Tula had finished her shift, she hadn't expected to be propositioned by Marguerite Marshall and brought here to Moor Court.

'I asked Dot. She says you're a hard worker, good with people, conscientious.'

'Ye-ees.' Tula nodded cautiously; was she about to be

headhunted? And just how much of a nerve did Marguerite have, asking Dot to recommend someone before attempting to steal her away from the hotel?

'Not full-time,' said Marguerite, answering that unspoken question. 'As and when. If people are coming here for meetings, small parties, whatever. I need someone to take their coats, organise the drinks, pass around canapés, that kind of thing. And be charming to the guests, of course. Good impressions are *so* important. Dot tells me your shifts are pretty flexible, so do you think you'd be interested? Because if you aren't, I'll ask someone else. Twelve pounds an hour,' she added.

'Brilliant. Definitely interested.' Tula nodded vigorously. 'Extra money's always good. I'd love to do it.'

'Excellent.' Marguerite gave a nod of satisfaction and said, 'Now, let's have a drink to celebrate.'

That had been over an hour ago, and she was still here. Marguerite had been asking all sorts of questions about her life, from upbringing to school days, from the different jobs she'd done to the various boyfriends she'd won and lost over the years.

'Can I ask you something?' said Tula. 'Am I being interrogated?'

Marguerite smiled slightly. 'Sorry, is that what I'm doing? We writers are nosy people. We like to know everything.'

Tula brightened. 'Are you going to put me in a book?'

'I very much doubt it. You're not interesting enough.'

'Thanks.'

'Just being honest. The female characters I write about are strong. They always get exactly what they want.'

'I've just got what I wanted.' Tula grinned. 'Another job.'

'Touché.' Amused, Marguerite topped up their glasses. 'Come on then, tell me some more about you.'

Over the limit herself, Marguerite had called Riley and asked him to drive Tula back to the hotel. When he returned, she said, 'That was quick.'

'Dropped her off, drove straight back.' Riley shrugged. 'Doesn't take long.'

'I thought you might have spun it out a bit, laid on the charm. Like you usually do.'

'I've tried. It didn't work. You know that.'

He'd told her, but he still hadn't told her why. Marguerite watched him examine a fraying hole in the sleeve of his favourite faded blue sweatshirt. 'I like her very much; she's a lovely girl. I'm sure you could win her over, you know.' Encouragingly she added, 'And we'll be seeing more of her now she's going to be helping me out here.'

There was a troubled look in his eyes. 'So it's all part of your grand plan, is it? Maybe you could go one step further and pay her to be my girlfriend.'

'Oh darling, I'm just trying to help.' The nicer Tula had turned out to be, the guiltier Marguerite had felt. Riley was normally so sunny-natured; she'd never seen him like this before.

'Well you can't help.' He shrugged. 'It isn't going to happen.'

'And it's all my fault.'

'What?' His gaze narrowed.

'I know why she won't take you seriously. I asked her and she told me.'

'Oh. Right.' He exhaled. 'It doesn't matter.'

'It does, though.' She couldn't bear to see him hiding his feelings. 'I can see what it's doing to you, how important this girl is.'

'Hey, don't worry. I'm me. I'll find someone else.'

Bravado. Did he think she was stupid? Marguerite took a deep breath and said, 'If you want, you can tell her.'

Riley froze for a moment. Then he slowly shook his head. 'No. We can't do that.'

'But if she matters that much to you . . .'

'Tula can't keep secrets. She told me so herself. She said she hates it, it's too stressful, and sooner or later things end up accidentally slipping out.'

'Oh,' said Marguerite.

285

'But thanks for offering.' He gave her a crooked smile.

'Oh darling. I do love you. So much.'

'I know. I love you too. Don't worry about it.' As he headed for the office to start work, he added, 'Really, I'll be fine.'

Marguerite watched him go with a heavy, guilty heart. If she hadn't known him so well, she might even have believed him.

Chapter 43

It was the bright corkscrew curls that did it; otherwise Sophie might never have made the connection.

The baby she never would have recognised, chiefly because he was no longer a baby; two years on, he was a big-eyed toddler in a turquoise all-in-one swimsuit, sitting at one of the tables outside the café eating an ice cream sundae. His older sister, who must now be five or six, was throwing bits of bread roll to the sparrows hopping around the table. She was wearing a green polka-dot sundress over her swimming costume and her red-gold ringlets gleamed in the sunshine, bouncing around her shoulders as she flung another piece of bread across the cobbles.

Yes, it was definitely them, presumably back on holiday again with their parents. The father was finishing a cup of coffee and putting away his phone. The three of them were getting ready to leave the café; now he was dropping a couple of pound coins on to a saucer for the waitress. The moment to act was either now or never; if she didn't say something, they'd be gone.

'Hello!' Sophie approached the children's father. 'OK, this might sound weird, but I've just recognised your daughter. I took a photo of your children on the beach a couple of years ago and I'd love you to have a copy of it.'

The man eyed her warily. 'I don't think we're interested, thanks.'

'Honestly, though, it's a brilliant photo. If I say so myself. I'm a photographer . . .' Rummaging in her bag for a business card, she belatedly understood his lack of enthusiasm. 'Oh, I'm not trying to sell you anything! I don't want any money. I just thought you might like it . . . I didn't expect to ever see you again. I love the photo so much it's on my living-room wall. I live just up there.' She pointed to the narrow street behind them. 'Or if you'd rather just give me an email address, I could send you a copy of it.' Or maybe not. She shrugged and gave up. 'But it's OK, you don't have to if you don't want to. You've probably got enough photos anyway.'

'Am I in it?' The girl with the ringlets sounded interested.

'You are. You're doing something very funny and a tiny bit naughty,' said Sophie. 'You're putting a bit of seaweed on your brother's head.'

'Am I?' Delighted, she turned to her father. 'I want to see the photo, Daddy. Can we go?'

He smiled at her, then at Sophie. 'I thought you were selling me something. Sorry about that. I'm too suspicious by far. If the offer still stands, we'd love to see the photo. And thank you. It does sound great.'

His name was Matt, she discovered on the short walk up the hill to her flat. The children were Georgina and Jamie, and this was the sixth day of their week-long holiday. Tomorrow they were heading back to London.

'So I found you just in time.' Sophie used the key on her silver bangle to open the front door. 'Now, just up these stairs . . . come on, sweetie, hold my hand . . . and here we are. Look, there's the photograph. And that's you!'

'Wow,' said Georgina. 'Hahaha, look at me putting seaweed on Jamie's head. And he doesn't know I'm doing it, hahahahaha!'

'And there's Bingo.' Matt pointed to the little dog with the naughty look in his eye as he made a grab for the last sandwich on the plate.

'He's our dog,' Georgina told Sophie. 'He likes sandwiches.'

'He likes any kind of food,' Matt said drily.

'And that's Mummy's foot there.' Georgina's arm shot up to

point to the pedicured toes in the bottom right of the picture. 'Look, Daddy! It's Mummy's foot!'

Matt nodded. 'Yes, it is.'

Sophie had briefly been tempted to Photoshop the foot out of the picture, but had finally left it in for balance . . . and because Photoshop always felt like cheating. She was also wondering where Mummy was right now; she could be sunbathing on the beach or back in London. Perhaps they were divorced. They hadn't mentioned her whereabouts and she certainly wasn't going to ask.

'Was Mummy watching me put the seaweed on Jamie's head?' Georgina regarded her with interest.

'I don't know. Maybe.' As Sophie said it, she saw Matt glance down at his daughter, checking she was OK.

'Mummy's dead,' said Georgina, staring once more at the photograph on the wall.

Oh.

Matt, who was holding Jamie on his left hip, rested his free hand on his daughter's head.

'How awful. I'm so sorry,' said Sophie. 'That's very sad.'

'We miss her very much.' Matt acknowledged her words with a brief nod. 'It happened just over a year ago.' Ruffling Georgina's bright ringlets, he said, 'Still getting used to her not being here with us, aren't we?'

Georgina nodded too. 'It's nice seeing Mummy's toes.'

'Well now I'm even more glad I recognised you,' said Sophie, 'so I can give you your photograph.' And reaching past them, she lifted the simply framed print down from its place on the wall. She turned to Matt. 'Here you go.'

'Thank you. Very much indeed.' He inclined his head. 'Only one problem: we don't have the car with us and I have to carry Jamie back to the house we're renting.'

'Well I could bring it over . . .'

'No, no, I can come by later and pick it up. Would you be around this evening if I called in?'

Sophie nodded; was it wrong to be wondering how his wife

289

had died? She smiled at him and said, 'No problem, I'm not going anywhere. Call round any time tonight.'

Matt returned shortly before eight o'clock, changed into dark trousers and a bottle-green shirt. His freshly washed hair was combed back from his face and he'd just shaved. He was also wearing nice cologne.

'OK, so here's the thing.' Wasting no time, he launched straight in. 'We're down here with my parents, who are babysitting tonight. As you can imagine, it hasn't been the easiest of weeks. Georgina was telling them about you, and my mum said why didn't I ask if you'd like to go out for something to eat this evening. Not on a date . . . I'm nowhere near ready for anything like that . . . but just as a way of thanking you for the print.' He paused, grimacing slightly. 'So I'm asking you, but feel free to say no if you don't want to. Believe me, I'll understand. It's hardly the most enticing offer you can think of.'

He'd stopped, run out of breath. Her heart sinking, Sophie said, 'Um . . . right . . .' This was when she really needed to be able to think up some kind of excuse, the perfect reason why she couldn't go out to dinner with this man.

'I know. God, I'm sorry. My mother just thinks I could do with getting out of the house, spending a couple of hours away from them. It's OK, though, I can see what you're thinking. Really, it's fine.'

Oh dear, what a shame, I have to stay in and wash my hair . . .

Oh what bad timing, I have to work tonight . . .

Oh no, so sorry, I've got friends coming over, they'll be here any minute now . . .

'Let's have dinner,' said Sophie. It was no good; this poor, poor man, how could she do it to him? Who would have the heart to turn him down?

By eleven o'clock, the restaurant was emptying fast.

'And you managed to stay awake the whole evening,' said

Matt. 'That's going above and beyond the call of duty. Well done you.'

Sophie grinned; it hadn't been the ordeal she'd expected. He'd promised not to embarrass her in public by bursting into tears, and he hadn't. As also promised, there'd been no flirting of any kind. Matt was still far too entrenched in his grief. His wife's name had been Louisa, and he'd thought they'd spend the rest of their lives together. Then she'd become ill and died. There hadn't been any more details than that, and Sophie hadn't asked. Now Matt was struggling to keep things going for the sake of Georgina and Jamie. Apparently one day he would begin to feel something vaguely approaching normal again, but at the moment that was as elusive as crawling towards a mirage in a desert. Every day was an effort. The bank where he worked had been great, but he sensed that some of his colleagues were starting to lose patience with him, not because they were horrible but simply because they didn't understand. They just wanted their old friend back to the way he'd been before.

'Anyway, thanks for keeping me company.' Having paid the bill, Matt said, 'We'd better get out of here. Looks like they're ready to close up.'

He'd driven over earlier, leaving his car parked outside Sophie's flat, and they'd walked down to the restaurant on the harbourside. Now they made their way back up the narrow cobbled lane.

'It's been a good night,' said Matt.

Sophie smiled. 'It has.'

'Isn't it weird? Tomorrow we drive back to London and the chances are that we'll never see each other again.' He paused. 'Could be why it's been so easy to talk to you.'

'Probably.'

'You haven't asked me how Louisa died.'

'Not up to me to ask that. It's none of my business.' *Oh, unless you murdered her . . .*

But he hadn't, she knew that. Poor man.

'Friends and family know. I've never told a stranger before.'

They were standing outside her flat now. Matt turned to her, a bleak look on his face.

'You don't need to tell me.' Louisa had been ill, then she'd died. Up until now, Sophie had assumed it was some form of cancer. But would that really be so difficult to say?

'I want to tell you.' She could see the tension in his jaw. 'You realise I'm using you to practise on. The first time has to be the worst.' Matt paused, then said in a rush, 'She had postnatal depression. I didn't know how bad it was. And then she killed herself. Oh God . . .' His voice began to wobble and crack. 'OK, said it now. She committed suicide, jumped off a bridge and left us, and I *know* it only happened because she was ill, but you can't imagine how it feels, knowing your wife would rather be dead than stay with you.' He shook his head, correcting himself. 'With *us*.'

Chapter 44

Dot and Antoine had bumped into some of Dot's old friends in the hotel bar and were busy catching up with each other's news, so Josh had volunteered to bring Griff out for his late-evening walk. They'd made their way along the beach and back, taking advantage of the tide being out. For the last forty minutes he'd been throwing Griff's ball across the wet sand and Griff had bounded after it, never tiring of playing his favourite game.

Now Josh was wishing he'd bribed one of the hotel staff to do the job instead.

OK, not quite true. Knowing had to be better than not knowing, surely.

But the sight had hit him like a punch in the stomach from a pro. There was Sophie, standing outside her flat fifty metres away, locked in a clearly emotional embrace with another man. Her hair gleamed pale gold in the reflected glow of the street lamp overhead. The man who was holding her was taller, darker and no one Josh recognised. It wasn't a normal hug between acquaintances, that much was obvious. They weren't letting go of each other.

And now, finally and with reluctance, they were. Words were exchanged; their heads remained close together, his hands still rested on Sophie's arms. Griff, suddenly realising who it was, pricked up his ears and let out a whimper of excited recognition.

'*Sshh*,' whispered Josh, before the dog could break into a giveaway volley of barks.

Together they watched as Sophie slipped the bangle off her wrist, fitted the key into the lock and opened the front door. The next moment she and the man had disappeared inside. Then the light went on in the flat upstairs and Sophie appeared silhouetted in the window, reaching up to pull the curtains closed.

Right, well that told him all he needed to know. Josh turned and gave Griff's lead a tug to show him they were heading home.

Fuck. Just what he hadn't needed to see.

Also, who *was* the man spending the night in Sophie's flat?

'Sorry about that.' Matt blew his nose on a tissue. 'So much for promising not to be an embarrassment. What a wuss.'

Sophie shook her head. 'You're not a wuss. Your wife died. It's allowed.'

'Haven't cried like that in months. Pretty brave of you, letting me into your flat.' He attempted a smile, took a mouthful of coffee and grimaced because it was now tepid.

'Do you feel better?'

'I think so. A bit. It's the guilt.' Matt sighed. 'The shame. The endless wondering if I said or did something to cause it . . . just one stupid, careless thing that tipped her over the edge.' He paused. 'And knowing that other people are wondering it too.'

Sophie said nothing. She couldn't tell him about Theo; the very last thing he needed was for her to try and compete. And how could she, anyway? His wife had died, leaving him alone to bring up two children. She couldn't begin to comprehend how that felt. All she understood was the guilt and the shame, coupled with the hideous inescapable knowledge that she most certainly *had* done something to cause her own husband to want to end his life.

'I'm seeing a grief counsellor,' Matt went on. 'I told him I wished Louisa had been killed in a car crash. Anything else would have been better than this.'

'Because then you wouldn't have had to feel responsible? You probably still would, though.' Sophie shrugged. 'One way or another you'd have found something to feel guilty about. It's what people do.'

Another wry smile. 'He said that too.'

'You can't see it now, but things will get easier. Eventually. Sorry,' said Sophie. 'I bet when people say that it just makes you want to stab them.'

'Sometimes. Not you, though. And I know.' Matt grimaced. 'There's no magic pill. I just have to get through it. My mother says she knows I can't imagine it now, but one day I'll meet someone else, fall in love again, maybe even get married . . .' He was shaking his head at the seeming impossibility of the idea.

'She's right.' Sophie's throat tightened. 'It'll happen. One day.'

Oh God, listen to me. What a hypocrite.

He left shortly after that, heroically finishing his cold coffee and thanking her again for listening to him. They exchanged another brief hug, she gave him the framed print and he carried it out to the car.

Sophie stood on the doorstep and waved as he drove off down the narrow street. Poor Matt. And what a lot of rubbish she'd told him. That was the thing about platitudes: they were easy to say, far less easy to put into practice.

Look at me, four years down the line and still completely unable to move on. What a pity I can't take my own advice.

The following morning Bonnie, Jem and Cal came to see Josh in his office.

It was decision time.

'OK, we've stuck to our side of the bargain.' Cal had his charming face on. 'We came all this way to see you, yeah? So you know how important this is to us. But we haven't hassled you, have we? We've stepped back and given you the time and space to, like, make up your mind.'

'Most generous of you,' Josh murmured.

They gazed at him uncertainly; getting to grips with the British sense of humour had always been beyond them.

'We've been nice to everyone.' Mindful of the time he'd called them ill-mannered spoilt brats, Bonnie flashed her ultra-white smile. 'Even the staff.'

'The whole time we've been here,' Jem chimed in. 'Nice nice nice, signing stuff, posing for photos, even when people were being really annoying. We've been, like, so *patient* with them.'

'Sounds like you're reformed characters. That's great,' said Josh. 'Good to know. Well done.'

'So?' Cal couldn't contain himself a moment longer.

'So what?'

'We want you to manage us again, man. Will you do it?'

Josh looked at them for a moment. Then he shook his head. 'No.'

'Why not? We came all this *way.*'

'That was your idea, not mine. You didn't have to come over,' said Josh. 'Could have just asked me in a phone call.'

'And you would have said no.'

'Yes.' He shrugged. 'I'd have said no.'

Cal's eyes narrowed. 'Why?'

'Because I've been there, done that, don't need to do it all over again. I like it better here.'

'Is there anything we can do to change your mind?' Bonnie's face had fallen; she looked as if she might burst into tears.

Feeling sorry for her, but not that sorry, Josh said, 'Afraid not.'

'Oh for Chrissake, I fucking knew it.' Cal aimed a vicious kick at the waste-paper basket next to the desk. 'You selfish fucking *bastard.*'

It hadn't taken him long to revert to his old ways. Faintly amused because it was no longer his problem, Josh pointed to Cal and said, 'That, too.'

'You think you're such a smartarse, don't you? Well you can kiss goodbye to the chrome limo,' Cal snarled. '*Loser.*'

'Can I? Really?' Josh raised an eyebrow. 'Thank God for that.'

Chapter 45

Fresh flowers had been laid on Aurora's grave. Top-of-the-range ones, at that. No prizes for guessing who'd put them there.

Lawrence quelled the immature urge to hide them behind the black granite headstone. The elegant arrangement of creamy calla lilies, perfect roses and pale exotic orchids put his own modest offering to shame. Which had perhaps been the intention.

But they were Antoine's style rather than Aurora's. The reason Lawrence picked flowers from the garden was because home-grown flowers were what she'd liked best. An exuberant mix of colours, shapes and sizes bundled gloriously together and spilling out of their stone vase. Friendly flowers rather than the severe, better-than-you, too-perfect kind.

Bending down, Lawrence moved the other arrangement a couple of inches to the left and lifted last week's dying bunch out of the vase. By the time he'd finished disposing of them, fetching fresh water from the tap at the far end of the graveyard and arranging today's offering of daisies, forget-me-nots, hollyhocks, gentians and foxgloves, he was no longer alone.

'Hello,' said Antoine.

'Hi.' Lawrence turned to acknowledge his presence before making further adjustments to the pink and purple foxgloves. It was unlikely to be a chance encounter; this section of the grave-yard was clearly visible from the end window on the second-floor landing of the hotel. At a guess, Antoine had spotted him and come down here to speak to him for some reason.

'Do you still miss her?'

For a split second, Lawrence thought he meant Dot. Then he realised . . . of course Antoine was talking about Aurora.

'Yes.' He nodded; either way, the answer would have been the same.

'I left those.' Antoine indicated the lavish arrangement swathed in cellophane.

'I guessed. Very nice.' See? He could be polite.

'Yours are charming too.' There was a fractional pause before the word charming.

'I know,' said Lawrence.

'It's been wonderful, getting to know Dot. She's an extraordinary person.'

Lawrence nodded briefly; he knew that too.

'In fact I'm taking her to Paris tomorrow. She doesn't even know this yet. It's a surprise.'

'Well, Paris is a great city.' Seriously, how did Antoine *expect* him to react?

'But of course. And Dot deserves a treat. She works hard.'

'Will she want to go? Who's going to run the hotel?'

'Don't worry, I've cleared it with Josh. He says it's fine.'

'OK. Well, that's good.'

'And don't worry about Dot either. I'll treat her like a princess.' A strategic pause. 'You should know, Lawrence, that my intentions towards her are serious. I would never hurt her.'

Unlike me, you mean.

'Right.' What else could he say? Lawrence realised that his short fingernails were digging into his clenched palms. Straightening up from the flowers, he looked Antoine in the eye and said, 'Well, have a nice time.'

As he walked away, he heard Antoine behind him say silkily, 'Thank you, I know we will.'

★   ★   ★

'Tula.' Josh paused at the reception desk, where she was helping out. 'OK to hold the fort for a bit? I'm taking Griff out for a walk.' He held up his phone. 'Any problems, just give me a call.'

'No problem, will do. Ah, wasn't it romantic this morning?' Tula said dreamily. 'I can't stop thinking about it. The look on Dot's face when she found out.'

'I know.' Josh smiled; it may have been orchestrated for maximum effect, but that was clearly Antoine's way. He'd made sure plenty of people were around to witness the moment he'd told Dot to pack a case and make sure she didn't forget her passport because they were off to Paris.

'Oh my word.' Dot's blue eyes had widened as she'd realised Josh was in on it. 'I can't believe it . . . I've never been whisked away to Paris before! I've never been whisked away *anywhere*.'

'Then that is a travesty,' Antoine had pronounced. 'And I'm very glad to be able to redress it. This shall be the first of many whisks away, I promise.'

An over-the-top declaration, but undoubtedly romantic.

Josh collected Griff, clipped the lead to his collar and was about to leave when Tula called out, 'Ooh, you wouldn't be going past Sophie's place, would you?'

The mention of Sophie's name sent a reflexive *zing* through his chest. 'Why?'

'I left my iPod at her flat yesterday. And I'm doing a double shift today, so I can't get down there.'

She was doing the double shift as a favour to him, helping to cover Dot's absence. Josh nodded and said, 'OK, I'll drop by and pick it up.'

'That'd be brilliant. Thanks. You're a star.'

Josh left with Griff. What if he rang the doorbell and the man who'd spent the night with Sophie was still there? And he had to be polite to him?

God, I must be some kind of masochist.

But in a weird way he did actually want to see him. This, after all, was the man who'd achieved the impossible task of seducing

Sophie Wells. Masochistic it might be, but he needed to know who he was, what he looked like.

Sophie didn't answer the door naked and wrapped in a sheet, which was something. Then again, it was four o'clock in the afternoon.

'Oh, hi. Hello, lovely boy!' She bent down and gave Griff's ears the kind of enthusiastic scratch that sent him into a frenzy of delighted squirming and tail-wagging.

Lucky, *lucky* dog.

'Tula asked me to drop by.' Was the man upstairs? Was he about to come face to face with him? Josh mentally prepared himself for the worst. 'She says she left her iPod here yesterday.'

'She did.' Straightening up, Sophie turned and beckoned for them to follow her. 'Come on in. You'll have to carry Griff – I've got stuff laid out all over the floor.'

Upstairs, there was no sign of last night's visitor. Josh held on to Griff and made his way between the groups of photos littering the carpet.

'Are you OK, can you manage? Sorry, it's just the best way to sort them into order.'

'No problem.' He looked at the expanse of geranium-red wall above the sofa. 'What happened to my favourite picture?'

Sophie had her back to him; she was busy rummaging through her oversized turquoise and silver bag. 'Which picture?' She turned to see where he was pointing. 'Oh, that one. I gave it away to its rightful owners. You won't believe what happened . . . I saw the two children sitting outside a café yesterday and recognised the girl from her hair. It wasn't until I'd told their dad and brought them back here to give them the print that he told me his wife died not long after it was taken. And it was her foot in the corner of the picture. He was really pleased to have it.'

'I bet he was. That's amazing.' *Had she ended up sleeping with the man?* It had certainly looked that way last night. Not that he could point this out. Josh said, 'So they just took the print and left?'

300

'He invited me out to dinner.' Sophie shook her head slightly. 'Poor guy, he's really struggling. His mum and dad babysat to give him a break and we went out for something to eat. OK, this is annoying, I could have sworn I'd put Tula's iPod in my bag, but now I can't find it anywhere. Let me think, let me think . . . what did I *do* with it?' She straightened up, clearly attempting to concentrate. 'I've put it in a safe place and now I can't remember where that is.'

The next twenty minutes were like a special form of torture for Josh, as Sophie searched all over the flat and changed the subject entirely to that of all the things she'd inexplicably lost over the years.

'. . . and once I lost my front door key and didn't find it again until I got the Christmas decorations out the next year and there it was all tangled up with the fairy lights – oh, *here* it is! Can you believe that? It was in the bottom of my bag all the time . . .' She pulled out the iPod and waved it at him with relief. 'I *knew* I'd put it in there!'

At last. *At last* he could casually return the conversation to the new owner of the framed print. 'So you went out to a restaurant with this guy.' His heart was speeding up but he maintained his outer cool. Drily he said, 'You, on a date. That's what I call a miracle.'

'Except it wasn't a date. In any shape or form. He just needed to talk to someone about the terrible time he's going through. It got pretty emotional.' Sophie paused and shrugged. 'Well, why wouldn't he be upset? Anyway, I'm glad I gave him the photograph . . .'

The words trailed away and Sophie gazed out of the window, mercifully oblivious to the tumultuous thoughts ricocheting around inside Josh's head. He slowly exhaled with relief; what he'd seen last night wasn't what he'd thought he'd seen. Just from the way she was, he now knew without question that there had been no sex, nothing physical of that nature. The prolonged embrace had happened because the man was grieving, overcome with emotion, possibly in tears and in need of sympathy.

And who better to comfort him than Sophie?

'How did his wife die?'

She glanced at him, hesitated for a fraction of a second, then shrugged. 'No idea. Didn't ask.'

It was five o'clock in the morning and Lawrence had had a terrible night's sleep. This was his punishment for buying a boeuf bourguignon ready meal for two and eating the whole lot himself. Indigestion had plagued him all evening and now he was awake again, unable to get comfortable in bed and haunted by thoughts of Dot in Paris, being treated like a princess by that smug French bastard Antoine Beauvais.

Lawrence exhaled and flexed his aching shoulders; all the tension in his muscles was making him bad-tempered. Because Antoine *wasn't* a bastard, not really. He just wished the man hadn't reappeared after all these years, turning up in St Carys like some knight in shining armour and effectively sweeping Dot off her feet.

Oh God, how had his life come to this? He'd done a bad thing and suffered a thousand times over ever since. And now, to put the tin lid on it, he was lying here all alone, battling with the worst case of indigestion known to man. The ache was worsening now, pulling at his chest, making it harder to breathe . . .

Lawrence stifled a groan of annoyance. Dear God, what was going on, what was happening to him? At this rate he was never going to get to sleep. If Dot were nearby he might have been tempted to give her a call . . . except she wasn't, was she? She was in Paris. And who else could he wake up at this time of night? Talk about making yourself unpopular.

OK, never mind, mustn't be a nuisance. Grit your teeth and get through it. If it was no better in a couple of hours, maybe he'd think about contacting Josh, asking him if he thought a visit from the GP might be in order.

Bloody hell, though, he'd never known indigestion like this before; it was like having cramp in your ribs . . .

Chapter 46

'Well? What do you think?' Antoine asked the question with justifiable pride.

The taxi had brought them up the steep twisting road and dropped them off just below the Sacré Coeur, at the best possible viewpoint. The sky was a cloudless cerulean blue, the sun blazed down and what looked like the whole of Paris was laid out before them.

Dot's eyes prickled with emotion at the sheer beauty of the sight. This surely had to be one of the most stunning views on earth. Antoine tilted his head so he could glimpse beneath the broad brim of her straw hat, then smiled at the expression on her face.

'It's just . . . perfect.' Dot shook her head. 'I don't know what else to say.'

Antoine gave her hand a squeeze. 'And you are perfect too.'

Which could have sounded nauseating, but somehow, when it was spoken in a French accent, managed not to.

'Thank you.' She returned the squeeze; he had taken so much trouble. Every detail of their trip had been planned to the nth degree. The hotel was wonderful, unbelievably French and luxurious. Last night Antoine had taken her on a boat trip down the Seine, followed by dinner at a jewel of a restaurant tucked away in the back streets of Saint-Germain-des-Prés. This morning they had strolled through the Luxembourg Gardens, and now he'd brought her here to Montmartre. Antoine was an excellent guide, full of information, determined she should enjoy every moment.

'I can't believe you've never visited Paris before.' He was shaking his head.

'I know. It's crazy.' Dot was still gazing at the view. It wasn't as if she and Lawrence hadn't taken plenty of holidays, just that somehow they'd always ended up going . . . well, somewhere else.

'And you see the Tour Eiffel?' Of all the landmarks, it was the one that had first caught her eye, but Dot nodded and obediently followed the line of his pointing finger. 'We'll be there this evening.'

'Really?' Dot wondered how well her feet would hold out. 'I've heard the queues for the lifts can be quite long.'

'Oh Dot, do you think I'd do that to you?' Antoine's eyes twinkled as he shook his head. 'We won't be queuing, *ma chérie*. There's a private lift that takes people up to the Jules Verne restaurant on the second level. It's the most magical place to eat . . . Michelin-starred . . . quite superb.'

'Oh my goodness, I've heard of it! One of our customers told me about the Jules Verne last year. But he said it's always booked up months ahead.'

'This is true, but sometimes it is possible to pull strings. For very special occasions and very special people.' His voice caressing her like silk, Antoine murmured, 'And some people are worth pulling strings for. I promise you, *mon ange*, this will be an evening you'll never forget.'

'How lovely. We'll have to take photos to show everyone! Ooh, and I can't wait to be in it when all the lights go into overdrive and the whole thing lights up like a giant sparkler!' As Dot mimicked the sparkling with dancing fingers, she heard her phone begin to ring inside her handbag. 'Sorry, better just see who that is . . . Oh, it's Josh. I hope everything's OK with the hotel . . .'

One moment she was answering the call, her gaze fixed on the higgledy-piggledy rooftops of heat-hazed Montmartre, the next moment she was listening to Josh's words and the ground was falling away beneath her feet. All around her, tourists joyfully exclaimed at the view, chattering away in a multitude of different languages as they held up their cameras and jostled for the best shots.

'What is it?' Antoine asked when she'd said, 'I'll call you back,' and hung up.

'Lawrence. He's in hospital. Heart attack.'

'Oh, that is a shame. Well, never mind. I'm sure he'll be fine.' He rested his hand in the small of her back. 'Wait until you see the inside of the Sacré Coeur.'

Dot turned to stare at him. 'What?'

'Its beauty is astonishing, truly beyond compare. Come, you will love it. The architectural style is Romanesque-Byzantine and the great bell, the Savoyarde, is one of the heaviest in the world at nineteen tons—'

'Antoine, did you hear what I said?'

He was looking at her, baffled. 'Of course I did. But it isn't going to affect our trip, surely. We'll be back in St Carys on Sunday night; that's—'

'I can't stay here,' Dot interrupted, her heart thudding. 'I have to go.'

'But you can't. Are you serious? *Ma chérie*, this is crazy; he's your ex-husband. You *divorced* him.'

'He's ill, he could die . . .' She could hear her voice wavering. *No, stay calm, be strong.*

'If he's going to die, it'll happen regardless, whether you're there or not. This is our weekend. *Your* weekend,' Antoine amended. 'Everything I've arranged is for you.'

A taxi twenty yards away was disgorging a gaggle of excitable Japanese occupants. Dot hailed it and hurried over. Antoine jumped in after her.

'Please don't go.' He clutched her arm. 'OK, we'll fly back tomorrow, how about that? But we have to stay here tonight. Truly, the Jules Verne . . . it's a once-in-a-lifetime experience. *Chérie*, you can't miss it.'

Dot looked at him and knew at once what was going on. Antoine might be a gourmand, but even he couldn't be *that* desperate to eat a nice bit of food. He'd arranged practically every minute of this trip with characteristically immaculate attention to detail. There had also been a declaration of love last week during which he'd hinted that although they'd only known each other a few weeks, when you met someone and knew they were The One, what would be the point in hanging around? Just because a romance was whirlwind didn't mean it wasn't real and couldn't last.

Antoine had evidently had Very Big Plans for this evening's trip to the Eiffel Tower. No wonder he was looking put out.

'Please.' He tried again.

Dot shook her head slightly. 'I'm going home.'

They arrived back at their hotel in the Latin Quarter and she began throwing everything into her case.

'He could be better by the time you get back.' Antoine was pacing the room like a supercilious panther.

'I hope he is.' As if her mind wasn't bursting with fear and anxiety and mental pictures of Lawrence being taken ill, wondering if he was about to die, being rushed into hospital then lying in bed facing his worst fears.

It was, of course, her own worst fear too. Lawrence could *die*.

'He doesn't deserve this.' Antoine indicated the open suitcase with irritation. 'Not after what he did to you.'

'Antoine, if you were going to ask me to marry you tonight . . .' Dot paused with a dove-grey silk dress in her hands. 'Look, I'm sorry, but I would have said no.'

He reacted as if she'd slapped him hard across the cheek. 'You would?'

'Yes.' She dropped the dress – ironically, the one she would have worn tonight – into her case.

'Why?'

Why? What could she tell him? That he was too perfect? Like a cut-out-and-keep version of the ideal partner?

'It's no good, I can't go into all this now.' Blindly, Dot shook her head. 'I just have to get to the airport. What's the number for the safe, please? I need my passport.'

Antoine had been the one to set the code. He crossed the room, pressed the buttons on the safe's digital display and opened it. From the other side of the bed, Dot glimpsed a small package wrapped in a distinctive – and instantly recognisable – shade of duck-egg blue. It was at the back, behind the other items. Then he closed the safe once more and held out her passport.

So he'd already selected her engagement ring from Tiffany & Co. Of course he would have gone to Tiffany's; where else?

The rest of the packing was finished in a matter of minutes and in a silence that wasn't exactly comfortable. Flipping the case on to its wheels, Dot said again, 'I really am sorry.'

'You haven't even booked a flight.' Antoine's shoulders were stiff, his jaw taut.

'I know. I'm just going to catch the first one I can.' She'd kept the taxi waiting while she packed; it was time to head off to Charles de Gaulle airport. Waiting there would be less unbearable than this. 'Thanks for . . . everything.' Dot hesitated; a kiss on the cheek probably wasn't appropriate under the circumstances. 'And I'll pay my half of all this, I promise.'

'I still can't believe you're going. I would have given you everything you'd ever wanted.' Antoine's voice registered frostiness tinged with regret.

It was no use; her brain was filling up again with images of Lawrence and what he was going through. Tightly clutching her phone, Dot prayed he was still alive. As soon as she was safely in the taxi she would call Josh back.

Aloud she said, 'I know you would.'

Chapter 47

Tubes.

Tubes everywhere, so many of them, coming out of Lawrence's mouth, disappearing into his veins, delivering oxygen and liquids and medication and monitoring his vital signs.

Dot's legs began to tremble again at the sight of him. Josh dragged a chair up behind her and she collapsed on to it, her heart hammering with terror at the sight of so much technology.

But Lawrence was still breathing, still alive. He'd been rushed here this morning, to the Terence Lewis Building at Derriford Hospital in Plymouth. It was the cardiothoracic centre of excellence for the south-west, and if anyone could get him through this, it was the staff here.

'You OK?' Josh murmured, keeping his arm around her.

Dot nodded, her mouth dry. At midday she'd been standing on the steps of the Sacré Coeur, gazing out over the city and thinking how happy she was with Antoine. Since then, she'd flown from Paris into Heathrow and travelled by train down to the south coast of Cornwall, to be met at the station by Josh. It had felt like the longest journey of her life, from sunny Montmartre to the cardiac surgery intensive care unit in grey, rain-soaked Plymouth.

'He's very poorly,' the doctor told them, 'but we're doing everything we can. And he's through the surgery, which is good.'

It was good. It was also a pretty idiotic thing to say. The

doctor looked too young to be allowed anywhere near a patient on his own; he hardly looked old enough to ride a moped.

Oh well, hopefully he knew what he was doing, had a few qualifications under his belt.

'A quadruple bypass,' said Dot. 'It just sounds so terrifying, so . . . major.'

'At least he got to us in time.' The doctor – a surgeon, presumably – nodded at Josh. 'Thanks to this one here.'

Dot nodded helplessly; Josh had already told her about Lawrence's call this morning, asking him to phone the surgery when he had a moment and see if he could be seen at some stage today. The moment Josh had heard the words *chest pain*, he'd hung up, dialled 999, jumped into his car and raced over to Lawrence's flat. With Lawrence unable to get out of bed, Josh had kicked down the door just in time to let the paramedics pile in.

Another couple of minutes, apparently, and Lawrence would have been dead.

Dot closed her eyes. It didn't bear thinking about.

Then again, the other thing that didn't bear thinking about was the fact that it could still happen.

He wasn't out of the woods yet.

It had been eight days since Lawrence's heart attack and subsequent surgery, but it was Marguerite's first visit. She paused at the entrance to the open-plan, state-of-the-art ward. This was exactly the kind of scene that could have featured in one of her books.

The once-philandering husband lying in his hospital bed.

The once-abandoned ex-wife sitting beside him, leaning forward and touching his arm. After more than ten years apart, they looked like a couple again.

And now: enter the new woman in this man's life, tall and striking, madly in love with him and furiously jealous of the ex-wife now threatening to steal back his affections.

You could turn it into one of those *Fatal Attraction* scenarios: Threatened and spurned, the new woman in his life walks the length of the ward, managing a tight, polite smile for the benefit of the nursing staff as she passes them . . . then suddenly produces a kitchen knife from the depths of her Mulberry handbag . . .

Oh well, you got the idea. Something like that.

Anyway, best get this over with. Bracing herself, Marguerite moved away from the door and headed over to join them. God, how she hated hospitals: that nasty disinfectanty smell, the unattractive decor, all the ill people needing constant looking after. So alien and uncomfortable and reminiscent of death.

The moment they spotted her, Dot guiltily slid her hand away from Lawrence's forearm and sat back in her chair. Lawrence nodded with a wary expression on his face and said, 'Hello!'

'Well look at you!' Marguerite cheerily dropped her Mulberry bag on to the other chair and manoeuvred her way past a drip stand. She greeted him with a kiss on each cheek, holding her breath in order to avoid the hospitaliness of his skin. 'I hear you're on the mend, which is excellent. Now, I *did* buy you flowers but apparently they aren't allowed on the ward so I've had to leave them in the car. I'll take them back home with me. But just so you know, the thought was there.'

'Thank you,' said Lawrence. 'I'm sure they're lovely.'

'Well they weren't cheap!' Oh dear, Riley was always telling her off for saying things like that, but she really couldn't help herself; sometimes these things just popped out. 'And I've brought you one of my books, seeing as you've never read any of them.' She took a hefty hardback out of the bag and placed it on the Formica cabinet alongside his bed. 'You really should give one a go.'

'Great.' He said it like a teenager being presented with a hand-knitted bobble hat by his gran. *Honestly, some men.*

'Sorry I haven't been able to get here before now, but I've been away on a book tour of South Africa.'

Lawrence nodded. 'Yes, I remember. You told me you were going.'

'It went *very* well.' Marguerite realised she was talking about herself rather than asking him how he was, partly out of guilt, because she'd actually arrived back from Cape Town three days ago. 'So anyway, how are *you* feeling?'

Lawrence shifted against the propped-up pillows. 'Well, not wonderful. But I guess things could be a lot worse.' He glanced over at Dot, who was apparently engrossed in reading the get-well-soon cards on the wall behind his bed.

'Must have given you a scare when it happened,' said Marguerite.

'It did. I thought I was a goner.' He shrugged and briefly touched his chest, bruised and scarred but healing after the surgery. 'Lucky to be here, I know that.'

Over a week had passed since it had happened. From her discussions with a doctor friend, Marguerite had learned that the danger period was now over; barring setbacks due to infection or clots, the prognosis should be good.

'Actually,' she looked at Lawrence, 'would you mind if we left you for a few minutes? I'd really like a word with Dot, if that's OK. In private.'

Together they took the lift down to the ground floor and sat on a bench outside in the courtyard garden. Dot looked like a captured spy preparing to be interrogated and possibly shot.

'Have you been coming here every day?' Marguerite opened the proceedings.

'Yes.'

'Travelling down or staying here in Plymouth?' She already knew the answer to this one.

Dot's spine was as straight as a debutante's, her hands clasped together in her lap. 'Staying. In a small B and B not far from here.'

'Why?'

'Because I can't bear not to be near him. Marguerite, I'm sorry if you're furious with me. I know you two were seeing each other and you probably think I have a damn nerve being here like this . . . but I can't help it.' Dot shook her head. 'I just can't.'

After a pause, Marguerite said, 'I hear you cut short your Paris trip.'

'I had to.'

'And how did the glamorous Antoine feel about that?'

'He wasn't tremendously impressed,' said Dot.

Nor had he returned to Cornwall, Marguerite knew that too.

'Is it over between the two of you now?'

'Yes.'

'And how about Lawrence? Do you love him?'

'Of course I do.' This time Dot didn't flinch. 'With all my heart.' She exhaled and said again, 'I'm so, so sorry.'

Marguerite shook her head. 'Don't be. It's fine. Lawrence and I did our best to make it more, but we were only ever friends. If anything, I'm relieved to be off the hook. Looking after someone who's ill isn't my thing. Just don't have the patience. And I can't stand hospitals.' She smiled briefly. 'So all in all, I'm glad you're here.'

'Oh thank *goodness*.' Dot clapped a hand to her throat. '*Thank you*. You'll never know how guilty I've been feeling. I didn't want you to feel . . . you know . . .'

'It's OK. Really. I'm happy for you.' Marguerite tilted her head. 'But I have to admit, also a bit puzzled. Lawrence has been in love with you all along. Everyone knows that. You could have had him back any time you wanted.'

'I know.' Dot carefully smoothed her skirt over her knees. 'But he broke my heart when he left. I was devastated, and there was Lawrence, madly in love and as happy as anything with Aurora. If she hadn't died, he might still be happy with her. But she did die. And it was Lawrence's turn to be devastated. Then, once he'd recovered from losing her, I saw the way his mind was heading. But I didn't want to be second best, option number two. And I still wanted to hurt him for doing what he'd done to me. Why should I make life easy for him? So I decided to punish him instead.' She paused, tipping her head back as if searching the sky for birds. Marguerite saw the glistening in her clear blue eyes and knew she was employing the tilt trick to stop the tears spilling out.

'Without realising how much you were punishing yourself,' she said gently.

Unable to speak for a moment, Dot nodded. Then she swallowed and said, 'Well, I did kind of know. But somehow it seemed worth it. Lawrence was always there, wanting me back and unable to have me. But then something like this happens,' she indicated the hospital, 'and it just hits you, out of nowhere. He's the only man I've ever loved. What if he wasn't around any longer? We so nearly lost him. And the thought of that . . . well, it would just be unbearable.' She managed a smile and a shrug. 'So that's how it happened. I realised I couldn't punish him, or myself, any more.'

'Well,' said Marguerite. 'What can I say? I should put the two of you in a book.' Her gaze softened. 'Lawrence must be happy about it.'

'He doesn't know yet. I haven't told him.'

'But you're staying here in Plymouth, visiting him every day. You left Antoine behind in Paris. He must have some sort of idea.'

'Who knows? He's a man; you can never be sure with them.' Dot looked mischievous. 'If he does suspect, he's far too scared to ask.'

Marguerite made her way across the car park, wearing wraparound Dior dark glasses. Dot had headed back to Lawrence in his ward on the sixth floor. There had been no reason to go with her; the deed was done now. And she hadn't been lying when she'd told Dot she was happy for her. Because she *was*.

Thank God, here was the car, tucked out of the way in a corner. Marguerite's hand trembled slightly as she pressed the key to unlock the door.

It wasn't until she was in the driver's seat of the Mercedes that she felt safe enough to take off the sunglasses and bury her face in her hands. Hot tears dripped through her fingers, and her shoulders shook with the effort of not honking like a goose.

So much for having allowed herself to think that maybe, just maybe, she and Lawrence might have stood a chance of happiness together.

It was never going to happen now. She'd known it the moment Riley had told her about Dot flying back from Paris.

When the outburst was over, Marguerite carefully wiped her face with a succession of tissues, cleaning away the mascara that had run into the wrinkles around her eyes, giving her the look of a centuries-old witch. Then she took out her make-up bag and painstakingly reapplied everything that had come off.

She might not have a man in her life – *again* – but there were still standards to maintain.

No more Lawrence, with whom she'd had such high hopes of building a proper relationship. It wasn't to be. Marguerite gave her mouth a final defiant slick of take-no-prisoners crimson lipstick.

Oh well, at least she still had her career, her fans and her dignity. She'd wanted Lawrence and been found wanting in return. But no one would ever know.

Chapter 48

'What are you thinking about now?'

It was evening, and visiting time was almost over. Dot looked at Lawrence and said, 'Why?'

'That little smile on your face. I like it. I want to know what made you smile like that.'

'OK, do I make something up or tell you the truth?'

'The truth.' Lawrence paused. 'Although now you've said that, I'm a bit worried I might not like the answer.'

What the hell, go for it. 'I was thinking about the time you asked me to marry you.' As she said it, one of the nurses arrived to check on Lawrence's drip.

'Ooh, marriage proposals, lovely!' Rose was a cheery soul who loved to chat. 'Was it wonderfully romantic?'

'He probably doesn't remember it,' said Dot. 'It was over half a century ago.'

The nurse feigned dismay. 'Oh Lawrence, surely you haven't forgotten! Have you?'

'I remember,' said Lawrence. 'I'm not that decrepit.'

'Go on then, tell me.' Rose beamed. 'I'm all ears!'

Her ears *were* actually quite large and sticky-outy. For a split second Dot and Lawrence exchanged a glance, silently daring each other to smile.

'It was a Saturday evening.' Lawrence held up his arm, allowing

Rose to get on with the task of unpeeling the tape holding one of the drip lines in place. 'Started off sunny, then the sky clouded over as we were setting out. We'd been invited to a party at a friend's house and my car had broken down the day before, so we had to walk there instead. It was about five miles away, but that was OK. We could manage it, no problem.' Drily he added, 'Back when we were young.'

'Wait,' said Rose. 'I need to know. Had you planned the whole thing? I mean, did you have the ring with you?'

'No.' Lawrence shook his head. 'We'd only known each other a few weeks. I knew I loved her, but that was as far as I'd got. So anyway, we'd walked a couple of miles along the cliff path when it started to rain. And Dot was wearing a new dress. A yellow one.'

Dot, sitting at his bedside, couldn't believe he'd remembered the colour of her dress.

'Pale yellow,' Lawrence elaborated. 'With white daisies on it. And pockets on each side.'

'It was the sixties,' Dot explained to Rose. 'Daisies and pockets were *very* popular back then.'

'When it started raining, she was worried about her dress getting wet, so I took off my jacket and let her wear it. But the rain came down harder. So then we tried to take a short cut, leaving the cliff path and cutting across some fields. Which would have worked well if it hadn't been for the locked gate.'

'Ooh no, what happened?' Rose was expertly retaping the drip line.

And now it was Lawrence's turn to smile. 'I was helping Dot to climb over the gate. But she was wearing white pointy-heeled shoes and she slipped on her way over the top bar. She went crashing down the other side, skidded, lost her balance and ended up sitting in a puddle, splashed head to toe in mud. Well, that was it; I knew what girls were like when their new clothes got wrecked. I was just waiting for her to go ballistic.' He shook his head, evidently visualising the scene. 'But d'you know what? She started to laugh instead. And there was mud all over her face . . . and her dress . . .'

'And your jacket,' Dot joined in. 'And you were still on the other side of the gate, looking *stunned* . . .'

'So then *I* climbed over the gate like a complete gentleman to haul her up. I grabbed hold of both her hands, and do you know what she did, Rose?' Lawrence raised an eyebrow at the nurse. 'Instead of letting me help her get back on her feet, she *deliberately* pulled me down into the mud.'

'Nooo!' Rose was agog.

'I mean, what kind of a girl does that?' He shrugged help-lessly. 'She dragged me down with her and laughed and laughed, then she kissed me and rolled me around until we were both completely covered . . . then she kissed me again and I knew exactly what kind of a girl did that.' Lawrence's mouth twitched. 'It was the kind I wanted to marry. So that was it, that was when I asked her. There and then.'

'In the mud and the rain,' said Dot.

'In an empty field.'

'And with our clothes ruined.'

'I couldn't have cared less.' Lawrence looked at Rose. 'She said yes, that was all that mattered.'

'Ah, that's so lovely.' Rose was clasping her hands together in delight. 'So you never did make it to the party.'

'Oh we did.' Lawrence smiled. 'We wanted to celebrate with our friends. Weren't going to let a bit of mud stop us.'

'They lent us a change of clothes,' said Dot. 'Weird clothes, but at least they were dry.'

'They gave you a giant pair of dungarees,' Lawrence remem-bered. 'And I had to wear a terrible pair of corduroy trousers. God, they were *purple*.' He threw his head back and laughed. 'But we still had the most brilliant night.'

'We did,' Dot agreed. 'Even if a couple of people thought we were far too young to be thinking about getting married and said it would never last.'

'Ha, and you proved them wrong!' Rose beamed. 'Look at the two of you now, fifty years later. Oh, I *love* stories like this. You give the rest of us hope, you really do!'

Dot opened her mouth to say, *except we aren't married, we're divorced*. Then she met Lawrence's gaze and closed it again. Why do it? Why disappoint Rose and prompt the question that would mean explaining all over again why their happy marriage had ended in unhappy divorce?

Instead she smiled and said, 'We just struck lucky, I guess.'

When Rose had finished and moved on to the next patient, Dot looked at her watch and said, 'They're going to be kicking me out soon.'

'Yes.' Lawrence paused. 'Thank you.'

'For what? The grapes?' Dot had eaten most of them herself. 'Sorry about that. I'll bring some more tomorrow.'

'Never mind them. Thank you for everything. Just . . . everything.' His voice cracked and he cleared his throat, embarrassed. 'Anyway, you should be heading off.'

To her lonely attic room back at the B&B. It was funny how a hospital ward, with all its bustle and chatter, could come to feel like home. She said, 'I suppose I should.'

'Thanks for keeping me company. Again. And for not telling Rose the depressing truth.'

'Didn't have the heart to disappoint her.' Dot lightly touched his wrist. 'I'm impressed, by the way, that you remembered what I was wearing when I fell over in the mud.'

'Just because I don't talk about things doesn't mean I don't remember them.' Lawrence shook his head. 'I'll never forget anything about that night.'

Dot reached for his hand, curling her fingers between his. She'd felt like the luckiest girl in the world that day. It had been the ultimate spur-of-the-moment proposal, followed by a wild impromptu celebration. Poor Antoine; all the immaculate planning and painstaking attention to detail in the world couldn't have matched it. She looked at Lawrence and said, 'I love you.'

Stunned, he gazed back at her. Finally he nodded and replied, 'I love you too.'

'Who knows how much time either of us has left? I don't think we should waste it.'

'Visiting time's over, you two lovebirds,' Rose sang out as she made her way back past them.

'Seriously?' Lawrence whispered.

'Absolutely.'

'Oh my God.' He squeezed Dot's hand. 'Are you trying to give me another heart attack?'

Dot spluttered; his sense of humour had always made her laugh. 'Do try not to have one.'

'Well, despite the fact that I'm lying in a hospital bed full of tubes,' said Lawrence, 'this ranks right up there as one of the best days of my life.' He raised his head from the pillow and she leaned over to kiss him on the mouth.

Eleven years since the last kiss. Dot closed her eyes; how she'd missed him.

Well, we're together again now. Until death us do part.

Her heart turned over. 'You know what? Me too.'

'And is Antoine . . . you know, definitely off the scene?'

'Absolutely definitely.'

'You mean, out of him or me, you chose me?'

'Looks like it,' said Dot.

'Wow,' said Lawrence. 'That's amazing. No accounting for taste.'

'I know. Weird, isn't it?'

He reached up and touched the side of her face. 'I'm the luckiest man in the world. I really hope I don't die just yet.'

Dot smiled, cupped her own hand over his and murmured, 'You'd better not. If you do, I'll kill you.'

Chapter 49

This time the shop was open. Since he wasn't stupid – not twice, anyway – Josh had called in advance to double-check.

And now he was here. It had begun to feel as if the fates were conspiring against him, but it was happening at last.

Please God, don't let Theo Pargeter refuse point-blank to speak to him when he found out the reason for his visit.

Josh braced himself. The conversation would be infinitely easier without other customers around. And it looked as if he were in luck; getting here this early seemed to have paid off. When he made his way through the gates, he saw only the one person in the outdoor section of the shop, busy unstacking a delivery of glazed planter pots.

'Hi.' Noticing him, Theo Pargeter straightened up and said in a friendly manner, 'Anything I can help you with?'

Just a bit.

'I hope so. But it's not to do with this.' Josh indicated the garden furniture surrounding them. 'More . . . personal.'

Theo looked taken aback. 'Oh? What kind of personal?'

OK, this was way more difficult than the meetings he'd had with entertainment industry bigwigs back in LA. Probably because the outcome was way more important.

'I need to ask some questions.' Josh cleared his throat, which appeared to have his heart beating away in it. 'About Sophie Wells.'

Theo went very still. The colour drained visibly from his face. At last he said, 'Why? Is she all right?'

'She's alive. Fit and healthy. I don't know about all right.'

'Who are you?' said Theo.

Honesty had to be the best policy. May as well go for it. 'I know her. We know each other. As friends,' Josh amended. 'I wish it was more, but it isn't.'

'Why not?' Theo was eyeing him warily.

'Because something happened in Sophie's past that . . . changed her. And I don't know what that something is, but I need to find out. Because I love her. And I think she has feelings for me, but she won't let herself get emotionally involved with anyone.' He shook his head. 'Not with anyone at all.'

The silence lengthened between them. Finally Theo said, 'Have you tried asking her why not?'

'Of course I've tried. She refuses to talk about it. And it's killing me,' said Josh. 'I need to know what happened. Maybe then I can help. Whatever it is, I just want Sophie to be able to put it behind her . . . because there has to be a way. If she can just get over it, she can be happy again.'

'Oh God.' Theo ran a shaking hand over his forehead. 'Does she know you're here?'

'No.' Josh knew he had to ask the question. 'Will you tell me? Did she try to commit suicide? Is that what happened?'

More silence.

Then Theo shook his head. 'No, Sophie didn't try to commit suicide. I did.'

In the frozen seconds following this startling pronouncement, a Kawasaki motorbike pulled into the parking area. A skinny lad removed his crash helmet and said, 'Sorry I'm late, a lorry broke down on Falcondale Road. Traffic was chaos.'

'Doesn't matter.' Theo shook his head. 'Roddie, can you finish unpacking these pots and take charge? I have to go out for a bit.'

Roddie, who evidently worked as Theo's assistant, shrugged and said, 'Cool, no probs.'

The two of them walked up the road to a small café and found a quiet corner where they couldn't be overheard. Then Josh sat and listened as Theo began to talk.

The whole story came out, jerkily at first, then faster and faster as it went along, fuelled by shame and remorse.

'It was my fault. All my fault. Sophie didn't do anything wrong. God, I had no idea. I swear I never thought it would have that kind of effect on her. I don't know how she stuck it out with me for as long as she did. I was a nightmare.' Theo grimaced at the memory. 'Well, I was ill. The doctors told me I'd had a complete nervous breakdown. It was hell for both of us. But after the overdose, when I told Sophie I never wanted to see her again, it was because I was so ashamed of what I'd done. And I told myself I was doing the right thing. I thought she'd be happy to be off the hook. The reason I left Birmingham was to give her some space. Well, I needed to get away too, take some time to sort myself out. Then after a while I heard she'd moved down to Cornwall. Is that where you're from too?'

Josh nodded, still taking in everything he'd heard. 'St Carys, on the north coast.'

'I know, I googled her name. She has her own photography business.' Theo's smile was brief. 'Good for Sophie. It's what she always wanted.'

Hmm, not quite true; what most twenty-something girls wanted was to live normal, happy lives and not be too terrified to allow themselves to fall in love.

'And how are you now? Are you happy?'

'Completely.' Theo shrugged. 'Everything's great. 'You don't think your life can change like that, become so much better; you just can't imagine it. But it can. It really can.'

'You could have sent Sophie an email,' said Josh. 'Just to let her know you were fine.' But he knew now, understood why that had never happened.

'It never occurred to me for a single moment that she'd be interested. I swear I just thought she'd be glad to have me out of her life. I caused her so much pain.' Theo had been shredding a paper napkin as he spoke; now he tidied the torn remnants on to his saucer. 'And I felt so guilty about that.' He paused. '*So* guilty. Why would she ever want to hear from me again?'

Josh looked at him. It was no one's fault. God, what a mess, all these years of needless misery.

Theo's phone beeped, signalling the arrival of a text. He checked it and said, 'Right, we need to get back.'

But when they returned to the shop, Theo walked past it and headed for the adjoining house instead, gesturing for Josh to follow him.

'Come along inside. There's something I want you to see.'

Chapter 50

'Oh wow.' Tula's mouth dropped open as she gazed around the hotel lobby, breathed in the smell of money in the air. 'How the other half lives.'

'Stop gawping,' said Marguerite. 'You look like a tourist.'

'I *am* a tourist.' The diamond-patterned black and white marble floor gleamed, chandeliers glittered above their heads and the wallpaper and furniture was like something out of a palace. A porter was wheeling a trolley piled high with Louis Vuitton luggage towards the lifts, and the chances were that it wasn't even fake. Every single person in this reception hall looked like a millionaire. Sliding her phone out of her pocket, Tula said, 'Am I allowed to take photos?'

'No you are *not*. Put that thing away.' Marguerite rolled her eyes at the very idea. 'Don't show yourself up.'

Tula grinned, because she was learning that Marguerite's bark was infinitely worse than her bite. 'Spoilsport. But don't you ever walk into a place like this and pinch yourself because you're here and it's just so incredible? Or are you so used to it by now that you don't even notice? I mean, *look* at it . . .'

'Oh, of course I notice.' Tula's refusal to be intimidated by Marguerite had, happily, resulted in the older woman relaxing and lowering her own guard. 'I may be rich on the outside but I still feel poor on the inside. You never forget your roots.'

'Well anyway, thanks for letting me come along.' Tula, poor

inside and out but used to it, added, 'You have no idea, this is so exciting for me.'

Marguerite was smiling at her now. 'Is it? Good. Ah, here comes Riley with the keys.'

Back from getting them checked in, Riley said, 'Here we go. We're on the third floor.' He looked at Tula's bag. 'Want me to carry that for you?'

A porter, materialising as if by magic at her other side, said, 'Madame, would you like me to take care of your bag?'

God, how mortifying. Not only did he look like something out of *Downton Abbey*, but her overnight bag was from Primark. 'Thanks, but it's OK. No need,' she reassured him. 'They're the guests. I'm staying somewhere else.'

As they made their way up in the unbelievably plush lift, Tula marvelled at the sequence of events that had brought her here to London and the Savoy Hotel. Forty-eight hours ago, Marguerite had hosted a book club event at Moor Court and Tula had been called upon to help out for the first time. The evening had gone well, everyone had enjoyed themselves and Marguerite had been on top lady-author form. Following the departure of the last few guests, however, she'd discovered that one of her diamond earrings had fallen out. Panic ensued. After twenty minutes of frantic searching, Tula had located the missing earring buried in the deep pile of the ivory carpet in the drawing room where the event had taken place.

Shortly after that, while she'd been washing up the perilously long-stemmed wine glasses, she'd listened while Marguerite and Riley, at the scrubbed-oak kitchen table, went through the appointments diary for the coming week. Thursday was publication day here in the UK for *Tell Me Now*, Marguerite's latest novel, and there was a ton of promotional work to be done. Interviews with journalists for newspapers and the most popular websites had been lined up. Videos needed to be made and posted online. There were book signings and an endless round of radio interviews . . .

'And on Thursday you've got the *EveryDay* show.' Riley moved on down the list.

'Right. Who am I on with?'

Tula's ears pricked up as Riley mentioned the names of the British-born Hollywood actor and the nation's favourite songstress.

'Well I've heard of the actor,' said Marguerite, 'but the other one . . . no idea. You'd better dig up some info for me so I have some clue who she is.'

'I will.' Riley nodded and scribbled a note on the page. 'Although the audience loved it last year when you asked Dustin Hoffman what films he'd been in.'

Dustin Hoffman. Tula almost snapped one of the long-stemmed wine glasses. *Imagine.* 'He was very nice about it,' Marguerite admitted. 'OK, carry on. What happens on Friday?'

'Can I just say something? You should be more excited than this.' Having finished rinsing the last of the glasses, Tula picked up a tea towel. 'Seriously, you're going to be on TV with really famous people and millions of viewers.' The *EveryDay* show was massively popular, an early evening magazine-style programme hosted by Jon and Jackie Jerome, a much-loved former comedian and his perky wife. 'I'd give anything to be on a show like that. Even being in a TV studio would be thrilling for most people. And you're not even excited.'

'It's just work. Selling books, that's all.' Sounding surprised, Marguerite said, 'Have you really never visited a TV studio?'

Hello? Real world? 'No! Believe it or not, most people haven't.'

'Well, are you free on Thursday? If you want,' Marguerite offered, 'you can come up with us.' She turned to Riley and said innocently, 'That'd be OK, wouldn't it? You wouldn't mind?'

Tula hid a smile; Marguerite the meddling matchmaker was up to her tricks again. Honestly, it was so obvious. But visiting the TV studio was an irresistible draw. Let's face it, offers like this didn't come along every day.

'After tomorrow I've got two days off, so that'd be perfect. If you're sure?'

'Of course I'm sure.' Marguerite indicated the list. 'We're booked into the Savoy, right?'

The Savoy? Yikes.

'We are.' Riley nodded. 'Two rooms.'

'Well that's no problem. She can share yours.'

Riley was visibly mortified, shaking his head. 'No, don't say that. It's just embarrassing.'

While Tula fleetingly imagined what it would be like to share a room – and a bed – with Riley. *In the Savoy.*

'Well she certainly isn't sharing with me,' Marguerite retorted.

'Honestly, don't worry,' Tula blurted out, distracted by the unexpected mental image of Riley without any clothes on – God, where had *that* sprung from? 'I'll sort out my own bed for the night.'

Which she had. But the urge to see *their* beds had been irresistible. And the two adjacent rooms were, as she'd known they would be, classy and immaculate in every way.

'Not bad, eh?' Marguerite joined her at the window as Tula gazed out at the view of the city skyline. The London Eye turned lazily on the South Bank, boats slid through the green-grey water of the Thames and sunlight bounced off the windscreens of the cars and lorries making their way across Westminster Bridge.

'It's amazing.' Tula pointed. 'Look, there's the Houses of Parliament! This is like being in a film!'

'I know. It's why I always stay here when I'm in London. The heart of the capital city,' Marguerite announced dramatically. 'The best view in the world.'

'Not quite,' said Tula. 'Not as good as the view of St Carys beach from the Mariscombe House Hotel.'

Marguerite smiled. 'You like it there?'

'Love it. More than anything.'

'So you're planning to stick around.'

'Why would anyone want to leave?'

'I know. I feel the same way. There's no place like home.' After a moment, Marguerite added drily, 'Even if things sometimes don't turn out according to plan.'

Tula instinctively knew what she was talking about; she gave the older woman's arm an impulsive squeeze. Lawrence and Dot were back together, a couple once more, and on the surface Marguerite had taken Lawrence's defection admirably well. But Tula sensed her feelings had been hurt rather more deeply than she'd let on.

'Anyway, I'm going to head off now.' Tula picked up the pink overnight bag that was looking so out of place in its plush surroundings.

'This is crazy. You don't have to go.' Marguerite gave it one last try. 'You can stay in Riley's room.'

Sharing a bed with Riley . . . their bodies accidentally touching in the night . . . ripples of desire she might not have the strength of will to control . . .

'It's fine, honestly. And my room's all booked. Forty-three pounds.' Tula said it with pride, having haggled the price down from fifty-five. 'Bargain!'

Marguerite suppressed a shudder of distaste. 'How ghastly. I can't imagine anything worse.'

'This is *soooo* exciting.' Tula whispered the words into Riley's ear so no one else in the studio audience could hear. She didn't want to sound like a complete dork.

Oh, but there was such a buzz of anticipation in the air. The cameramen were manoeuvring their cameras around the studio floor like Daleks; the presenters, Jon and Jackie, were making last-minute adjustments to their scripts and a make-up girl was busy dusting mattifying powder on Jon's forehead. In three minutes the show was set to start and they'd be live on air. The atmosphere was electric.

'Calm down,' Riley murmured back. 'You aren't actually going to be on TV yourself.'

'I know.' He'd found it amusing earlier that she'd changed into a nice dress and put on make-up. 'But I could be, that's the thing. Look at us, right here in the front row. If the show started and I suddenly jumped up and ran up there, they couldn't stop me. I could rip off my clothes and streak across the stage . . . by the time they realised what was going on . . . *pah*, it'd be too late.'

'All the same, probably better if you don't do it.' Riley seized her hand, his warm fingers closing around hers. 'In fact I'm going to keep hold of you, just to be on the safe side. Apart from anything else, Marguerite wouldn't be too thrilled if you stole her thunder.'

'True.' Tula settled back in her seat; it wasn't as if she was actually planning on doing a streak across the studio on live TV. But having her hand held by Riley was nice, and easier to cope with than those vivid mental images of being naked in bed with him . . . *Uh oh, whoops, and now it's happening again* . . .

'Sorry, can I squeeze in?' Suze, who worked in the publicity department of Marguerite's publishers and had been waiting backstage with her, made her way past them and settled into the empty seat on Riley's other side. She glanced at their entwined hands and switched off her phone before dropping it into her bag.

'How is she?' said Riley. 'OK?'

'Quite nervous, actually. More than usual.' Suze shrugged, not particularly concerned. 'Probably because she's on with Tony Weston. I think she finds him rather attractive.' Her eyes danced. 'Sadly, Tony has his lovely wife with him . . . Ooh, here we go now, show's about to start.'

Chapter 51

Marguerite waited in the green room, pretending to read texts on her phone in order to avoid having to make polite conversation with anyone else. Her mouth was dry and her palms were damp. She'd never been one for spur-of-the-moment decisions before, but it was happening now. Less than an hour ago, she'd realised what it was she had to do.

OK, not *had* to. But it needed to be done.

Oh yes. Definitely.

'Hi,' said Tony Weston, appearing before her and making her jump. 'In case I don't get a chance to tell you later, my wife's a huge fan of your books. She wanted you to know how much she loves them.'

'Really? Thank you so much. That's lovely to hear.' Having done her homework and studied the information Riley had printed out for her, Marguerite knew that Tony Weston had met his wife Martha just four years ago. A strikingly attractive woman of Afro-Caribbean descent, she was a successful artist in her own right. Their first meeting had taken place on Primrose Hill in north London, and as far as Tony was concerned, it had been a case of love at first sight. By all accounts they were idyllically happily married.

Which was lovely in one way, of course, but disappointing in another.

Some people just had it so easy, didn't they?

And then there's me, thought Marguerite, at the other end of the scale. *Why can't I have a fraction of their luck?*

'Ms Marshall?' A studio runner wearing the obligatory headset and clutching a clipboard, said cheerfully, 'Time to take you downstairs. Shall we go?'

'Absolutely.' Now that she'd made up her mind, the fear fell away. It was like waking up and finding yourself miraculously twenty years younger. Rising to her feet, Marguerite smoothed down her skirt and said, 'Let's do this thing.'

Tony Weston's smile was unintentionally encouraging as she turned to leave the green room. 'Have a good one.'

'Don't you worry,' said Marguerite. 'I will.'

The show had begun. The hosts had had their three minutes of playful husband-and-wife banter and were now announcing who would be on the show tonight. The audience, whose job it was to generate maximum enthusiasm, went wild. Listening to them from backstage, Marguerite wondered if this was how it felt to have an out-of-body experience. Her agent would be at home now, watching the show. As would her editor.

As would her fans, those faithful readers all over the country who for years had bought and adored her books.

'Ms Marshall?' said the runner. 'Are you feeling all right? You're looking a bit pale.'

Was she? Marguerite considered the options. What was the worst that could happen? She could faint on stage, on live TV. Sometimes people lost control of their bladder when they fainted; *that* would generate a few headlines.

Although maybe not the kind you'd want to read.

Oh what the hell, she wasn't the fainting kind.

And as for the headlines . . . well, they weren't exactly going to be flattering anyway.

'Don't worry.' Marguerite checked her mic pack was secure. 'I'm fine.'

'. . . And now please welcome into the studio one of this country's most successful novelists, with twenty-five million books sold worldwide . . . the marvellous, *magnificent* Marguerite Marshall!'

The audience cheered and applauded and Marguerite made her way on to the set. She exchanged air kisses with Jon and Jackie and took her place on the purple suede sofa. A pocket of extra-enthusiastic cheering in the right-hand section of the audience alerted her to the fact that her fan club was in; thirty or so women who lived and breathed her books and hired minibuses to attend as many of her public appearances as humanly possible. Six of them, she knew, had travelled down from Scotland for this evening's show.

Who else would be watching from the comfort of their own homes? Lawrence and Dot? Loyal readers who had queued in the cold and the rain to have her sign books for them? Old friends from years gone by with whom she hadn't bothered to stay in contact after her career as a best-selling author had taken off?

OK, this was like drowning and having your whole life flash before you. Time appeared to have slowed to a crawl. Marguerite glanced at the front row and saw Suze, still clapping madly. Because she worked in public relations and it was her job to applaud.

And there, next to her, sat Riley and Tula, the sides of their legs almost but not quite touching. As she looked at them, Riley leaned over and murmured something and Tula tilted her head close to his in order to hear what he was saying. Then she broke into a smile and gave his knee a playful nudge with hers.

Marguerite, who had spent the day paying *very* close attention to the way they interacted, knew she was about to do the right thing. The chemistry between them was unmistakable. Tula might be doing her level best to deny it, but to a novelist – a professional observer of body language – the signals were definitely there.

OK, *ex-novelist*.

'Wow, Marguerite, that was quite some welcome,' Jon enthused when the applause finally died down. 'Not that you're anywhere near old enough, but that kind of reaction means you're practically a national treasure!'

'It's very kind of them.' The blood in her veins was racing around her body at Formula 1 speed. Smiling apologetically at the audience, Marguerite said, 'Thank you. I really don't deserve it.'

Which prompted cries of 'Yes you do!' from her adoring fan club.

'Well I *love* your books,' Jackie chimed in, as bubbly and effusive as ever. 'Once I start reading them I just can't stop! I once missed a flight to New York, that's how engrossed I was!'

'And that was our honeymoon!' Jon quipped. 'Now, the new book is published today.' He held up a copy of the hardback for the benefit of camera three. 'Unbelievably, it's your thirty-ninth novel, and this one's called *Tell Me Now*.' He paused, twinkly-eyed. 'So, Marguerite, tell *me* now, what's the secret? How *do* you keep on doing it?'

If she'd written the script herself, she couldn't have engineered a better opening line. OK, here goes. Marguerite fixed her gaze on twinkly-eyed Jon and said, 'I don't. I get someone else to do it.'

Everyone burst out laughing. If a stand-up comedian had said it, it wouldn't have been funny. But when a non-comedian said something faintly amusing, the response was greater. Like when a tennis player at Wimbledon dropped a ball thrown to him by a ball boy and pulled an *oops* face, and everyone on Centre Court cracked up.

'No, don't laugh.' Marguerite shook her head at Jon and Jackie. 'I'm not joking. It's the truth.'

The weird thing, Tula couldn't help noticing, was the way everyone in the audience was laughing except Riley. He'd suddenly become very still. Glancing at his profile, she saw him staring intently at Marguerite on the purple sofa, his high cheekbone accentuated by the overhead lighting. A muscle was twitching in his jaw.

'Are you OK?' she whispered, her own cheek brushing his shoulder.

He nodded without replying.

Up on the stage, Jon was now saying jovially, 'You mean if you get a bit stuck every now and again, you have a brainstorming session with your editor?'

Then Tula saw that Marguerite was shaking her head, very firmly indeed.

'No, nothing like that. It's been bothering me for a while; I'm a very proud woman, if not always an honest one. But it's time to come clean. I suffered a horrible case of writer's block and haven't managed to write a book since. In fact it's been six years now . . .'

Marguerite wavered and paused, raising a hand to signal that she needed a moment to compose herself. Tula wondered what was going on; was Marguerite drunk, or having some kind of breakdown? The audience had now fallen silent too.

'Um, so I know this is going to upset my readers and I'm really sorry, but there it is. I can't write any more. At all. It just won't . . . happen.'

'Well, this is quite an announcement,' Jon said quickly. 'I think it's fair to say we're all pretty surprised by this news. Can I ask how your publishers feel about it? I mean, presumably they hired a ghostwriter to do the job on your behalf, but did they have any idea you were coming here tonight to reveal the big secret?'

Tula glanced across at Suze, who was looking as frozen now as Riley had done earlier. It was safe to say the answer to that question was no.

'My publisher didn't hire a ghostwriter,' said Marguerite, 'because they didn't know I needed one. They weren't aware there was any secret to reveal.'

God, this was getting weirder and weirder. It was unbelievable. Tula put her hand on Riley's forearm and felt the rigidity of the muscles beneath the surface. Leaning in to him, she whispered, 'Is this true? Did she tell you about this? Did you *know*?'

'So, Marguerite.' On the purple sofa, Jackie assumed her professionally mystified face. 'In that case, who *has* been writing your books for you?'

Marguerite turned her head to look out into the audience, and Tula felt the muscles in Riley's arm tighten to the next level. Then Marguerite raised her left arm and pointed directly at her.

'Right there. See? Sitting in the front row.'

'*Oh shit.*' Tula gasped as Suze jerked round to stare incredulously at her. 'This is mad, it's not me . . . She can't make me pretend I wrote her books!' There might be some situations you could blag your way through, but this definitely wasn't one of them.

Then she became aware of a noise like compressed air escaping from a car tyre and realised it was coming from Riley's throat.

As the floor manager frantically gestured for camera two to swivel round and face the audience, Marguerite pointed again and jabbed her finger. 'That's who's been writing the books. Over there. My nephew, Riley.'

Chapter 52

OK, now Marguerite really had lost it. Either that, or she was playing some kind of bizarre, improbable joke. Except there didn't appear to be any discernible punchline.

Then Tula looked again at Riley, saw him shake his head in resignation and heard him say under his breath, '*Fuck.*'

Not in an it's-not-true way. More of a cat-out-of-the-bag one.

Tula's eyes widened in disbelief. 'You? *You've* been writing Marguerite's books?'

The idea of it was on a par with a Labrador suddenly breaking into a tap dance.

Then she flinched as the overhead spotlights swivelled, their brightness illuminating the audience. Specifically, the front row. The cameras had swung round too, cables snaking behind them. Up on the stage, Marguerite's voice broke as she said, 'I'm sorry, I'm so ashamed, I've felt terrible about it for years. I just didn't want to disappoint my readers . . .' She stood up, struggling to disentangle the mic pack from beneath her pink jacket. 'We didn't mean to trick anyone; it was just my own stupid pride. OK, I can't do this any more, I have to go now before I make even more of a fool of myself . . .'

There were gasps as Marguerite succeeded in separating herself from the mic pack and left the stage, leaving Jon and Jackie staring helplessly after her. There was a moment of stunned silence, then Jackie jumped up and moved quickly over to the audience. Reaching for Riley's arm, she said, 'Well you can't leave us guestless! Come on, if you write the books for Marguerite, you can stand in for her on the sofa.'

She must have been stronger than she looked, because Riley didn't appear to have any choice in the matter. The moment the cameras panned away from the audience, Suze shot out of her seat and disappeared, clutching her phone and looking as if she'd swallowed a hedgehog.

The next few minutes surely ranked among the most surreal of Tula's life as she sat and listened to Riley explain how the switch had come about. If Jon and Jackie seemed amazed, it couldn't begin to compete with her own astonishment, since they didn't know Riley and she did.

Except she hadn't, had she? Her heart thumping against her ribs, Tula realised she hadn't known Riley Bryant at all.

Then the interview was over and Jon was wrapping up this segment of the show with, 'Well, I have to say, ladies and gentlemen, that wasn't something I'd planned on happening tonight, but I guess that's live television for you. Expect the unexpected, eh? Riley, good luck with everything, my friend.' Cheerily he added, 'And tell Marguerite we forgive her for pulling the wool over our eyes all these years, even if her publishers don't!'

The audience broke into jerky applause and Riley left the set, to the accompaniment of stifled sobs and angry mutterings from Marguerite's fan club, who evidently weren't taking it well. Someone said in a shocked voice, 'All this time she was just lying to us . . . I can't *bear* it.'

And then there was one. Tula wondered what she was meant to do now. Jon and Jackie were already gearing up to introduce the female singer, their next guest on the show. Then someone in the row behind Tula tapped her on the shoulder and whispered, '*Psst,* he's over there by the fire exit.'

Tula looked and saw Riley beckoning to her. As she crept out of her seat, the girl who'd given her the tap on the shoulder said enviously, 'Is he your boyfriend? You're so lucky. He's, like, totally hot.'

The fire exit door closed behind her and Riley said, 'Come on, we need to find her.'

He looked serious. And concerned. And gorgeous. The girl sitting behind her had been right; he *was* totally hot.

Anyway, never mind that now. Together they made their way along corridors and past members of staff who allowed them through security doors when they realised who Riley was. They reached the green room and found Suze pacing up and down, speaking urgently into her phone, her body radiating tension. The female singer's entourage was clustered around the TV, watching her performance on the show. Marguerite was sitting on a black leather sofa, wiping her eyes with a tissue and talking to a middle aged Afro-Caribbean woman in a long crimson cotton dress.

Tula said, 'Who's that with Marguerite?'

'Tony Weston's wife. Her name's Martha.' As they watched, Martha wrapped motherly arms around Marguerite and drew her into a sympathetic embrace. She murmured words of comfort as Marguerite broke down and sobbed on her shoulder.

'Oh God,' Riley said under his breath.

He'd taken Tula's hand. She squeezed his in return. Marguerite had always been strong, fearless, super-confident and utterly invincible. Seeing her in tears was all kinds of wrong.

Then Tony Weston crossed the room carrying a brimming, fizzing tumbler.

'Here you go.' He held it out to Marguerite. 'Gin and tonic, strong enough to stun a tiger.'

Martha released her hold on Marguerite and rummaged in her bag for fresh tissues. 'If my husband's good for anything, it's mixing a hefty gin and tonic. There now, sweetie, dry your eyes.' Glancing over at Riley and Tula, she said, 'Ah look, your boy's here.'

Your boy. Martha had the warmest, gentlest voice you could imagine. They saw Marguerite mentally gather herself, dab the tissue beneath her heavily mascaraed lashes and take a huge gulp of her drink. Then she looked up.

Riley said, 'I've just been interviewed on TV.'

'I know. We saw. Sorry about that.'

'You could have warned me.'

'You were great,' said Marguerite. 'You're a natural.'

Riley paused, shaking his head. 'Why did you do it?'

A longer pause. Then Marguerite replied steadily, 'You know why.'

Tula, who *didn't* know why, gave Riley a nudge and hissed, 'Give her a hug.'

Riley ignored her, continuing instead to gaze down at Marguerite. 'Talk about risky. What if it doesn't work out? You'll have done all of this for nothing.'

'Maybe I have. But I don't think so.' A glimmer of a smile lifted the corners of her mouth. 'I'm pretty good at sussing out what's going on. Trust me, I used to be a writer.'

'You're completely mad,' said Riley. Then he let go of Tula's hand, made his way over to Marguerite and hugged her tightly. From ten feet away, Tula thought she heard him murmur beneath his breath, 'But thanks.'

Honestly, what *were* they on about? This was a conversation badly in need of subtitles.

'Right!' Switching off her phone, Suze announced efficiently, 'I've spoken to your editor, the publishing director and the MD. They're all on their way over . . . they'll be here in twenty minutes. We'll have a meeting and decide what to do. Obviously Riley needs to be included—'

'Not me,' Riley interrupted. 'Not tonight.'

Suze was visibly alarmed. 'Oh, but—'

'Nor me,' Marguerite said firmly.

Suze's eyes widened in horror; this time she looked as if she might pass out. 'Marguerite, they're on their way now. As we speak. You can't do this. You have to talk to them!'

'Not if I don't want to.'

'But—'

'Come on.' Marguerite knocked back her gin and tonic. 'Let's get out of here.'

'Marguerite, please!' Panic-stricken and begging, Suze's voice rose. 'They'll be here *any minute*.'

Having kissed Martha and Tony Weston goodbye, Marguerite said briskly, 'All the more reason to leave now.'

Outside, Riley flagged down a black cab, and the three of them travelled back to the Savoy in silence. Marguerite gazed out of the window, lost in her own thoughts. When they'd reached the hotel and navigated the heavy revolving doors, she said to Riley, 'I'm going to my room now. The rest's up to you. Can you ask them to send up a bottle of something decent and not put through any calls? I don't want to be disturbed.'

Riley nodded and headed over to the reception desk, leaving Marguerite and Tula together.

'No way.' Tula shook her head. 'We're not leaving you on your own.'

'How sweet you are.' Visibly touched, Marguerite said, 'But I'm not planning on killing myself, if that's what you're worried about. Truly, not my style at all.'

'Well, good.' And thankfully she sounded as if she meant it. 'But listen,' said Tula, 'I know it might not feel like it at the moment, but you'll be so glad you did this. It's all out in the open now. No more subterfuge, no more guilty conscience.' Desperate to reassure Marguerite, she added enthusiastically, 'Trust me, it's a good thing and you're going to feel a million times better. So don't worry, everything'll turn out fine.'

'Really? Sure about that?' Marguerite's expression softened. 'After all this palaver, let's hope so.'

Chapter 53

'Shouldn't we stay with her?' said Tula when the lift had closed, whisking Marguerite up to her room on the third floor. 'Will she be OK?'

Riley nodded and indicated his phone. 'She's fine. I'll check on her later.'

'Good.'

'Shall we get out of here?' He gave her a nudge in the direction of the revolving doors. 'Come on, let's go.'

They left the hotel and headed along the Strand, then turned down a narrow street and reached Victoria Embankment Gardens. Tula paused, the Thames glittering before her, the ripples in the water reflecting the setting sun.

At her side, Riley said, 'What are you thinking about?'

Tula shook her head. 'I just can't believe it. Any of it. I mean, I know it has to be true because Marguerite said it was. But is it *really* true?'

'Yes.'

'You actually write the books?'

He nodded. 'I actually write the books.'

'I mean, not being funny . . . but it's kind of like me saying Stephen Hawking's been having trouble with his latest thesis on black holes so I've been helping him out with the tricky bits.'

Riley shrugged. 'I know. It is like that.'

'It's like Darcey Bussell twisting her ankle just before the start of *Swan Lake* and me going on instead.'

'Well, Darcey Bussell's retired now, but—'

'Or Beyoncé getting stage fright and not being able to sing at the Superbowl, so I have to jump up on to the stage and—'

'OK, I get the message,' said Riley. 'It's pretty unlikely. But it's the truth.'

'And Marguerite's always gone on about how hard she works, how many words she's written.'

'That's the way she always used to be. She just carried on saying it. Otherwise people would have wondered why she'd stopped.'

'And all this time you've been doing her job for her.' Tula paused, the implications beginning to fully sink in. Up until now, her concerns had been for poor guilt-ridden Marguerite. 'I had no idea.' She experienced a jolt in her chest. 'You should have told me.'

Oh, you really should . . .

'I couldn't tell anyone,' Riley said simply. 'It had to be a secret.'

'You could have told me.'

'You don't like having to keep secrets, remember?'

'I don't *like* having to keep them. But I would have done.' She raised her arm, lifting her hair away from the suddenly overheated nape of her neck.

'You told me you always end up accidentally letting things slip,' said Riley.

'*What?* Well I don't know why I'd have said that, because it's just not true,' Tula said indignantly. 'I'm brilliant at keeping secrets if they're important enough.'

'And if I had told you, what kind of difference would it have made?'

It was a rhetorical question, surely; he knew perfectly well how she felt. A lump sprang into her throat as a whoosh of emotion surged up. Out of nowhere, Tula was suddenly terrified she might burst into tears.

'Well?' Riley was watching and waiting for her reply.

'It would have made all the difference in the world,' she blurted out. 'You know it would. And it's nothing to do with money either. The way I felt about you . . . God, didn't I tell you enough times? There you were, perfect in every way except one. I couldn't handle the fact that you were a lazy bum with no ambition, too idle to even be interested in holding down a job . . . like all the men who wrecked my mum's life.'

His gaze was unwavering. 'And now?'

'And now . . .' Tula took a deep breath. 'Well, it turns out you aren't a lazy bum after all.' Adrenalin was zapping around her body. All this time she'd worked *so* hard to ignore her attraction to him, had refused to allow herself to weaken because he was so incontrovertibly off limits.

'Right.' Riley nodded. 'Well, just so you know, I used to be.' He shrugged. 'And I might have carried on being a lazy bum . . . playing around, having fun and not worrying about the future . . . if the thing with Marguerite hadn't happened. But it did. And I suppose that's when I grew up.'

Tula remembered something else he'd said to Jon and Jackie on the show. 'And you do most of your writing at night. How many hours?'

'Between eight and twelve. It varies.'

'Every night?'

'Pretty much.' He raised an eyebrow. 'So it makes a difference then, does it? To my prospects?'

He was attempting to make a joke of it, but Tula sensed the tension beneath the surface. The handsome, hopeless case she'd tried so hard not to fall in love with was a hopeless case no more. She didn't have to hold back any more; the reason she'd held back no longer existed.

Oh God. He was perfect.

'It could make a difference.' She nodded fractionally in agreement.

'You don't have to be polite. Only say it if you mean it.'

Up this close, she was able to see the darker flecks in his sea-green eyes. His lashes were thick and long, tipped with gold, his skin poreless and caramel-tanned. He had possibly the most perfect mouth she'd ever seen on a man . . . and as for the golden stubble on his chin . . .

Without even realising she was doing it, Tula reached up and ran her hand lightly over his jawline. The sensation of warm skin and the gentle rasp of stubble against her fingertips caused the breath to catch in her throat. She brushed her thumb across his lower lip and inched closer.

Then waited.

After a while, Riley said in a low voice, 'In case you were wondering, this is killing me.'

'Sshh.' Tula rested her hands on his shoulders. 'This is the best bit.'

'Sure about that?' His smile was crooked. 'Oh God, don't tell me you're into that tantric malarkey.'

'Don't make fun of it. We're going to be standing here for the next six hours.' Moving closer still, so their faces were almost but not quite touching, she whispered, 'Like this. It'll be worth it.'

'Sod that.' Riley's arms encircled her waist and he pulled her properly against him, his mouth closing over hers. Tula's insides dissolved; this was it, this was what she'd longed for and denied herself for so long.

And if this is just a kiss, imagine the rest . . .

When they finally came up for air, Riley said, 'So does this mean you like me now you know the truth?'

Tula ran her fingers down his forearms. 'I liked you before. That was the whole problem.'

'You mean I wasn't suitable then.' His mouth twitched. 'But I am now.'

'You are.' She tipped her head back, gazing at the cloudless blue sky, the birds wheeling overhead, the slowly revolving Millennium Wheel on the other side of the river. 'I keep thinking

I'm dreaming. I still can't believe this has happened. It's like you were a toad before and now you've turned into a prince.'

'Thanks. You definitely have a way with words.'

'We're here in London,' Tula marvelled, 'and you're not the man I thought you were. God, and I don't even know why you like me so much, when you could have all the blonde modelly types you want.'

'I don't know either,' said Riley. 'I just know I do. You're beautiful.'

'I'm no model.'

'You're more fun than any other girl I've ever met. I like everything about you.' He shrugged helplessly. 'Every single thing.'

'You're so smooth,' said Tula. 'I bet you say that to all the girls.' *Oh God, what if he did?*

'That's where you're wrong. I've never felt this way about anyone.' Riley was shaking his head. 'And I never want to feel it again. I don't like being turned down one bit.' He kissed her again, lingeringly, then gazed deep into her eyes. 'I'm telling you now, you're stuck with me.'

Two teenage boys, zigzagging their way along the path on skateboards, whistled loudly and yelled out, 'Oi! Get a room!'

'Actually,' said Riley when they'd whizzed past, 'that sounds like a pretty good idea.' He stopped and looked embarrassed. 'Sorry, is that crass? I shouldn't have said it out loud.'

'But it was in your head?'

'Of course it was in my head.'

'I was thinking it too.' Tula laced her fingers through his, feeling deliciously wanton. 'And the good thing is, we already have a room. Maybe we should do as they say.'

'Great idea.'

'I'm full of great ideas.' Still holding his hand, Tula swung round and turned to the right.

Riley stayed put. 'Where are you going? The hotel's in that direction.' He pointed over his shoulder, to the left.

'Yours might be. Mine's this way.'

'Mine's closer,' said Riley.

'Let's go to mine.'

'How many stars has yours got?'

'Two,' said Tula. And the owner had presumably stolen them from somewhere.

'And you'd really rather go there than to the Savoy?'

'Yes. Is that a problem?'

His expression softened. 'Not at all. I just think you're mad. I've got one of the most fantastic hotel rooms you could possibly ask for, but you'd rather we went to yours.'

'Yes,' said Tula.

'In that case, what are we waiting for?' Riley slid his arm around her waist and gave it a squeeze. 'This is still turning out to be the best day of my life. Let's go.'

The look on Riley's face was a picture when he saw her room. 'Wow. This is . . . quite something.'

'Forty-three pounds,' Tula reminded him gaily. 'Can't say that about the Savoy, can you?'

'This is true. And they can't even begin to compete in the swirly-carpet stakes.'

He had a point; this was possibly the swirliest swirly carpet ever. There was also paint peeling from the ceiling, the seventies paisley wallpaper was curling at the edges and the view from the window was of an assortment of bins against a grimy brick wall.

'The bed takes up most of the room,' Riley observed.

'I know. It's all part of their fiendish plan to hide as much as possible of the carpet.'

He smiled and began to undo the buttons on her shirt. 'I know why we've come here, by the way.'

'You do?' Tula's skin tingled at his feather-light touch.

'Oh yes.'

'Bet you don't.' *Not long now.* She quivered in anticipation as he slid the shirt off her shoulders.

'You'd be wrong.'

346

'Tell me, then.'

Riley's green eyes glittered with amusement as he trailed an index finger lazily along the line of her collarbone. 'I'll tell you later. Right now there's something else I'm far more interested in doing . . .'

'OK,' said Riley. 'If it makes you happier, you were right and I was wrong.'

Had she *ever* been happier? Tula lay on her side, half covered by the white sheet, and said, 'Get used to it.'

'Basically, if you're with the right girl, it doesn't matter where you are.' He pulled her closer into the crook of his arm and kissed her again for about the millionth time. 'You're amazing. I can't believe we're here. I thought this was never going to happen.'

'You're not so bad yourself.'

Riley checked his watch. 'It's ten o'clock. Does this place do room service?'

'No, but there's a vending machine downstairs.'

'Fantastic.'

'Actually, it is pretty fantastic. It has Caramacs,' said Tula. 'I've never seen Caramacs in a vending machine before.'

'Do you know what they have at the Savoy?'

'Tell me.'

'Everything. Everything you could possibly ask for.' Riley paused. 'But it looks like we're staying here.'

She nodded. 'Yes.'

'Because you wouldn't feel comfortable having Marguerite in the room next door.'

Tula burst out laughing because he'd known all along. 'Exactly that reason.'

'It is the Savoy,' Riley pointed out. 'The walls are thick, the beds don't creak. She wouldn't be able to hear anything.'

Except once you'd pictured Marguerite with an upturned glass pressed to the wall, there was no way of unthinking it.

Tula said, 'It just wouldn't feel right. She'd still *be* there. I couldn't relax.'

'OK, I get it. But she's going to be so pleased about this. Her plan worked out. You do know, don't you, how much Marguerite wanted this to happen?'

'I had an inkling. She was pretty miffed when I told her you weren't my type.' Hastily she amended, 'That was before I knew you *were* my type.'

'It's why she invited you up here. Well, she can relax now; it's happened. Job done.' Throwing back the sheet, Riley jumped out of bed and pulled on his shirt and jeans.

'Where are you going?'

'If we're staying here tonight, I need to buy a toothbrush.'

'And a bottle of wine.'

'Good idea. Let's make it champagne to celebrate.' Reaching down to give her another kiss, he said, 'Anything else you want?'

'I can't believe you're even asking that question,' said Tula. 'Hello? *Caramac.*'

Chapter 54

He didn't snore. That was good. Then again, the way she was feeling right now, Riley could probably get away with snoring like an angry tractor.

Tula smiled to herself, giddy with wonder and joy. Last night had been, hands down, the single most perfect night of her whole life. This was the happiest she'd ever felt; the connection between Riley and herself was just magical. For the first time she understood what people meant when they said *when you know, you know*.

And now, amazingly, she knew too.

A muffled *ting* announced the arrival of a message on Riley's phone, wherever it was. Following the sound, Tula reached over the edge of the bed and located it on the swirly carpet beneath randomly discarded clothes.

She wasn't being nosy, it was just normal human instinct; if there were words on a screen it was hard not to glance at them. Especially when they came from Marguerite.

Mission accomplished? Result! Makes it all worthwhile. Xx

Amused, Tula put the phone on the rickety bedside table. Honestly, what was Marguerite like? Once she had her mind set on something, there was no stopping her.

It was almost seven in the morning. Riley was still fast asleep, hardly surprisingly after the night they'd had. The only reason she'd woken up was because she was bursting for the loo.

Maybe she'd have a shower too, while she had the chance . . .

The thought occurred to Tula halfway through her shower.

Mission accomplished? Result! Makes it all worthwhile.

Around midnight last night, Riley had admitted that it hadn't only been her guilty conscience that had prompted Marguerite's shocking confession. She'd done it for him. Which had been a pretty major deal to come to terms with, but at the same time it did make sense that she should have come clean. It was only right that sooner or later the truth should come out.

Last night it hadn't occurred to Tula to question it. Now, her brain buzzing with fresh doubt, she stood motionless and let the water stream over her as an alternative scenario presented itself.

Oh God, oh God. Sick with fear, she examined the possibility. Please don't let it be true.

Surely it couldn't be.

But when you were up against someone as determined and unstoppable as Marguerite Marshall, nothing was beyond the realms of possibility.

Because Marguerite adored her beloved nephew; everyone knew that. Basically she worshipped the ground Riley walked on. So . . . what if she were only *pretending* to have lost the ability to write her books? Had they cooked up this whole charade between them purely in order to make her, Tula, believe that Riley Bryant wasn't a world-class shirker after all?

Tula was seized with panic. *OK, breathe slowly, get a grip.* It was, she knew, a far-fetched and completely ridiculous idea. But the trouble was, now she'd thought of it, there was no way of *unthinking* it. As mad and out-there as it might seem, it was now lodged in her brain.

Needing time to think, and desperate not to wake Riley, Tula dressed, let herself quietly out of the bedroom and ran downstairs. Out of change for the vending machine, she left the hotel and picked up bottled water and a packet of biscuits from the news-agent's next door.

Too confused to go back to the room, she began to walk.

OK, there didn't appear to be any way of finding out the truth. If she asked Riley, he would only reiterate what he'd already told her.

As would Marguerite.

And they'd already announced that no one else had been aware of their deception. Which meant, basically, that there was no way in the world of proving that they weren't lying.

And if this sounded like a wild hypothesis . . . well, it actually wasn't as far-fetched as the idea that Riley had been writing Marguerite's books in the first place.

The trouble was, short of physically tying him to a chair and standing over him *forcing* him to write . . .

Tula felt sick. Oh God, *had* it all been a ruse? Please don't let this be true . . .

She'd been wandering in a daze and had now reached Westminster Bridge. It was seven forty and the height of the rush hour. Traffic clogged the road across the bridge and the walkways on either side were full of people in smart business suits hurrying to work. Everyone was preoccupied, in commuter mode, either concentrating on their mobiles or lost in the music feeding into their brains via headphones.

With her wet hair, white lacy sundress and lime-green flip-flops, Tula realised, she wasn't dressed like anyone else. As always, she was the odd one out. Where was she even headed, anyway? How was aimless wandering going to help? All these busy people surrounding her, tutting with annoyance because she'd now stopped walking and was getting in their way; were any of them as muddled and conflicted as she was? And what was that? Oh God, her phone . . . was this Riley calling to find out why she'd done an early morning runner?

Tula fished the phone out of her bra, earning herself a look of disgust from an immaculate brunette with a brown leather briefcase that exactly matched her sensible hair and shoes.

Then she exhaled with relief, because the incoming call was from Sophie.

351

Tula moved out of the way of the steamroller tide of commuters, leaned against the bridge's green-painted balustrade and said, 'Hi, you.'

Because Sophie was good to have around in a crisis. Maybe she'd be able to help and advise her, even though there was obviously no way of answering the unanswerable question about whether or not Riley had—

'OH MY GOD,' Sophie bellowed down the phone from Cornwall. 'I was out working last night and I completely missed the show! Hazel from next door just called in to borrow some milk and she told me all about what happened! Were you there in the studio when Marguerite said it? Can you believe it's been going on for so long? Isn't it just completely brilliant?'

Hmm. Brilliant if it's true.

Tula gazed across the river at the London Eye. Prevaricating, she said, 'In what way?'

'Because Riley's crazy about you and you really like him too but you didn't want to be stuck with a no-hoper . . . except he *isn't*,' Sophie exclaimed triumphantly. 'He's been working his socks off all this time, just to help Marguerite out. Which makes him even more perfect. Just think, slogging away, putting in all those hours and getting none of the recognition.'

'I suppose so . . .'

'Oh come on! Don't you see? It's like a dream come true for you!'

Oh God, and now she was going to have to confide her doubts to Sophie, like the world's biggest spoilsport. Tula pressed the phone to her ear, gazed up at the Houses of Parliament and said miserably, 'I know, but the thing is, what if—'

'And it's a relief for me too,' Sophie blurted out. 'Now I don't have to feel guilty any more about not telling you!'

A fat businessman shoved past, almost sending Tula flying. Regaining her balance, she said, 'Not telling me about what?'

'I knew! I found out two weeks ago! And I knew it was a secret and I couldn't breathe a word to anyone, but I really wanted you to know because it would make all the difference. But now it's OK, everyone knows!'

Sophie had what? She'd *known* the truth? Tula's head swam with disbelief. Stunned, she said, 'How . . . but *how* did you find out?'

'It was when Marguerite asked me to take photos of that mystery bird in her garden. Riley didn't know I was there. He was working on the computer in Marguerite's office . . . I had a long lens on my camera and I saw what he was doing. Well obviously I thought at first I was having some sort of hallucination, but I wasn't. It was actually true. What's that noise?' Sophie said abruptly. 'Are you sniffing? Have you got a cold?'

On Westminster Bridge, with no tissue to wipe away the tears streaming down her face, Tula had to do the best she could with her free hand. 'I'm fine. Just . . . h-happy. So happy you can't imagine.' Oh help, and now her nose was running too; talk about the epitome of glamour.

'Good, I'm glad.' Sophie sounded as if she was smiling now. 'If anyone deserves to be happy, it's you.'

'You went away.' Riley was sitting up in bed when she arrived back at the hotel ten minutes later.

'And now I'm here again.'

'I woke up all on my own and didn't know where you'd gone.' He drew her on to the bed beside him. 'Never do that to me again.'

Tula breathed in the scent of him. 'I won't.' Oh God, his skin smelled irresistible.

'Where were you?'

'I went to buy us some water and biscuits for breakfast. And then I ate them. Sorry.'

'This is a terrible hotel. I don't want to stay here any more.' Riley kissed her. 'Let's check out and go and see how Marguerite is this morning. Then once she's gone downstairs to breakfast . . .'

There followed a meaningful pause. Tula looked at him and said innocently, 'Catch up on some sleep?'

'Hey, it's the Savoy.' Riley's smile was equally innocent. 'And the beds don't creak. We can do whatever we like.'

Chapter 55

It was Sunday afternoon and the beach was crowded with holidaymakers. A light breeze coming in off the sea ruffled Tula's hair as she shielded her eyes from the sun and watched Sophie emerge from the water in her black swimsuit.

OK, this was a secret it was *definitely* killing her to keep. With a bit of luck she wouldn't have to do it for much longer. Since Josh had confided in her on Friday evening, she'd been buzzing with the knowledge, bursting with it and simultaneously terrified she might accidentally let slip something that would give the game away.

Except it wasn't a game, was it? It was important, and please God, everything that had gone so horribly wrong years ago was finally about to come right.

Tula double-checked that everyone was in position. Yes, there they were, sixty or so metres away to the right. And over there to the left, sitting in the shade of the café, were Josh and Riley. *Her perfect Riley . . .*

OK, and here came Sophie now, shaking the sea from her hair as she made her way back up the beach. Reaching Tula, she picked up her purple towel and quickly dried off before sitting down.

'You should have come in. The water's fantastic.'

Thank goodness for dark glasses. Tula grimaced. 'Didn't feel like swimming today. Too lazy.'

'It's good exercise.'

'I've been getting plenty of good exercise, thanks very much.'

'You're smirking again.'

'Can't help it. I'm very smug.'

Sophie smiled. 'Ever been happier?'

'No.' Tula shook her head. 'Never. Honestly, nothing's ever felt so right.'

'Ah, that's good. You deserve it.'

'So do you.' She hadn't meant to say it; the words had slipped out. God, just knowing what was about to happen was getting her jittery. Sitting up and arranging herself on the pink rug, Tula said, 'How am I looking? Pretty good?'

Sophie said teasingly, 'Like a woman in love,' and flicked the ends of her hair at her, showering her with droplets of water.

'Go on then, take some pictures of me. Flattering ones.' Tula nodded at the Nikon in its case. 'Make me look fantastic.'

Luckily Sophie never turned down a photo opportunity. She reached for the case and took out her favourite camera. Tula's heart broke into a panicky canter, because she'd just set the train of events in motion. Plus she knew Josh and Riley were watching from the café. *Please let it work.*

'OK,' said Sophie, moving backwards and fiddling with the buttons on the camera. 'Turn your face up to the left, rest your arm on your knee, just relax . . .'

Tula did as she was told. *Oh, but how could she relax?*

'What's wrong?' Sophie lowered the camera.

'Nothing.'

'You need to loosen up. Let your shoulders go back. And just dangle your hand.'

Tula had another go, but it was impossible. The harder she tried, the more scrunched up she became. Her fingers had completely lost their ability to dangle.

'You're not on your way to the electric chair,' said Sophie. 'Just try to smile in the normal way.'

'I am.'

'No you aren't.'

Tula tried again. Sophie took some shots and said, 'Now you

356

look like a dog that's secretly eaten all the biscuits and is waiting to be found out.'

'Thanks a lot.' She glanced at the pictures Sophie was showing her on the screen and winced. 'Eww.'

'See what I mean? I've never seen you like this before.'

'I don't know why it's happening.' And now even her mouth felt strange; oh help, this was impossible. Hastily Tula rubbed her hands over her face to hide the guilt. 'OK, give me two minutes to stop feeling awkward . . .'

'Take deep breaths,' Sophie said helpfully. 'Give your arms a shake, stop thinking about the camera and just relax.'

Were they all watching her from their various viewpoints? Did they appreciate how incredibly stressful this was?

'It's no good. Don't worry about it. Take photos of someone else instead.' Tula waved a dismissive hand and began to scan the beach, casually and taking care not to zone in too fast. Kneeling on the rug, she noted the relevant targets and took a deep steadying breath. Then she pointed and said in a voice barely recognisable as her own, 'Oh look over there at those little ones in the matching pink T-shirts!'

'Where?' Sophie raised the Nikon and followed the direction of her gaze.

'Just in front of the big sandcastle, see? Next to that yellow beach ball.'

'Got them. Oh, cute. They're twins! Ha, look at the one on the right, she's about to trip over that bucket of water . . . whoops, there it goes.' Laughing, Sophie began happily clicking away, oblivious to the fact that Tula was no longer watching the two small girls. Instead, her gaze was fixed on Sophie, waiting for the reaction that would surely come any second now . . .

And then she saw it. The lens moved a fraction to the right. The clicking of the camera abruptly stopped. Glancing over her shoulder, Tula saw Josh and Riley in turn watching Sophie.

How on earth was she feeling now? It was anyone's guess.

★　★　★

Sophie stared through the viewfinder, her index finger frozen in mid-air, her entire body stiff with disbelief. She'd only meant to glance fleetingly at the twins' parents, but that was because she hadn't expected one of them to be her ex-husband.

Theo.

Theo.

I'm not dreaming. It is actually him.

Looking the same, apart from a bit older. God, though. He was here. In St Carys. With a woman. And two small children. And now one of the twins was waving a blue plastic spade at him and he was laughing, *actually laughing* as he pretended to reach over and grab it away from her.

The sound filling her ears, Sophie realised, was that of her own rapid breathing. An overload of information had caused her to lose track of time. Slowly she lowered the Nikon and rested it on her bare thigh.

The penny wavered. It wasn't until she turned to look at Tula that it finally, properly dropped.

Tula, despite her best efforts, had always been the most hopeless fibber in the world.

Sophie gripped the camera with both hands to make sure it didn't fall. Within the space of the last minute her emotions had ranged from shock and fear to curiosity and unfolding realisation. Her mouth dry, she said, 'You knew.'

Tula was the picture of pink-cheeked guilt. It was blindingly obvious now why she'd been unable to relax enough to have the photos taken.

'Oh my God.' Sophie stared at her. 'Did *you* do this?'

'No.' Tula shook her head. 'But I knew it was being done.'

'It's Theo.' OK, stupid thing to say, but she needed to spell it out for herself. 'And he isn't here by chance. I don't believe this is happening . . .'

'Take another look at him,' Tula prompted. 'Go on. How does he seem to you?'

How does he seem? Slowly Sophie brought the camera back up to eye level and searched through the viewfinder until she found him again. Theo was wearing a white T-shirt and knee-length navy board shorts. He was now filling a blue plastic bucket with sand with the help of one of the small girls, while the other proudly waved a shell at him. She said something to Theo, who threw his head back and laughed.

Sophie felt the backs of her eyes prickle with heat; during the last four years she'd thought of Theo thousands of times, but never had she pictured him laughing. In her imagination he'd always been sad, despairing, angry or just plain stony-faced and sullen. Not once had it even occurred to her to think of him as being happy.

Then again, nor had she imagined a scenario like this.

And now the little girl was offering him the shell, curling her chubby arms around his neck and planting a kiss on the side of his face. Whereupon Theo scooped her up into his arms and tickled her until she collapsed in fits of giggles against his chest.

Watching them, Sophie's heart turned over. The smile on Theo's lips, the look of absolute love in his eyes was just wonderful to see. Unable to help herself, she clicked the shutter and captured the moment.

Theo had twin girls. And a partner, too. Shifting focus, Sophie studied the woman sitting beside him. Chestnut-brown hair, sparkling eyes and a pretty, smiley mouth. She was wearing a sea-green vest top and cream shorts. Good legs, bare feet, tanned arms and . . . yes, a wedding ring on the appropriate finger.

Just to be sure, a quick check of Theo's left hand confirmed the presence of a matching gold band.

When she moved the angle of the lens to take another look at his face, she got the shock of her life.

He was gazing straight at her.

Sophie almost dropped the camera in her haste to look away. 'Shit, he knows I'm here!'

'Of course he does,' said Tula. 'How else would Josh have managed to set this whole thing up?'

'*Josh?*' But the idea that Josh had been behind this was oddly inevitable. Sophie's heart was racing; of course it had been him. She might not know how, but she knew why. Aloud, she said, 'How did he find him?' Because *she* knew where Theo had been living, but it was beyond her how Josh could have tracked him down.

'Um, not sure.' Tula shrugged. 'But he did. Because it matters to him too, in case you hadn't noticed. *You* matter to him. And don't worry,' she added, 'everything's fine. Theo wants you to know how sorry he is. Will you speak to him?'

He's sorry.

Sophie swallowed, her mouth dry. 'Is he OK?'

'Look at him. Of course he's OK. If you don't want to do it, you can just leave the beach.' Tula's voice softened. 'But you really should meet him. Have a talk.'

Of course she had to. In a daze, Sophie passed over the camera. In return Tula handed her the navy cotton kaftan she'd taken off before diving into the sea. Yes, that was a good idea. She pulled it on over her head.

'If you'd rather not do it in front of his wife, just go for a walk along the water's edge and he'll join you,' said Tula.

Everything had been worked out, each eventuality planned for. God, this was *so* surreal.

'It's all right, I'd like to meet her too.' Sophie took a deep breath and brushed dry sand off her legs. 'OK, wish me luck. Here goes.'

Josh had never watched anything so intently in his life. At his feet, Griff was wagging his tail and gazing adoringly up at him in the hope that a bit of stick-throwing might be about to happen. Then he jumped up and rested his paws on Josh's knee, as if this might spur him into action.

Not a chance, not at the moment. Don't even think about it.

Sophie was making her way over to Theo and his family. She looked so effortlessly beautiful, with her tousled sun-bleached hair and slim tanned limbs. It was probably a good thing that Tula had given her the kaftan to put on over her swimsuit.

'You know, if I was writing this in a book,' Riley said cheerfully, 'they'd take one look at each other and fall madly in love all over again. Which would leave you looking like a right idiot and it'd be all your own fault.'

'Great. Thanks for that. I feel so much better now.' Josh nodded. *As if the exact same thought hadn't already crossed his mind.*

'No problem.' Grinning, Riley finished the last mouthful of his chicken sandwich. 'But it's the obvious twist.'

Josh said drily, 'I think I liked you better when you were just a lazy beach bum.'

'Don't tell me you haven't thought about it,' said Riley playfully. 'They were married, after all.'

'If that happens, it happens.' Josh reached down to ruffle Griff's ears. 'It's a risk I have to take. OK, there's a chance I might lose her, but up until now she hasn't been mine to lose anyway. I still won't have her.' Shaking his head, he said, 'But thanks for reminding me.'

'Hey, that's just the worst-case scenario. You never know, it could all work out fine. Are you hungry?' Riley reached for his wallet on the table in front of them. 'I could do with another sandwich.'

As if he could eat a thing. Josh's chest tightened as he saw Sophie approaching Theo. 'No thanks. Not right now.'

'Sure?' Riley turned his attention to Griff and said, 'Sandwich?'

'*WoofwoofWOOF!*' His tail going into metronome mode, Griff promptly bounced over, abandoning Josh in favour of Riley.

'See? As fickle as a girl.' Riley's white teeth flashed as his grin broadened. 'One minute he liked you best, and now he prefers me.'

Chapter 56

'Hi,' said Theo.

'Hi.' Sophie wondered if anyone was watching her knees, because they definitely felt as if they were knocking together like castanets.

'I'm so sorry,' said Theo.

She nodded, and managed a wobbly smile.

'BUGGER,' yelled the nearer of the two small girls playing on the picnic rug between them.

Which was unexpected.

'Hello,' Theo's wife chimed in. 'It's so lovely to meet you. I'm Lorna. That one's Emmy,' she pointed to the other twin, 'and this is Kate. She's trying to say bucket, by the way, but it's not coming out terribly well.' Reaching for the yellow bucket and passing it over to Kate, she said, '*Bucket*, sweetheart.'

'BUGGER,' Kate screamed happily.

'They're beautiful,' said Sophie. 'How old are they?'

Listen to me, I'm talking as if we're strangers. Which we are . . . except also kind of not . . .

'Sixteen months. They keep us busy. Poor you,' added Lorna sympathetically. 'You're looking a bit stunned. Are you still in shock?'

'I think so.' Sophie smiled, instinctively liking her.

'Anyway, thank goodness you came over. We were worried you wouldn't. Now, I'm going to stay here with the twins and I think

362

you and Theo need to go for a walk and have a bit of time together. Talk things through. But let me just say, he never meant for any of this to happen. He was completely mortified when Josh told us about you. Am I talking too much? Sorry, I'll shut up now. You two head off. Take as long as you like. We'll be here waiting for you when you get back.'

'She's lovely,' said Sophie, once Lorna and the twins were out of earshot. 'You have great taste in wives.'

'I do.' The tension in Theo's face dissipated. 'Lorna's amazing. It was her idea that we should come down here, you know. Once Josh had explained the situation. I thought I should email you or maybe call, but she said that something this important needed to be done properly, face to face.'

'That's really good of her.'

'It's the kind of person she is. Lorna means the world to me. Well, her and the girls. Can you believe how much my life has changed? How much *I've* changed?'

They'd reached the water's edge and were walking along it now, navigating small children and collapsing sandcastles.

'I can believe it. I can see it with my own eyes.' Sophie inwardly marvelled at the realisation that there wasn't the faintest flicker of attraction between her and this man she'd once been married to. All that remained was fondness; it was like bumping into an old, entirely platonic, friend. 'And now tell me everything,' she said, stepping over a carefully dug trench decorated with shells. 'I want to know it all.'

It hadn't taken that long, really. Together they'd walked and talked and Theo had brought her up to date with everything that mattered. He kept apologising too, until Sophie made him stop. She also discovered that as soon as Lorna had said they must come down here to see her, Josh had insisted they stay at the hotel as his guests.

'It was really kind of him,' Theo added. 'We've never been away anywhere before, what with getting the business up and running, then having the twins. We did try, but he refused to take any money.'

'Josh is kind.' As Sophie nodded in agreement, she felt her heart give a little squeeze.

'He's crazy about you. You do know that?'

She hesitated, then slowly nodded again.

'He's done all this because he's trying to cure you.' Theo was surveying her closely. 'Also, because he's in love with you.'

Oh good grief. Sophie watched her bare toes squish into the wet sand as she stopped walking. 'Did he tell you that?'

'Come on. He doesn't need to say it, does he? It's so obvious. Are you blushing or hot?'

'Both.' It was a lethal combination.

'Look, you've accepted my apology—'

'*All* of your apologies,' Sophie interjected.

'And now I need you to promise me something,' said Theo. 'I've managed to wreck the last four years of your life, but it has to stop now. Don't make me feel worse about it than I already do.'

A lump the size of a conker expanded in Sophie's throat. She shook her head.

'It's no way to live.' His voice was gentle but firm.

She knew that too; it really *hadn't* been any way to live. Well, it had been OK until Josh had burst into her life. Since then, her tangled emotions had made the last few months a lot harder to bear.

'Hey, look at me,' Theo prompted. 'It's OK, it's all over now. You don't have to worry any more.'

'Don't I?' Sophie felt the old familiar stirrings of anxiety. 'But what if it happens to me again?'

Theo placed his hands on her shoulders, forcing her to pay attention. 'Right, now listen. I may have only just met Josh Strachan, but I can tell you categorically that he'd *never* do anything like that. And you know it too,' he went on steadily. 'You just have to get over the fear, learn to relax and enjoy feeling normal again.' He smiled and raised his eyebrows. 'So, do you think you're going to be able to do that?'

He was OK, he was fine, he was *cured*. Gazing at his oh-so-familiar face and hearing the sincerity in his voice, Sophie realised she could do it. The time had come to let go of the guilt.

She breathed out and said, 'Yes, I can.'

'Promise?'

Sophie nodded; it was as if the anxiety of the last four years had magically released its hold on her body.

Aloud she said, 'Promise.'

She felt lighter, exorcised, *free*.

'Well, good. Glad to hear it.' There was no need for a hug; Theo gave her shoulders a brief reassuring squeeze, then let her go. 'That makes me feel better too.' He paused for a moment. 'So on a scale of one to ten, how much do you like Josh?'

This was Theo. They'd been through so much together, she could be completely herself with him. Sophie said, 'Seven. Maybe eight.'

It was a measure of how close they'd once been to each other that Theo didn't bat an eyelid; the ability to know when she was joking hadn't been lost. He regarded her with amusement. 'And the real number is . . .?'

'Out of ten?' Just the thought of Josh made her heart contract with emotion. She smiled at Theo and said, 'Sixty?'

The problem with other people taking control of your life and making things happen is that it might not actually be the best time for it to happen to you.

As they made their way back along the beach to where Lorna and the twins were waiting, Sophie saw that the party had expanded. Tula had joined them, as had Riley and Josh, along with Griff. Yesterday when Tula had casually asked her if she was free today, she'd said yes, because she *had* been free. Until a regular client had rung last night asking to be squeezed in for a sitting at four o'clock this afternoon. And it was now twenty past three.

Hardly ideal.

Furthermore, since the client, Gloria, was forty-one weeks pregnant and keen to be photographed in all her voluptuous, about-to-give-birth glory, it wasn't the kind of appointment you could risk putting off for another day.

Sophie's pulse began to race as they neared the group. Griff was perched on Tula's lap, his stumpy tail wagging as one of the twins stroked his back. The other twin was up on Riley's shoulders, squealing with delight. Josh and Lorna were sitting together, deep in conversation.

'Yay, you're back!' Tula had spotted them.

One of the twins waved at Theo and yelled, 'Da-da!'

'So you two didn't run off together,' said Riley. 'Damn, I lost my bet.'

Lorna looked at Sophie. 'How are you feeling now?'

OK, this was weird. But nice. In fact, nice was an understatement. 'Better.' Sophie smiled at her. '*So* much better.'

'I knew it!' Jumping to her feet, Lorna gave her a warm hug.

'*And?*' said Tula meaningfully, gesturing in less than subtle fashion at Josh.

'And I have a client booked at four. Which means I need to leave pretty much now.' Sophie turned to Josh. 'Can we meet up later? If you're not busy?'

He gazed at her for several seconds, then nodded. 'OK. That's fine. Just let me know when you're ready.'

Sophie nodded too; basically she was ready – more than ready – now. All she wanted was to get this whole thing sorted out at last.

But there was no time. It would just have to wait. *God, it was going to kill her.*

'I'll see you in a bit.' Suddenly unable to look at Josh, she picked up the bag and camera Tula had brought over and gave an awkward teenage wave encompassing everyone. 'OK, thanks. Bye.'

Chapter 57

When Tula and Riley arrived back at Moor Court, Marguerite came rushing out to greet them.

'And? Tell me everything! We're *dying* to know.'

'We? Who else is here?' Riley looked around; there were no other cars on the driveway.

'Not *here* here,' Marguerite said impatiently. 'I meant Baz. We're on Skype!'

'Again? Has he asked you to marry him yet?'

'Oh *shush*.' But Marguerite's eyes were sparkling as she shook her head at Riley; her Skype calls with Baz were rapidly approaching marathon status. 'We've been talking non-stop since midday.'

Tula marvelled at the change in Marguerite; the last week had been eventful to say the least. Following her shock confession on the *EveryDay* show, the backlash had been swift and brutal. Her fans had felt cheated and betrayed, and coruscating journalists berated Marguerite for lying to her readers and treating them like gullible fools.

People who'd never read any of her books piled in to condemn her, and the hatred gathered pace to such an extent that she was practically public enemy number one.

This continued for forty-eight hours and could well have carried on had Bertha Mulligan, Marguerite's deadliest and most vociferous rival in the world of contemporary women's fiction, not launched her own personal attack. Bertha was singularly self-important, and her latest facelift had left her looking like a bulldog wrapped in cling film. Miraculously, it was the utter viciousness of her comments that caused everyone to take against her and decide they'd far rather be on Marguerite's side instead.

Sympathy then turned to admiration when Marguerite refused to retaliate and Bertha found herself an object of ridicule and distaste.

The general public, who had always admired and respected Marguerite, now decided to love her instead. An underdog for the first time in her life, she found herself taken to their collective hearts. Her publishers, needless to say, breathed a hurricane-sized sigh of relief.

At the same time, interest in Riley had grown at a rate of knots, book sales rocketed and the publishers had already suggested that if he wanted to divide his time between co-authoring Marguerite's books and writing something else in a different genre under his own name, they would back him to the hilt. It was an idea Riley had never considered before, but their support – and Marguerite's – had inspired him to begin plotting out an action thriller with a hero who could feature in future books.

The other exciting development had occurred last week when Marguerite's agent had been contacted by a US-based film producer keen on turning her life story into a movie.

This wasn't unusual in itself – options on her books had been snapped up over the years by various TV and film production companies – but the difference this time was the man doing the snapping. Baz Kingsley had emailed Marguerite, then he'd phoned her . . . and phoned again, swiftly establishing a rapport. In no time at all they'd progressed to video calls, and now Baz was flying over next week to meet her in person. They were as besotted with each other as teenagers, completely smitten.

Which was wonderful in one way – Baz was ruggedly good-looking, hugely successful and had his own teeth *and* private jet. The slight down side was the fact that he had five ex-wives.

Five.

Frankly, it was a miracle he had any money left at all.

Having been updated with the details of Sophie's meeting with Theo on the beach, Marguerite said, 'Poor darling, what that girl's been through.' She looked at Riley and raised her eyebrows. 'We could use it in our next book.'

'No we couldn't.' Riley shook his head firmly. 'That's not on.'

'Spoilsport. Oh well, I suppose you're right. I've invited a few people down from the publishers next week, by the way. So they can meet Baz. I'd better get back to him; he'll be wondering where I've got to.' Taking a crimson Dior lipstick from her skirt pocket, she applied it with a practised flourish, then bared her teeth tigerishly at Tula. 'Am I OK? Any on my teeth?'

'No, you're fine.' Tula did her best to keep a straight face as Marguerite patted her hair and pinched her cheeks in order to make herself camera-ready once more for Baz.

'Oh stop it, I know you're laughing at me. I know how crazy this whole thing probably seems to you. But that's because you're young,' Marguerite chided, 'and I'm not. And I've never felt this way about any man before. Not any of my husbands,' she announced defiantly. 'Not even Lawrence. This thing with Baz . . . OK, I know we haven't met in person yet, but it just feels so different; it's like the moment I first saw him . . .'

'We know.' Riley winked at Tula as Marguerite gazed off dreamily into the distance. 'We can tell. It was love at first Skype.'

Chapter 58

It was six o'clock when Sophie left her flat and walked up the hill towards the hotel. The shoot had gone well. Gloria had been thrilled with the pictures of her with her impressively large bump. In one of the photos Sophie had even managed to capture the moment when the baby had been kicking and flailing, so that pushed-out hand and footprints were clearly visible on the outside.

Which had been both miraculous and a little bit weird.

'You can't imagine how it feels.' Gloria had run her hands lovingly over her watermelon-sized stomach. 'You just have to wait until it happens to you.'

And for the first time – the *very* first time – the idea of it didn't fill Sophie with terror.

Everything felt different now. It was incredible. She felt as if she were starting a whole new life of her own.

Arriving at Mariscombe House, Sophie glanced down and stopped in her tracks. Oh brilliant, so much for calm and in control. From the ankles up she was OK, wearing a sleeveless lilac dress and a bit of make-up, no problem there. But from the ankles down . . . well, one orange flip-flop and one purple one probably was a bit of a giveaway.

How had that even happened? Oh well, never mind, too late now. She pushed open the door and made her way through the hotel out on to the broad terrace at the back, boasting the best views in St Carys.

She waved at Dot and Lawrence, sitting at a table at the other end of the terrace. Home from hospital now, Lawrence was recuperating nicely, and he and Dot were inseparable. It made your heart sing to see them together, reunited at last.

There were plenty of other guests out here too, eating and drinking and enjoying the early evening sunshine. Sophie spotted the ones she was looking for and went over to them.

Back from the beach, Theo and Lorna each had a twin on their lap.

'Hi.' Sophie opened her turquoise and silver bag and took out an envelope. 'Can't stop, but I just wanted you to have this. I took it earlier, kind of by accident. Thought you might like it.'

Theo slid the glossy enlarged photo from the envelope. He studied the picture of himself smiling and gazing lovingly into his daughter's eyes as she lay cradled in his arms, clutching a shell and giggling with delight.

'Wow.' Leaning over to take a look, Lorna said, 'That's fantastic.'

Sophie shrugged. 'I couldn't help myself. You just looked so happy.'

'I am.' Theo nodded. 'You know, you're pretty good at this. You should think about taking it up professionally.'

'I may just do that.' Sophie turned to leave, smiling at Lorna and waggling her fingers at the girls. 'See you later.'

Back inside, she stopped at the reception desk and said, 'Hi, is Josh around?'

The new receptionist shook her head. 'He isn't in the office.'

'Oh.' Sophie's heart was clattering around inside her ribcage like a church bell; please don't let him have gone out.

'He's busy upstairs in his apartment, said he had some very important work to be getting on with.' The girl was new and hesitant. 'I could call him if it's really urgent, and ask him to come down.'

There was no going back now. Sophie said, 'It's OK, I'll head on up.'

'But . . . do you know him?'

'I do.' *And I'm about to get to know him even better.*

The receptionist said helplessly, 'Should I give him a ring first?'

'No, let's make it a surprise.' Sophie was already halfway up the first flight of stairs.

'Um, excuse me, you've got different-coloured flip-flops on!'

'I know,' Sophie called over her shoulder. 'It's a style statement.'

She reached the door on the third floor and knocked straight away. *Here I am, here we go, it's happening at last.*

Josh looked surprised when he opened the door. 'Hi. I thought you'd call first.'

Ah, look at him, look at that face, those incredible eyes . . .

'Couldn't wait.' Her mouth curved into an unstoppable smile. 'Besides, I wanted to see what you were up to. The receptionist says you're busy doing some *very* important work.'

With a whiffle of delight, Griff bounced off the sofa and trotted over to see her. She bent and tickled his ears.

'Hey, sweetie, what's this incredibly important work that's being dealt with up here, hmm?'

The TV was on, showing an old film starring Frank Sinatra. Josh's computer was also open and she got to it before he could shut it down.

'Ah-ha, Angry Birds.' Sophie nodded triumphantly. 'Very busy, very important work.'

Josh closed the lid of the computer and gave her a long look. 'It's all right for you, you've had something to distract you. I've spent the last three hours wondering when you might turn up or even *if* you'd turn up, and what you might say if you did.' He paused to take a steadying breath. 'Because that's the thing about you . . . I never know what you're going to say. Apart from *no*, rather more often than I'd like.'

Sophie gazed up at him. Josh Strachan, impulsive and impatient by nature, had been infinitely more patient than she deserved. A lesser man would have given up on her months ago.

But that was the thing about Josh, he wasn't a lesser man. He was strong and honest and knew what he wanted. He was also a problem-solver, and somehow, miraculously, he had managed to sort out her problem.

He'd freed her from the cage she'd built around herself.

'I'm going to say thank you,' said Sophie. 'For everything.'

She stepped forward, wrapped her arms around his neck and kissed him on the mouth. Oh wow, and there it was, happening again, fireworks exploding and every molecule in her body fizzing with adrenalin . . . The sensations were just overwhelming and it felt like coming home.

Was it possible to be happier than this?

'You see?' When the kiss finally ended, Josh held her face between his hands. 'That's the kind of answer I like. It's the kind of answer worth waiting for.'

He smiled, and the look in those glittering dark eyes made Sophie's insides melt with love.

'Thanks for finding Theo and making it happen. Thanks for understanding how I felt.' She had never felt so elated, so helium-filled with joy. 'Thanks for hanging in there. It means the world to me. You're everything I ever wanted.' Her eyes were prickling this time, with tears of happiness. 'And everything I thought I could never let myself have.'

'You're worth it.' Josh tucked a strand of hair behind her ear and gazed at her. 'Honestly? I didn't even know the kind of girl I was looking for. And then you came along, and you were it. You were just perfect. So I really didn't have any choice.'

'I'm not perfect.'

'You are to me.' He paused and frowned. 'Apart from one slight problem . . .'

'Oh?' *Were her boobs too small?*

Josh moved back, glanced down at her feet. 'Want to tell me what happened? Or are they meant to be like that?'

'I was on my way here to see you.' Sophie smiled and slid her arms around his waist. 'Obviously I was distracted. Don't worry, I didn't do it on purpose.'

'Good. Glad about that.' His smile broadened. 'It does look a bit . . . you know, eclectic.'

Griff, his tail wagging, was still dancing excitedly around them. They'd reached the stage, Sophie felt, where some alone-time might be preferable. Bending down, she eased off the flip-flops and sandwiched them together, then offered them to Griff. The little dog, who loved *all* footwear with a passion, gave an ecstatic wiggle and grabbed them, cigar-style, between his teeth.

'What are you doing?' Josh watched as she crossed the room and opened the door to let Griff out.

'Sometimes,' said Sophie, 'three's a crowd.'

They heard the clatter of claws on polished wood as Griff disappeared downstairs with his fabulous treasure of one orange flip-flop and one purple one.

'You're mad,' said Josh. 'He could take them anywhere; you know what he's like about burying things. You might never see them again.'

Sophie closed the door and turned the key in the lock so they couldn't be interrupted. 'Don't worry about it.' With a playful smile, she made her way back to Josh. 'I've got another pair just like them at home.'

If you enjoyed

THE UNPREDICTABLE CONSEQUENCES OF LOVE

look out for the new *Jill Mansell* novel

THREE AMAZING THINGS ABOUT YOU

Out in January 2015

Turn the page for the first chapter...

You can order

THREE AMAZING THINGS ABOUT YOU

now

www.headline.co.uk

www.jillmansell.co.uk

🐦 @JillMansell

📘 /OfficialJillMansell

Chapter 1

OK, this is it, confession time. For the last two years I've asked all of you to tell me three things about you. And in return I've never told you anything about me. Which probably hasn't seemed very fair, has it?

But it's currently one o'clock in the morning, I'm in the back of a car being driven down to London and I've decided to come clean.

So here we go:

1. I'm twenty-eight, I have cystic fibrosis and I never actually expected to live this long.
2. The hospital transplant coordinator called two hours ago – they have a new pair of lungs for me.
3. I've never been so scared in my life. Also, excited. But mainly scared. Because this is a big thing that's about to happen and since I'm a coward I can't help picturing the worst-case scenario.

So now you know the reason for the full disclosure. Basically, if this turns out to be the final entry on the website, you'll understand why. Needless to say, I really hope it won't be.

One more thing. Thank you, thank you, THANK YOU to the wonderful family of the donor for giving me this gift, this incredible chance. I'll be grateful until the day I die and

Hallie paused, reread what she'd written and deleted the last sentence. In its place she typed: *I hope you know how amazing you are. Your courage, kindness and generosity will always be remembered*.

Droplets of light summer rain speckled the windscreen of the car. Hallie gazed out into the warm night as a sign saying *London 25 miles* loomed out of the darkness towards them and slid past. Street lamps glowed amber and houses showed only occasional lights in their windows; almost everyone at this time was asleep. Soon, though, dawn would lighten the sky, alarm clocks would wake them and they'd carry on living their normal lives without even pausing to think how miraculous their normal lives were.

Just being able to breathe in and out, that was pretty miraculous . . .

The finality of it all hit her afresh. There was still a chance, of course, that the tissue match would turn out not to be good enough and the transplant wouldn't go ahead. Which was why she wasn't uploading her post to the website just yet. But a few short hours from now, she could be in the operating theatre receiving another person's lungs. And who knew what might happen after that?

How many people would read what she'd written? What would they think?

Sitting back, Hallie thought of the line she'd deleted and wished she could as easily erase the song now playing in her head. It was a great song, one that people loved to sing during karaoke sessions. Everyone always joined in enthusiastically with the chorus.

She wasn't sure of the exact lyrics, but the last line of the chorus went something like: *This could be the day that I die . . . this could be the day that I die . . .*

Oh well. Seemed like her brain still had a sense of humour, at least.

Before

'Hey, hi, how's things? What are you up to?'

Hallie brightened at the sound of Bea's voice. 'You really want to know? OK, I'll tell you. But I'm warning you now, you're going to be *so* jealous.'

'Fire away.'

'I'm in Venice, sitting at a table outside Caffè Florian in St Mark's Square. The sun is shining, church bells are ringing and the waiter's just opened a bottle of ice-cold Prosecco.'

'Is the waiter handsome?'

'What do you think? This is Venice! Of course he's handsome. He's giving me one of those handsome-waiter looks,' said Hallie. 'With his *eyes*.'

'Hmm, and is he listening to you saying this?'

'It's fine, he doesn't speak a word of English. I may seduce him later. He has a look of Bradley Cooper about him.'

'Sure you don't mean Tommy Cooper?'

'Shut *up*.'

'Are there pigeons there?'

'Yes, loads.'

'My mum went to St Mark's Square once. A pigeon did a poo on her head.'

'Lovely.'

'She was so mad,' said Bea. 'She'd had her hair done specially for the trip. I wouldn't stick around there if I were you. Get out while you can. Those Italian pigeons are evil.'

'Fine, you've convinced me. I'm going to jump into my helicopter now and fly home.'

'I think you should. Shall I come over after work this evening?'

'That'd be good.'

'Around seven then. See you later. Bye-eee!'

Hallie put down the phone and straightened her duvet, which had gone crooked again. She pulled herself into a more comfortable sitting position and did her best to adjust the pillows too. There was a definite art to staying in bed and not having to endlessly rearrange yourself, and she'd yet to master it. Back-arching, shoulder-stretching, bottom-wiggling and neck-tilting all played their part.

Having stretched and wriggled and got herself half sorted, Hallie looked out at the indigo sky as darkness fell. It was the week before Christmas, and multicoloured fairy lights were being switched on. From here, she had arguably the best view of the village: to the left, the high street; to the right, the River Windrush with its low stone bridge and the row of honey-coloured shops, hotels and houses on the other side of the water. She could watch everyone coming and going, keep track of people she knew, and also view the progress of tourists making their way around Carranford, the self-styled jewel in the north Cotswolds' crown.

Not so many visitors during the winter months, of course, but still enough to keep the people-watching interesting and the tourist-friendly shops open. A coachload were currently milling around, taking endless photographs, diving in and out of shops and buying souvenirs they didn't need, as well as Christmas presents for friends and relatives back home. By the looks of things, plenty of them would be opening a festively wrapped umbrella this year, printed with scenes of Carranford. Bea must have sold over a dozen today alone.

Eight days to Christmas. Hallie tried not to wonder if this one might be her last, basically because such thoughts were unanswerable and never helpful. Apart from anything else, the answer was always *possibly*.

Then again, that applied to everyone on the planet.

Banishing the question from her mind, Hallie switched on

the iPad and checked her emails instead. Several more had arrived this afternoon from visitors to the website. Brilliant, something to keep her occupied until Bea turned up. Never mind wondering if this Christmas would be her last; there were far more important problems to be sorted out, like how a girl should handle the discovery that she's inadvertently been dating twin boys, and the best way for a middle-aged man to divide his time over the festive season between his dull wife and his enthralling mistress.

Hallie had set up the website during a prolonged and particularly tedious hospital stay. Didn't everyone enjoy reading advice columns? She always had. She loved them, and loved coming up with solutions to problems too. When the columnist neglected to mention a useful suggestion, it always killed her not to be able to jump in and add a reply of her own.

The answer to this particular dilemma had, therefore, been to create the web page and begin dispensing advice herself.

She hadn't done it as poor-tragic-Hallie-with-the-manky-lungs-and-limited-lifespan either. This would only have inhibited questions; she'd known that from the word go. No, when people had problems in their lives, those problems were overwhelmingly important to them and everyone simply had to respect that. They certainly mustn't feel as if they couldn't compete with the person doling out the advice.

So she'd been anonymous from the start, and had remained so. All her readers knew was that she was female. The website was called www.threethingsaboutyou.com, and everyone writing in for advice with a dilemma was asked to include three things about themselves. Whether they chose to reveal big or small details was entirely up to them, but it was always an interesting indicator of character, and Hallie used them to more fully understand the people who were asking her to advise them.

Of course, for the first few weeks there hadn't been any readers, nor any problems being sent in, simply because no one knew the website existed. She'd had to make up dilemmas, borrow and adapt some from old magazines and reply in her own words to people who'd never confided in her in the first place.

But before long, interest had started to grow. Thanks to the power of social networking, people slowly discovered the website and, deciding they liked it, spread the word to their friends. The number of hits steadily increased, and readers began submitting their own problems, which was good of them and freed Hallie up to spend more time researching the relevant issues and compiling the best possible answers.

Since then, the popularity of the website had continued to grow. Hallie was known to her readers as Rose, which was her middle name. Visitors to the site were welcome to contribute their own advice, but she was the one who decided whether or not it was posted. It was generally agreed that Rose's replies were great and her rapport with the contributors second to none. She had warmth, wit and compassion, and the readers appreciated this.

Almost as much as Hallie appreciated them in return.

She clicked on the first email:

Dear Rose,

1. I'm a fireman.
2. I play rugby.
3. I'm afraid of the dark.

I'm forty-six, married for almost twenty years, and my wife doesn't know I like to wear women's underwear. Well, no one does. My problem is that last week my mother-in-law took it upon herself to wash and clean my car while I was out at a work event. Being the thorough type, she took out the spare tyre in the boot and found the bra and knickers underneath.

She has now accused me of having an affair and is demanding I confess all to my wife. I know what my mother-in-law is like – she won't rest until I do. So which do you think I should admit to being, Rose? An unfaithful husband or a transvestite? I honestly don't know which option she'd find easier to accept.

Okaaaaay.
The second email said:

Dear Rose,

1. I'm ugly.
2. I'm fat.
3. I hate my life.

There's this boy in my class and I really like him but he never looks at me. I thought it was because I wasn't skinny enough because he seems to only like thin girls, so in October I stopped eating and now I've lost three stone but he still isn't interested.

What's wrong with me and how can I make him fall in love with me? I just want to be happy. Do you think it'll happen if I lose more weight? Help me, Rose, I'm so miserable I just want to die. Please please tell me what to do.

Hallie's heart went out to the desperately unhappy teenager. She would answer this one first. Poor girl, a bit of love-bombing probably wouldn't go amiss.

JILL MANSELL

Don't Want To Miss A Thing

Dexter Yates loves his fun, carefree London life. But everything changes overnight when his sister dies, leaving him in charge of her eight-month-old daughter Delphi.

Comic-strip artist Molly Hayes lives in the beautiful Cotswold village of Briarwood. When it comes to relationships, she has a history of choosing all the wrong men.

Leaving the city behind, Dex moves to Briarwood – a much better place to work on his parenting skills – and he and Molly become neighbours. There's an undeniable connection between them. But if Dexter's going to adapt, he first has a lot to learn about Molly, about other people's secrets . . . and about himself.

Just *Heavenly*. Just *Jill*.

Everybody loves Jill Mansell's novels:

'A skilfully constructed, believable and brilliantly written tale about love *****' *Heat*

'A warm and thoughtful read, populated with engaging characters . . . I raced through it' *Daily Mail*

'Another compulsive page-turner from Mansell' *Daily Express*

978 0 7553 5589 1

headline
review

JILL MANSELL

A Walk In The Park

This was her guilty secret . . .

It's eighteen years since Lara Carson vanished into the night, leaving first love Flynn Erskine with lots of questions – and no answers. He's stunned by her return to Bath and can't deny the spark between them. But is there something she isn't telling him?

Lara's childhood best friend, Evie Beresford, is thrilled to welcome her back – especially as she's about to walk down the aisle with her dream man, Joel. But life's never that simple, is it? Things are about to change drastically for everyone involved. And it all starts on the morning of Evie's wedding . . .

Just *Heavenly*. Just *Jill*.

Some of the warm acclaim for Jill Mansell's novels:

'As frothy and moreish as a summer cocktail . . . your beach bag will be empty without it' *Heat*

'A warm and thoughtful read, populated with engaging characters . . . I raced through it' *Daily Mail*

'Smart and grown-up chick lit at its very best' *Good Housekeeping*

978 0 7553 5585 3

headline
review

JILL MANSELL

To The Moon And Back

When Ellie Kendall tragically loses her husband she feels her life is over. But eventually she's ready for a new start – at work, that is. She doesn't need a new man when she has a certain secret visitor to keep her company . . .

Zack McLaren seems to have it all, but the girl he can't stop thinking about won't give him a second glance. If only she'd pay him the same attention she lavishes on his dog.

Moving to North London, Ellie meets neighbour Roo who has a secret of her own. Can the girls sort out their lives? Guilt is a powerful emotion, but a lot can happen in a year in Primrose Hill . . .

Everybody loves Jill Mansell's novels:

'This is a warm, witty and romantic read that you won't be able to put down' *Daily Mail*

'The perfect pick-me-up. Utter indulgence' *News of the World*

'As frothy and moreish as a summer cocktail . . . your beach bag will be empty without it' *Heat*

978 0 7553 5581 5

headline
review

You can buy any of these other bestselling books by
Jill Mansell from your bookshop
or *direct from her publisher*.

FREE P&P AND UK DELIVERY
(Overseas and Ireland £3.50 per book)

Don't Want To Miss A Thing	£7.99
A Walk In The Park	£7.99
To The Moon And Back	£8.99
Take A Chance On Me	£8.99
Rumour Has It	£8.99
An Offer You Can't Refuse	£8.99
Thinking Of You	£8.99
Making Your Mind Up	£8.99
The One You Really Want	£8.99
Falling For You	£8.99
Nadia Knows Best	£8.99
Staying At Daisy's	£8.99
Millie's Fling	£8.99
Good At Games	£8.99
Miranda's Big Mistake	£8.99
Head Over Heels	£7.99
Mixed Doubles	£8.99
Perfect Timing	£8.99
Fast Friends	£8.99
Solo	£7.99
Kiss	£8.99
Sheer Mischief	£8.99
Open House	£7.99
Two's Company	£8.99

TO ORDER SIMPLY CALL THIS NUMBER

01235 400 414

or visit our website: www.headline.co.uk

Prices and availability subject to change without notice.